Mary Wesley was born near Windsor in 1912. Her education took her to the London School of Economics and during the War she worked in The War Office. She has also worked part-time in the antique trade. Mary Wesley has lived in London, France, Italy, Germany and several places in the West Country. She now lives 'rather a hermit's existence' in Devon. She has previously written for children and claims that her 'chief claim to fame is arrested development, getting my first novel published at the age of seventy.' That first novel was *Jumping the Queue*. Her later novels, *The Camomile Lawn, Harnessing Peacocks* and *The Vacillations of Poppy Carew,* are also published by Black Swan.

Author photograph by Kate Ganz Dorment.

Not That Sort of Girl

Mary Wesley

BLACK SWAN

NOT THAT SORT OF GIRL
A BLACK SWAN BOOK 0 552 99304 2

Originally published in Great Britain by
Macmillan London Limited

PRINTING HISTORY
Macmillan edition published 1987
Black Swan edition published 1988
Black Swan edition reprinted 1988 (six times)
Black Swan edition reprinted 1989 (twice)

Copyright © 1987 by Mary Wesley

Black Swan Books are published by Transworld Publishers
Ltd., 61–63 Uxbridge Road, Ealing, London W5 5SA, in
Australia by Transworld Publishers (Australia) Pty. Ltd.,
15–23 Helles Avenue, Moorebank, NSW 2170, and in New
Zealand by Transworld Publishers (N.Z.) Ltd., Cnr. Moselle
and Waipareira Avenues, Henderson, Auckland.

Printed and bound in Great Britain by
Cox & Wyman Ltd., Reading, Berks.

For Kate

I

Nicholas Thornby peered needle-eyed into the delicatessen. The narrow shop was full of customers competing for the attention of servers behind the counter; he squinted in, his view partially obscured by his reflection in the glass door. Recognising several people he had no wish to talk to, he decided Emily's shopping list of smoked cod's roe, soused herrings, Tiptree cherry jam and truffle chocolates could wait until later. Before moving on, he smoothed a hand over his stomach, congratulating himself on its flatness, comparing his reflection favourably with his contemporaries inside the shop. There was no need, he thought disgustedly, to droop round-shouldered, bulge like pregnant women, lose sight of your feet. Pleased with his ghostly reflection, Nicholas moved on before he could be seen, hailed, button-holed, bored. He could guess what was being said inside the shop.

But as he entered the wine shop he found Ian Johnson behind him.

'Morning, Nicholas,' Ian said, following him in. 'I've only just heard of Ned Peel's death. Harold Rhys told me. Poor, poor Rose. How ghastly for her.'

'I dare say he's left her pretty well off,' said Nicholas cheerfully. 'What price the Beaujolais?' He addressed the lady behind the counter.

'I might take some round to the old girl to cheer her up. I'll take six.'

'It's hardly a celebration,' said Ian.

Nicholas laughed, showing no proper feeling. 'Who told you? I thought you were away,' he said. 'I wonder what else we need?' He looked around the shop.

'I was. Harold Rhys in the delicatessen.'

'It's in *The Times*, if you'd looked. Thanks for reminding me I have to go to the delicatessen. I am getting so forgetful. I'll get Rose some of her favourite pâté.'

'You know her well?' asked Ian. 'Still?'

'Since we were children. Yes, please,' to the girl at the counter, 'I'll take six. Can you give me a box, I don't trust carrier bags? We knew her long before she married Ned.'

'Poor Rose. What did Ned die of?'

'The usual. Accumulation of years, that sort of thing. Will you take a cheque?'

'Of course, Mr Thornby.'

'Poor, poor Rose. She will be lost,' repeated Ian. Nicholas did not answer, he was busy writing a cheque. (Nicholas Thornby is so original, he refuses to carry credit cards, pays for everything by cheque.) Nicholas clasped the box of bottles to his chest, left the wine shop and headed for the delicatessen. I'll buy her some flowers, he thought. This is quite like old times. In imagination he saw himself buying wine, pâté and flowers for Rose in his bright and springy youth before her marriage: it did not matter that in reality this had never happened. What mattered was that he and his sister Emily had known Rose for many, many years. Piling his shopping into the boot of his car Nicholas smiled secretly and mimicked 'Poor, poor Rose,' in Ian's lugubrious accents. He remembered Rose shy but merry, easy to tease. Could she have done better than marry decent, honest, nice-looking, well off, unquestionably dull old Ned who was not even particularly faithful? She had been such a pretty girl. Nicholas Thornby drove the three miles out of the market town to Slepe, Ned and Rose's house; now, he supposed, their son Christopher's.

Taking his parcels from the car, Nicholas rang the bell and walked into the hall, calling as he did so, 'It's only me, Rose, Nicholas.'

Faintly, Rose answered from the floor above, 'I'm in the bath.'

'Can I come up?'

'Of course.'

Nicholas put his parcels on the hall table, climbed the stairs to Rose's bedroom and went in, rapping his knuckles on the door as he did so. He walked across the large light room and looked out of the window at Ned's fat acres. Through the bathroom door he heard Rose splash in the bath: 'I won't be long,' she called.

Nicholas thought, When we were all young Emily and I would sit on the edge of her bath and gossip or she would sit on the edge of ours and gossip with us. In actual fact, Nicholas had not been there on the edge of the bath, but being so close to his sister he had been there in spirit.

'Do you remember the enormous bath we had at home?' he called over his shoulder to Rose, still invisible in the bathroom.

'Of course I do.' Rose, wrapping herself in a robe, came in from the bathroom. 'How daring you were; what would your sainted father have said if he'd known about you and Emily?'

Nicholas and Emily's parent had been the rector of the parish, later to evolve into a minor bishop when his wife, who had the undeserved reputation of holding him back, had died.

Nicholas evaded Rose's question by asking, 'Rose, are you not asking for trouble leaving the front door open? What would you do if a burglar took it into his head to walk in while you lie there in the bath?'

'The dogs would bark.'

'Oh, Rose . . .' Nicholas watched Rose sit suddenly on the edge of her bed and begin to cry.

'All of them in one week.' She wiped her tears with the sleeve of her robe. 'Pass me those tissues.'

Nicholas obliged and watched her blow her nose. ('That stupid thoughtless Christopher,' Emily had said. 'Letting the dogs loose on the main road, he must have been drunk.')

'Was Christopher drunk?' asked Nicholas.

'No, squabbling with Helen. He has always been cack-handed with dogs, and Helen . . .' Rose stopped crying at the thought of her son and daughter-in-law.

3

'Are they still here? I didn't see their car.' asked Nicholas.

'Went back to London last night, that's why I overslept. Christopher has a lot to do in London and Helen was anxious to get back to her job and the children. She has to plan her life.'

'Ah.' Nicholas drew out the word. 'Aaah . . .'

'Actually, it's been rather marvellous to have the house to myself. Will you turn your back, Nicholas, while I dress?'

Nicholas turned to look out at Ned's acres, watching a slow flock of sheep drift nibbling from right to left. Behind him Rose dressed in faded blue jeans, cotton shirt and striped red and fuschia sweater. At sixty-seven she was still nice-looking, with clear eyes and hair that had once been ash blonde and was now completely ash, with lots of lines round her eyes and rather large mouth. Her hands betrayed her true age.

'They will be back at the weekend,' she said to Nicholas's back, stooped towards the view, his sparse white hair in need of a cut, 'to take over.'

'So soon?' Nicholas span round, shocked.

'The sooner the better. What is there to keep me here?' She spread her hands. 'I can't wait.'

She was amused, laughing at Nicholas. He does not realise, she thought, watching her childhood friend, that when the dogs were killed I was finally alone, far more so than when Ned died. The dogs were the last strand of the persistent thread which has tied me here.

'Who arranged the funeral?'

'Helen, of course . . .'

'I thought Harrods . . .'

'She orders the best, she does her best, she . . .'

'Knows best?'

Rose laughed.

'Why do you let your son and daughter-in-law treat you as though you were half-witted?'

'It makes them happy. They feel useful. Besides,' said Rose, justifying her young, 'all this is theirs now. Helen might as well begin as she means to go on. She likes to be bossy.'

'And Christopher?'

4

'Christopher is guided by his wife.' Rose failed to keep the zest of acidity from her voice.

'What shall you do?' Nicholas asked. Then, sensing that she was unlikely to tell him: 'I've brought you some pâté and Beaujolais from the town. Ian Johnson was in the wine shop. Harold Rhys . . .'

'It's their wives' day for the hairdresser.'

'Harold Rhys had told him about Ned. He kept saying "Poor Rose, poor Rose, what will poor Rose do?" Were they such great friends of Ned's, still?' said Nicholas, remembering Ian.

'Well, friends. Yes, I suppose they were in a way. They all played together, were in the war together and latterly fished together. They are poor old men.'

'Not so much older than us,' said Nicholas, smiling.

'But they know they are old, Nicholas. You and Emily never think of your age.'

'And you?'

'Rarely.'

'Were Ian and Harold . . .' Nicholas watched Rose, sitting now at her dressing table, brush her hair 'your . . . ?'

'I did not meet either of them until I married Ned. Did you say Beaujolais and pâté?'

'Yes.'

'Then let us telephone Emily and picnic in the kitchen, if that suits. Unless,' said Rose, 'you would like to invite old Harold and Ian?'

'You know we don't like them. What's more, Rose, they do not like each other. It was Ned who held them together.'

Ned's death, thought Rose, has unleashed more than just me. 'Then go and ring Emily, and what about Laura, would she like to join us?'

'I doubt it,' said Nicholas. 'I had thought of taking you out to that new restaurant on the river, it's said to be good; but I thought it wouldn't, be quite *comme-il-faut*.'

'Damn *comme-il-faut*. You sound just like my old father. No, we must eat here because I haven't time for anything else, I am going away as soon as I have packed my bag.'

'So soon? Where to?'

'I haven't decided yet. Use the telephone in the hall, Nicholas. I need to concentrate on what to take.'

Nicholas left the room.

Rose sat on in front of her mirror, her hands in her lap. Looking deep into the glass at the reflections of the room, she murmured, 'You, I'll take you.' She got up and took from the wall a small picture and, after wrapping it in a nightdress she took from a drawer, put it into an overnight bag, padding it protectively with underclothes and jerseys. Then, fetching her washing things from the bathroom and adding them to the bag, she zipped it up and left the room without a backward glance. Running down the stairs she met Nicholas on his way up from the hall. 'She's coming,' said Nicholas, 'let me take your bag.' Rose let him take the bag so that he turned to descend the stairs again. She had no wish for inquisitive Nicholas to note the picture's absence from the wall. 'Is this all you are taking?' asked Nicholas. 'It's not much.'

'I shall not be much away.'

'Where?'

'Just somewhere quiet. The telephone has hardly stopped. I need to be alone. I thought just for once the solitude of a good hotel . . .'

'You could come to us, dear Rose.'

'But I would not be alone, dear Nicholas. Come now and use your expertise with Ned's frightful corkscrew while I make toast for the pâté.'

'Perhaps, since Ned is no longer here, I could use one of the many efficient corkscrews I have given him over the years, or would that be tactless?'

'It wouldn't be tactless. But didn't you know? Ned made a habit of giving your corkscrews, so hintingly given, to friends for Christmas.'

'The old swine!'

'No, no. He would not be drawn, that's all.'

'He didn't like me, did he?'

'He never said so,' said Rose, cutting bread for toast.

'Where will you scatter his ashes?' asked Nicholas spitefully.

Rose did not reply.

'What hotel shall you go to?'

'I'll find one, I haven't thought.'

'How long will you be gone?'

'Only a few days, Nicholas. Do stop asking questions.' Rose's voice trembled.

'Same old secretive Rose,' said Nicholas. It angered him that whereas Rose knew most of what there was to know about his sister Emily and himself, there was precious little either of them knew about Rose that was not public property since her marriage to Ned in 1939. 'Here comes Emily,' he said, waving towards a white Ford car coming up the drive.

2

'There she goes.' Emily Thornby stood with her brother Nicholas watching Rose's car disappear. 'Can you see which way she is going?'

'No. The hedge hides the crossroads.'

'It would be nice to know where she has gone,' said Emily wistfully. 'Do you imagine she has an assignation?'

'Rose! At her age! All that sort of thing is long past, if it ever existed.'

'So we believe,' said Emily.

'And there never was anything of that sort. She has been the model wife, she will now make an ideal widow. Rose's love life never amounted to much, her life has been an open book.'

Emily snorted. 'That was one of your theories when you called her the ideal daughter . . .'

'When we were far from ideal,' agreed Nicholas. 'Mind you, I've always thought her father was preferable to ours, I rather envied Rose her father's death.'

They had sat with Rose at her kitchen table and eaten the pâté provided by Nicholas. Emily had mixed a salad. Both women had watched Nicholas struggle with Ned's corkscrew to uncork the Beaujolais. He had only succeeded after breaking the cork and had to decant the wine, straining off the bits of cork through muslin.

Rose did not drink more than a glass, while Nicholas and his sister finished the bottle and opened another. Now moderately inebriated, they stood on the steps outside the door which Rose had locked as she left the house. In the hall behind them the telephone rang unanswered, as it had all through the meal, as it would until Christopher, the new owner, the heir, took over or Rose chose to return.

'I bet Christopher installs an ansaphone,' said Emily.

'Ned's carefulness with money!' said Nicholas irritably. 'No ansaphone is on a par with his manic use of second-class stamps and re-use of envelopes. Just listen to it! How could Rose sit there all through lunch and not answer?'

Emily laughed: 'I never told you about Rose and the crabs, did I? I was sure that no one, not even you, would believe me, so I kept quiet about it.'

'What are you talking about?' asked Nicholas, suspicious of his sister's tone.

'I am suggesting,' said Emily, 'that Rose has not been the ideal wife we have watched all these years. I am suggesting that there is more to Rose than meets our eyes.'

'Let us sit on her doorstep while you tell me then,' said Nicholas, lowering himself onto the stone steps warmed by the afternoon sun. He drew his sister down beside him. 'We shall not sit here so intimately when Christopher and Helen are masters but for the moment there is nobody to bother about us.' He smiled appreciatively at his sister, seeing in her delicately-pointed nose, narrow-lipped mouth, high forehead and inquisitive brown eyes a feminine version of his own beloved self. I wish, thought Nicholas, that I could tint my hair as she does, then we might still be taken for twins. 'The chaps in the town are saying, "Poor, poor Rose, she will be lost." ' Nicholas laughed and Emily, sitting down beside him, laughed too.

'It's nice here.' She stretched her legs out beside her brother's, admiring her neat ankles and small feet.

'So, go on. Tell me,' prompted Nicholas, 'about the crabs.'

'Some years ago,' Emily turned towards her brother, 'I was taking the short cut through Bennett's passage into Waycott Street and up it, you know how steep it is, a Land-rover was slowly towing a small trailer. The trailer was open and it was full of crabs destined, one supposes, for one of the hotels, or more probably 'the fish restaurant in Jude Street. Actually, where it was going doesn't matter. I came out into the street as the Land-rover slowed to turn right into the High Street. There was nobody about except Rose walking up the hill ahead of me. As the trailer drew level with her, quick as a flash, she helped herself to crabs as they went by, putting them into her shopping trolley. Then the Land-rover went on round the corner and Rose walked on with her booty.'

'Were the crabs cooked?'

'Yes.'

'She didn't see you?'

'She didn't see me.'

'And?'

'That was it. But later I met those boring fishing friends of Ned's, Arthur and Milly, and they told me what a marvellous crab supper they had had chez Ned and Rose.'

'Oh.'

'And Milly said she was particularly impressed because usually she did not think Rose put herself out for them as they were so much more Ned's friends than hers. Hadn't much in common, was how she put it.'

'How marvellous, how absolutely marvellous.' Nicholas, who had been holding his breath, let it out in a gust, then leaned his head back against the closed front door and whinnied with laughter.

Emily looked pleased, but Nicholas, recovering from his mirth, said, 'If there were this side to Rose which was unknown to us during her married life . . .'

'Forty-eight years.'

9

'Yes, forty-eight years! How can we be sure we really knew her before she married? Was there a Rose we did not know? Have we ever known her?'

'Of course we know her. We knew her as children, as we grew up. We knew the men, such as they were, who might have married her. We knew everything she did. She confided in us, we were her friends. We knew she was a cold fish. Not for Rose the adventures and risks we took. Rose is conventional, she always was, she played safe, got herself married to Ned Peel and all this.' Emily nodded back at the house behind them, waved her arm towards Ned's acres. 'Find me a better example of her breed and upbringing.'

'But,' said Nicholas, 'with your crab story, you have been suggesting otherwise.'

'It must be the exception, the slip which proves the rule,' said Emily, feeling a little annoyed with her brother.

'All the same.' Nicholas was intrigued. 'I would give a lot to get back into the house and go through her things. There might be a ribboned packet of letters, a precious clue which would lead to the discovery of the Rose who would steal crabs, a Rose who has conned us.'

'If you went through the house with a fine comb,' scoffed Emily, 'you would find everything in order, in its place. Ned's farm accounts perfect, their income tax paid. You would find bundles of receipts but no love letters.' Now Emily wished she had not presented well known old Rose to her brother in a new and intriguing light; she feared her tale of the crabs had in a sense boomeranged. 'We know Rose,' she said with conviction, permitting the smallest note of patronage into her tone.

'Maybe you are right.' Nicholas stood up. 'It's getting chilly, shall we go home?' Probably, he thought, knowing his sister as well as he knew himself, the crab story never took place. It's more likely Emily saw the load of crabs herself, was tempted to help herself and attributed a non-existent act to Rose. It is the sort of story I make up myself.

'Come on,' he said, holding out his hand. 'Time to go home.'

Emily took his hand, pulled herself up and walked with him hand-in-hand to their cars.

As they walked, it occurred to Nicholas that Rose had deliberately let the telephone ring all through lunch to put a stop to conversation.

3

'Would it be possible to have a sandwich in my room?' Rose asked, handing back the pen she had borrowed to sign the register. 'Or is it too late?'

The manager, who was also the owner of the hotel, flicked a quick glance at the book as he turned it back towards him, changing his mind as he did so as to which room to offer his guest.

'Would a smoked salmon sandwich and a glass of wine be all right?' (She looked exhausted.) 'Half a bottle of Muscadet?'

'Lovely.'

'And a little fruit? Peaches, grapes? Brown bread or white? Coffee?'

'Perfect. Brown, please, no coffee.'

'I'll lead the way.' He picked up Rose's bag. (Goodness, it looks tatty; I've been meaning to replace it for years.) 'I will put you in a room on the ground floor. You look out on the creek and can step out into the garden. It has its own bathroom, of course.'

'Thank you. I am quite tired.' Rose followed the manager along the passage. 'I shall enjoy the quiet.'

'Would you like to be called in the morning?'

'No,' said Rose. 'No, thank you. I wake.' The trouble is, she thought, unpacking her few belongings, I don't sleep.

She busied herself putting toothbrushes and sponge in the bathroom, laying her nightdress on the bed, keeping her thoughts at bay, as she had managed so successfully on the long drive from Slepe, a drive to nowhere in particular until at the end of the long afternoon she had seen the sign which said 'Hotel', and followed a winding lane down a wooded valley to arrive at this place, hitherto unknown to her.

She opened the window and looked out onto a lawn sloping down in the dusk to the water. A swan, its head tucked under its wing, drifted close to the bank; further out the cob swam placidly. Across the creek she could just make out the silhouette of a heron, immobile on a branch overhanging the water.

'How long is she going to stay?' asked a woman's voice from further along the building, its tone of irritation amplified by the water. 'I have just got that room ready for the Dutch couple who are booked for Tuesday.'

'Then you will have to get it ready again, won't you? She didn't say.'

'Why,' a note of rising ire, 'why did you not ask her?'

'Hurry up with those sandwiches, don't forget the lemon. I put her there because she looks the sort who will recommend us to her friends,' the manager snarled.

Leaning out of the window Rose listened for a contemptuous snort, smiled.

'With those clothes? With that shabby bag?' asked the woman. 'Why is she travelling alone?' Her suspicion was almost tangible. One of them, Rose presumed the husband, banged the window down. Out on the creek, a coot cried and was answered. There was a knock on the door.

Rose drew away from the window. 'Come in.'

'Your sandwiches.' She recognised the voice. 'Is there anything else you would like?' The woman wore good looks masked by an expression of martyrdom.

'No, thank you. This looks delicious. I will put the tray outside the door when I have finished. Have you had a very busy season?' The trick of making herself agreeable was automatic.

'You can say that again,' exclaimed the woman. (For two cents she will tell me how she hates her husband, how overworked and unappreciated she is.) 'Shall I turn the bed down? Have you enough towels?' The woman peered into the bathroom, assessing Rose's toothbrushes and Greek sponge.

'No, no thank you. It's all lovely; thank you so much for all your trouble. Good night.' Rose sat by the tray that held the sandwiches. She was suddenly ravenous and began to eat as the woman went out and closed the door.

Outside it was now dark. She finished eating, poured herself wine, went and stood by the window. Shafts of light illumined the grass, the angry voices were stilled, a secret cat crossed the beam of light and rejoined the night. I am travelling alone, thought Rose, and waited for memories of Ned to crowd into her mind, but all she felt was a surge of heretical pleasure at being properly alone for the first time since 1939.

Sipping her wine, she looked out at the water glittering blackly and savoured her pleasure. Her wine finished, she put the tray outside her door, locked it, switched the telephone by the bed to 'Off', undressed, brushed her hair, went to the bathroom to clean her teeth and wash, smooth cream into her face, slide the nightdress over her head.

Ready for bed, she reached into the overnight bag for the picture she had taken off her bedroom wall and put it propped on the dressing table where she could see it from the bed. She got into bed, switched off the bedside light, pulled the bedclothes up to her chin, lay back, closed her eyes and courted composure. Then, remembering Nicholas and Emily's expressions of pain as she let the telephone ring loud, intermittent, unanswered all through lunch, she began to laugh so that under her the bed shook. The probability was that all the messages would have been more or less identical, safe enough for the pricked ears of Nicholas and Emily. Yet one of the callers might have been Mylo. The risk of its not being Mylo had been so great that she had left the telephone unanswered.

4

'Have you definitely made up your mind?' Mylo held her against
him, teasing her hair through his fingers, bending to nuzzle her
neck. 'Snuggle up close, then you won't feel cold.' He leaned
back against the tree, feeling the bark rough against his spine.
'Answer me, Rose.'

'No, no, oh, Mylo.' She put her arms round his neck, reaching
up to him. 'It's so difficult, so hard.' She pitied herself.

'No, no, you won't marry him, or no, no, you haven't made
up your mind?' He pulled away from her, trying to see her eyes
in the dark. 'It's not hard. You don't love Ned Peel, you love me.
He's an old man, you can't . . .'

'He's only thirty-one.'

'And you are eighteen. It makes me ill to think of him touching
you; you can't possibly marry him,' said Mylo violently.

'My father . . .'

'Your father thinks you will be safe with him. I bet that's what
he says.' (He would say: I want to die feeling that you are safe,
that you are provided for. Were it not for this 'cancer' I would
not press you to make a decision. I am anxious for you. There is
going to be a war. Married to Ned, you will be safe and with my
'cancer' I cannot ensure you will be. And so on and on, with the
repetition of the dreaded word in inverted commas, the stress on
security.) 'He knows the man,' Mylo went on, 'he has this house
in the country, he knows he is well off, he will have informed
himself, spoken with Ned of marriage settlements. Of course he
has, I've heard of his kind. He knows Ned's job, knows what he
earns, knows the form. Has he any idea what being in bed with
Ned will be like? Has he put himself in your shoes?'

Rose giggled. 'I can't see Father and Ned tucked up together.'

Mylo shook her. 'Rose, stop it. You know you love *me, me*.'

14

'Yes,' she said, 'I do.'

'So what's so difficult?'

'It's all difficult,' weakly, for she was tired. Rose began to cry. Impossible to repeat her parents' opinion of Mylo. (A nice boy, of course, but only nineteen, no prospects, no money, no family, no job, hasn't even been to university, good looking in his way, speaks French. The speaking of French was somehow derogatory, louche, dangerous.) Their argument had gone on the whole evening, all through dinner in the restaurant and in the car driving out of London to the relatively quiet spot where they now stood on Wimbledon Common. She felt that all she wanted was to go to bed and sleep, forget her father, forget Ned Peel, even forget Mylo. 'He is dying,' she said, as she had said several times before, 'he has cancer.'

'I don't believe he has cancer. I think he is using a rather unsubtle blackmail. I think your father is a snob. He is impressed by Ned Peel and his worldly goods. It's a very old story. He'd like to boast about "my son-in-law, Ned Peel", look him up in *Who's Who*.'

'He'd never say that.'

'Not in so many words. It's the elevation by implication . . .'

'Anyway,' Rose said bitterly, 'he couldn't say it, he'd be dead.'

A car passed along the road; the tears on Rose's cheeks glittered in its headlights. The driver, a happy man, seeing the lovers, gave an appreciative toot on his horn.

'I bet you he will live for years and years,' said Mylo nastily, 'the old fraud.'

'Mylo!'

'He will, like to bet?'

'You are calling my father a liar.' She swung away angrily.

'I am. You wouldn't be so angry if you didn't know it's true. Your father would absolutely panic that you would ruin your prospects – that's how he'd put it – by marrying me. He knows I have no money, he'd think me far too young, nothing alarms a solicitor more than insecurity.'

'Take me home.' Rose walked to Mylo's little car parked on the grass verge. 'I've had enough of this, I shall do what I please.

I do not belong to you; all you do is make me miserable. It's terribly late and I promised I would be in by twelve. The aunt I am staying with is extra respectable and quite strict, she thinks late nights are immoral.'

'One can also be immoral by day,' said Mylo caustically, 'not that you go in for it, silly little prude.'

Rose said nothing, biting back a mixture of hurtful and/or loving, joking retorts. How on earth, she asked herself, have we got ourselves into this misery?

Mylo drove back into London. He had said too much, gone too far. 'I am off to France,' he said. 'I've got a job.'

Rose's heart turned over.

'I wanted it to be a surprise,' said Mylo. 'Now I shan't see you again. I wanted to take you with me. We could have managed; it would have been fun.' (It was unlikely he would be allowed to take Rose, but never mind.)

Rose sat beside Mylo saying nothing, feeling a void opening in the heart that for the whole year had overflowed with Mylo.

'It's pretty stupid,' said Mylo conversationally, keeping his eyes on the road, 'we haven't even slept together. There has never been anywhere to go and I do so terribly want you . . .' He gripped the wheel tightly. They were crossing Putney Bridge, a flock of gulls flew down river. 'It's all right, I shan't drown myself or anything. It just seems so wasteful that I have never held you naked in my arms, never spent a whole night with you, never learned with you how to make love. We could have learned together.' He guided the car into the King's Road, past the World's End. 'World's End,' he said. 'Well, our bit of World looks like ending. Where are you staying, I forgot to ask?'

'Chester Street.'

'I dare say Ned Peel knows how to book in for a night at an hotel with a girl without curling up with embarrassment in inexperienced agony. He is not nineteen, he's an experienced man of thirty-one. It's possible, though he doesn't look the type, that he's done it often. He really does look reliable and safe, one can see the charm he holds for your father. I dare say your respected Pa is absolutely right. Here's your aunt's street, what's the number?'

The bitterness in Mylo's voice was dry and crisp as the east wind.

'Twenty-two. The green door, by the pillarbox, just here.' Rose got out of the car. 'It's dreadfully late. I must creep in and not wake her. Good night.' They did not kiss.

'I'll wait and see you safely indoors,' he said.

'I have a key.'

'I'll wait.'

Rose fumbled in her bag for the latchkey, put it in the lock, turned it, pushed the door. 'I'm locked out,' she said incredulously.

'Ring the bell.' Mylo watched her.

Both were astonished when the door suddenly flew open and Rose's aunt let fly.

'I hadn't realised she was like that,' said Rose presently, standing by the coffee stall at Hyde Park Corner sipping boiling tea from a china mug, still so shocked by her aunt's invective that she had to hold the mug with both hands for fear of letting Mylo see how they shook. 'What a surprise,' she attempted a joke, 'she slammed the door like an expert chucker-out.'

'I thought whore, prostitute and tart all meant the same thing; her vocabulary isn't exactly original,' said Mylo. 'Where did she get her ideas about sinful and loose-living youth?'

'Father says she was unhappily married, distrusts men.'

'Perhaps her husband had lots of outside sexual encounters. Where shall I take you now? What about Nicholas and Emily, aren't they friends of yours? You could come with me to France, of course.'

'No, I can't go to them.' Rose shied from the suggestion of the Thornbys, ignored the allusion to France.

'They don't seem the type to think I'd robbed you of your virginity in Park Lane.'

'She didn't say Park Lane, she said "dingy nightclub". I said I'd rather not go to Nicholas and Emily's.'

'She implied every conceivable indecency, suggested things I'd never heard of.' (As though there could ever be indecency between me and Rose.) 'Don't let's think about her, she's a nasty old woman,' said Mylo.

Will she write or telephone my father? Rose wondered. He is so ill, it would be the last straw.

Mylo read her thoughts. 'She won't bother your father; that sort of person keeps the hatch on her sewer. More tea, my love?' Rose shook her head. 'I am staying with an aunt too, another sort of aunt, I'll take you there. She will give us breakfast and lend you money to get home. Come along, it's across the park, she lives in Bayswater.'

As they drove across the park, Mylo said quietly, 'Rose, don't rush into marriage with Ned. He's a nice chap; I'm jealous, that's all. There's nothing really wrong with him, but you are only eighteen. Even if you don't want me, you may find you want somebody else. There's the whole world, Rose, all your life.'

Rose did not answer.

Mylo stopped the car by the Serpentine bridge. 'Let's be quiet a minute and watch the water.'

The park was empty at this early hour, nobody about, London as still as it ever is.

'Shall we walk a little way?' Mylo got out of the car and held out his hand to Rose.

They strolled by the water, watching the water fowl. Ducks cruised, coots paddled in desperate haste to reach the reeds, calling to each other with sharp querying cries.

Under the bridge Mylo stopped and kissed Rose gently.

'I warn you, I shall have at least one more try before I give up,' he said, 'in any case even if we never meet again I am in your bones. It can't be helped. I know it, and you would too if you were honest. We can't escape. I will go to France. You may marry Ned. However unhappy we are, and I hope we won't be, we shall always have each other. Tell you what,' said Mylo, laughing now, 'I will telephone from time to time all through our lives.'

'All down the years?' Rose mocked, yet felt a lift of spirit.

'You never know,' said Mylo. 'But the first time will be soon, you won't have long to wait.'

Rose was uncertain how to take this. 'Is that a threat or a promise?'

Mylo grinned. 'I shall marry too, perhaps find myself a beautiful girl, kinder than you.'

Rose drew in her breath.

'You can't have it all your own way,' mocked Mylo. 'I can't delay my sex life indefinitely, can I?'

Rose did not answer.

'Besides,' said Mylo, walking her briskly back to his car, 'there are more things than marriage to worry about. There will be a war soon; that will keep us busy.'

'Ned is in the Territorials.'

'Ned would be; his future role tidily arranged. My darling, do you realise what an utterly conventional life you are letting yourself in for?'

'I may enjoy it.' She was defensive.

'We were going to travel the world, I seem to remember. Visit Russia, explore the Balkans, discover Greece, cross the Andes, explore Tibet.'

'I shall travel with Ned.'

'I dare say you will and at the back of your mind you will always be wondering whether it would not be more fun to be with Mylo.'

'Shut up.'

'Get into the car, my love.'

Mylo drove slowly towards Bayswater. By the look of the sky it was going to be a beautiful day.

'And, in bed with Ned, you will wonder whether this curious act of sex would not with Mylo turn into something sublime.'

'Shut up.'

Mylo stopped the car outside his aunt's home.

'Promise me one thing, Rose, you owe me that.'

'All right.'

'When I send for you urgently to come and meet me, you needn't do anything you don't want to do, but just come.'

'How can I?'

'You will manage.' Mylo had confidence.

5

Stretching her legs down into the bed, Rose tried to remember Ned. Easily she visualised his upright figure in greenish tweeds. The ancient but beautifully cut coat. The knee breeches he affected, ribbed stockings, brogue shoes, if it were fine. If wet or cold, he would wear a green quilted waistcoat, green gumboots and a greenish waxed rainproof jacket with poacher's pockets. Round his neck the soft scarf she had given him, dark red this, underneath a checked Viyella shirt and either a knitted tie or his old school tie, which he wore as unashamedly as had been the mode when he was a young man; topping the lot would be a checked cap or a tweed hat with flies stuck in it.

Ned's face was harder to remember than his clothes. A narrow-lipped mouth, watery blue eyes giving the impression that he drank, which he did not, a thick reddish nose which by its coarseness spoiled his otherwise rather distinguished appearance. His chin, a good feature in his youth, had mysteriously doubled, mysterious since he was not a fat man, more on the spare side.

More on the spare side, Rose repeated to herself while she waited for the memories which should now come flooding into her widowed mind.

Since no memories came, she tried dressing Ned in his London gear (they had after all lived much of their life in London), but although she could see Ned well enough in his navy pinstripe, his charcoal – almost black – suit, his Prince of Wales check, his camel-hair overcoat, even in his boring old striped pyjamas, Ned steadfastly refused to come to life. Which, thought Rose, as she lay in the strange hotel bed, is quite natural since he died ten days ago and is cremated.

She got out of bed and padded to the window, opened it to let in the night. The air rushing in was chilly; getting back into bed she switched on the electric blanket. This hotel was a lucky find – every comfort. '*Tout confort.*' Who said that? Mylo, of course. '*Tout confort,*' he had said, holding her tightly in his arms that first time in that fearfully uncomfortable hotel in the shabby little port where they had their first rendezvous.

Suddenly Ned materialised in her widowed mind's eye. Ned watching her read the letter from Mylo with its neatly worked-out instructions for the intricate journey. 'You take the boat as usual from Dunoon to Glasgow; from Glasgow you take the 11.30 train to Crewe. At Crewe you wait an hour, then catch the train for Holyhead. I shall be waiting on the station platform. You need do nothing you don't want to, but I absolutely must see you before I leave the country. This may well be our last chance to meet.' Had Ned, watching her read Mylo's letter, also heard her answer the telephone two days before? The unexpected, for she had taken care not to tell him the Scottish address, call from Mylo, long distance. He had said, 'I am in Dublin. I have written the trains and boat you must take to meet me. Do not fail me.' And, clever Mylo, he had rung off before she could prevaricate or protest or get his number to ring back.

She had felt unease that he was in Dublin when she had believed him to be in France. Her thoughts when they strayed to Mylo had crossed the Channel, even caught the boat train to Paris. What was he up to in Dublin?

What had Ned been thinking as he watched her read the letter? Her heart jolting in her chest, she had said, keeping her voice casual, 'Oh, damn, I had quite forgotten, how awfully rude of me. The Wigrams are expecting me on Wednesday. I shall have to leave a day early. They are my father's greatest friends' (well, they might be, if they existed). 'I am so sorry, how maddening.' She had held the letter out to Ned as though it was a nothing letter, a letter from an expectant hostess, taking the risk that Ned would take it, read it, but more probably not since he read with difficulty without his glasses and with luck would have left them upstairs. With her heart in her throat, Rose gambled on Ned's eyesight and good manners.

'Of course you must go,' he had said, 'but this means I cannot drive you home.'

'Oh,' she had said, 'I'll take the train – she says I have to change at Crewe.'

'I promised to give Nicholas and Emily a lift home and we cannot make them cut their visit short, they are relying on me.'

'Of course. Never mind. It's not for long. You can't let them down, they can't afford the train.' Gratefully she thanked God for the Thornbys' sponging habits, their continual cries of poverty.

'Poor you. How boring for you.' Emily with her usually needle eye had noticed nothing. 'The separation,' said Emily, 'will add spice to your engagement and, who knows, some good may come out of your duty visit, a sumptuous wedding prezzie, perhaps?'

Ned had proposed to her the evening before, walking along the river valley. Weighed down by her father's cancerous wish Rose had accepted him to the sound of curlews crying in the bog further up the hillside.

It was not an entirely fraudulent thing to do, thought Rose, lying alone in the strange hotel, part of me wanted to marry Ned. Much of me longed for the security, a house in London, the house in the country; the big wedding was tempting, the clothes I had never been able to afford. I was almost in love with Ned in August 1939 in Scotland at the house party for the grouse shooting, surrounded by his approving relations who thought I would do very well for Ned. (A nice little thing, quite pretty, she'll shape.) They had known, those relations, what was required of Ned's wife. At eighteen, thought Rose, I hadn't the remotest idea.

Lying in the dark Rose thought she heard a curlew cry and into her mind's eye came Ned's face, not as it had been when he died, but as he was in 1939 before his hair thinned and greyed, before his face grew lined. He was an awfully nice man, she thought. I was very fond of him, what a lovely friend he would have made; I must have been mad to marry him. I did not hear a curlew cry, I imagined it.

Ned had driven her to the boat at Dunoon, giving up a day's shooting to do so. Her future aunt- and uncle-in-law had pressed upon her two brace of grouse to take to her imaginary hostess,

Mrs Wigram. Rose remembered gulping back laughter, a tearful attack which was assumed to be sorrow at the parting with Ned. 'No need to cry, dear, you will see him in a few days.' Her future aunt-in-law had pressed her against her large and rather squashy breasts, smacking her lips in the air with a parting kiss. 'There!'

Nicholas and Emily had come for the drive and to do some desultory shopping in the town. Even then, thought Rose amused, they were prying inquisitively into my life. Ned's relations had stood on the front steps waving goodbye, pleased that Ned's future was settled, regretful that she must depart a day early but, good manners apart, impatient to be off for the day's shooting; a group of ghillies and beaters were waiting. And who else, thought Rose, peering back down the years, who else was there?

Ned's cousins, two soon to be killed in the war, and yes, of course, Harold Rhys and Ian Johnson, jolly high-spirited bachelors in those days, Ned's friends. It would not be long before they too married and began the long decline towards arthritis, piles, deafness, obesity, operations for this and that, collections of grandchildren, irritating sons-in-law, the decline which turned them into what they were now, dull old men. But, in those days, Rose remembered, they felt it their right, their duty, too, to make a pass at every girl in the house party and they expected the girls to be flattered.

Why did I tell Nicholas this morning that I did not know Harold and Ian until after Ned and I were married? He was hinting, was he not, that I might have flirted, had an affair with one or both of them. Poor Nicholas, he is obsessed, as is Emily, with my secret life for which there is no evidence. They sniff the air, they ferret from force of habit. I was careless, upset thinking of the dogs, my dear dogs crushed by tne lorry. He will remember Ian and Harold were there in Scotland, for he was there too. My mind slips as I grow old.

She saw herself sitting beside Ned in his open car driving over the hills to Dunoon. She watched herself boarding the boat carrying the grouse, the boat drawing away from the quay; Ned, Emily and Nicholas waving; Ned shouting that they would choose the engagement ring when they met soon in London; she had waved back, and then alone at last on the boat she had faced the day-long journey to Holyhead with a mixture of trepidation and joy.

Only a very naïve person would get away with what I did, thought Rose. It would not have occurred even to Nicholas and Emily that I was not on my way to stay with the Wigrams, a duty visit to my father's friends, but that I was travelling to meet Mylo.

The charm of the situation had been that Nicholas and Emily hardly knew of Mylo's existence in her life, and neither did Ned. Remembering the journey Rose relived her fears. The fear of discovery by her parents or Ned, but principally the fear that at the end of the journey Mylo would not be there.

Rose remembered putting the grouse on the rack on the train from Glasgow to Crewe. At Crewe she had deliberately left them there, but a fellow passenger had shouted as the train drew out of the station, gesticulated, thrown the dead birds to a porter. Oh, those bloody birds, thought Rose, and tried to remember how she had rid herself of them, and could not. (The gaps in the memory as one grows old.) My fears, thought Rose, remembering vividly, my fears were so great.

And then at the end of the everlasting day as the train drew into the station at Holyhead, Mylo was on the platform, his face drawn and strained: 'I thought you might not come,' he had said, and later in the awful little Commercial Hotel they had gone through the brownish hallway which smelled of stale tobacco and beer, of years of vegetables cooking and failure, up the straight stairs to a room with a double bed. He had shut the door. 'It's pretty shoddy, I'm afraid.' Then holding her, sitting on the bed, bouncing to test it, he had said, his voice rasping, a little husky, '*Tout confort*,' trying to lighten their situation, their love, their fear, their ignorance.

Who in these days, Rose wondered as she listened to the night sounds, the small breeze which now whispered through the reeds by the water, who in these days would credit that a girl of eighteen and a boy of nineteen should both be virgin? For that fear, the exquisite fear of the actual act of making love, terrified them, she remembered, though Mylo who assumed he knew how to set about it pretended not to be afraid (and so to be fair, did she).

'What did the man at the desk think?' Rose had whispered. They had signed the register with trepidation.

'Thinks us a honeymoon couple,' answered Mylo stoutly.

'Arriving separately?' Rose had jeered. 'Oh, Mylo.'

'It doesn't matter, forget him. You are here now. Kiss me.'

They had hugged and kissed. Then, Rose remembered his arms round her, that his ribs were quite painful against her chest. They had drawn apart breathless, laughing.

'The bed's pretty lumpy,' Rose had said. Then, 'Shall we go out before it gets dark, go for a walk along the cliffs?'

They jointly put off what was to come.

I have never been back, thought Rose, the town must have doubled, trebled in size, perhaps even the cliffs where we walked have changed since that summer nearly fifty years ago.

They had wandered along the clifftop hand in hand, listening to the seagulls, meeting no one, leaned over looking down and watched the seals bobbing innocently below them close to the rocks, their faces turning this way and that on thick necks, rolling their oily eyes.

In the late afternoon they had clambered down to a stony cove and Mylo said, 'Let's swim.'

'No bathing things,' she objected.

'Naked then, nobody to see us.'

Greatly daring, she undressed near the water's edge, waded quickly in, the stones hurting her feet. The water was ice cold. She looked back, saw Mylo naked, magnificent. She had never seen a naked man, was aghast at the size of his sex.

She swam a few strokes out, turned, came back, climbed up the stones raking up and down in the swell, dried herself inadequately with a handkerchief, dressed.

But Mylo, confidently treading the cobbles, dived shallowly, swam out strongly. She watched his body gleaming silvery through the green water.

The seals had gone; she climbed the cliff, watched Mylo swim, waited for him to return.

He had said 'You needn't do anything you do not want,' but she knew, want to or not, she would do it.

Oh, poor us, moaned Rose, nearly fifty years later. What a shambles in that lumpy bed. How ironic the '*tout confort*'. How frustrating for Mylo, how painful the whole experience.

'You are nervous, my sweet, try and open up, be happy.'

'Happy,' Rose murmured, now in recollection. 'Happy,' she thought wryly; what was needed was a tin opener. If I was hurt, what about Mylo, what about him? He too must have been sore. Funny, she thought, now in the present lying alone in recollection, I never asked him whether he hurt himself. Eventually he had slept, his head on her breast, his arms around her body and she, wakeful as now, listened to his breathing, as now she listened to the night and smiled at their tragi-comic abortive attempt at making love.

Mylo had left in the very early morning on the boat to Dublin and she had caught the nine-thirty train to London where three days later Ned took her to Cartier to buy the engagement ring, putting on his glasses to inspect it.

Three days after that, Mr Chamberlain declared war. They were married at the end of September.

6

Mr Chamberlain's declaration of war delighted Rose, it relieved her mind, put paid to the possibility of questions such as How was the journey to the Wigrams? Had she enjoyed herself? Who else was staying there? Had they been pleased with the grouse? Nobody was interested in her mythical visit, everybody was adjusting to the war; those with the more active imaginations, for imminent death. For Rose the war was of secondary importance; filling her mind was the paramount question – was she or was she not pregnant?

The relief after ten days of crippling fear at the arrival of her period was so great that she was slow to take in the movement set in train by Ned and his family conjointly with her parents towards a wedding, hers to Ned. Ned insisted on an early date. He was joining his regiment immediately, he would get leave for his marriage then install Rose at Slepe, where she would live while he was away. She was not consulted, her agreement was taken for granted.

Ned, with his sensible orderly mind, had, it seemed, not only anticipated the war but made his preparations. Deploring the idea of evacuees in his beloved house, he had months before arranged for the greater part of it to be taken over by a branch of the Ministry of Information, only keeping a minimum of rooms for his own use and now, of course, for Rose.

Emerging from her fog of secret fear, rejoicing over her blood-stained knickers, Rose discovered that a lot had been going on without her. Her parents and the Peel contingent brushed her lovingly aside. 'We are managing very well.' The words 'without you', while not actually voiced, were implied. The advent of war demanded short cuts, fast action, no hanging about. There was no time for prevarication on the bride's part; it would be best for her to keep quiet and let those who knew what's what to get on with it. Rose could usefully answer the telephone and relay messages, said her mother. So she fidgeted about the house waiting for the telephone to ring, answering it breathless in case the caller was Mylo: it never was.

If Mylo had got in touch, if I had heard his voice, Rose asked herself fifty years later, would I have gone to him?

The question nagged intermittently over the years, receiving no clear answer. A second question for which she had no answer was how and why had she so weakly – as she thought in the strength of old age – allowed herself to be steam-rollered by that inexorable tide of goodwill? Why had she not spoken up loud and clear, said quite simply, 'I do not want to marry Ned'?

While dallying with the idea of getting engaged to Ned she had dreamily anticipated a long engagement during which there would be pleasurable shopping for a trousseau, time to acquaint herself with Ned's friends and relations, time to decide whether his ideas and hers agreed in principle (did I have any ideas?). Whether their tastes were similar, time to get to know each other. Above all, time to change her mind, time to break off the engagement.

It seemed, though, that during the ten days of what she later thought of as her phantom pregnancy an unstoppable juggernaut of family custom had started to roll. She and Ned would be married in the church where all Peels got married (no time for the banns to be called, a special licence was obtained). A bishop who was also a Peel would officiate, on condition he skipped the reception and caught the train at Liverpool Street to dash back to his diocese. She was to wear a veil of Peel family lace and round her neck the Peel diamonds whipped out of the bank for the occasion. Ned's Aunt Flora's French dressmaker was willing to run up the wedding dress in record time provided the design was plain (Rose later had it dyed black and wore it for years). The honeymoon would not be spent in some exotic location but at Slepe, the marriage beginning as it must go on, at home.

Rose spoke up once, her voice squeaky with nerves, to her mother busy writing the wedding invitations; 'I can't think what you want *me* for, couldn't you hire a model for the day?'

Without looking up, her mother had replied, 'Don't be difficult, darling. If you've got a pain go and lie down with a hotwater bottle; if not, you can make yourself useful addressing these envelopes. Here's the list.'

I lacked gumption, thought Rose in old age, I dithered. The parents and Ned were so enjoying it all it would have been wicked to spoil their pleasure, deny them their wedding.

And still during those long hot September days, while Whitehall wrapped itself in sandbags and the population of London began to dress in khaki and blue, the telephone rang, but it was never Mylo.

Hard as it is to credit now, thought Rose, I was moulded by custom and family pressure, by what was right and proper for them, by what was expected of me from the moment of my conception: not unlike an animal, a pig, a racehorse, a prize winner at Crufts.

Yet there was Mylo who did not conform, and Nicholas and

Emily who even then could scarcely be accused of conformity.

Rose turned on her side in the strange bed, pressed her cheek into the pillow remembering Emily's sharp nose, bright enquiring eyes when she pottered in to ask, 'What are you going to do in the war?'

'I'm getting married.'

'I know that, I mean war work.'

'I hadn't thought. What shall you do?'

'We are considering possibilities, finding out what will be the most amusing for us.'

'Us?'

'Nicholas and me?'

'Won't he join up?'

'Nicholas does not want to do anything dangerous, neither of us do. We leave that to the Hoi Polloi.' Emily managed to give this description of her fellow-men capital lettering. Rose remembered being jolted by Emily's honesty.

'There are lots of reserved occupations, we shall stay together,' Emily had said.

'Oh,' Rose had said. 'Oh,' rather shocked by Emily's independent spirit which about that time was beginning to show itself openly.

But Emily had switched her attention from herself and her brother to Rose. 'Rose,' she had said. They were sitting in the hall of Rose's home attending to the telephone which was at that moment idle. 'Rose,' lowering her voice slightly, for Rose's mother was reputed to have the hearing of a bat. 'Rose, do you know anything about sex? We are worried for you.' She leaned towards Rose, looking her straight in the eye. 'Do you?'

'Of course I do.' Rose had flushed. 'I am getting married, aren't I?'

'That's why I asked, why we worry. I bet you know nothing. That's why I came round especially to see you, we . . .'

'We?'

'Nicholas and I. We don't think you know the first thing. Have you for instance ever seen a naked man?'

'I have.' (Oh, exquisite Mylo!)

Emily laughed. 'Rubbish. Statues perhaps. The real thing is different. Statues have very small cocks. Honestly, Rose, we are concerned about you. What has your mother told you? I bet she's told you nothing. I bet I'm right.'

'She said she supposed I knew all about such things.'

'What things?'

'I supposed she meant – you know.'

'And you said?'

'I said Yes, I did.'

'I bet you did.' Both girls went off into a fit of high-pitched giggles. Rose's mother called from upstairs, where she sat at her desk addressing the last of the wedding invitations. 'What are you girls laughing at, what's the joke?' not expecting an answer. Emily, recovering her composure whispered, 'She didn't even tell you to buy a pot of vaseline?'

'Whatever for?'

'Oh, we were right! You know nothing, nothing at all. Nicholas and I have a bet on it.'

'I suppose you two know it all,' Rose had said huffily. (Never, never would she divulge about Mylo.)

'We thought we had better tell you before you get too great a surprise, getting married might be quite a shock.'

'No thanks, it's no business . . .'

'We don't want a repetition of when you started the curse,' said Emily relentlessly. 'If your mother couldn't bring herself to tell you about that she won't have told you what happens in bed with Ned or any other man for that matter, though Nicholas swears you will never commit adultery, we have a bet on that too.'

'I . . .' Rose remembered the humiliating experience of getting her first period while staying the night at the Rectory. Nicholas and Emily had been surprisingly informative and kind, they had not mocked. Her mother, when she returned home with the news, had said awkwardly, 'I had meant to tell you some time.' Perhaps, Rose remembered thinking, perhaps some time after her marriage to Ned her mother would break to her the rudiments of sex. 'All right,' she said grudgingly to Emily, 'fire away.'

Listening to Emily she was amazed by Emily's powers of invention. Some of it may be true, she had thought, but she's crazy if she thinks it's fun. When Emily stopped for breath Rose asked, 'How d'you know all this?'

'We . . .' began Emily, then stopped, laughed in what for her served for embarrassment, altered course. 'We have made you an appointment with Helena Wright.'

'Who's she when she's at home?'

'The contraceptive doctor, she's famous,' Emily whispered.

'Oh.'

'We thought we'd give you that as a wedding present. Something practical to remember us by.'

'How thoughtful.' Rose was overwhelmed by their interference. Even for Emily and Nicholas this was going too far. Could they have guessed at her phantom pregnancy? 'No, thank you,' she exclaimed. 'Please don't.' She realised that to accept such a present would connect Emily and Nicholas for ever with her every sexual experience, making of them some sort of godparents. Five decades later Rose thought she might not have been sufficiently grateful for their imaginative suggestion. She had postponed making an appointment for herself until after her honeymoon when she had become more brusquely aware of what Emily referred to as 'the facts', a belated act which might if she had married some man other than Ned have cost her dear, precipitating Christopher into the world before his time. But Ned, so sensible, was also cautious; just as he had prepared for war so he prepared for marriage.

I remember little of my wedding, thought Rose, lying solitary in the hotel bed. My mother chose the hymns, Ned's Aunt Flora chose the flowers (I hated gladioli then, I have hated them unforgivingly since). I remember Ned's bishop uncle gabbled the service; was he afraid of missing his train? I remember walking down the aisle on Ned's arm with the Peel veil tossed back so that I was able to see, as I had not been able coming up it with my father, searching the congregation for Mylo, but he was not among them and he was not in the small crowd which had gathered to gawp outside the church. He was not there.

7

'I think that went off very well.' Ned took his hand off the wheel and felt for Rose's hands folded in her lap; he squeezed the fist they made. 'Happy, dear?'

'Yes.'

That might have been the moment when she could have told Ned that she detested being called 'dear', simply loathed it. Being called 'dear' made her curl up. But it was already too late. She would learn to smother her irrational dislike of this endearment and be glad that 'darling' belonged to Mylo. When Mylo said darling in the voice which sounded like honey kept so long in its jar it had become gritty, her whole being responded.

So in late September 1939, driving out of London on their way to Slepe when Ned squeezed her hands and said, 'Happy, dear?' Rose answered brightly, 'Yes.'

Thanks to Ned's planning the wedding had gone off without a hitch. Ned liked planning; his attention to detail would presently stand him in good stead in the Army just as it already did in business. By the end of the war he would be a staff officer. He congratulated himself that his decision to get married put in train by a conversation with his Scottish uncle was working out so well.

Some time previously, on a bitter January day, Ned had sat with his Uncle Archibald Loftus on the sofa at the top of the stairs in the vestibule of the Hyde Park Hotel watching the people coming in and out from Knightsbridge. They had lunched at his uncle's club, where over potted shrimps and steak and kidney pudding Uncle Archibald had suggested that now Ned had reached the age of thirty and come into his inheritance it might be advisable for him to marry. It was Uncle Archibald's habit to tender some piece of useful advice to his nephew on the rare occasions when they met. Ned had already agreed in principle and they had returned to the hotel where his uncle and aunt were staying on a foray south to the capital from their home in Argyllshire. Now they sat amicably digesting their lunch and mulling over Uncle Archibald's views on the relinquishment of celibacy.

'Find a girl,' he had said. 'She need not be particularly pretty – that can be a nuisance – from a decent family, of course, she needn't have money, you have plenty, this widens your field. Healthy, of course, no skeletons in cupboards, and as young as possible.'

'Why?'

'It's like buying a puppy or a horse,' said Archibald Loftus impatiently, 'you train 'em to your ways. If you take on a girl who has had the time to have other affairs she'll make comparisons, derogatory, unflattering. No, no, the younger the better. It's like buying fish, you look for the sparkle in the eye and make sure the sparkle is for you. Ask your Aunt Flora.'

'Was that how you set about it?'

'Practically snatched her from the schoolroom.' Archibald Loftus stretched out his long thin legs, thoughtfully lit his cigar. 'Like a brandy?' he asked. Ned remembered that while accepting the brandy he had realised his uncle had something more to say. Some pearl of wisdom, he had told himself, amused. 'Your aunt won't be back for a little while,' said his uncle, confirming Ned's suspicion. They had sat in silence until the waiter had brought the brandy and gone away. 'There's one more thing you may find useful,' said Uncle Archibald, warming the brandy between his hands, sniffing it with his long predatory nose. 'You may remember that my mother originated in Austria, was half Viennese?'

'Yes?' Ned, puzzled by this tangent, sniffed his brandy, waited for his uncle to go on.

'Well, her uncle – we are going back to my marriage to your Aunt Flora, dear boy – my mother's uncle, a good chap wholly Viennese and a great chap with women – but I digress – gave me a priceless piece of advice. Would you like me to pass it on?' He swivelled a glance at Ned.

'I shall be grateful.'

'Needn't take it, of course; it's a bit, shall we say, continental.' Uncle Archibald had laughed.

'Oh.' Ned had hoped that he did not sound doubtful; there were times when his uncle could be rather too robust.

'Shall I go on?' Ned nodded. 'I don't know how you feel about foreigners; being a Scot I have a soft spot for them, feel more at home with them than you people down here in London do.'

'Make yourself clear, Uncle Archibald.'

'I will, Ned. I am not a politician; when I make something clear it is clear, not some damn euphemism for muddle.'

'Please go on.' If he goes on like this I shall be late back at the office. 'Go on, what was your mother's Viennese uncle's advice?' Better listen to the old boy, Ned had thought, I respect his advice as a rule.

Uncle Archibald lowered his voice so that a group of people passing on their way to the lifts should not overhear. 'On the morning of your wedding you fuck another woman.' He breathed in at his cigar. 'If you have a mistress it's easy of course, but if not, fix yourself up with someone handy.'

'Why?' Ned remembered asking stupidly.

'Dear fellow, think.' Uncle Archibald was exasperated. 'If you've already had a go you're not in a rush, you don't spoil your wedding night by fruitless impatience, you can afford to wait, take it slow. You are, one assumes, marrying a virgin.'

'Oh,' said Ned, getting the gist. 'Ah.'

'Naturally if you are marrying a widow it doesn't apply. No need to take my tip, of course. I just pass it on in case it's of use.' Ned's uncle had sipped his brandy, puffed at his cigar.

'Did you act on this tip?' Ned had enquired.

Archibald Loftus had laughed. 'Flora and I have been happy. Ah, here she comes.' He got up to greet his wife, Ned's Aunt Flora, coming in from the cold street laden with parcels but wonderfully fresh surfacing from the January sales.

'My Uncle Archibald and Aunt Flora are a good example of a happy marriage, aren't they?' Ned broke the silence between himself and Rose as he drove her towards Slepe and their wedding night.

'Yes,' said Rose.

'Are your parents happy?'

'I've never really thought about it,' said Rose. 'They don't quarrel, so I suppose they are.'

'We shall be happy,' said Ned, driving along feeling grateful to his Uncle Archibald. 'I want you to be happy and I want you to love Slepe.'

'I am sure I shall. I've only seen it from the outside, as you know.'

'I want it all to be a beautiful surprise,' said Ned.

'It will be,' she assured him. 'It looked lovely in the distance; I saw it from across the valley when I was riding with Nicholas and Emily.'

'How well do you know those two?'

'More or less all my life, it's propinquity. Their father was our rector. My father is his solicitor. I haven't seen so much of them since he became a bishop. They are neighbours. Why? Don't you like them?'

'So you wouldn't have chosen them as friends?'

'Maybe not. I've never thought about it. Why? Don't you like them?' Rose asked again.

'They're all right,' said Ned, 'not exactly my sort. I thought since you asked them up to Uncle Archie and Aunt Flora's that you were close.'

'They invited themselves,' said Rose, 'it was nothing to do with me.' (Nicholas and Emily are not close to me, thought Rose, nobody is close except Mylo.)

'Oh,' said Ned, rearranging his thoughts. 'Oh,' and 'I see.' He drove without speaking for several miles while he stilled a faint feeling of unease. 'I have arranged that the fires will be lit for us when we arrive and I thought it would be nice to find supper left ready for us, something simple we can heat up ourselves. We have no servants as you know, just the Farthings.'

'The gardener and the wife who cleans?' Rose hoped Ned would not tell her yet again about the Farthings who had cleaned and gardened for the distant cousin from whom he had inherited Slepe. She was already rather in dread of them or the idea of them, having recently read about malign old retainers in one of Daphne du Maurier's novels.

'Yes, them,' said Ned. 'We shall be alone. Nobody knows we are here, I told everyone we would spend our first night in the Ritz.'

'So did I,' said Rose, who had been looking forward to the Ritz, never having stepped inside its portals, but was, she hoped, too tactful to show Ned her disappointment.

'So here we are!' Ned had said, swinging the car off the road and up the drive. 'There's the house, there's Slepe.'

'Yes,' said Rose, looking at its seventeenth-century charm. 'Does it know we are coming?'

'Nobody knows except the Farthings. I hope you will be pleased.'

'I trust the house will be pleased,' said Rose, running up the shallow steps, pushing open the front door, crossing the flagged hall to the log fire, looking round at what was to be her home for fifty years, 'and of course *I* am.'

Ned carried in their bags, slammed shut the door. 'Alone at last,' he said. He took Rose in his arms: 'Welcome to Slepe, Mrs Peel.' He kissed her; 'Mrs Peel.' (He had rehearsed this sentence in his mind and was pleased now to voice it.) 'There's a parcel for you,' he said in irritation, looking over Rose's head towards the hall table.

'Oh?' Rose detached herself, looked at the packet: 'It doesn't look important,' she said, keeping her voice uninterested; 'I expect it's just something I've left behind.' Ned did not seem to notice the ineptitude of this remark; he was adding logs to the fire. 'These seem a bit damp, I would have thought – Come, dear,' he took her arm, 'let me introduce you to the house so that you get to know each other.'

'I am coming,' said Rose, feeling that the house would have to get to know Mylo as well as herself. She was unaware that beside her Ned ungratefully felt a third party present. Someone 'handy', had been Uncle Archibald's expression.

'Isn't it marvellous to be on our own at last,' said Ned on a rising note.

'Yes,' said Rose, 'isn't it.' As she walked past the parcel on the hall table she idly turned it over. She noticed that the stamps on it were French. So he's reached France, she thought, retrieving her thoughts from Dublin and sending them on a swift journey across England (he must have passed within a mile of me and I did not know), across the Channel – was the crossing rough? – and on to Paris. 'Show me everything,' she said, slipping her hand into Ned's. 'Show me the house and show me the garden before it gets dark and then let's have supper . . .'

'. . . and go to bed,' said Ned.

'Ah . . .' said Rose (would it be better here than in the Ritz or worse?) 'and . . .'

'And a bottle of champagne with our supper,' said Ned. (Somebody had said 'prime her with booze': Uncle Archie probably.)

'I think I had enough at the reception,' said Rose.

'Oh, no, dear, you didn't,' said Ned.

Now, lying in the hotel bed, listening to the night sounds whispering through the open window, Rose tried to remember her wedding night.

Ned had been gentle. His ears had been cold. He had fallen asleep quite soon. Why do I only remember his cold ears? she asked herself lying wakeful as she had fifty years before. If I wrote my autobiography no reader would find the temperature of Ned's ears particularly enthralling.

8

Rose on her wedding night was grateful that Ned was a kind and caring man (he had that reputation). Aware of her inexperience, she crossed her fingers and hoped. She was anxious to co-operate, to make things easy for him, start on the right footing – though how feet came into what she vaguely termed as 'things', still shying from the word sex, she did not know.

Although she had put off a visit to the birth-control doctor, she had not been idle. On an afternoon when she was supposed to be running errands for her mother, she had searched the shelves of Foyles bookshop, found a sex book for beginners. This manual she had perused locked in the lavatory, puzzling over the diagrams which bore no resemblance to her memory of flesh and blood Mylo. She looked up words she did not know in her father's dictionary, but was left little the wiser. Having memorised the necessary information, she disposed of the book in a rubbish bin in the park, not trusting her mother's cook general who had a way of throwing kitchen implements, even silver forks and spoons, into the waste bin and later retrieving them. The book left her half-mystified, half-repelled, but she approved its lack of romance. Romance, joy, delight was left to the reader to practise and discover in his or her own good time. Rose felt she must rely on Ned to show her how this aspect of sex, this happy state, was achieved.

In bed with Ned, his arms around her, she tried to stop the nerves bunching her body into the stiffness of a cadaver. She bore in mind that the book stressed the need of relaxation for both participants. 'Take your pyjama trousers off, Ned, you will get wound up in the cord.' He had laughed, freed himself from the trousers, switched off the light, said, 'That's better,' relieved, kissed her, she had kissed him back, felt him relax.

'Where d'you get your hair oil?' She sniffed at him, an unconscious delaying tactic, nuzzling his neck.

'Trumpers, sometimes Penhaligon's. Why?'

'I like the smell. Smells matter to me.'

Ned stroked her, gently running his hand down her flank, pausing on her hip, letting his thumb halt near her sex. Had Ned also read the manual? Rose stifled a laugh, her tense muscles loosening. 'You can't be a very faithful man if you go to both shops.' Still she put off the inevitable.

'But I am faithful.' Ned stroked some more. 'Is that nice? Tell me.'

'Yes.' And it was quite nice.

'If we stick a pillow under your bottom, it will be more comfortable.'

He *had* read that book. She reached for a pillow, fumbling in the dark, shaking with a mixture of amusement and fear. 'That better?'

When Ned slept, Rose lay listening to the magnolia which grew against the house rustling and scraping its stiff polished leaves against the old stone wall. In her mind a voice spoke, '. . . and in bed with Ned you will wonder whether this curious act of sex would not with Mylo turn into something sublime.'

She was assailed by a sense of desolation.

Anguished, she had carefully got out of bed; leaving Ned deep in his private sleep, and leaned from the window feeling the night air cool on her hot cheeks, smelled the piercing scent of magnolia flowers, felt rather than seen the moths fluttering about them, felt pity and tenderness for Ned, shivered as the magnolia leaves stirred, climbed back into bed.

Half waking, Ned had clutched her. 'Who? That you? Is it Rose?'

'Yes. Yes, it's me.'

'Where have you been?'

'Just to the window . . .'

'Rose, don't leave me.'

'Why should I?'

'Promise never to leave me, promise . . .'

'Of course not.'

'Swear.' He was sitting up now. 'Say it, say: I swear never to leave you.'

'Don't be silly, Ned, you are half asleep.' She felt protective, maternal.

'No, I'm not. I am very much awake. Swear, say: I swear never to leave you.'

'I did, at our wedding, in church . . .'

'You weren't paying attention, you were distracted, your mind was miles away.' (How had he known?) 'Come on, swear it to me now.' He was insistent, almost bullying.

'All right.' She felt afraid. 'I swear never to leave you. What about you? What do you swear to me?'

'No need for me . . .' He was content, slipping back into his sleep, leaving her later, much later, to find her separate sleep from which she woke to a sunny morning with Ned up and dressed, confident and cheerful, bringing their breakfast into the room on a tray. 'Wake up, Mrs Peel, we have this one day to explore . . .'

'And the other days?' she asked, pouring coffee, handing him his cup.

'The other days I must spend putting you in the picture for when I shall be away.'

'And I am to stay here alone?' She knew this, had she not agreed, liked the idea, seeing freedom from her family, insisted that she would manage, would be all right.

'You said you would rather be on your own, but it's not too late. We can find someone to live with you, a girl friend to share . . .'

'Who, for instance?'

'Emily.'

'Why do you suggest Emily?'

'Isn't she a friend?'

'Not particularly. What I'd like is a dog, or two dogs.' Rose visualised a pair of companionable animals.

'Or a pack!' Ned laughed. 'Remember the war, dear. We shall have food rationing soon; one dog should be more than enough.'

'Oh, rationing,' said Rose, privately deciding to have as many dogs as she wished.

'Yes, rationing,' said Ned, 'we shall have to learn to live with it. Which reminds me, I must show you where the petrol is.'

'What petrol?'

'I've hidden a lot of jerrycans in a shed in the copse.'

'Isn't that illegal? You have a hoard?'

'I did it before rationing started.' Ned sensed disapproval. 'I foresaw rationing so I laid in a store.' (This may not be strictly true, he told himself, but she is not to know.) 'If we are invaded, we might have to make a quick getaway, or you might if I am gone?'

'Are you suggesting the Germans will invade us?' she said incredulously.

'If things go badly,' said Ned, who had listened to talk in his club.

'Golly.'

40

'It will come in useful anyway,' said Ned. 'This isn't going to be a short war, whatever people say, but what I am sure of is that everything will be in short supply; sensible people are stocking their store cupboards.'

'Rich people! Well,' said Rose, 'I shall hoard tinned dog food for my dogs.'

'You should have a dog,' said Ned, as if the idea was his. 'I would be happier when I'm away if you had a dog. I will buy you one.'

'Let me find my own dog . . .' cried Rose before she could stop herself, knowing that Ned's choice of dog would not be hers.

'All right,' said Ned, 'if you insist.' He felt cheated, rather hurt, feeling that he had planned to buy her a dog, an alsatian or a labrador.

Feeling the drop in temperature, Rose said, 'More coffee?' holding up the pot (George III, recently inherited along with the house). Ned passed his cup. 'Yes, please.' Why not let her choose her own dog, he thought indulgently; it was a lovely day, last night had gone off well, he felt contented, uxurious, Rose looked very pretty sitting up in bed with the tray across her lap. He had enjoyed last night rather more than he expected. This marriage, entered into with care and consideration, was off to a good start. Uncle Archibald was a wise old bird. 'We will choose a nice puppy,' he said, 'if you promise to be careful of the rugs.'

'Rugs?' She pretended not to understand.

'When I take you on a tour of inspection, Mrs Peel, I will show you the rugs, some of them are very valuable, they should really be hung on a wall.'

Rose wondered how long it would amuse Ned to call her Mrs Peel. 'I've read,' she said, 'that in Turkey they pen geese on new rugs to make them look old, then, when they've been thoroughly shat on, they are washed in the Bosphorus.'

'I don't like you using that word,' said Ned.

'All right,' said Rose, 'I won't. I'm going to get up now. There's no hurry about the dog. I think I'll have a bitch. A dog might lift his leg against the Chippendale chairs. Don't look like that, Ned, I'm only teasing. Here, take the tray.' She thrust the tray towards him. 'Let me have a bath and then I want to be shown round the house, introduced to every stick of furniture, every picture, every rug.' She laughed, pushing the bedclothes back, exposing her legs. Her nightdress had ridden up her thighs; Ned could see her dark bush as she kicked clear of the bedclothes. 'Give me half an hour, I'll meet you in the garden.'

Ned would have liked to catch hold of her but his hands held the tray; he watched her skip into the bathroom and close the door, shutting him out.

Carrying the tray downstairs, Ned told himself that Rose was very young, malleable, that loving him she would also love his possessions. He put the tray on the kitchen table where Mrs Farthing would find it, then walked through the house and out into the garden.

While delighting in his inheritance, Ned did not feel passionately about the garden. Flowers were insubstantial, they faded, got eaten by slugs, died. It was natural to feel strongly about pictures, furniture, silver and rugs. Ned winced at the memory of Rose's vulgar use of English. The garden, while aesthetically beautiful, was of no intrinsic worth apart, of course, from its value at so much an acre. Ned had a sneaking feeling that here he was lacking in sensitivity, that he ought to feel as passionately about the garden as he did for the house and its contents. Sitting on a stone seat in the sun, he tried to puzzle out this lack in himself, to pin it down. He picked up a stick and swished at a late wasp buzzing near some Japanese anemones. The wasp put on a burst of speed. Ned watched it go. Putting a value on his garden, he ruminated, was as slippery – slippery being the unwelcome word which came to mind – as setting a price on Rose. But surely not, he thought, kicking at a pebble on the path at his feet. He had picked Rose, chosen her with care, taken advice, used his judgement, his wits. I kept my wits about me, thought Ned, sitting in the warmth of late September watching butterflies swoop and hover over a clump of michaelmas daisies. I decided to have her, I picked her out of the crowd at that party, I made up my mind.

'What are you thinking?' Rose joined him sitting at the end of the stone seat, turning towards him: 'You look so serious.'

'I was thinking of the Malones' winter tennis party where I first met you and . . .'

'And?'

'And I fell in love with you.'

'Ah,' said Rose disbelieving, and then, 'I remember, I remember it well.' She let out her breath in a sigh.

They had sat, the newly married pair, each remembering the winter tennis party.

9

Ned remembered Uncle Archibald had said, 'You have to start somewhere,' holding out the invitation to the Malones' tennis party. 'There may be some possible girls. I know the Malones, they are old friends, they built that indoor court just after the war. Their winter tennis party is an event. They get people down from London and mix them with the local talent. It's an annual do not to be missed, a compliment to be invited.' He was enthusiastic.

'I am asked because I have inherited Slepe.' Ned turned the invitation this way and that with suspicious fingers.

'Quite so, and I am asked because we are old friends. We played tennis before the war. His standard was high, almost Wimbledon.'

'Does he still play?'

'No, too arthritic, but he likes to watch the young people. Flora and I always go if we are down south. We will come along with you, if you like. Motor down for the day.'

'I'm not fearfully keen.'

'Come on, Ned, you have to get to know your neighbours at Slepe. The Malones have sons and there will, as I say, be girls.'

'Oh.'

'The sort of girls you should be taking out in London, suitable girls,' said Aunt Flora.

'I sense a trap,' said Ned amused.

'Good God, Ned, the girls won't bite you, you play a decent game of tennis, you have to make a start, it's a year since I advised you to marry, this tennis . . .'

'On Boxing Day? In midwinter? So soon after Christmas dinner? I am more used to a Boxing Day meet or a day's shooting.'

'It's an indoor court, Ned, marvellous to play on. It's wood, makes the game very fast, even quite poor players put up a good show. When you are playing in there and it's blowing and sleeting outside, you will be pleased you came. See more of the girls than muffled up to the eyes and miserable on a shooting stick or bouncing along on a horse they can't hold when all you see is their bums. I've nothing against bums, of course, but a tennis dress in the warmth shows them off better . . .'

'Honestly, Uncle Archie . . .'

'I shall accept for you,' said Ned's uncle. 'I have to ring him up anyway. You get a good lunch,' he added consolingly, 'as well as the exercise, and there's a dance in the evening for those who stay on.'

There had been a men's four, Ned remembered; he had been partnered by Richard Malone against Nicholas Thornby and a visitor from London. The court, as his uncle had said, was marvellous; he found himself playing well.

There were, beside himself, George and Richard Malone, three men from London staying in the house, four vivacious girls, friends of the Malone sons, Emily and Nicholas Thornby, and a very young, very shy Rose, brought in as a stop-gap to fill the place of a girl cousin who was down with flu. Ned enjoyed himself presently, partnering Emily in a mixed doubles. She played a spirited game. Ned noticed that she did not wear a brassière; he was used to girls wearing brassières and found its absence a little disturbing. Twice he missed an easy backhand while thinking about this. Nevertheless, or because of it, he later suggested she might come out to dinner when next she was in London, he not yet being properly installed at Slepe; would she like to dine and dance or go to a theatre?

Later, when Emily and three of the girls from the house party played a women's doubles, Ned watched while Richard Malone sat whispering into his favourite girl's ear, reducing her to fits of giggles. Of the women's four, Emily had been by far the keenest player, leaping up and showing a lot of leg as well as the disturbing breasts, reaching up to smash difficult balls which did not necessarily land in court and might well have gone out if she had left them. Ned noticed Emily again when partnering one of the girls from London; he played against her and her brother Nicholas. They made a curiously cohesive team, giving no quarter.

Of the girls from London, Ned got to know two, later taking them out and receiving invitations back into their milieu. Emily came to London often and when she did she rang him up so that over a period of months he grew to know her fairly well. Imperceptibly she latched on to the group of friends he now saw most often.

It was quite untrue that he had, as he now told Rose, fallen in love with her at the winter tennis party. He had barely noticed her. In any case, during much of the tennis Rose, already rendered invisible by shyness, had absented herself.

It was much later, at another party – Ned had by this time become friends with the Malones – that Ned overheard Mrs Malone say to a friend, 'Isn't it extraordinary that a plain little thing like Rose Freeling should suddenly blossom into a positive beauty.'

'She must be in love,' said Mrs Malone's friend, staring across the room at Rose.

'The boys say not. They say she has no one in particular; both George and Richard find her unapproachable; they both find her extremely attractive.'

'Who is she?' asked Mrs Malone's friend.

'Nobody much,' said Mrs Malone, 'the family is all right, I suppose, but there's no money. The father is a solicitor, not successful, rather ill, on the way out, they say. The mother is a stick. One feels sorry for the girl, she doesn't have much fun. We asked her to the tennis last Boxing Day when some girl fell out. She didn't seem to make much of a mark, but we thought we'd give her another chance and then the boys found her quite ravishing.'

Mrs Malone's friend said, 'Being ravishing isn't everything. One needs money to carry it off.'

'True,' said Mrs Malone, watching Rose across the room standing with a group of men. 'It's funny, though, she was so shy as a child, she was quite ugly, but now . . .'

'I thought Emily Thornby was supposed to be the local beauty,' said Mrs Malone's friend, 'not that she is exactly beautiful.'

'There's not much money there either,' said Mrs Malone, 'but she and that brother of hers have lots of push.'

Ned, overhearing this conversation, began to watch Rose and presently took the opportunity of asking her to dance, preparatory to getting to know her better.

Rose was not wearing anything under her dress, neither brassière nor knickers, but since she did not think about it Ned did not notice, yet he was suddenly anxious to make an impression. The ease with which Rose had stood among the group of men had annoyed him.

So it came about that when for their annual house party for the grouse shooting in Argyll, Uncle Archie and Aunt Flora invited two of Ned's friends, Harold Rhys and Ian Johnson, to form a leaven of young people among their middle-aged friends, Aunt Flora added two of Ned's cousins and let Emily and Nicholas fish successfully for an invitation. It was Uncle Archie who had noticed Rose at the Boxing Day party and been astonished that Flora had not added Rose's name to the list. Although getting to know Rose, Ned was not moving fast enough. 'Quiet girls like Rose Freeling slip through your fingers,' he said, 'get her under the same roof as Ned.'

'But she has no money,' said his wife, who had had none herself and knew this disadvantage.

'In Ned's case it doesn't matter. I thought we were agreed.'

'Very well, I'll write,' said Flora, who had only brought up the lack of money to test her husband. 'You may be right,' she added. 'Ned is the sort of man who gets hooked by an unsuitable girl; I am not sure I should have invited the Thornbys.'

'I find them a lively pair,' said Archibald Loftus, 'the girl makes me laugh.'

'A bit too lively,' said Flora, 'though I can't put my finger on why I think so.'

Touched by his relatives' machinations for his welfare, telling himself that their anxiety was superfluous, Ned after considerable havering had decided to pick Rose from the choice presented to him. He was never in any doubt that she would accept him.

Thus, sitting on the stone seat in the garden at Slepe, the morning after their wedding, Ned honestly believed himself when he told Rose that he had fallen in love with her nine months before at the Boxing Day tennis party.

10

Rose's recollections of the winter tennis party bore little relation to Ned's; perhaps all that they had in common was their initial reluctance to go to it.

Mrs Freeling had answered the telephone and accepted Mrs Malone's last minute invitation on Rose's behalf.

'That's extremely kind of you,' she enthused. 'I am sure she will be delighted. Oh, yes, she plays a reasonable game, though that sounds boastful on my part. Be there by eleven-thirty? Yes, of course she can. The Thornbys will give her a lift? How kind of you to arrange it. Of course, my husband would have brought her, but he's not very well at present. Rose will be thrilled.'

'I am not thrilled,' said Rose, overhearing.

'You should be, you have never been invited there before. The Malones' winter tennis is an event,' said Rose's mother.

'As a stop-gap,' said Rose. 'Barrel-scraping only.'

'What does that matter?' snapped her mother, who felt perpetually guilty that she had not got what she thought to herself as the nerve to launch Rose socially. Rose made no effort herself. 'You make no effort, here's a chance to meet new people. You know how difficult it is for me to give parties for you with your father so unwell and . . .'

'So little money.' Rose knew the litany.

'Really, darling!'

'I don't want to go,' said Rose. 'Tennis in midwinter is ridiculous.'

'It's a covered court. I've heard it's beautifully warm. There will be a house party from London. Nice young people.'

'Don't I know it.' Rose already felt her toes curling with horror at the prospect of meeting sophisticated strangers from London.

'And the Malone boys, Richard and George, you hardly know them since they've grown up. This is a chance to get to know them better.'

'They have had every chance to get to know me all these years, Mother, and they haven't bothered.'

'Rubbish, Rose.' Mrs Freeling stifled her agreement with this statement. When they were little she had invited the Malone boys to the children's party she forced herself to give once a year for Rose, her only child, an enormous effort this, after which she would relapse into her habitual lethargy, feeling that she had done her duty.

'The only time they ever came to this house George Malone threw jelly at the other children and shouted that this was the bloodiest party he had ever been to,' said Rose.

'Well, yes, darling, but he was very young, only eight or ten. Mrs Malone rang up and apologised. She did. I remember it well. The poor little boy was over-excited and had a temperature.'

'Ho!' said Rose. 'Ha!'

'Rose!'

'They made excuses for ever after when you invited them, they never came again.'

'Well, darling, they are grown up now, it's quite different.'

'So am I,' said Rose. She had admired George's action, remembered it with glee, pink and yellow jellies had flown through the air, splattering against the walls of the dining-room, and lodged

48

in nice little girls' hair. George had been right: her mother's parties were of an extreme awfulness. 'He's grown up jolly boring,' she said, 'more's the pity.'

'You don't know him well enough to judge,' said her mother.

'I have no tennis clothes,' said Rose.

'That is not true, you bought new shoes in July.'

'No dress.'

'Rose, you are being difficult.'

'No racquet.'

'You can borrow mine,' said Rose's father, looking up from *The Times*, hoping to put a stop to the argument. 'I shall never use it again,' he said with self-pity.

'Oh, Father,' cried Rose, 'don't!'

'Just go to the party; please your mother; you will find you enjoy it.'

'So you want me to go?'

'I should like to think that my racquet is being used,' said Rose's father, spoiling his otherwise generous offer by his tone of voice, wringing his daughter's heart.

'All right, I'll go,' said Rose. (And why must he wring my heart with his bloody racquet? Why must he thrust his cancer down my throat, she cried to herself as she watched her father fold his newspaper and limp from the room. Why does supposed cancer of the stomach make him limp?) 'I am not going to wear white,' she told her mother.

Mrs Freeling did not answer. Let Rose go wearing every colour of the rainbow, so long as she went. People as rich as the Malones did not invite inconspicuous, shy and – let's face it – moneyless girls like Rose a second time. It was not often one of their guests went down with flu at the crucial minute, leaving a heaven-sent gap. Fate, Mrs Freeling told herself as she made her way to the kitchen to make her shopping list, was not always malign.

If there should be some personable young man at the Malones' party, he might just possibly be attracted to Rose. Ask her out when they got to London. Perhaps Rose was not destined, as she felt herself to have been destined, to be crushed by life. I never had any real opportunities, Mrs Freeling told herself as she

49

planned the day's meals; I have always been crushed.

Mrs Freeling at that time felt particularly harassed since the specialist had said that her husband's only chance was an intensive course of treatment in London. In a week's time they were to move into an expensive flat for half of every week so that Rose's father could receive this treatment, returning to the country at intervals to keep a toehold in his ailing practice.

What harassed Mrs Freeling even more than her husband's probable cancer (there was no certainty yet that he had it), their impecuniosity and Rose's rebarbative shyness was her subconscious wish that her husband would quite simply drop dead, that her long sad unsatisfactory marriage would come to an end while she was still of an age to have some fun. Naturally Mrs Freeling did not know she harboured such thoughts; they milled about in the recesses of her unconscious.

Sulkily, Rose went to the cloakroom where her father's racquet hung in its press. She took it out and twanged the strings.

Upstairs, she fished her tennis shoes out from the back of her cupboard. She had put them away dirty, they were stained green; she laid them aside to blanco. She pushed aside her winter clothes, and pulled out the only summer dress she liked, a simple cotton dress in a deep rose colour made by the village dressmaker the previous summer. Her mother had misjudged the amount of material, bought too much; there had been enough left over from the frock to make matching knickers; it was this that made the dress her favourite. Her mother had bought the material for her and for once she had not questioned her mother's taste. Laying the garments on the bed to be washed and ironed, Rose almost began to look forward to the party.

'My mother,' she said to her reflection in the glass, 'hopes I shall meet Mr Right. God, my hair's a mess!' She went to the bathroom to wash it. 'It's greasy and the ends are splitting.' She was still at the age when girls dramatise their hair; her hair was not in the least greasy, nor were the ends split.

'What are you doing?' Her mother's voice floated up the stairs.

'Washing my hair,' Rose shouted, her head in the basin.

'Don't use all the hot water.'

'It's automatic, it's automatic, she doesn't even think!' Rose plunged her head down in the basin so that water sloshed out onto the floor. As she came up for air, she heard her mother's voice again. 'What?' she shouted. 'Can't hear. What did you say?'

'I said,' Mrs Freeling stood in the bathroom doorway, 'I said Ned Peel is going to be at the tennis party. Oh, look what a mess you've made of the floor. You will mop it up, won't you?'

'Who is Ned Peel?' Rose worked shampoo into her hair.

'Is it good for your hair to wash it so often? You only washed it two days ago. Ned Peel is the man who has come into Slepe, old Mr Peel's heir.'

'So what?'

'Don't be rude, Rose. I was making sure Emily and Nicholas will pick you up tomorrow. Emily told me that he is to be there.'

Rose said nothing, rinsing her hair, rubbing her head with a towel, jerking a comb through the wet hair. 'Don't do that, darling,' said Mrs Freeling, 'let your hair dry naturally; wet hair is so brittle.'

'Mother!'

'All right, darling, I will leave you. I only want you to enjoy yourself . . .' Mrs Freeling retreated. Rose ran after her, flung her arms around her and hugged her. 'Oh, darling, you are making me all wet,' said Mrs Freeling.

'Oh, oh,' whispered Rose, watching her mother go down the stairs, 'neither of us ever gets it right.' She watched her mother's diminishing back with pity. 'Poor Mother, am I supposed to be gobbled up by this Ned Peel?' She began filing her nails, waiting for her hair to dry. I'd better shave my armpits, she thought. And what about my legs? She pulled down her stockings and eyed the soft almost invisible hairs on her legs. No, leave the legs hairy. She went back to the bathroom and stole one of her father's razor blades. After shaving her armpits, she took the blade out of the razor and put it in her purse. A desperate idea had occurred to her.

11

One of the mysteries about Nicholas and Emily was that in spite of their perpetual cries of poverty, they always managed to look chic; they exuded an aura of confidence and one-upmanship which Rose found unnerving. Arriving to fetch her in their father's respectable old Morris, wearing immaculate white tennis clothes under twin camel-hair coats, they jumped out to greet her, showing themselves off.

Rose often thought of them as saplings planted too close together, growing up entwined. She grinned at them posing, their arms round each other's waists. 'Willows,' she said, 'wandlike, unpollarded.'

'What?' asked Emily.

'Nothing,' said Rose.

Nicholas cried, 'How pretty you look, Rose,' meaning: look at us, are we not pretty?

'Shall I sit in the back?' asked Rose, drawing her old school coat around her, muffling it over the pink dress. 'What are the suitcases for?' she asked, squeezing into the back seat, pushing aside tennis racquets and suitcases.

'There's usually a dance in the evening,' said Emily, getting back into the car. 'We've brought our evening clothes to change into.'

'Oh,' said Rose, surprised.

'It's for the house party, but we are prepared, if asked, to stay on for it,' said Nicholas, settling himself in the driver's seat. 'Come on, you old rattler.' The car shot forward.

'I see you've got your father's racquet,' said Emily, whose beady eye missed nothing, 'his new Slazenger. What happened to yours?'

'Bust,' said Rose, feeling inferior. If they had told me about the

52

dance I would have cried off, she thought, seeing in her mind's eye people dancing in evening clothes while she still wore her pink cotton. (She would have sweated under the arms by then, or spilt something down her front.) She said, 'Nobody said anything about dancing to me.'

'Never mind,' said Emily, who had discussed with Nicholas whether to tell Rose and voted not to. (Nothing worse than an odd girl to upset numbers.) 'Nicholas or someone can run you home. We got our racquets in the end of summer sales,' she said, 'they are brand new.'

'They smell nice.' Rose sniffed the leather on the racquet handles. 'Delicious.'

'Father is letting us have this car for ourselves from now on; the diocese are providing him with a new one now he is a bish,' said Nicholas.

'Oh,' said Rose, impressed. 'A car for nothing.'

'We will swop it soon for something more dashing; it looks a bit too churchy, don't you think?' said Emily. 'We want a red sports.'

'One could have guessed,' said Rose.

'A soupçon of vulgarity suits,' sang Nicholas.

'And,' said Emily, leaning over from the front seat, 'Father is sinking his savings in the Rectory.'

'What do you mean?'

'The new parson wants a smaller house. Father is buying the Rectory from the Church Commissioners and putting it jointly in our names. He's heard this will save death duties.'

'Very thoughtful is Father,' said Nicholas.

'We are going to live in it, just us two,' said Emily.

'The real reason is he would find us an embarrassment in the Bishop's Palace,' said Nicholas. 'Not that he actually says so.'

'Why,' asked Rose, bewildered, 'should he?'

'If you don't know, we shan't tell,' said Emily in the tone of voice which would lose her many a friend through life.

Nicholas sniggered.

Rose wished fervently that she had not let her father work on her feelings. 'Have you been to this winter tennis before?' she asked dubiously.

53

'Oh, yes, often,' said Nicholas.

'Several times,' said Emily.

Once, perhaps, thought Rose.

'I hear Ned Peel is going to be there. I hope we shall like him as a neighbour,' said Emily. 'I plan that he shall be an asset.'

'I quite took to him when I met him,' said Nicholas, who had happened to sit next to Ned on the London Underground on a brief journey between Knightsbridge and Piccadilly and seized the opportunity to introduce himself. 'I met him in London not so long ago. Of course, he never came down to Slepe before his uncle died.'

'The old man was a recluse,' said Emily, 'never entertained. Ned hasn't opened the house properly yet, let's hope he's not like his uncle.'

'Oh, no, he's not at all like the old man,' said Nicholas, 'he's entirely different.'

'All the old man liked was his garden, they say,' said Emily. 'He kept a full-time gardener but no proper servants. I bet the house is in a state.'

'Supposed to be full of lovely things,' said Nicholas, double de-clutching around a corner. The Morris, unused to such grand treatment, screeched its gears like a demented turkey and stalled its engine.

'Poor old dodderer, outlived his welcome in this world,' said Nicholas, re-starting the car. 'High time there was some young life at Slepe.'

What a lot they know, thought Rose, wondering whether the skirt of her dress was the right length, sure that it wasn't, fingering her father's racquet as it lay across her knees. It's too heavy, she thought, it's a man's racquet, I shall never be able to play with it, I shall look a fool, I wish I had not come. Then she thought, Nobody will notice me, they never do, they will notice Emily who is so lively, she will hold her own, outdo the girls from London, why the hell should I bother? Then again, she thought, they will all wear white. I shall stand out like a sore thumb. My pink dress will make me obvious when I do something awkward, I don't want to be noticed, and Emily does, they will notice Emily if only because she is wearing white and has a new racquet, I wish I had the nerve to ask Nicholas to drop me by a bus stop to find my way home. (There is no bus stop.)

Nicholas drove the old Morris up to the Malones' front door. 'Here we are, girls, let battle commence.'

They had arrived too early.

George Malone, coming round the house from the stable yard, found them grouped on the doorstep waiting for the bell to be answered.

'Hullo, hullo,' said George, 'you are early birds, we don't start play until twelve, but do come in. Everybody will be changing. I bet some of the girls are not even up yet, there were faces missing at breakfast; we went to a party last night and got to bed in the small hours, but, tell you what, I'll get Betty to take you round to the court, you'd probably like to knock up or something, get your eye in. Will you show them the way, Betty?' said George to the maid who had appeared to open the door. 'You haven't been before, have you?' he said to Emily.

'It's Rose who hasn't been before,' said Emily quickly, 'I know my way to the court. Come on, Rose, I'll lead the way.'

George smiled at Rose and said, 'Does your mother's cook still make those stupendous jellies?' And to Nicholas he said, 'I must rush up and change. Mother likes us to be ready to greet our guests.'

This is where if I liked Nicholas better I would feign a pain and ask him to drive me home, thought Rose, but he would see through me. Why, oh why, do he and Emily make me feel so provincial? She followed Nicholas, Emily and the maid through the house, out through a side door, across a stretch of garden to the building which held the covered court. Here the maid left them.

Nicholas and Emily took off their coats; Nicholas measured the height of the net, adjusted it, bounced several times on the balls of his feet, swung his racquet serving an imaginary ball.

'Isn't George an old comic,' said Emily, swishing her new racquet. 'What was that reference to jellies, Rose?'

'I don't know,' said Rose, remembering with relief that Nicholas and Emily had not been at the party where George had disgraced her mother, but been in bed with mumps.

'Let's knock up,' said Emily, swishing her racquet again. 'Where are the balls?'

'Here.' Nicholas opened a box of new balls. 'Come on, girls, I'll take you both on.'

'No, you and me against Rose and her father's wonder racquet,' cried Emily, 'let Rose Freeling take on the Thornbys.'

'Why not,' said Rose, fiddling with her shoe laces, standing up to confront Emily, gripping her father's racquet. The handle was too thick, intended for a man's hand. It occurred to her that one reason she had so enjoyed George's awful performance with the jellies was that Emily and Nicholas had not witnessed it; life unwitnessed by Nicholas and Emily was tolerable. Nicholas was already on the court practising his service. 'Why don't we play a single and let Rose ball-boy?' Nicholas was furious with George for belittling his sister, snubbing him for his ineptitude at arriving early, and for having secret knowledge of Rose (what's this about jellies? I must find out). He knew George only pretended to think this was Emily's first visit; he had once overheard George tell another man that Emily was a pushy little tart who could do with taking down a peg. Hitting the ball as hard as he could, Nicholas vented his anger. Rose could be whipping boy.

Stepping onto the court, Rose felt Nicholas's enmity linked with Emily's malice; she mistrusted them. She felt the spring in the wooden floor communicate itself to her legs. She swung her father's racquet, returned Nicholas's serve, enjoyed the whizz of the ball, the impact on the strings of the racquet, the feel of the sinews in her wrist reacting. 'I'll take you both on,' she shouted on a rise of spirit.

'Ho! Listen to her! All right, little Rose, we take you at your word. Shall you serve first?' Nicholas patronised.

'No, you.' Rose stood ready near the back line.

'No quarter,' said Nicholas.

'No quarter,' answered Rose.

Emily danced from one foot to the other near the net, looking mockingly at Rose.

Nicholas served, putting all his strength into it.

Rose returned the serve, flukily driving the ball hard and low.

The strings of her father's racquet parted with a twang. The ball, driven across the net with the combination of Rose's strength and the weight of the racquet, thumped into Emily, hitting her hard between her breasts. Emily yelped. 'My breast bone!'

'Sorry!' cried Rose. 'Oh, look what I've done to Father's racquet. Oh, bother, I'll go and see whether I can borrow another from somebody.' She ran lightly from the court, making her escape. Behind her, Emily groaned and Nicholas sympathised. I must get away, thought Rose, running across the garden and into the house. She doubled along a corridor and opened a door at random, shutting it quickly behind her. She was in Mr Malone's library. There was a log fire burning in the fireplace, the smell of hyacinths dotted about the room in large bowls, no sound except the faint ticking of a bracket clock on the mantelshelf and the rustle of ash as a log settled in the grate.

Rose put the broken racquet down on a table, leaned forward on her hands and let furious tears fall onto the polished wood. She stood thus for several minutes, drawing her breath in long shuddering gasps, loathing Nicholas and Emily.

Presently she wiped her eyes with the back of her hand and straightened up.

A yard from her nose across the table were a pair of men's feet, bare, high-arched, long-toed. The heels rested on a copy of the *Field*.

Rose said, 'Oh, my God,' and froze.

The feet disappeared as the legs they belonged to were lowered. A young man stood up, holding the book he had been reading against his chest.

Rose stared. He was not much older than she. Tall, thin, dressed in clothes she had only seen worn by French workmen, baggy cotton trousers in faded blue, a baggy jacket to match over a dark flannel shirt, collarless, fastened at the neck with a bone stud. He had thick, almost black hair worn rather longer than most people, a thin eager face, longish nose, wide mouth and black, intelligent eyes.

They stood staring at each other across the intervening table. On the mantelshelf the clock ticked on while their eyes meeting measured, assessed, questioned.

Then he smiled. 'I must put on my socks. *Je m'appelle Mylo, et vous?*'

'Rose,' said Rose.

'Lovely,' said Mylo, sitting down on the sofa which had hidden him from Rose. 'I have a bloody great hole in the toe of my sock.'

'Oh,' said Rose.

'Why don't you sit down,' said Mylo. 'You could mop your tears with this.' He reached across the table to a blotter and eased out a sheet of blotting paper. '*Comme ça,*' he said, blotting the tears which marked the table. 'Salt isn't good for furniture or cheeks. Salt dries and becomes uncomfortable.' He handed Rose the blotting paper. 'Try it.'

Rose took the sheet of blotting paper and dabbed her face. 'Thanks.'

'Excellent, and now the socks. Just look at that for a hole.' He wiggled his toe through the hole.

'Are you French or English?' Rose moved round the table, nearer the fire.

'Both,' said Mylo. 'French mother, English father. And you?'

'English.'

'Come for the tennis?'

'M-m-m.'

'Bust your racquet on purpose?'

'I had a razor blade with me just in case, but it broke anyway. It's my father's. I was annoyed with somebody.'

'You will have to go back . . .'

'M-m-m.'

'But not just yet. Come and sit here.' He patted the sofa.

Rose sat in a corner of the sofa and drew up her legs. 'Are you going to play?'

'Lord, no. No fear. Not me. I am only the tutor.'

'The what?'

'Tutor. I am here to babble French at George to help the final hoist into the Foreign Office. I am paid for my pains on condition that I don't let a word of English pass my lips. That colour suits you.'

'Oh? Thanks.'

'And you don't really belong in that *galère*. Not for you the marriage market, not for you the auction.'

Rose looked at him in silent question.

'You know that's what it is, don't pretend. I bet your mother or your father pressed you to come to this party.'

'They did,' Rose admitted, 'I suppose.'

'An opportunity to meet . . .'

'Oh, yes,' said Rose impatiently. 'Shut up.'

Mylo manoeuvred the sock so that his toe was no longer exposed, put on its mate. 'It happens in the best societies,' he said, 'a marriage of convenience is a marriage that is often convenient for all, parents, children, everybody. In France where I've lived, it's out in the open, everybody knows. It's decent. In this country it's wrapped up, disguised, cocooned in things like winter tennis parties. I wonder why you were invited.'

'I'm a stop-gap,' said Rose, 'some girl has flu.'

Mylo laughed. 'That explains it.' He began fumbling around to find his shoes. One shoe, after the malicious manner of inanimate objects, had hidden itself under the sofa. Rose observed the back of Mylo's neck while he reached for it. His hair grew down in a point. 'Got it!' He sat up and laced the shoe.

Watching his long fingers lace the shoes, Rose felt inexplicably consoled, then a swift spasm of pleasure. Mylo sat back, straightened his legs stretching them towards the fire, turned towards Rose and observed her.

Rose sitting with her legs tucked under her let her eyes travel from Mylo's feet, now decently shod, past his waist where the too wide trousers were belted in by a leather belt, up over the heavy cotton jacket, going slower now, to his eyes.

'There now,' said Mylo, his lips twitching into a smile. 'We could marry?' he suggested.

'What?'

'What is your attitude to marriage?'

'Trepidation.'

'Both intelligent and beautiful. What do you say, though? Yes or no?'

No one had ever supposed her intelligent; the suggestion coupled with beauty made her laugh. Mylo laughed too. 'My

French side is practical. I have no money, we shall have to wait, but there is nothing to prevent us loving meanwhile, is there?'

'Are you making fun of me?'

'No, I am not. There is nothing funny about love. My father told me. He also told me that it can be extremely painful.'

'Ah.' She had not considered pain in relation to love. 'Oh.'

'I think, before they miss you, you had better go back to the tennis. Then, after a decent interval, come back. You can tell me about yourself and I will tell you about me. Go on, Rose, go.' (I need a moment to think.)

'Must I?' (This is a lunatic conversation.)

'I fear so.' (What am I letting myself in for?)

'All right.' She stood up. 'I'll go.' (Perhaps he's not quite right in the head?)

'But come back.'

'Yes,' she said, 'of course.' She knew she would.

As she turned to go Mylo said, 'This person who annoyed you just now . . .'

'Two people. Nicholas and Emily Thornby.'

'Are you afraid of them?'

'Of course not.'

'What do they do to you?' He did not believe her.

Rose was irresolute. Why expose her frailty, why clarify the Thornbys to this stranger? 'I've known them all my life,' she said defensively. 'Their father was our rector; we were expected to be friends.'

'Give me one example that explains why you are afraid of them.'

'I am not,' Rose denied hotly.

'Come off it.'

'All right. Years ago . . . it was a joke. We were all about six or seven, I was at a convent day school, they were at a progressive school down the road.'

'Yes?'

'I don't see why I should tell you, it's all forgotten years ago,' she back-pedalled.

'You seem to remember.'

'It's pretty silly.'

'Go on . . .'

'They boasted that my nuns were dull and that at their school they learned lots of jokes and funny stories which they brought home to tell their parents and they all laughed at the stories together.'

'That sounds all right.'

'I thought so.'

'Go on.'

'I've never talked about this since it happened. I don't know why I'm telling you now.'

'Do get on with it.' (She looks distressed.)

'Well. They told me their *best*, actually I paid them sixpence for it, they said if your nuns laugh you'll get your sixpence back, I said, Of course my nuns would laugh, they often laughed, they were on the jolly side, those nuns. I thought that I'd try it on my parents first and if they laughed, the nuns would be sure to, my father and mother never laugh much, you see. So I paid my sixpence and Nicholas and Emily told me their story.'

A flash of suspicion. 'Did you understand this story?'

'Of course not, but I couldn't say so, could I?'

'Tell it me, if you remember it.'

'I remember some of it.'

(I bet she remembers all of it.) 'Go on, then.'

'It was about a man and a girl in a punt. They get in the way of a barge and the bargee shouts, "Seeing as how you've a cunt in your punt, I won't say what I was going to say but what I will say is . . ." I really have forgotten the rest . . .'

(Liar.) 'But you told your parents, you remembered it long enough for that.'

'Yes. They had some people in for drinks.'

'And?'

'My father whipped me, and my mother kept me in my room for two days.'

'So the nuns never heard it?'

'No.'

'The nuns might have been kinder.'

'They might not have known the words either.' (It's a funny thing that my mother did.)

'And you were still expected to play with these charmers?'

'Of course. My parents thought I'd heard the story from a rude Catholic child; they complained to Reverend Mother and took me away; there was a hell of a shemozzle.'

'And you never let on?'

'I couldn't let Nicholas and Emily crow.'

'What charming innocent children.'

'Perhaps they did not cry at their baptisms,' said Rose.

'Perhaps you will get your revenge one day.'

'Perhaps I shall,' said Rose, grinning. 'It would be worth my sixpence.'

'I love you.'

'Pulling my leg.'

'No.'

Rose turned again to go. It was too early to tell him that she still did not know the meaning of the offending words; she had not been able to locate them in a dictionary. She had risked her naïvety far enough.

Mylo watched her move towards the door; by the door she looked back. It struck them both that they had not touched, their hands had not even met when he gave her the blotting paper.

'Later?' she said, looking across the space between them.

Mylo nodded.

'And the dangers?' she asked, as though she had previous experience of love, of life.

'We brave them together,' he waved her on her way with his book, 'all of them, Emily and Nicholas, the lot.'

Rose laughed.

'Tell them, out there at the auction, that you have a reserve on you,' said Mylo.

'Then I shall not mind the dangers,' she said. Then, 'Is the reserve a large one?'

'Limitless.'

12

Mylo tried to switch his mind back to his book but it was no use; he laid it down. I will make George read it aloud, he thought, pounce on his terrible accent. While he reads, I can dream. He stood up and paced the room; he felt threatened. A hitherto independent future had become in one instant fused, interlaced with that of the girl in the rose-coloured dress who had burst into the room, disrupting his solitude.

As he paced Mylo remembered his father philosophising on love, on its aspects tragic, comic, pleasurable, painful. A lecture on love as they sat at a café table under plane trees in Provence, his father drinking pastis, his mother stitching to mend a rent in his shirt, his best, which he hoped to wear at the fête that evening. Now and again she stopped stitching to bite a thread and smile quizzically at her husband lecturing their son of ten years on the pitfalls and delights of love, urging him to enjoy but to take it lightly. He must have been a little drunk, thought Mylo, remembering the clouded pastis in the glass, the dappled sunlight slanting across his father's face, lighting his mother's eyes. 'Beware,' his father proclaimed, 'love can alter your whole life, make you change direction, trap you.'

'C'est juste,' said the café owner, pouring his father another drink.

'Your father, of course, never changes direction,' Mylo's mother said, mocking her husband whose chief characteristic was volatility.

'There you go, mock me, sweep the ground from under my feet,' Mylo's father had caught his wife's eye, smiling at her with complicity over the rim of his glass, 'as usual.'

Mylo's mother blushed, returning his father's glance. The café proprietor flapped his napkin remarking, 'C'est un beau *discours*,' and went back inside the café chuckling. Watching his parents Mylo had realised with shock that his parents were in love. He was amazed. Amused by his stunned expression, his mother had said gravely, 'Listen to your father, Mylo, he warns you of this terrible danger which you must avoid at all costs.'

'It is only right that he should be made aware of the risks,' protested his father, 'when he meets . . .'

'This girl like me?' She had let the hands which held the sewing fall into her lap. 'Remember that, Mylo, when the trap closes, *gare à toi*, take note of your papa's warning.'

'But it will be too late,' cried Mylo's father dolefully. '*Il sera foutu*,' and his parents had laughed, watching his puzzled face.

The wonderful thing about them, thought Mylo as he paced Mr Malone's library, had been that their love for each other had buoyed him up, included him, carried him with them. (A stupid unnecessary accident had killed them both, leaving him to face the future by himself at sixteen. There had been enough money to finish his education at the lycée, but none for university. He learned to consider the years spent with his parents in France, England, Germany, Italy, and briefly South Africa, travelling with his father, a peripatetic freelance journalist, as important experience, the University of Life – that humdrum cliché. Bilingual in French and English, he could get by in three other languages.) He had seen his mother insulted as a Jew in Germany, watched the fascists in Italy perform their deadly pantomime, accompanied his father to illicit political meetings in Spain, to incipient Marxist get-togethers in the black parts of Cape Town, grown up to think of himself as English, 'Even though,' as his mother would say, unable properly to pronounce her 'th's', 'they are slow sometimes, they are your people. *Je te donne ton pays*.'

She was an anglophile, his father complained, who longed to live permanently in the filthy English climate rather than that of her native France.

Mylo stopped pacing to stare out at the Malones' garden, neat clipped hedges, raked gravel, orderly flower beds. What would have happened to my mother, he wondered, in the war that is coming? How would things have gone for her as a Jewess in

64

France? Jews are not going to have a very nice time. There is the possibility that unless there is a miracle the villages of England and France will have notices at the crossroads prohibiting Jews, as there are in Germany. And my father, thought Mylo, who wrote exposing the false tricks and hypocrisies of governments, how would he have fared? Could he, would he, have adapted? Most unlikely, thought Mylo, smiling in recollection of how his father had been if not exactly evicted, asked none too politely to leave South Africa. As he looked out at the frosty garden Mylo hummed the song he had helped his father record, a song sung at those secret meetings:

> Tom blows hot,
> Tom blows cold,
> Ev'ry time poor Tom gets so-old,
> Therefore, brothers, black and white,
> Workers of the World unite!

He wished as he sang the words softly that there was a way of indicating to his parents that the hitherto academic experience of which they had laughingly warned him had hit him. 'Bang, smack, wallop,' he said out loud.

'What?' asked Rose, coming into the library.

'What a long time you've been,' he cried.

'I had to play two interminable sets, every time I thought I had nearly lost, my partner won a rally.'

'It's getting dark outside.'

'Yes.' She moved towards the fire. 'I must go home.'

'Not yet!' he cried with pain.

'Mrs Malone said that if I looked in the library I would find a young man called Mylo Cooper. She didn't know that I already had.'

'And?'

'To ask you whether you had had any lunch . . .'

'I haven't.'

'And, if you had not, to drag you away from your books, take you to the kitchen, and get cook to give you tea on a tray. I don't notice you buried in your books.'

'I was thinking of you.'

65

'Oh, good — and she said you were funny about meeting people.'

'It's she who is funny about my meeting people; it's my clothes, I disgrace her socially.'

Rose laughed. 'I thought so. I like them. Then she said that I was to ask you to drive me home, when you've had some tea, that is.'

'And you, too.'

'And she said to take her car, not her husband's.'

'Right. When are you expected home?'

'Not at any particular time. If my mother knows there's a dance, she will hope I will be asked to stay on for it. I do know and I don't want.'

'So we can get ourselves tea, take as long as we like, and you can tell me the story of your life.'

'It's very short and dull.' They stood looking at the garden in its winter sleep. A blackbird alighted on the grass, stood listening, then ran a few paces. A second, stronger bird came flying down and ran aggressively towards the first bird, who flew off cackling.

'I still have not touched you. I am putting it off,' murmured Mylo.

Rose shivered. 'Do you think I'll explode, disappear?'

'You might. This whole thing frightens me,' said Mylo. 'Let's get some tea. I have so much to tell you. I feel faint with love.'

'If you've had no lunch your faintness may be due to hunger,' said Rose, reaching for the mundane.

From the warmth of the Malones' kitchen they had brought a tray laden with teapot, buttery crumpets, bread and butter, strawberry jam, wedges of Christmas cake and mince pies. In the light from the log fire and the frosty starlight of the winter's evening, they ate sitting side by side on the sofa.

It did not seem necessary to talk — the whole of the rest of their lives stretched ahead.

When they had finished Mylo took the tray back to the kitchen. Rose sat waiting for his return, listening to the distant sound of the house party, no longer playing tennis but fooling and flirting in the drawing-room at the other end of the house.

Emily and Nicholas had knit themselves into the company, making their mark with the girls from London, consolidating themselves with the Malones, forgetting her. Waiting for Mylo, Rose felt an elation and trepidation which was entirely new to her, scary.

Mylo, coming back, switched on a lamp, bringing light to pry into dark corners and illuminate Rose's eyes and mouth. He knelt beside her on the hearth rug. '*Elle est belle à la chandelle*,' he quoted.

'*Mais le grand tour gâte tout*,' she carried on.

'So you know Molière?' He was surprised.

'A little. Nicholas taunted me with those lines when I was fifteen . . .'

'I was not going to quote further than the first line. Shall I get even with him for you?'

'I think life will do that. Tell me about you.'

'Where to start?'

'Your parents, perhaps. People always seem to docket one by one's family – it is not always fair.'

'They are dead,' said Mylo.

Rose said nothing.

'I will try and bring them alive for you. While you played tennis I was thinking of them. They once, when I was small, tried to tell me about love. I will tell you what they said some day, but not now.'

'They warned you?'

'They could not warn me against something they cherished so . . .'

'Oh, fortunate people,' Rose exclaimed.

Mylo stared at Rose. 'Yes. My father was clever, rash, impetuous. A burster of bubbles, a reporter of uncomfortable facts. He loved ideas. He was traveller, linguist, lover. He adored my mother, and she him. My mother was Jewish, beautiful, French, determined; she built around us a barrier of love. They had great ups and downs,' said Mylo, 'because my father would not compromise, nor would my mother have allowed him to.'

'And they made you happy?'

'Very happy. You would have loved them, and they you.'

'Thank you for telling me about them.'

Mylo put logs on the fire, stacking them in the glowing ash so that the draught would reach them and they would flare up. 'And you?' he asked gently. 'Shall you tell me about your parents?'

Rose drew a long breath. 'My father is dying of cancer, at least he thinks he is; I find it hard to believe, but that's the general idea. He is a solicitor, not successful, I don't know why. Yes, I do, I must be honest. He is unsuccessful because he is all things to all men, and people don't really like it. He tries to please people when they want plain facts, even nasty ones, so they do not trust him (and nor do I, she whispered). Then he is a snob. It matters very much to him who people are, how much money they have. Why are you laughing?'

'I am not laughing,' said Mylo, who had gasped at the pain in Rose's voice.

'My mother is much the same,' Rose went on, 'but she is shy and awkward. When she has people to the house, she infects them with her embarrassment. I have never spoken of my parents like this before. She is desperately anxious that I should get married to a man with money. She forced me to come to this tennis today; she thought I would meet someone suitable. You *are* laughing.'

'You have met *me*.'

'In her eyes or my father's you would be a calamity,' cried Rose in anguish, 'and awful though I have made them sound, I suppose I love them but,' she cried, 'they do not love each other. The idea of cancer is a plot to escape each other.'

'Oh, my love.' Mylo put his arms round Rose. 'There,' he said, kissing her, 'there, I have touched you at last.' Locking her in his arms, consoling her. 'Oh, my love.' He did not know whether he consoled her for her parents or for his love.

'Mylo, Mylo, Mylo,' Rose loved his name, her arms round his neck, her face against his.

'Listen . . .' he said.

Trooping from the drawing-room through the hall they heard the house party in high-pitched badinage, George's laugh, Richard shouting some fool joke, Nicholas sniggering, the girls answering with coos and yelps, abrupt screams. 'They are going up to change. There is to be a dance.'

'Not for us,' said Rose smugly.

'Shall I drive you home? Fetch your coat and meet me in the back drive by Mrs Malone's car.'

'I must say goodbye and thank her. I'll be quick.' She could not bear to part with him.

'Goodbye,' she said to Mrs Malone, sitting tiredly in the drawing-room, 'and thank you for a lovely day.'

'Pretty boring, I'm afraid, you did not play much tennis. You must come again.' Mrs Malone's head ached; she planned a drink of stiffish whisky while she had her bath. The Freeling girl seemed anxious to leave. And I don't blame her, thought Mrs Malone. All the boys do is work the girls up until they become noisy and shriek, high time they got married, this one seems quiet enough.

Rose fled through the house to join Mylo. 'You will have to remember the names of the suitable people you played tennis with,' he said.

'Tomorrow. Not now.' She slammed the car door shut, sat beside him.

Mylo kissed her, holding her face in his hands. 'Who else have you kissed, Rose?'

'The only person who kissed me did it for a laugh under the mistletoe. He had a wet mouth and a moustache; it was horrible.'

'I can't be jealous of him.'

'There will never be anyone for you to be jealous of . . .'

'Oh, Rose . . .'

How innocent we were, thought Rose half a century on, lying in the hotel bed. Pathetic in a comical way. Embarking on the rapids which crashed us together, tore us apart. In the stillness of the night, from the woods across the creek, there was the sudden shriek of a vixen calling for a dog fox, the blood-chilling scream which has terrified many a city dweller into fits (somebody is getting murdered out there). Rose stiffened in sharp recollection. The vixen screamed again as her ancestress had screamed the night she first met Mylo. Rose lay back, straining her ears. Who am I listening for? Ned? Mylo? Poor Ned, gone. Ned, cremated, dust, dust.

'I won't come in with you,' said Mylo as they drove, 'I will come and see you as soon as I can escape my tutorial duties.'

'It would be better not,' Rose agreed. 'They will not like you,' she said. 'I don't want this day ruined.' My mother, she thought, or my father could sully Mylo with one derogatory glance. I shall feel stronger tomorrow.

'You can regale them with your exploits at tennis.'

'I broke my father's racquet and can't remember who I played with.'

'You will remember by the morning. Shall you tell them about me?'

'Oh, no, they would try and spoil you, you don't know them. I will tell them nothing. I know it is best so.'

'I could shout my joy from the housetops.'

'Better not. When you meet them, you will understand. You could have told your family. I cannot tell mine. They are destructive.'

'Then we shall be secret to one another.'

'Promise?'

'I promise,' said Mylo who, young as he was, knew the dissipating power of gossip. 'It may not be for very long,' he said, 'but I shall keep mum.'

'Stop here,' said Rose. 'There is a short cut through the wood.'

They got out, leaving the car by the side of the road and walked up a grass ride, their feet crunching on the brittle frozen grass. They held hands, walking in silence, then a full moon dodged suddenly from behind a cloud, lighting the bare branches of the trees, exposing their faces to each other so that they stood and stared and examined each line and hollow, every curve of lip and cheek, taking note for their future. Then Mylo held her close and hugged her, and Rose discovered the joy of pressing against him, warming her cold nose against his neck as he nuzzled and kissed her. It was then the vixen screamed. Clinging together, they whispered, 'Hush, listen, will he

70

answer?' And again the vixen screamed.

'Oh, Mylo,' said Rose, 'I hope I never call for you and get no answer.'

'Only death would stop me, although,' said Mylo, laughing now, 'in the nature of things I might get delayed, my love, but I will come, I won't be long.'

How long is fifty years? Rose asked herself, lying sleepless in the hotel bed. How does one calculate the passage of time and retain one's sanity?

13

Mrs Freeling woke early, as was her habit, and heaved herself up on one elbow. Two yards away, her husband slept on his back, his mouth open, his breath going in-out-in-out in lugubrious rhythm.

At this hour before she had collected them, her thoughts wandered stumbling along the route beyond the noticeboard which said, No trespassing. The first unformulated thought said: I wish, if he is going to die, that he would, not hang about like this.

The second said: At least in London we can have separate rooms that will lead without quibble to separate rooms here. Then, if he should die, I could sell this house and move into something smaller, easier to run. Or a flat.

And next: If Rose would only get married, I could live alone.

Then she thought: I did not hear her come in last night; I wonder whether she got to know any new people at the party? She's pretty, it should not be too hard to marry her off to someone suitable. I really must do something about it. I wonder how one begins? I'm so bad at that sort of thing.

Here Mrs Freeling permitted her dream to present her with a

son-in-law who, besides taking Rose on, would gratuitously produce a rent-free house or cottage for his mother-in-law. But that was going too far, too fast. Just let Rose marry.

Mrs Freeling sank back on her pillows and breathed deeply and slowly from her stomach in-out-in-out thirty-six times which should, she had read somewhere, induce beautiful thoughts and peace of mind. Perhaps, she thought, marriage would be all right for Rose; perhaps she would not mind the physical part – so messy at best, so painful at worst. There were women who did not seem to mind. It must be terrible to be raped, thought Mrs Freeling, thrusting into her unconscious the belief that her husband had raped her on their wedding night (and subsequently), and that Rose's birth, another agonising incident, was its direct consequence.

Time to get up.

Mrs Freeling swung her legs over the side of the bed and felt for her slippers. I was stupid, she told herself, getting into her dressing gown, to put up with a double bed all those years. It's been much better since we had twin beds. If Rose marries, I shall advise twin beds from the start.

Mrs Freeling set off to the bathroom.

As she cleaned her teeth, Mrs Freeling thought, Rose should be able to find a husband; if she were ten years older, it would be another story, she would be up against the shortage of men since the last war. There had been 'ten million surplus women, ten million surplus wives' in the words of the music hall song. They didn't know their luck, thought Mrs Freeling, spitting into the basin, rinsing her toothbrush under the tap.

As she dressed, Mrs Freeling shed her waking thoughts, resumed with vest, knickers, suspender belt, stockings, shoes, tweed skirt, blouse and cardigan, her proper persona. Then she knelt briefly by her bed to say her morning prayers, Our Father forgive us our trespasses, before trotting briskly downstairs to see whether the maids had her husband's breakfast tray ready.

'Morning, girls.'

'Morning, madam.'

'I will take it up to him,' she said, supervising the lightly boiled

72

egg, toast, butter, marmalade and china tea, 'he likes me to be there as he wakes. I like to see him.'

'Yes, madam,' said cook.

The house parlourmaid said nothing; she had had a letter from her mother in Wales and felt homesick.

Mrs Freeling carried the tray upstairs. As she passed Rose's bedroom door she rapped on it smartly. 'Time to get up,' she called, 'breakfast is ready.'

Rose groaned, a groan she had perfected during adolescence, knowing the groan was expected. On no account could she let out the shout of, 'I'm in love, I'm in love, I'm in love,' which welled up. Damp it down, treasure it, keep it secret.

'Here we are, darling, here's your breakfast. How did you sleep? Let me plump up your pillows. Wait a sec, here are your teeth – how do you feel this morning, my poor darling? Is that all you need? Yes, I'll ask her at breakfast and get her to come up and tell you all about it. Oh, you'll be up? That's good. Feeling better today? How wonderful. Soon be in London and get started on the treatment. Sooner the better. I'll just open the window a crack, it's a bit fuggy in here. I'll get you a shawl to put round your shoulders . . .'

'Don't fuss me. Leave the window as it is.'

'Oh, very well. I'll send Rose up for the tray presently . . .'

'I'm getting up. Why don't you listen?'

'Of course you are, sorry. It's a lovely morning. I can't wait to hear how Rose got on.'

'I can. She broke my racquet.'

'What? How do you know?'

'Couldn't sleep. Got up and went downstairs to read for a bit. Saw it on the hall table. Brand new Slazenger.'

'Oh, dear, I wonder how it happened?'

'Broke it over some young fool's head.'

'Nonsense, darling, Rose would never . . .'

'Where's *The Times*?'

'Oh, sorry, I forgot to put it on the tray. I'll send Rose up with it, then you . . .'

'Don't bother, can't read the paper properly in bed, uncomfortable.'

73

'I wish. I wish.' Mrs Freeling trotted downstairs to her own breakfast in the dining-room. She would have been horrified if anyone had told her that what she wished was her husband dead. 'We have been married nineteen years,' she often told people, 'and never a cross word.'

'Ah, Rose, are you there? Did you have a good time? Don't come into the room yawning. Was the dance fun?' She offered her cheek for Rose to kiss.

'I didn't dance.'

'Then how was it you got home so late?'

'Oh, Mrs Malone – you know how it is – there were a lot of people – a lot of waiting about – then her car . . .'

'Didn't the Thornbys bring you home?'

'No, Mrs Malone got someone who is staying there to drive me back in her car.'

'How kind of her. One of the young men staying there?'

'A tutor person,' said Rose astutely.

'Oh, really.' Mrs Freeling's interest dimmed. 'You must tell us all about it. Pass the milk, darling. Do sit up, don't slouch, it's so ugly. Your father says you broke his racquet.'

'Yes, I did this tremendous drive. I hit the ball so hard the strings bust.'

'Oh, oh dear.'

'Does it matter? He won't ever need it.'

'Rose, how *can* you!'

'Oh, Mother, don't cry – please don't cry.'

'It's just, it's just all so awful.'

'Oh, Mother, stop. Please. Look, I'll tell you about the tennis party. George Malone asked if cook still makes her jellies, and the new man at Slepe, Ned Peel, was there . . .'

'Ned Peel, did you talk to him much?'

'Not really, no. Not at all, actually.' Rose, hoping to comfort her mother, was sorry to disappoint her.

74

14

I usually managed to disappoint my mother, thought Rose lying in the hotel bed. She had propped the window wide now and thought she could really hear, was not imagining, the rustle of the reeds as they swayed in the still night.

I disappointed my father also, she thought, but not so much. He had his work to think about and his supposed cancer. I wonder whether he did have cancer? Whether it might not have been ulcers or something of that sort? He died of a stroke. I remember my mother's resentment when the bill for the cancer treatment had to be paid. Had all that money been wasted? It's curious how little I know about my parents. Rose abandoned sleep, surrendered to a wakeful night.

They disliked each other, those two, she thought. It was rather dreadful the way they pretended not to.

Presumably they never had any fun in bed. If they had, there would have been ups and downs in their relationship. Lively shouting matches to break the monotony. Their rows were tamped down, never allowed to surface, just the sort of thing to produce ulcers.

Those quarrels, thought Rose, yearned for a bout of healthy fucking. I bet my mother never had an orgasm. My poor Pa would not have known how to set about giving her one. An orgasm for a woman of my mother's generation was a matter of chance. She almost certainly went to her death with an undiscovered clitoris. She always said she was unlucky. I wonder, mused Rose, how much the younger generation's aptitude for guitars has contributed to sexual bliss. I must enquire of Christopher. No, I can't, he would find my question in poor taste. There is too much of Ned in Christopher. No wonder Helen has such a grip.

The least disappointing time for my parents, thought Rose, was the period between the winter tennis party and my marriage to Ned.

It was extraordinary in retrospect how Ned had insinuated himself into the Freelings' lives. Had there been a moment when it would have been possible to put a stop to Ned, choke him off without irreparably hurting him? Dear kind Ned. Was there a moment when I could have cried halt? It was my fault, thought Rose, I was inattentive, I should have seen that his strength was his apparent vulnerability. I used him to deflect attention from Mylo. I trailed Ned as the lapwing trails her wing.

She tried to remember when it had become unremarkable, accepted, for Ned to come constantly to the house.

At first it had been George and Richard who came on one excuse or another on their way to the Thornbys, or bringing some message from their mother to hers in a friendship destined for an early demise, blossoming briefly, to die when Rose married Ned.

Sometimes George and Richard brought Mylo, practising their French. At other times Nicholas and Emily would be there and other young men whose names and faces now eluded her. I was in love, thought Rose, that made me attractive to other men, that is the way it works, just like the animal world.

Mrs Freeling had been delighted, made references to moths and candles, causing her daughter to wince. The advent of this modest number of young men had excited her, increased her subtle pressure for Rose to marry. She picked over the young men deftly. This one's father drank, that one had an uncle who was an undeclared bankrupt, another's mother was rumoured to have Indian blood. How had she discovered these things, to which grapevine did she connect? For an unsociable, retiring woman, she was no slouch. She shuffled the pack, conjuring to the fore the two Malones (the jelly incident forgotten), only to push them aside when Ned appeared and re-appeared, became constant.

She never really noticed Mylo, thought Rose. No warning bell sounded. Rose chuckled forty-eight years later.

Mylo came, dressed now as were all the others in the dress of the day. Tweed jacket and grey flannel trousers, a uniform as ubiquitous as jeans. There had been a brief parental bristle. Wasn't he rather foreign? Jewish, perhaps? No family. No money (poor boy, how worn his shoes). No proper job. No university degree. Frightfully young.

This quasi-invisible put-down, which applied in varying degree to lots of people, was enough for Mylo to steer clear, for them to meet secretly where they could be together unobserved: in the woods in fine weather, in churches when it rained. They pretended an interest in brass rubbing if anyone chanced to interrupt them absorbed in talk, sitting entwined in the most comfortable pew or reading aloud to each other. Our love, like prayers, must have soaked into the walls of those churches, stirred the loins of the long dead under the brasses, thought Rose.

Mylo had acquired his little car so they travelled far afield. It had belonged to a friend of Mylo's father who, owing him a favour, repaid it to the son.

When the Freelings moved to London for Mr Freeling's cancer treatment, they met in the museums, picnicked in the parks, strolled hand in hand in Kew Gardens, lolled in Richmond Park. Mylo by this time had finished his stint at the Malones (George never acquired a good accent, but was famous for fluency) and was looking for a job.

While Rose floated on cloud nine, Ned grew closer. Kind and friendly to her parents, consistently attentive, taking her to Quaglino's, the Écu de France, to dine and dance at the Berkeley, to lunch at the Savoy. To the regatta at Henley (surprising in his pink socks), to the Eton and Harrow Ball, to the Air Show, to Wimbledon, to theatres and cinemas, displaying the kingdoms of his world. Had she played him off against Mylo, had she been seduced by Ned's offerings?

If only I had not been a virgin, thought Rose. If only I had known what I learned later, that the hungry coupling of the young which failed us in that smelly little hotel could become a glorious leisurely indulgence.

How had the trap closed? Was there a day when Mylo gave up? Did he stand back, angry? When had she decided to opt for safety and pleasing her parents? (Be fair, I was pleased too.) Impossible now to put a finger on it, enough that she had said, 'Yes, all right,' walking with Ned in the dusk, in his Uncle Archibald's glen with the curlew crying.

It was then, Rose thought wryly, that her parents had stopped feeling their disappointment, had quite liked each other, basking in a joint glow of parental success.

I was so young, Rose excused herself, and Mylo was so young too. If only we could have waited.

My parents' liking for each other did not last. But the trap closed and I, thought Rose, grew fond of my jailer. Mylo, angry and estranged, absorbed by the war, disappeared; he might, in his silence, have been dead, so totally did he withdraw.

The telephone had rung while she was in her bath before dressing for her wedding.

'Somebody wants you on the telephone, he won't give his name' – her mother had been irritated – 'won't give a message.'

Wrapped in her bath towel she had heard his husky voice: 'Meet me at the corner of the street. It's not too late. Come quick, don't stop to think. I've got the car.'

'How can I? I'm in my bath. I . . .'

'I shan't bother you again, then.' He was furious.

'Oh, please, please, don't go, don't say goodbye,' she had screamed, regardless of her mother listening on the stair.

'I am not saying it . . .' He had rung off.

One of Ned's secrets was a sense of insecurity. He needed to be reassured, pampered. Something of a parvenu – he was only a distant cousin of the old Peel, had not grown up expecting to inherit – he enjoyed obsequious waiters bowing to his money as they pulled out chairs, flapped napkins, proffered menus, and I, thought Rose, was too young, too naïve to observe this until later. Poor Ned, I no longer mind but there were times when I deeply resented the asking and the giving of that promise. Poor old Ned, poor Ned.

I wonder, thought Rose jerking awake before she finally drifted into sleep, where I put Ned's ashes?

I am growing so forgetful, she thought worriedly, I am for ever losing things.

Then, How stupid of me. How could I forget? Helen took charge of them. Helen would, thought Rose, smiling none too kindly in the dark. One wonders, does Helen pleasure Christopher? He wears such a discontented expression. He was such a dear little boy. Now he has a sad look to him. Does Helen look covertly at me and wonder how Ned and I got on in bed? Will she care for Slepe as I did? Where will she decide to put Ned's ashes? Is Ned, in ash, feeling more secure? There was never any need for Ned to worry.

Through the open window came the hotel cat, viewed on his way to hunt the night away. Now he sprang onto Rose's bed, stepping onto her body to tread and purr, pressing down his claws to clench the bedclothes, catching and extracting them, purring and rumbling in ecstasy and Rose, released by surprise, wept for Ned for the first time since he had died.

15

'So,' Ned said, relinquishing his imprecise memories of the winter tennis, 'shall I show you round the house? Shall we do the grand tour?' He was impatient, proud of his possessions, anxious to show them off, present Rose with her future.

Rose jumped up. 'Could we walk round the garden first?'

'If that's what you'd like.' He would indulge her. 'I know nothing about gardens,' he said, striking at a passing bee, swishing the head off a Japanese anemone.

Rose retrieved the decapitated flower. 'Nor do I know much, but I am ready to learn.' She walked ahead of him.

The paved path led through the garden to wrought-iron gates leading into a second garden. 'How lovely,' Rose exclaimed, 'two walled gardens, what riches, what wonderful flowers.' She looked around, pleased.

'It's very disorderly.' Ned looked about critically.

'That's what's so exciting,' said Rose. 'I like it.'

'There's a third and larger garden for vegetables and fruit,' Ned said. 'It should be useful if food gets short as it did in the nineteen-fourteen war. I hope Farthing knows his onions. Ah, there is Farthing – we'd better say hullo.' He took Rose's arm above the elbow, 'This is my wife, Farthing, Mrs Peel.'

'Ah,' said Farthing, looking Rose over (as though I need pruning, Rose told herself). Farthing was a man of sixty with leathery outdoor skin, small bright eyes, a puckered mouth and obstinate chin. He was a very small man, no taller than Rose.

Rose took his hand. 'Your garden is gorgeous.'

'Who did that?' Farthing's eye seemed to slide down Rose's arm to the flower head in her hand.

'An accident.' She would not betray Ned.

'I saw him,' said Farthing. 'Bees is useful animals.' He had witnessed Ned swish at the bee.

'He missed.' Rose grinned. 'Do you keep bees?'

'Two, three hives, depends.'

'How are the vegetables, has it been a good season?' Ned felt excluded.

'Veggies is all right.' Farthing was studying Rose.

I wish he'd call me sir, thought Ned. 'We should concentrate on vegetables from now on,' he asserted his authority.

'But not to the exclusion of flowers, Ned, bees need them and honey is frightfully important; sugar is going to be rationed, and without disturbing the flowers, there are lots of vegetables which can be grown among them, aren't there, Mr Farthing?'

'Hadn't thought to do that, Miss, good idea. Farthing will do, Miss, just Farthing.'

'Mrs,' corrected Ned, 'since yesterday. Mrs Peel.'

'Ah,' said Farthing, 'um.'

He is teasing Ned, thought Rose. 'Will you teach me to work in the garden?' she asked Farthing. 'When I'm on my own.'

'Ah,' said Farthing, 'veggies is through there.' He nodded towards a door in the wall. 'Nice crop of onions and shallots; my old gentleman was fond of garlic too.'

'Good,' said Rose. 'Come on, Ned, let's look.' She led the way into the kitchen garden. 'This is all jolly orderly,' she said, pointing at the rows of vegetables. 'What a lovely man; isn't he nice, Ned?'

'He will have to get used to me,' said Ned, 'he misses my uncle.' Lovely was not, he felt, an applicable word for the gardener.

'Of course he does. One can read his feelings, his love in the gardens.'

'I can't say I can, but he seemed to take to you . . .'

'Come on, Ned, don't be grumpy, just look at that crop of onions! They would win prizes anywhere.'

(I am not grumpy.) 'I'd rather show you the house, come along . . .' Ned walked her past the rows of onions ripening in the sun, turning his eyes away from the fruits of Farthing's labours. 'Fortunately Mrs Farthing has looked after the furniture rather well. The house needs a lot doing to it, but we shall have to wait until after the war. All I've done so far is to put in an Aga. My uncle made do with a monumental Victorian range. It all needs modernising.'

'Is Mrs Farthing pleased?'

'She should be. Of course she is. Here, come this way into the house, by the side door.' Ned led the way. 'When you get to know the house you shall help me decide what needs doing to it. This is the kitchen. Hullo, Mrs Farthing, this is Mrs Peel.'

Rose and Mrs Farthing shook hands. 'How do you do,' said Rose.

Mrs Farthing, thin, wiry, tall and energetic, stood defensively by a kitchen table scrubbed pale. Rose could imagine Mrs Farthing's bony hands wielding the scrubbing brush which had worn the grain of the wood into almost parallel lines. At the moment Mrs Farthing made show of making pastry; Rose felt she intended to be found at work. The legitimate occupier. Newcomer keep out. 'A lovely kitchen.' Rose genuinely liked it.

'We must modernise it,' said Ned, looking round, 'get advice.'

'I expect Mrs Farthing can tell you what needs to be done, she would be the person to know.' She had noticed the older woman flush.

Mrs Farthing did not relax. 'Our cottage kitchen is as we

wanted it, our Mr Peel did that for us.'

If she snubs him as hard as that, there will be out-on-your-ear trouble. 'Do you have a cat in your cottage? A kitchen should have a cat; there should be a cat here, shouldn't there, Ned?' Rose burbled nervously.

'Do you want a cat?' asked Ned doubtfully.

'We have our cat in the cottage, Miss, expecting kittens, Miss.'

(Another one calling her Miss; she's a married woman, I made her so last night. Ned tingled in recollection.)

'Would you let me have one, or two, perhaps, to keep each other company?'

'Yes, Miss, if you like, Miss. Farthing was going to drown . . .'

'Oh, no!'

'Steady on, I said I'd let you have a dog, we'll be eaten out of house and . . .'

'I love cats. My mother never let me have one. They earn their keep, don't they, Mrs Farthing?'

Mrs Farthing's mouth semi-smiled. 'Of course, Miss.'

Ned siphoned air up his nose, as Rose had known her father do when particularly irritated. (I bet her cat is fat as butter, and no great mouser.) 'Show me the house,' she said quickly. 'Come on, Ned. I want to see everything, the pictures, furniture, silver, glass, rugs, the lot.'

Mrs Farthing watched them go. 'She may do,' she said to her husband coming into the kitchen with a trug of vegetables. 'Wipe your feet.'

'Ah,' said Farthing, 'give her one of they honeycombs for her tea.'

'Oh, my,' said his wife sarcastically, 'charmed already!'

'Makes a change,' said Farthing, kicking off his boots, 'we must learn to call him sir, if we want him happy.' Farthing was sardonic.

'And her Mrs?'

Husband and wife doubled up in wheezy mirth.

'I shall be alone in the house when you are gone, with the Farthings in their cottage, just me with my dog and my cats,' said Rose.

'Shall you be nervous?' Ned was uneasy.

'I like being alone.' (Surely Mylo will be here sometimes, if only in my thoughts.) 'What is this room?' Rose opened a door.

'The drawing-room. When you have the lay of the house, I want to decide what rooms to keep open. When the Ministry people move into the back, they will have their own entrance, but everything from that part of the house must be stored. So Rose, pay attention, there really isn't time to look at the view, this is not an ordinary honeymoon . . .' He let irritation escape.

'No.' Rose turned back from the window. 'It's not.' She stopped looking out at the garden which she would grow to love. (He has already decided what rooms to keep in use, where to store the furniture.) 'What's the matter, Ned?'

'I want you to like it here, it's yours as much as mine, you know it is.' He caught hold of her and held her.

'No, it's not.' She drew away.

Ned curbed his irritation. I am not doing this right. She doesn't know what this house means to me, she has no idea of the sanctity of inheritance. 'It's ours, dear, and will be our children's.'

Rose turned back towards the garden which enchanted through the window; unbelievably she had not envisaged children (why must he call me 'dear'?) 'Oh, Ned.' She looked away.

'I had so hoped you would like it.'

'I do. I do. Give me time. It's such a lot to take in. Start telling me. Who, for instance, is the privileged gent above the fireplace watching us now?'

'Augustus Napley. He married Angelica Peel. They did not get on. My uncle moved her matching portrait into the dining-room, said they looked much happier apart. My uncle was inclined to be whimsical, a fanciful old man.' Ned was disparaging of his relation.

'I would have liked him.'

'Maybe you would. Shall I go on?'

'Do.'

Ned led her about the house explaining, naming, and describing his treasures. Rose stopped listening, content to wear an intelligent expression; later, by herself, she would get to know the house, develop her own rapport.

After lunch they strolled across the fields to the farm so that Ned could introduce her to his farming tenant and his wife. 'The Hadleys have farmed here for years; you will not go short of milk, butter, eggs and cream.'

'How you harp on about food.'

'I thought you might like to send me hampers when I'm with the regiment,' said Ned huffily.

'Ensuring your popularity.'

Ned looked at her sharply. He had not realised that she was so, so un-meek.

The Hadleys, John and Tina, were both large and friendly, their several children friendly also. Ned talked farming with John Hadley; Rose saw that he was at ease with them, quite knowledgeable on farming. He expanded in the farmhouse atmosphere and made earthy jokes which made the Hadleys laugh, but not Rose; she did not understand them. Watching Ned with the Hadleys she wondered whether they were as bucolic as they seemed, or putting it on to please Ned. When they left, the Hadleys told her to come over whenever she pleased, there would always be a welcome.

Walking back to Slepe, Rose said, 'I like them, but they are not as interesting as the Farthings. The Hadleys are open, the Farthings closed.'

'I can't say I find the Farthings likeable, but they do their job; everything is above board at the farm; the Farthings are different.'

'That's what I like,' said Rose.

'I hope you will not be bored when you are on your own.'

'Of course not. I shall find plenty to do.'

'You are only twenty-five miles from your parents.'

'Yes.'

'And five from the Thornbys.'

'Yes.'

'And ten from the Malones.'

'I'm not madly sociable, Ned.'

'I shall be able to get home whenever I get leave, so long,

that is, as we are in England.'

'Of course.'

'There is talk, strictly between ourselves, of France.'

'When?'

'Soonish.'

'France!' (Mylo is in France. That parcel . . .) 'How soon?'

'Any time now, I fear. Damn, who is that over there in the drive waving?'

'Emily Thornby.'

'One would have credited her with more tact,' exclaimed Ned, furious, 'than to call on the first day of our honeymoon.'

'You did say it was no ordinary honeymoon,' said Rose unkindly.

'Hullo,' shouted Emily, advancing. 'I was just passing, thought I'd stop and see how you are getting on.'

'Very well, thanks,' Ned said with chill.

'I shan't stay,' said Emily laughing, 'I can see I am not welcome.' Her eyes danced brightly from Rose to Ned and back to Ned.

'Come in and have a drink,' suggested Rose.

'Thanks. I've our wedding present in the car. Nicholas and I were late buying it, couldn't make up our minds or raise the cash. Like to fetch it from the car, Ned?'

Ned moved off towards Emily's car, grudging every stride.

'Eventually we managed to charge it to Mrs Malone's account,' said Emily, grinning. 'It's all right, she'll never notice.' She watched Ned's back. 'How are you? What's marriage like?' Emily lowered her voice an octave. 'Do you think you can manage?' Her eyes swept over Rose from head to toe, then up again.

'What's the present?' asked Rose, feeling herself flush.

'A lamp from Peter Jones, Fortnums wouldn't charge to Mrs Malone. It's a Tiffany copy guaranteed to give a soft glow. Nicholas tried it, it's quite sexy. Are you all right?' she persisted.

'Of course I am,' said Rose, stung into replying.

Emily made a moue and giggled. 'That's good.' She was watching Ned's return with a cardboard box in his arms. 'We hoped you would be, Nicholas and I . . .'

Ned put the box down beside Rose. 'I'll walk you to your car, Emily.'

'Oh,' said Emily. 'Rose has just suggested a drink.'

'Some other time,' Ned had her by the elbow, 'not today.'

'Oho,' said Emily, tossing her narrow nose upwards, 'so that's how it is.'

'That's right.' Ned opened Emily's car door and started pushing her in.

'What's she like then, Ned?'

Ned smacked Emily's bottom hard.

'Ouch!' cried Emily.

'Be off,' said Ned, good humoured, and slammed the car door.

'That's better,' murmured Mrs Farthing, watching from a window, 'maybe he will do.'

'What did you want to do that for?' asked Rose as Emily drove off.

'She had it coming,' said Ned, rubbing his hands together. 'I quite hurt my hand, she has a hard bottom.'

'I thought men like you never hit women,' said Rose, wondering why the curious little scene with Emily disturbed her.

'It depends on the woman.' Ned closed the subject.

'I know I am very naïve,' said Rose.

'Bless you,' said Ned. He put his hand, which still stung, around Rose's waist and drew her towards the house. 'Come indoors, it's getting chilly. Your naïvety is part of your charm,' he said.

As she walked towards the house, Rose wondered whether in similar circumstances Mylo would have smacked Emily. I do not know why Ned should want to hit her. She is irritating, but surely – and would Mylo? In the hall Rose stood still and suddenly she shivered. I must stop thinking of Mylo, stop making comparisons. It isn't fair. I have promised Ned. Promised. She was hit by a wave of anguish. I must keep Mylo separate, or I shall go mad.

'What's the matter, Rose, are you cold? Are you tired? Why do you shiver? A goose, is it a goose?' Ned, unnerved by Rose's distraught expression, tried a joke.

Rose shook her head. 'No goose,' she said, 'no grave. It's

nothing, perhaps I need a jersey.'

'Are you sure?'

'Let me take it easy, Ned. I hadn't realised how much there is to this marriage business. Your house, your possessions, your people . . .'

'Well, dear . . .'

'I will work it out, I will, I won't let you down.' Rose held her hand out to Ned. 'I am being silly.'

'Yes,' said Ned, puzzled, 'you are.'

She wondered whether he was being obtuse on purpose, whether he was trying to protect her as already she found herself protecting him. Last night, she thought, I tried to pretend it was Mylo; it didn't work. There is no way being in bed with Ned could ever resemble being with Mylo. He is gone anyway, she told herself bitterly, all that talk of phoning was just eye-wash.

'I think I'll have a bath and warm up,' she said.

'You do that. Then come and join me in a drink.' Ned moved towards the drinks in the drawing-room. We must shut up this room, it's too big, he thought, stack the furniture, use the old man's library for the duration. He let his mind snake through the rooms, deciding what furniture to move, what to store, which rooms to keep in use. He poured himself a drink, wandered back into the hall, shouted up the stairs, 'Don't take too long, I need you with me.' Listened for Rose's faint answer, wandered slowly back to the fireplace. I need to imprint my house on Rose, he thought as he stood listening for her return, but all he heard was the mocking clack of jackdaws coming down the chimney. He struck a match and bent to light the fire. 'That'll put paid to you.' He watched the smoke curl up.

16

The Farthings watched Ned enjoy his honeymoon with detachment. It amused them to observe the satisfaction he derived fitting Rose in among his property. He manipulated her with the same care that he lavished on the Sheraton desk, the sofa table, the Regency commodes, the sofa, armchairs, bookshelves and rugs with which he furnished the room that had been his uncle's library, moving and removing until he was satisfied that each piece was in an appropriate position.

He led Rose about, showing her every room, satisfying himself that she belonged in it, then walking her through his fields, showing her the boundaries of his property, bonding her to his land.

Just as they had noticed him adopt with his uniform a military persona, so, surrounded by his inherited possessions, they watched him cherish them and with them his appendage wife, making complete his role as landed gentleman. For a man who had until lately scarcely put foot outside London, they granted that Ned did not do too badly.

It entertained the Farthings inordinately when Ned took an almost womanly interest in his household, making lists of stores which could be hoarded prior to rationing and probable shortages, ordering, besides groceries, large stocks of coal and anthracite, arranging with the Hadleys to stockpile logs for winter fires. He even, much to Mrs Farthing's delight, checked and criticised Rose's meagre trousseau, telling her that she must as soon as maybe get herself more warm clothes, thick sweaters, trousers, fur boots to overcome the absence of decent heating at Slepe, a draughty house with several outside doors.

'Thinks of everything,' said Farthing, laconic.

'Grocery list as long as your arm,' said his wife, extending her arm in sardonic gesture.

'Knows it all,' said Farthing.

'Not quite,' said Mrs Farthing and waited until Ned had come back with Rose from depleting the stocks in the market town, to suggest a fresh list of stores, without which she maintained the war could not be weathered. Olive oil, cans of golden syrup, rice and sugar.

None too pleased, Ned took Rose on a second foray and was even less pleased when she, entering into the spirit of things, added to the list lavatory paper, candles, dog food in tins, and Roget et Gallet bath soap.

'But there is no dog . . .' protested Ned.

'There will be . . .'

'She'll grow up,' said Farthing, taking time off from the garden to help his wife stack the stores in the pantry cupboards. 'Fact is, her's begun.' Farthing liked to talk yokel on occasion.

'My poor back!' Mrs Farthing straightened up, groaning. 'We'll teach her when he's gone to put butter down in salt and pot eggs *and* he's made no provision for ham and sides of bacon.' Mrs Farthing eased herself, her hand pressed against the small of her back.

'A pig?' suggested her husband.

'Too soft-hearted, I'd say.'

'Um. Farm pig, then?'

'That'll do.'

'Who's it all for? Won't have evacuees.'

'Wants to have his fellow officers to stay. Heard him telling her.'

'What did she say to that?'

'Yes, Ned, why don't you. As though she's not to live here herself.'

'She's only half here. Think she'll settle when he's gone?'

'Dare say she will find her own way; hers is not his, that's for sure.'

On the last evening of Ned's leave he led Rose to an outbuilding in the copse behind the garages. 'It's in here,' he said, unlocking a padlocked outhouse. 'I will show you where I keep the key.

The petrol is in those tanks.' He showed her two large galvanised iron receptacles. 'You will see, if you climb up those steps, the petrol is in the jerrycans stacked inside them, a hundred gallons.'

'Golly!' Rose peered down from the steps. 'What a lot.'

'I got one of the chaps from the regiment to help me put it there; the Farthings do not know, of course.'

No 'of course' about it, thought Rose, watching her husband lock the door.

'You are only to use it in case of dire emergency,' said Ned, 'it's not for joy-riding.'

'What would dire emergency be?'

'A German invasion.'

'So I could hop it to Scotland?' Rose was amused.

Ned did not care for her frivolity. 'It's more than a possibility, from what I hear from the War Office.'

'Do you have a direct line?' Rose teased.

'One gets one's information,' said Ned.

Does one indeed? thought Rose.

'Should I be posted overseas, I shall lay up my car; it eats petrol; I am getting you a small Morris of moderate consumption.'

'Oh. How moderate?'

'It's a surprise. The garage will bring it tomorrow.'

'I am surprised. Thank you, Ned.'

'It's not new, it's second-hand.'

'Good enough to bolt from the Germans in a dire emergency.'

Ned was not sure what to make of his wife's tone. He looked at his bride sharply, trying to read her thoughts.

A dire emergency, Rose was thinking as she turned smiling eyes on her husband, would be if I had to rush to Mylo, but I cannot rush as I do not know where he is; I cannot rush into a void.

'I am sad,' she exclaimed with sudden passion.

'I am only going as far as Aldershot.' Ned misunderstood her. 'I am, too, but I shall be home whenever I can. One gets leave. I shall bring people to stay. You will not be lonely long. I will ring up.'

'You will ring up?'

'Of course I shall. I shall telephone often, every day probably.'

'Oh, Ned. Yes, of course. I had not thought of that.' (And Mylo? When will he telephone?)

'If you find you're lonely, there's your family. The . . .'

'I shall be all right, Ned, I am looking forward to being alone,' she said hurriedly. 'I don't want . . .'

'That's nice!' exclaimed Ned, hurt.

How did I let that slip? 'You know I don't mean looking forward to being without you. I mean that I am quite happy on my own, I am used to my own company. I am an only child, Ned.'

'Dear,' said Ned, 'it's my last evening.' He put his arm around her. 'Come to bed.'

Tomorrow, thought Rose climbing upstairs, when he is gone, I shall open the parcel. Perhaps it will tell me where Mylo is. There will be a message. There is bound to be a message. 'All right, hurry up,' she said to Ned to hasten his departure.

Ned took her hand and ran up the last few steps with her, misunderstanding. In the large rather lumpy fourposter Ned took Rose then, assuaged, lay sleepily considering his honeymoon which had passed so swiftly and busily. He was content as he reviewed the rearrangement of the rooms, the storing of the stores, the plans of what he had yet to do when he came on leave. 'It's wonderful,' he said drowsily, 'how well you fit in to Slepe, it's as though you had been here for ever, you belong here.'

Rose gritted her teeth, biting back the rejoinder, I am not one of your Regency commodes. 'I think one of the things I must do is get a new mattress for this bed,' she said. 'It's bloody lumpy.'

'It seems all right to me.' Ned was nearly asleep (he must teach her not to swear).

Rose lay wondering what was in Mylo's parcel. Perhaps there would be a message to come at once and she had already waited seven days to open it. Perhaps she would go in the car Ned was giving her, treating her flight as a case of 'dire emergency'. But I cannot, I promised not to leave; promises cannot be broken. Had Ned, poor kind Ned, sleeping now, an inkling of what he had done by extracting that promise?

Do I like or loathe Ned? Rose asked herself, and unconsciously kicked her foot towards him, jerking as a dog jerks in his dream, withdrawing her foot in shame as her toenail grazed his calf. Ned did not stir.

In the morning when he had dressed in his uniform, buckling his Sam Browne belt, brilliant with polish, when he had jerked the tunic down to lie flat over his chest as yet bare of medals (those would come), put on with the uniform his military air, driven away in his car to join his regiment, and with it after many false alarms the war, Rose, barely waiting for him to be out of sight, bounded upstairs three at a time to take from where it lay hidden in a drawer under her nightdress Mylo's parcel.

Mylo had sent her a Bonnard lithograph.

Tearing away the wrappings, turning it over, she found no message, no hint of an address.

She sat staring at the picture, disappointed. Then as she looked she became aware that there was no need of written word. The tenderness with which the lover in the picture encircled the girl with his arm, the way she looked down into his face told her all that was needed.

Thus we sat in that glade in Richmond Park, so we lolled on the lawns of Hampton Court, it was like that in the gardens of Kew, in the country round my home, so it will be, said the picture Mylo had sent her, for us two, for our lives, for ever.

Her promise to Ned must be kept, but it would in no way alter the love she had for Mylo.

Presently, carrying the picture, she went down to the kitchen to borrow a hammer and beg a nail from Mrs Farthing. Then to her bedroom to hang the picture where she would see it last thing at night and first thing on waking.

'Looks happier now,' said Mrs Farthing to her husband. 'Don't bring in all that mud, wipe your feet.'

'Hang that picture?' asked Farthing, aware as was his wife of everything new coming into the house.

'Looks so,' said Mrs Farthing.

'M-m-m . . .' muttered Farthing, satisfied that his swift brain and x-ray eyes had deduced the content of the foreign parcel to be a picture.

17

The prospect of exploring her new home without Ned held considerable allure. There were parts of the garden where he had prevented her lingering, a room opening out of their bedroom she would like to turn into a sitting-room for herself and furnish with small pieces of the furniture he had covered with dust sheets; she would extract them from the sad mass in quarantine for the duration. There was also the Farthings' pregnant cat to be visited.

When the car Ned had promised her was delivered she would drive up to London to choose a new mattress for the bed. I have nothing against the bed per se, she told herself, it is the mattress which is bloody awful. I want to be rid of the mattress Ned just fucked me on. (I will use words he deplores if I wish; he is mealy-mouthed.) All the same he is thoughtful to give me my own car, I should be more grateful. The sooner the car is delivered, the better.

As she waited for the car she wandered about the garden, then sat watching a pair of blackbirds gorging on fallen mulberries scattered like clots of blood under a tree. 'What a mess,' Ned had remarked disgustedly, 'something must be done about that.' The blackbirds were doing something.

The driver of the car hooted as it drew up at the house. Rose ran to meet it. She was disappointed to see Emily; she had expected a mechanic from the village garage. 'Brought your surprise.' Emily stepped out of the car which had been her father the bishop's. 'Ned's present.'

Hard on Emily's heels came Nicholas driving a shiny MG. 'Hail the bride!' Nicholas shouted, bringing the MG to a halt beside his sister. 'Is Ned gone? Does the bride grieve for her groom? Actually,' he said, stepping out of the car, 'we know he is gone, we passed him on the top road.'

'He looks very fine in uniform,' said Emily. 'Larger, somehow. Don't you find him larger than you expected, Rose?'

'No,' said Rose, watching her neighbours' (she did not at that moment look on them as friends) faces. This is some trick on somebody's part, she thought, but I shall not delight them by letting on and rising to their bait. 'I see you have acquired your slice of vulgarity,' she said, gathering her nonchalance about her, managing to ignore Emily's double entendre. 'I trust you have filled the tank with petrol, topped up the battery, checked the tyres? Have you brought its insurance papers and so on?' she asked coolly. 'Or did you give them to Ned?'

She walked round patting the bishop's car as though she was pleased with it. 'Dear old thing,' she said, 'it reminds me of the Malones' winter tennis where I first met Ned' (and my darling Mylo) 'and we fell in love. If you didn't know Ned as well as I do, you would not credit him with sentimentality, would you?' Rose looked smiling at Nicholas and Emily standing now by their red sports car. She began to laugh, forcing herself. 'Sorry I can't ask you in,' she said, 'I was only waiting for you to bring it to be off to London. Let's see you drive away in your new-found vulgarity – oh, I must not be unfair to the car. I have a whole day's shopping and I'm late already. We were expecting you earlier, but Ned couldn't wait.' (How am I doing?)

Nicholas and Emily's eyes met.

They were not expecting that, thought Rose, they now don't know whether I knew what Ned had done or not. Maybe I shall like the bishop's car, he is a rather nice old man. Later I may be able to work out whether Ned tricked me, or they tricked Ned.

'Are those its papers? Thanks, Nicholas.' She took the car papers from Nicholas.

The way Ned smacked Emily's bottom has something to do with this, she thought, but it doesn't matter, it is not as though I were in love with Ned, none of them know how safe I feel.

Rose stood contemplating Nicholas and Emily, who growing uneasy under her amused scrutiny now wished to be away. What had seemed a splendid jape had in some peculiar way backfired. It was not Rose who stood surprised, disappointed and cut down to size, but themselves.

From the open window of the library, the telephone pealed. 'I must answer that, it will be Ned,' Rose exclaimed. 'Goodbye, thanks, see you soon.' She leapt up the front steps into the house and shut the door, leaving them in the drive.

'Oh, God, let it be Mylo,' she prayed as she ran, but God was not answering prayers that day; it was Ned.

'Rose, I should have told you about the car.'

'Should you?'

'It occurred to me as I drove that I should have explained to you that I had bought the Thornbys' car.'

'Did it?'

'Yes. I thought you might . . .'

'Might what?'

'Might have expected something better, I . . .'

'Oh?'

'It's in frightfully good nick. The bishop . . .'

'And ultra respectable.'

'What?'

'Everyone will expect me to wear gaiters.'

'What?'

'What?'

'Are you disappointed? I rather wondered as I drove along whether you were expecting something better.'

'Oh, no, Ned. Why do you repeat yourself?'

'They had set their hearts on . . .'

'I know, Ned.'

'So you don't?'

'No, I don't.'

'Well then, I . . .'

'Where are you, Ned?'

'Half way to Aldershot, why?'

'Then go the whole way. I am going to London to buy a mattress and swop a few wedding presents.'

'Oh, Rose, which? We didn't discuss . . .'

'Nicholas and Emily's, for a start; they charged that lamp to Mrs Malone's account.'

'I can't believe . . .'

'I can.'

'Your time is up,' said the operator, bored.

'Oh, Rose!'

And did they charge the MG to your account at the garage?
Rose replaced the receiver.

18

Life which had been as it were nibbling at Rose's edges took off.
During the first six to eight months of the war she grew up.

The tide of evacuee children from London which engulfed the
neighbourhood at the outset of war ebbed and retreated as the
expected mass bombing and poison gassing of major cities failed
to materialise. Of the first exodus, only two waif-like children
remained to lodge with the Farthings and grow, by 1945, as
countrified and robust as any local child.

Ned, who his neighbours had been inclined to vilify for his
selfishness (and foresight) in making over the major part of his
house to the Ministry of Information, was now envied for his
perspicacity in avoiding the problem of giving houseroom to
children who might have infested heads or wet their beds. That
nobody had actually had experience of such children was neither
here nor there. The whole country was rife with horror stories of
evacuees, just as later it would be with personal bomb experi-
ences. During the lull known as the phoney war householders
with spare rooms filled them with old aunts or maiden cousins
who would join the Red Cross or WVS and make themselves
useful to their hosts, as domestic servants vanished.

Rose, new to her role in the neighbourhood, was barely
aware of the discussion and general upset, accompanied by self-
justification, that went on; she was occupied learning to run a
house as large and inconvenient as Slepe, catering for Ned's
friends when he brought them on leave clamouring for drinks, hot

meals, hot baths, warm beds. At night Ned would expect what he called his 'roll in the hay', regimental life having the effect of making him much randier than had been his pre-war mode.

Lying in Ned's uxurious embrace Rose tried not to listen for the telephone. As the months passed she disciplined herself to listen less, not to run when it did ring, nor lose her breath as she snatched up the receiver.

The Finnish war began and sadly ended. Winter grew vicious. It snowed and froze, pipes burst when it relaxed temporarily before freezing harder. All over England plumbers who had not joined the forces became the kings of society.

Ned and his regiment were moved at short notice to France.

Rose was alone at Slepe, listening to the radio, gleaning news of a frozen Maginot Line, of ice-bound northern Europe. She brought two of Mrs Farthing's kittens into the house and stocked up with hot-water bottles. Huddling in her bed with the cats and hot bottles she shivered as the wind howled round the house and whoofed down the chimneys. Still the telephone failed to deliver Mylo's voice. Seeking comfort from the lithograph he had sent her, she staved off loneliness.

There were times waking in the night when she questioned whether he had sent the Bonnard. There had been no written word inside the parcel. Almost his last words, she remembered with desolation, had been, 'I shall not bother you again.'

From time to time, mindful of soon-to-come petrol rationing, she drove to London to pay a duty visit to her parents who since her marriage remained permanently in town, her father concentrating on his cancer treatment. (It did not seem to be doing him much good, nor did he appear worse.) She drove into a London whose streets, parks and squares were deep in frozen slush, stained grey and brown with grime.

She brought her parents cream and butter from the farm and on occasion a fowl. ('I fear,' she warned them, once, 'that this is the last time I shall come by car; it will be more difficult to bring you things by train.' 'Nonsense,' said her mother, 'you are a strong girl; your father needs a bit extra.')

She stayed with them for as short a time as was decent. Visiting her parents confused her. Then she fled their probing eyes, their unspoken questions. When she reached the street she muttered her answers: 'No, I am not pregnant, and no, I am not happy.'

After one such visit, walking down Sloane Street, she ran into Mrs Malone. The older woman was struck by Rose's pinched appearance. She stopped, chatted, invited her to lunch near by. 'The Cordon Bleu is still functioning.'

Rose was about to refuse, say that she had a full day's shopping ahead, that she was not hungry. They were standing downwind from the Kenya Coffee Shop; a customer coming out brought into the icy street a waft of coffee. Rose's mouth filled with saliva. 'Thanks,' she said, 'I'd love to.'

They sat in the restaurant and ordered their food. Rose told Mrs Malone that she had been visiting her parents, so explaining her presence in London.

'I hear that they have let their house,' said Mrs Malone, 'for the duration of the war, and might sell.'

'They have not told me,' said Rose, surprised.

'Not wanting to bother you.' Mrs Malone buttered her bread; she was hungry and could not wait for the waitress to bring the ordered dish. 'Your mother,' she said munching, 'would rather live in London, she expects your father to die.'

Rose, who also expected this but had never voiced the eventuality to anyone other than Mylo, said nothing; she did not feel she knew Mrs Malone well enough to discuss death.

'You should call me Edith,' said Mrs Malone, 'that's the name I'm stuck with.'

'Oh,' said Rose. 'Edith, thank you.'

The waitress brought their order. Edith Malone began to eat. 'Go ahead, eat. It is easier,' she said, 'to talk about your father dying to a comparative stranger than to your mother.'

'I suppose . . .' Rose took a mouthful of food; it was good, its goodness made the topic of her father's demise worse. 'I suppose . . .'

'Of course, your mother's trouble is that your father is not dying, he has not got cancer.'

'Oh.'

'I know his physician. This situation is tough on your mother, she had hoped to become free . . .' Mrs Malone munched on.

'How do you . . .?'

'I know, but I do not suppose your mother does.' Edith masticated slowly. 'If she does, she suppresses it. Your mother tries to be good, she had a Christian upbringing no doubt, is repressed, and is constipated.'

'She is continually dosing herself.' Rose could not help her laughter.

'There you are. I wonder whether they have any profiteroles, so delicious, or has the war put a stop?'

'A stop,' said a passing waitress who seemed to know Mrs Malone.

'Then, coffee for two,' said Edith. 'Black. Your mother now hopes that if they stay in London the God of War will oblige with a bomb and remove your father.'

'There are no raids.' Rose was convulsed with merriment.

'There will be,' Edith assured Rose, delighted to have made her laugh.

'Then what does she do?' Rose warmed to this new version of Edith Malone.

'Oh, then she will start *living*,' said Edith, sipping her coffee, 'but,' she was suddenly sad, 'she may find that life when lived resembles coffee in that the smell is more delicious than the liquid. You didn't know I was so wise, did you?'

'No.' Rose grinned at her. 'I didn't.'

I wish, thought Edith, that stupid George or idiot Richard had snapped this girl up before letting Ned Peel get her. Why did I never notice her properly? I could have done something about it. 'If you have nothing better to do,' she said, 'come with me to Harrods. I want to stock up with toys.'

'Toys?' Rose was mystified. 'Why?'

'There may be a shortage presently, bound to be. Already this morning I found there are no glass balls for the Christmas tree. All made in Germany by our *enemies*! Ridiculous, isn't it, what brings home the reality of war.'

'Yes,' said Rose (the reality of war for me is no Mylo).

'When this phoney war is over, there will be another wave of evacuee children. I plan to fill the house. I did not want them any more than anyone else. I am now rather ashamed. I am stocking up with toys and presents for them. Will you help me, give me your afternoon?'

'I would love to.'

'Good,' said Edith, paying the bill. 'We can house ten children; they can use the tennis court as their playroom.'

'I didn't know . . .' began Rose.

'Didn't know a woman like me could have a social conscience? Don't be fooled. I am going to enjoy those children just as much as your mother will enjoy her widowhood.'

Rose, shocked and pleased, asked, 'What about Mr Malone? Does he know?'

'He will enjoy them. I haven't told him yet. He never had much time for George and Richard when they were small, too busy making money. It's much easier to enjoy other people's children, one isn't ultimately responsible. Come along, we are wasting time. Have you a car?'

'Yes, the bishop's. Why?'

'I can load you up with my parcels.'

'Of course, but wouldn't you rather have Harrods deliver?'

'There might be a raid which would prevent them,' said Edith hopefully. 'Rather fun, is it not, not knowing from one moment to the next whether or not we are to be raided?' Then, noting Rose's puzzled expression she said, 'Come, my dear, it's no use being glum, it's better to get the maximum enjoyment out of every situation – in this case, the war.'

'I had not pictured things that way.'

'Then do start. Enjoyment is good for morale. Good morale wins wars. By the way, did you say the bishop's car? The Thornbys'?'

'Yes. Ned bought it from them.'

Or they sold it him, thought Edith. 'See a lot of those two? Nicholas and Emily?'

'Not all that much.'

'You'll get a fresh insight into life there too, I gather. Something that boy we had to tutor George in French said about them rather interested me. An observant fellow, that.'

Rose looked away, biting back her longing to talk of Mylo to this new Edith Malone, but it was risky, she must not. She followed Edith into Harrods thinking that if Edith was able to present her with a novel view not only of herself but of her parents, she might well be capable of unveiling a new Mylo, but he is all mine, she thought, only I must discover him.

Presently, loading Rose's car with her parcels of toys – she herself would be returning to the country by train a day later – Edith Malone thought it would not be wrong to suggest to George and Richard that they should take Rose out, enliven her grass widowhood. 'Come over to supper one day,' she said. 'I will ring up and fix it. George and Richard will be on leave soon, they would like to see you.'

Rose rather doubted this. 'I have not seen them for ages. What are they doing?'

'George is soon to be posted abroad, and Richard has at last got himself into the Wavy Navy. You will come, won't you?'

'I'd love to,' said Rose.

So life nibbled a little further, but reserved its fiercest nips for later.

19

Rose caught a bad cold towards the end of the winter. She would have shaken it off if she had, as Mrs Farthing suggested, stayed in bed or in one room in an even temperature; but this she would not do. She moved, sneezing, from the kitchen which was warm through icy passages to the library, which was too hot near the log fire but refrigerating if you moved six feet away from it. She tramped about the garden making plans with Farthing, although she knew he would only pay lip service to her and carry on in his own way. She visited the farm where she got in the Hadleys' way. She needed to acquaint herself with Slepe as she saw it, not as Ned had shown it her; she was not used to the responsibility thrust on her, and would take time to bear it. In Mrs Farthing's book she crowned her stupidity by going to London to meet Ned coming on leave from France, hanging about a draughty station waiting for his train. It was an hour late after a mine scare in the Channel.

Their journey home was slow, the train crowded and cold.

Ned wanted her with him every moment of his leave, whether in the house or tramping the estate. He was gloomy, depressed and unusually silent. The campaign in Norway was raging disastrously and he was convinced that when the weather broke there would be fighting in France. He was pessimistic about the war, derogatory about the government. He confided his fears to Rose, snuffling in his arms. He did not like the new mattress she had bought at Heals and did not hesitate to say so. He banished the kittens from the bedroom, refusing to let them in when they scratched temperately but persistently at the door in the watches of the night, causing Rose to screw up her toes with suppressed fury. He was afraid too of catching Rose's cold. 'I shall give it to everyone in the mess,' he grumbled.

'I am sorry, Ned. I can't help having a cold. I didn't plan it on purpose.'

'You've no idea how cold it is in France. I shall probably develop pneumonia,' Ned grumbled louder, shifting his position and snatching the bedclothes round his shoulders and away from his wife.

'Then you can get invalided out of the war,' she tried to cheer him as she pulled the sheet back.

'I shan't catch pneumonia until we are overrun by the Germans. Then it will be too late . . .'

'Ned, do stop moaning, you haven't caught my cold yet, you may be immune to my germs. What's the matter with you? I've never known you like this, tell me for God's sake.'

Instead of answering Ned rolled over her and made love, climaxing with a grunt and collapsing on top of her so that her face was squashed against his shoulder and with nasal passages blocked with mucus she nearly suffocated.

'For heaven's sake get off.' She dug her nails into him.

Ned shifted a little. 'What's the matter?'

'You are squashing me. I can't breathe, move over. These acrobatics are supposed to be pleasurable and romantic. Oh, God, where is my handkerchief, where's it got to?' She found it and blew her nose violently.

'Damn you, blast you, fuck you, bugger you and your cold,' cried Ned and began to weep with great gulping sobs. 'Oh, shit.'

'Ned!' She had never heard him swear. 'What's the matter? What is it? I'm sorry about my filthy cold.' Nor had she ever known a man cry.

Ned went on crying.

Rose sat up and cradled his head against her chest. 'Ned, tell me, what has happened to you?'

Ned's sobs subsided; he circled her with his arms, pressing his face against her breast, his copious tears soaking her nightdress. Presently he fumbled for her handkerchief and ignoring her germs blew his nose. Then he lay back with his head on his arms drawing himself away from her. 'The truth is,' he said, 'I am afraid. I am afraid of the war. I am scared. I lie awake in France imagining what it is going to be like, what it will be like to be wounded. What it will be like to die. I can't discuss it with anyone. I wish I had not told you. You will now, I take it, want nothing more to do with a coward.'

Rose felt a rush of affection for Ned. 'Ned, darling, I love you. I swore I would not leave you, don't you remember?' (I could let her off her promise, thought Ned, no, no, I couldn't.) 'I am sure you won't get wounded, why should you? Everyone says this war is going to be quite different to nineteen fourteen, no casualties.'

'That's what they say . . .'

'You won't get killed. I'm sure of it. You are not a coward. We are all frightened, all of us, I am afraid all the time and especially at night, that's why I have the cats for company.' In speaking of fear she dredged up terrors as yet suppressed, she would share them with him, offer them to him.

'You use your cats as hot-water bottles. How do you know I won't get killed?'

'I just know it.' She sought to be robust.

'I may be maimed. I may get my legs blown off. I may be

blinded. I may be deafened. There's a fellow who trod on a mine near the Maginot Line who had his legs blown off and is now both blind and deaf.'

'How near are you to the Maginot Line?'

'About a hundred miles.'

'Oh, Ned . . .'

'I am glad you are afraid, too. I thought it was just me. There's no need for you to be afraid here at Slepe.' Almost he was jealous of his fear, unwilling to share it.

'We are all afraid. We wouldn't be human else.'

'Sure you won't leave me?'

'I promised.'

Ned sighed, turning towards her: 'I can hear those fucking cats scratching at the door. Shall I let them in?'

'Yes, please, Ned.'

He got heavily out of bed, crossed the room and opened the door: 'Come in, you little bastards.' He closed the door on the feline entry and got back in bed, bringing with him a cold draught. He lay holding her hand.

'What started all this bad language, Ned? It's not you.'

'What is me? What am I? Everyone swears, with the men every other word is fuck or bloody, it's catching.'

'Like my cold.'

Ned laughed. 'Everyone . . .'

'They are afraid, too. They have the horrors, too.'

'Glad, glad to hear it.' Ned fell asleep breathing deeply, absorbed by his sleep. Rose listened wakeful to Ned's breathing, felt the cats' stealthy approach, the light leap onto the bed, the rhythmic treading of paws, the soft purr in kitten throats as they settled in the hollow between husband and wife.

Three days later at the end of his leave she went with Ned to London. He was cheerful, almost exuberant. They went to his tailor and ordered a new uniform, then on to Wiltons for lunch. They ate a dozen oysters each and Ned made a tasteless joke about the waste of the sexual effect now that they were to part. Rose was not hungry and watched him eat her brown bread and butter with his own and drink two pints of Guinness. She went with him in the taxi to Victoria and was still chatting from the draughty platform when the guard blew his whistle. She tiptoed up and kissed him goodbye. The train drew out. She waved until it was out of sight.

There had been no further mention of Ned's horrors. She felt extremely ill.

She crossed to Paddington in a taxi and caught the afternoon train home.

When Mrs Farthing sent for the doctor he came two days later; he was rushed off his feet, both his partners had joined up. He took Rose's temperature and listened to her chest.

'You've got bronchial pneumonia; I fear there is no available bed in the hospital.'

Rose croaked that she was glad to hear it, she would rather die in her own bed in her own good time. The doctor turned the cats out of the room. Rose crawled to the door to let them in again while Mrs Farthing saw the doctor out. When Mrs Farthing came back with a fresh hot-water bottle and a hot honey drink she raised her eyebrows. 'What you want is for Farthing to make a hole in the door, then they can come and go as they please. Won't make a mite of difference to the draughts.'

'Thanks,' Rose whispered.

'Farthing's taking the bishop's car to fetch you your medicine.'

'Thanks.'

'What you need in here is a nice fire going.'

'Lovely . . .'

During the days that followed Rose listened as she fought for breath to the radio announcer describing the retreat from Norway and was glad good kind Ned was not there. Once she woke in the night screaming that Mylo was drowning in a cold fiord. She put on the light and keeping her eyes on the Bonnard lithograph knew that he had sent it even though he sent no word. She decided that as she was so near death, she must do something about it. She made up her mind to think positively about life after pneumonia; it was just possible it would be worth living.

When the train pulled out of Victoria Ned pulled up the window and straightened his back, cricked from the drawn-out farewell to Rose. It was amazing how plain a head cold could make a girl look. He undid a couple of uniform buttons, sat back and shook out his evening paper. By some fluke he seemed to have the carriage to himself. He felt very well after his lunch of oysters and wished retrospectively that he had taken more advantage of his marital rights while on leave. It had been irritating of Rose to have such an awful cold.

When the door from the corridor slid open and a girl backed in Ned put down his paper and stared. She was adjusting a notice on the glass door which said 'Reserved'. She stepped over his legs and stuck a similar notice on the window beside him.

'Hullo, Ned,' said Emily.

'What are you doing here?'

'Same as you. Travelling to Dover. My job is peripatetic.'

'Where did you get those notices?'

'We had an uncle on the board of GWR, Nicholas pinched them when he showed us behind the scenes at Paddington. We find them jolly useful in wartime.' Emily now pulled down the blinds on the corridor side of the carriage.

'What are you doing that for?'

'The blackout.'

'It's still daylight.'

'I thought it would be nice for us to be private.' Emily looked as alert as a blackbird listening for a worm. 'Ghastly cold poor old Rose has got, hope you haven't caught it. I was watching you from along the train.'

'You are not really going to Dover to work.'

'How did you guess?'

'You followed me.'

'Flattered?'

'Why did you?'

'Ask a silly question,' said Emily pertly. 'I thought it would be nice for us.'

'Oh.' Ned edged away as Emily settled on the seat beside him.

The train rocked over some points, gathering speed. Emily edged back closer.

'I'm a married man,' said Ned stiffly.

'So you are,' Emily agreed.

'I'm in love with my wife, she's very much in love with me.'

'If you believe that, you'll believe anything.'

Ned raised an angry hand.

'No need to hit me.' Emily let her hand rest in Ned's lap. 'What have we here?'

'Emily, do behave.' Ned began to laugh.

'Why don't we behave as we feel. Why don't we have an enjoyable journey, fill in the time usefully?'

'In a train? One can't . . .'

'There's precious little one can't do in a train.'

'Emily. No.'

'Come on, Ned – by the way, what made you hit me like that the other day? You hurt me.'

'I meant to. I hurt my hand. What *are* you doing, Emily?'

'Unbuttoning your flies. Oh, look!'

'Where d'you learn all this?' asked Ned presently.

'Never you mind.'

'I'm sure this position is a sexual deviation.'

'Suitable for trains.'

'Really, Emily, I . . .'

'If your boat to France gets delayed by mines in the Channel, we could put up for the night in that lovely hotel. Last time Nicholas and I were there we stuffed ourselves with oysters. Isn't it marvellous, they aren't rationed?'

'Rose and I had oysters for lunch.'

'Rather wasted on Rose. Will she be faithful to you?'

'Of course she will.'

'You sure?'

'Of course. We're married. She promised.'

'And men are different?'

'Men – well, yes – men have different habits.'

'In that case . . .'

'I warn you, Emily, I shan't let you become a habit,' said Ned firmly.

'Who suggested such a thing? What a silly idea,' said Emily, putting on lipstick, powdering her nose, combing her hair. 'I'm not a habit. Not me. I'm a pastime.'

'A passing fancy,' said Ned hopefully.

'Possibly.' Emily licked her finger and smoothed her eyebrows, peering at her reflection in the looking glass above the seat.

Ned patted her behind as she adjusted her skirt. 'Perhaps there will be mines in the Channel,' he suggested.

But Emily had found the journey to be just the right length. 'I have to meet a chap from the Min of Ag,' she said. 'Sorry.' She kissed Ned lightly. 'Goodbye, Ned. Thanks a lot. I really do have a job,' she said, 'he's one of the loonies who want to plough up the South Downs, but you try the hotel if you are delayed.' She slipped out of the train as it drew into the station and ran towards the exit.

Ned wondered as he took his luggage down from the rack and struggled into his greatcoat why he tolerated Emily's behaviour, why he found her wantonness amusing. Thank God, he thought, there's nothing like that in Rose and smiled as he summoned a porter at the recollection of Rose's red and swollen nose. A bad cold is better than any chastity belt, he thought, following the porter along the platform and, pleased by his wit (could he call it an epigram?), decided to store it and air it in one of the conversations which tended to arise on guest nights in the mess.

The crossing to France was cold and rough. Ned sheltered from the wind in the lee of a funnel, preferring to stay on deck wrapped in a sense of well being. He thought fondly of Rose. As he passed through Paris there might be time to buy her some decent scent. (Emily had smelt rather nice.) As Uncle Archie had predicted, an inexperienced bride was what was needed; he was grateful to the old rascal. My marriage is working out well, he thought, remembering Rose with more tenderness than he had felt when he was with her. He slept in the train to Paris, huddled in a crowded carriage, and woke feeling calm. Somehow his leave had kitted him out for the war. He forgot the terrors he had confided in Rose and congratulated himself on the episode with Emily, thinking that he had handled her rather well. It did not occur to him that he owed his new confidence to one or other or both girls; he was too nice a man to go in for much soul-searching.

20

George Malone, sent by his mother to invite Rose over for the weekend, was horrified to find her so ill.

'Lord, Rose, you do look a dying duck!'

Rose wheezed, coughed, struggled to hitch herself higher on her pillows, flopped back fumbling for her handkerchief, her mouth full of phlegm.

'Here, wait . . .' George bent, heaved her up, piling and patting the pillows behind her. 'That better?'

Rose spat into her handkerchief, nodded. Her face, George noted, was grey, translucent. 'Who is looking after you?'

'Mrs Farthing.' Her voice was a hoarse whisper.

'What about your mother?'

'Sent a message – can't – Father's ill, too.'

'That old chestnut!' George had heard of Mr Freeling's poor health for years and was disinclined to believe in it. His father had often remarked, Whenever Freeling has something he wants to do, especially if there is money in it, he becomes quite well. 'We've all heard that one.' He pulled up a chair, took Rose's hand and rubbed it between both of his. 'What does your doctor say?'

'Bronchial pneumonia,' whispered Rose and was off again, coughing, wheezing, fighting for breath.

'You should be in hospital.' George was alarmed.

'No. Hate them . . .'

'Surely it would be . . .'

'No, bossed about . . .'

'True.' George looked around the room. 'Are you warm enough?'

'Yes.' Rose lay with her eyes closed. 'Cats, hot-water bottles . . .' she smiled, 'wouldn't be allowed in hospital.'

'They would not.' George's eyes, getting used to the lumps and bumps in the bed, noted the cats staring across Rose's body with a mixture of apprehension and insolence. 'The passages in this house are like a morgue,' he said. 'Let me make up your fire.'

'Thanks,' she said croakily.

George poked the fire, laid on fresh coal and logs, watched it flame up. 'I'll just go and see Mrs Farthing.'

'They are not well either.'

Finding Mrs Farthing in her cottage, George said angrily, 'Mrs Peel is bloody ill.'

'No need to swear. Farthing is ill too and so are the children, I'm doing all I can.'

'She shouldn't be alone in that cold house.'

'Listen,' said Mrs Farthing aggressively, 'to that.' She pointed to the ceiling and George listening heard a coughing chorus. 'Can't cut myself in two,' said Mrs Farthing. 'Her mother won't come, she doesn't like her anyway. Doctor says it's an epidemic and the last bed in the hospital is gone. She wouldn't go, said she was waiting for a telephone call. I could have sent Farthing or one of the little girls.'

'From Ned?' George was not interested in the little girls.

'Didn't say. Don't think so. She won't let me tell him.'

'I heard on the radio this morning that all leave is stopped; he'd only be worried sick,' said George. 'They must be expecting some movement over there. A push, perhaps.'

'Huh,' said Mrs Farthing, 'might do him good to worry.'

George let this pass. 'What does the doctor say?'

'Keep her warm. Give her her medicine, lots of liquids and hope for the best.'

'And your husband? The children?'

'Same thing, but it's only flu; she's got pneumonia.'

Mrs Farthing, George realised, was near exhaustion. 'I'm sorry I was so abrupt,' he said. 'What about you? You don't look good.' Upstairs one of the children began to cry. 'Would it help if I stayed?' he asked. 'I can keep the fires going, give her hot drinks. I'll telephone my mother.'

'You could, I suppose,' Mrs Farthing admitted. 'If the fire was lit in the hall, it would warm the house a bit and there's the Aga in the kitchen.' She sounded more grudging than grateful. 'It's worrying when she's delirious.'

'Delirious?'

'Looks so, keeps saying, "I should have been more tender" over and over.'

'I'll go and telephone my mother.'

Back in the house George built up the Aga, lit the fires in the hall and in the library, went back to Rose's room and stood watching as she slept. She looked awful, he thought, remembering her cheerful and pretty. She was not pretty now.

He telephoned his mother.

'Oh dear! Your leave. Never mind, it can't be helped. I'm waiting for Richard to arrive, then we'll come over and take it in turns.'

'I can manage.'

'Don't be silly. Did you say the girl's mother won't come? Really, that woman! All she wanted was to get Rose off her hands – I'm sure her husband is not ill – well, we had better be neighbourly. I wonder whether the Thornbys would help. They live much nearer. No,' she answered herself, 'much too selfish.'

Too ill to notice what was going on, it was days before Rose realised that the Malones had come en bloc to care for her. Edith sent Mrs Farthing away to care for her own family, dealt with the doctor, miraculously organised warmth in the house and nursed Rose, bashing up her pillows, blanket-bathing her, overseeing the intake of medicaments while her husband and sons answered the telephone, ran errands and stoked the fires. Since it was Richard's leave and George was expecting to be sent abroad, the Malones kept together, the anxiety of war giving the family even greater unity than usual.

Edith allowed herself a number of uncharitable criticisms when she thought of Rose's neglectful parents. If I was her mother, she thought, or if I was her mother-in-law, and she looked reproachfully at her bachelor sons, blaming them. Slow in the uptake, slow off the mark, she thought.

After four days the doctor pronounced Rose out of danger. The elder Malones withdrew with Richard, who was due in

Plymouth to join his ship. George was left to fetch, carry and tempt Rose to eat.

George sat with Rose and read aloud passages of *War and Peace*. While she lay ill, one of the telephone calls had been for him; he was posted to Moscow; must leave in two weeks. 'One should know something of their literature . . .'

'Do you speak Russian?' Her voice was gaining strength.

'Only French. My French is pretty good. You will not remember, but I had a French tutor.'

'Did he telephone?' She raised herself on the pillows.

'The tutor? Why should he? Oh, you mean Ned. No, he didn't. Too busy, I expect. If one can believe the news, things are on the move over there or will be soon.'

No telephone. 'Send me an Astrakhan hat.' Her voice drooped.

'I'll try.'

'There's the telephone!' She struggled to sit up, to get out of bed.

'Lie still,' he pushed her back, 'I'll answer it.' George left the room.

Rose listened, straining her ears. 'Who was it?'

'Nicholas and Emily asking whether they can come over and have a bath. After much grovelling they've got the plumber to mend their burst pipes, but he's making a meal of it, he's cut off their water. What shall I say?'

'Let them come.'

'Selfish beasts, they could have come before, I told them you were ill.'

'It doesn't matter.'

George went slowly down again. He did not want Nicholas and Emily to come over. He heard himself telling Nicholas that it wouldn't be possible for them to come that day: 'Come when I'm gone,' he heard himself say. 'I'll leave a list of jobs for you with the Farthings.' This is my last afternoon with Rose, he thought. He was half way up the stairs when the telephone rang again. Rose should get an extension put by her bed; all this haring up and down stairs was ridiculous. 'Hullo,' he shouted unnecessarily loud. 'Who is it? Rose is ill in bed.'

'Tell her,' said Mrs Freeling, 'that her father is dead.'

'Wolf, cry wolf,' George murmured as he went back to Rose. 'Who was it?'

It occurred to George that she was expecting a telephone call; he remembered a lovesick teenage cousin wearing just such an expression. 'Your mother, she . . .'

'Is my father better?'

'Dead,' said George, embarrassed.

'Oh.' She lay back. 'Cancer?'

'Doesn't sound like it. She said she went into his room this morning with his breakfast tray, his usual lightly boiled egg, and found that he had died in his sleep, a stroke. A coronary, perhaps?'

'What else did she say?'

George debated whether to gloss over what Mrs Freeling had said. 'If you give me your hot-water bottle, I'll take it down and refill it,' he prevaricated.

Rose fumbled for the bottle, come to rest under the cats, pulled it free and handed it to George. 'What else did she say, George?'

'What a waste of an egg when they are in such short supply.' George snatched the hot-water bottle and left the room. His laughter exploded on the stairs.

Bringing the fresh bottle after a decent interval, George apologised. 'I should not have laughed. I'm sorry.'

'How could you help it. Oh, George!' Rose too began to laugh. She reached up, caught his hand. 'Oh, ho, ho, ho. Hold my hand a moment. My mother has been hoping for this for so long. What a shock. They are not like your parents, George, they don't get on, he was so difficult to please. I never – oh, where is my handkerchief?' She was crying now, her abrupt laughter changed to tears, runny nose, sobs. 'I never pleased him, I was a rotten daughter. All he ever wanted was for me to be safe, he kept on about it, he was so glad when I married Ned, he thought all that mattered was safety, I never loved him much. I feel so guilty . . .' The rest of Rose's declaration was drowned by sobs. George saw himself gathering her in his arms to comfort her, lashing out with his foot to kick away the scalding hot-water bottle, pushing aside the cats. It seemed simpler to console Rose in her bed; she would not catch cold that way. Rather warm though. Easier if he took off his trousers. This is not really my style, he thought, but all the same it's pretty good and my word it's oh, ah, oh. 'Heavens, Rose, I did not really mean to do that. I hope you don't think I set out to – I hope I've not made your pneumonia worse – here, hang on while I retrieve that hot-water bottle, oh, good, it's still warm, oh, Lord, look at the cats, what an unfeeling . . .'

'Stop burbling.' Rose straightened the bedclothes as he got back into his trousers, pulled her nightdress down and the sheets up, settled the hot bottle by her feet, reached for a comb, ran it through her hair. 'Could you bring me a hot sponge?' She was startled into feeling almost well. George ran the hot tap, squeezed the sponge under it, brought it to Rose, watched her wipe her face, erase the tears, wondered what he should do or say.

'Oh, George.' Rose looked up at his anxious face, handed back the sponge. 'I'm so hungry.'

From time to time through life George would be tempted to tell the tale of how he had found the barrel of oysters left for Rose's convalescence by his mother. Of how they had feasted together, she in her bed, he sitting beside it. When people remarked jokingly on the aphrodisiac qualities of oysters, George would say he wouldn't know about that but he had heard they were wonderful for convalescents. In old age, if reminded by the taste of oysters of the episode with Rose, he would puzzle as to whether it had really happened, whether he had mixed fact with fiction to make a good story. Was it likely he would ask himself that he would find oysters fresh in a barrel in such circumstances? Or probable that he would seduce a friend's wife when she was ill with bronchial pneumonia? In any case it was not the sort of story one could tell anybody. Was I that sort of fellow? he would question, looking at his beloved wife, splendid sons and daughters, charming grandchildren. 'When I was posted to Moscow in the war,' he would say, steering his train of thought into safer waters, 'I spent

a lot of time trying to find an Astrakhan hat for the wife of a
friend of mine.'

'And did you succeed?' one or other of them would ask. 'Were
you in love with her?'

'I can't recollect. I don't suppose so. One had many more
serious worries; there was after all the war – no, it wasn't love.'

But Rose remembered.

When people discussed tonics, pick-me-ups after severe illness,
she kept to herself the prescription of a quick dip in bed with
someone you liked but were not in love with. A short shock of
sexual astonishment which could make you feel surprisingly well
and high spirited.

After her little brush with George she found herself well
enough to attend her father's funeral, console her mother for
never noticing that he had a bad heart, help her find a convenient
flat in which to spend her widowed days.

In actual fact the funeral and Mrs Freeling's move from Kensington to Chelsea took place over a period of months with
many visits from Rose during the summer of 1940. But memory
being what it is, her mind concertinaed the funeral and her
mother's move into briefer space. What she chiefly remembered
in age was returning to Slepe after the funeral with a sense of
liberation, and her extreme annoyance at finding Nicholas and
Emily in occupation, having invited themselves while the plumber sorted out their burst pipes.

21

The first indication that her privacy had been invaded was the
sight, as she drove up the drive, of the MG parked askew at the
front of the house.

'Damn.' Rose parked what she continued to think of as the
bishop's car beside the MG. She hefted her bag and went in. She

stood in the hall listening. There was no sound. The bud of a late camellia fell with a plop onto the hall table. The water in the vase was low and the flowers Edith Malone had arranged two weeks before were browning and dead. Farthing had resentfully watched her cut the camellias, making it plain by the twitch of his nose that camellias lasted longer left where they belonged. After the fall of the flower, the silence was absolute.

Rose looked in the library. Nobody. Nor was there anyone in the kitchen.

She carried her bag upstairs, anxious to change from her funeral clothes. She supposed the Thornbys to have gone for a walk while waiting for her. She would offer them tea then pack them off home. They had not bothered to come to her father's funeral. They could, she thought resentfully, have made the effort. Other people had. Ned's uncle and aunt from Argyll, for instance, who scarcely knew her parents.

Crossing the landing to her room she saw the door of a spare room ajar and moved to shut it, but first she glanced into the room in case the cats had strayed; shut in, they might make a mess. She was surprised to see clothes thrown casually about, an open book on a chair, brushes and combs on the dressing table. The bed dishevelled. She closed the door, frowning.

Then from across the landing, from the visitors' bathroom, she heard a gurgle of laughter, Emily's laugh. What bloody cheek. She strode into the bathroom, furious.

'Oh, Rose.' Nicholas reached up from the bath to grip her wrist. 'So you're back. How did it go? We knew Ned would want us to make ourselves at home, so we've done just that. Sit and talk to us, sweetie. This is the first bath we've had for weeks – can't tell you the bliss of a good wallow after washing in parts and boiling water in a kettle – one gets so cold – one feels so deprived.' He pulled Rose nearer the bath. 'Sit down, lovey, while we tell you about our resident plumber; he makes surreptitious eyes at Emily and she encourages him.' He jerked Rose down onto the chair by the bath.

'Hullo, Rose.' Emily lay in the bath facing Nicholas. She had put a cushion from the spare room to protect her head and shoulders from the taps; its fine brocade was soggy. 'Keep us company,' drawled Emily, 'tell us the latest.' She grinned glee-fully up at Rose. 'Remember how we all had our baths together as children? Pity there isn't room for you now. Weren't you a coy little thing!'

'You cried, didn't you, Rosie?' Nicholas kept hold of Rose's wrist.

Rose remembered her agonised embarrassment when, an only child, she had found herself expected to share the bath with the Thornby children, stranded with them for the night after a party (her father's car had broken down; he had not been able to fetch her home). She had reacted violently, made a scene, refused to undress, screamed. Nicholas and Emily's nurse had teased her for hiding her body, mocked her infant modesty. 'What have you got to hide?'

Nicholas and Emily had followed suit, chanting, 'What have you got to hide,' in loud sing-song. 'Take off your knickers. What have you got to hide?' They were not hiding much now.

Rose snatched her wrist free, remembering how Nicholas, excited, had threatened to pee in the bath water. The nurse had smacked him twice, once on each buttock; she had been shocked and curiously excited.

She stood up. On no account was she going to betray her surprise at seeing them together in the bath, lay herself open to taunts of lack of sophistication. 'Ned couldn't get back for the funeral,' she said, not prepared to endorse or deny his possible invitation. (I do not yet know Ned well enough, she thought.) She forced herself to look calmly down as they lay in the steam-ing water, Nicholas caressing his sister's neck with his toe, she idly soaping her leg, then her brother's. Apart from the obvious difference in sex, they were remarkably alike.

'Ned didn't exactly invite us – to be honest,' said Emily, laugh-ing, daring Rose to be shocked. 'Notice the difference?' she asked, following Rose's glance.

Rose realised with fury that one part of her mind had been noting that Nicholas, unlike Ned, was circumcised. 'Oh, I shouldn't bother to be honest, Emily, it's not you, is it?' She bent and removed the cushion from behind Emily's head with a jerk, at the same time pulling up the bath plug. 'This had better dry off in the hot cupboard.' She ignored Emily's squeal of protest as she dodged to avoid the hard taps against her head and neck. She squeezed the cushion over the bath. 'When did you arrive?' she asked, keeping her voice casual. 'Or should I say move in?'

'Yesterday,' said Nicholas quickly. 'Mrs Farthing said . . .'

Told her we'd invited them, thought Rose. 'Maybe you'd do better to keep an eye on your plumber,' she suggested, watching Nicholas get out of the bath, noting his weedy legs, making it plain as she ran her eye over him that his compared ill with Ned's physique. 'Ned wasn't exactly the soul of welcome last time you called, was he, Emily?'

'Not on *that* occasion.' Emily got out of the bath, hinting that there had been other occasions (and I don't care, thought Rose, if there were). 'Don't let me hurry you.' Rose watched Emily look around for a bath towel. 'I remember now, I told George to tell you you could come over some time. How silly of me to forget. Oh, d'you want a towel?' she asked, as though to need a towel was somehow remarkable, that ordinary people shook themselves like dogs when they got out of a hot bath.

'We should have brought our own.' Nicholas had ceased to enjoy the situation, was beginning to shiver in the prevailing Slepe draught.

'Oh, no, no, no,' said Rose. 'I'll fetch you some,' she said graciously as she went out, leaving the door open, letting the draught increase, taking her time to cross the landing, open the hot cupboard door, place the damp cushion to dry, extract two of the least good bath towels. 'Here you are,' she said, strolling back. 'I'd ask you to stay,' she said, 'but I'm expecting Ned at any moment and we will want to be on our own, you know how it is – or perhaps you don't?'

'Thanks.' Emily snatched a towel and wrapped herself in it.

'And Nicholas . . .' She held a towel out to Nicholas. 'My poor Nicholas, you are all goosefleshy.' She looked despisefully at his exposed person. 'There,' she said, 'I'll give you tea before you go. I'll go and put the kettle on.' She forced herself to walk out of the bathroom slowly, go steadily down the stairs. Half-way down, her rage at their solipsistic behaviour overwhelmed her; she was affronted that they had come uninvited, shared the bath, and by the look of things the bed also.

'Emily,' she shouted up the stairwell.

'Yes?' Emily, half dry, leaned over the banisters. 'What is it?'

'Clean the bath before you go, strip the bed and put the used sheets in the laundry basket.' To suggest disinfectant would be overdoing it.

'Oh,' said Emily, 'the famous Slepe hospitality!' But she went obediently back, and Rose heard her splash water in the bath and use a disagreeable tone to Nicholas.

Rose put the kettle to boil and laid out two cups and saucers; she would not join Nicholas and Emily to drink tea. She was amused to find herself as fiercely possessive of Ned's Slepe as though it were her own.

Mrs Farthing came in from outside. 'Glad to see you back. They invited themselves, said Mr Peel had ...' her nostrils twitched, 'and that you said ...'

'Don't worry,' said Rose, 'they are on their way.'

'H-m-m-m.'

'I'd rather Ned were not told.'

Mrs Farthing relaxed a few folds round her mouth into a smile. 'Shall I get the cake out?'

'Certainly not.'

'Honeycomb?'

'For you and me later.'

'Hah!'

'And we'll make that bed up fresh. Ned may come home; he might bring someone with him.'

'Worried, are you? About the war?'

'I think the war is hotting up. Yes, I *am*.'

'They do say,' said Mrs Farthing, dodging away from Rose's anxiety, 'that vicars are given to having funny children, maybe bishops is more so.'

A car hooted in the drive. Rose ran out to find Uncle Archibald stepping backwards out of the station taxi. At the sight of his reassuring back, Rose gave a shout of joy. 'Oh, Uncle Archie.' She had never called him uncle before.

Archie enfolded her in his tweedy arms. He smelt of heather

and whisky. He hugged her close and patted her back. 'Flora suggested I should come and see you before I go back north; she's gone ahead.'

'Kind, kind. Come in and have tea.' Joyfully Rose hugged the old man. 'Oh, I am glad to see you.'

Renewing his hug, holding Rose with one arm while he fumbled in his trouser pocket for change to pay the taxi, Uncle Archie watched Nicholas and Emily slink out of the house, get into their M G and drive away.

'Got visitors?' he asked.

'Some neighbours who came for a bath; their pipes burst in the freeze-up; they have only just got the plumber.'

Leading Ned's uncle into the house, Rose put the Thornbys out of her mind. 'Come in. Mrs Farthing is making tea, and we have one of Farthing's honeycombs. You will stay, won't you?'

'Glad to, just for the night.' He liked the way Rose led him into the house, holding his hand. The girl had changed, he thought, grown up, matured; she must be in love with Ned; good show.

Rose was interested by the way she led Ned's uncle indoors, that she made much of him for her own sake, not Ned's. I am turning into Ned's wife, she thought. 'Tell me what you have heard about the war,' she said. 'I'm sure you know more about what's going on than what's on the radio or in the papers.'

'Ah,' said Uncle Archie sitting down to his tea. 'Yes. France. Can't say I know more than you, my dear.'

Rose sighed. Quite irrationally she had hoped he would have news not necessarily of Ned, but of Mylo.

'I only half trust the French,' said Uncle Archie.

Mylo is half French, thought Rose forlornly.

'Flora wondered,' said Archibald Loftus, accepting his cup, 'whether you might not be lonely with Ned away and your father just dead and so on. Wondered whether you would come back with us and stay for a few weeks?'

'Oh, I can't go so far. It's terribly kind; I'm not lonely. I have to wait. I don't think I'd better go further than London – my mother and so on – I'm waiting for news.'

'He writes, of course?'

'No. Yes, I mean yes. Of course he writes.'

'But can't give news? Censors are over-zealous. Yes, please, I'd like some of that.' He helped himself to honey, stirred his tea, drank, wiping his moustache with a silk handkerchief. She's not worrying about Ned in the way one would expect, he thought. Is it her father's death that's bothering her? She wasn't close, from what one's heard. Boring sort of fellow, not our type at all. 'This war jangles people up,' he said. 'People will feel better when it's really started. They're all feeling a bit disappointed at the lack of action; when it comes they'll perk up no end; it's like waiting to have a baby.'

Rose laughed. 'I wouldn't know about that.'

So she's not pregnant; about time she was. 'He will be back soon,' he said. Better do his stuff then, he thought, I could drop him a hint.

'Could someone just disappear?'

'No, my dear, oh, no, don't start getting fanciful ideas. The Army's got its head screwed on, it's good at its paperwork, Ned won't disappear.'

But Mylo *has*, thought Rose, not a word since that last telephone call when he was so cross, and he's not in the Army.

Uncle Archibald started telling Rose what friends at his club had told him about the Norwegian campaign. 'Most unfortunate, but a great deal of gallantry. Lucky Ned wasn't there. If he had been, there really would have been cause for worry.' As he munched his bread and honey, moved on to Mrs Farthing's cake, Archibald Loftus thought, This Rose of Ned's is a dark horse; it's a waste of breath wondering what's going on in her head; what could she mean 'disappear'? People like Ned don't, far too solid and mundane. He resigned himself to enjoying what he knew of her and his tea.

'What you need, my dear,' he said, 'if you won't come up to us in Scotland, is some fun; try and combine some fun with visits to your mother.'

'I shall take your advice,' said Rose, 'if opportunity arises.

Meanwhile stay here with me for a night or two, come and look round the garden.'

'I'd like to listen to the news first.'

'Very well . . .'

22

Listening to the news, Archibald Loftus became seriously worried. (Why was bad news worse in beautiful surroundings?) The Slepe garden was awash with spring, the smell of Farthing's wallflowers pervasive. Archibald did not, as Rose did, study the flora; he fretted. The news was not so much serious as potentially disastrous. Rose strolled peacefully, sniffing at flowers, picking little bits off herbs, bruising them with her fingers, adding her quota of scent to the evening. She kept Archie silent company, made no attempt at conversation, leading him away from the house out of reach of the radio.

Archibald appreciated silence in a woman; he was married to a chatterbox. But tonight he wished this girl of Ned's was not quite so reserved. This surely showed some pent-up emotion and fret? How was it that he got the impression that whatever was bothering her was not bother on behalf of Ned? He broke the silence: 'I don't think you should stay here on your own.'

'Why ever not?'

'Things look very black over there.' He jerked his chin in the direction of France.

'It's difficult for me to make out what's going on,' she said.

'There is every likelihood that our armies will be defeated. I distrust the French,' he said, as he had said before.

'Ah.' She was not paying attention; she was listening to a blackbird singing its heart out on the branch of a flowering cherry.

'The Germans may invade,' said Archibald bluntly, 'it's more than a probability.'

'That's what Ned suggested,' she agreed.

'Then he is cleverer than I thought.'

Rose felt tempted to mention Ned's hoard of petrol but thought better not, he's a magistrate or something up in Scotland, and Ned said to keep it secret. She thought with amusement of her husband and his secret hoard supposedly unknown to the Farthings.

'You are not listening,' said Ned's uncle.

'Yes, I am.'

'What did I say last?'

Rose laughed.

'I was saying, Rose, that if and when the Germans invade you would be better off up north with Flora and me. Please be sensible and come.'

'I must look after Slepe, Germans or no Germans. Besides, Ned will get back. I have to be here when he arrives.'

'Let us pray he does.' Archibald could not shake off his gloom.

'Of course he will.' Of course. People like Ned don't get lost, but Mylo, what of Mylo?

'Come up to London with me,' said Archibald urgently. If I can get her as far as London, I can persuade her on to Argyll, he thought.

I wonder what he would look like without a moustache? Rose was thinking. I have never kissed a man with a moustache, except for that scuffle under the mistletoe. I have not kissed many men. It must be like kissing a doormat. 'I must stay here.' She looked at Ned's nice uncle (I hope Ned is as attractive as that when he's old). 'I would like to, but I can't, thank you. It's very kind of you and,' she added, 'Aunt Flora.' (I wonder what she would say if I was suddenly planted on her?)

Archibald Loftus, admitting defeat, grunted.

The following day he left. On his journey north he sat in the train watching the fields rush by and thought that it would be nice to be young again and seduce Ned's wife, that she was just the sort of girl he could have left Flora for, that perhaps it was as well she had not been born when he met and married Flora, they had been pretty happily married. He had never had a mistress like his Viennese uncles (missed something there, no doubt), there had never been enough temptation. All the same, he thought – does Ned realise? Does he treat her properly? Does he? I am jealous of Ned, he thought with amusement, jealous! He left his seat and walked up the train to the restaurant car and ordered a large whisky. As he drank he let his mind dwell on Rose and speculated on whether she would be one of those rare women who are as attractive in age as they are in youth. And would she know it, and profit by it? He felt the prick of desire as the train rushed north, and watching the speeding fields he noted that he was not done for yet if a girl like Rose could make him feel like this and although it was in a way uncomfortable, it was also pleasurable. Then he thought of his dear wife Flora, grown thick-set and bristly in her tweeds and brogues. Desire evaporating, he ordered another drink.

Alone once more Rose wandered about the garden, played with the cats, came restlessly in and listened to the news. While Uncle Archibald travelled north to Scotland, the collapse of France already under way was admitted. There was congestion on the roads, the Belgians asked for an armistice, the French and British were encircled as they retreated towards Dunkirk, and the evacuation began as lovely day followed lovely day and the birds sang.

Mrs Freeling telephoned to say that she was taking a gamble (Mrs Freeling!) and buying the leases of two flats, not one. If one was to get bombed, she would move to the other.

'And if neither gets bombed?'

'I shall rent one to the Germans and take lodgers in the other.'

'Oh.' Mother making jokes! What next!

'As everybody who can is getting out of London, I am getting the two flats dirt cheap. There will never be such a chance again.'

'I had not realised you had such a – a – perspicacious business sense.' Rose was amused.

'Nor had I. Isn't it fun?'

'Fun?' Rose was amazed at this new version of her mother. 'Aren't you afraid of air-raids? Of getting killed?' she enquired.

'Of course I am, but I can't let that stop me. I have been dammed up too long.'

'Where are these flats?'

'One in Chelsea, the other is in Regent's Park. I had thought of Hampstead, but then someone said there are a lot of Jews there and the raids may be directed at them. If I can sell the house in the country, well, I might try and find one in the Holland Park area. It shouldn't be difficult.'

'A *third* flat?'

'Why not? Nothing ventured . . .'

'I wish you luck,' said Rose respectfully. So that's what she's been, dammed up. Well I never, thought Rose, and went again into the garden where now the syringa was mingling with the wallflowers and a mistlethrush sang with heart-rending sweetness. Will my spirit be dammed by Ned as hers was by Father? She pondered the prospect as she paced the stone path. When the telephone rang at last, she ran.

'Hullo?'

'Rose?' A man's hoarse voice.

'Yes?'

'It's me, Ned. I'm at some bloody place in Kent but getting a miraculous lift home.'

He arrived hours later exhausted, sunburned from his wait on the beaches, still damp from wading through the sea to the rescuing boats, in high spirits.

'Weren't you frightened?' she asked tentatively.

'Terrified by the bombing. It was really scary because my tin hat was full of gooseberries I had picked in an abandoned garden. I wanted to bring you some but the chaps ate them on the ship.'

A new mother, a new Ned.

'What is it? What are you thinking?' He was pulling off his uniform sticky with salt. 'Oh, I know. No, it's all right,' he said, 'I am not afraid any more. Once it begins, there's no time and when there is time it is never anything like what I expected or imagined. Piece of cake, really.'

'I'm glad.'

'Run a bath for me. Luckily I haven't much imagination, I think I've spent what I had these last weeks.'

She brought him a drink as he lay in the bath. 'Mrs Farthing is keeping food hot for you.'

'What I need is sleep.'

'Eat first.'

She watched him eat, thankful to see him whole. Fond of him, rather proud, liking him in a comradely way, not at all jealous for Mylo. (All this is separate.)

Ned slept for fifteen hours. Then kissed her goodbye, hurried to rejoin his scattered regiment like a boy to a football game.

Rose went back to listening to the news. France collapsed. Paris fell. Mr Churchill flew to and fro. The evacuation of half a million men continued from Cherbourg and St Malo. Mr Churchill made his blood and beaches speech. Rose's mother furnished her flats, moved out of the flat her husband had died in (what a waste of money all that cancer treatment, had he ever had it?) and sold the house in the country at profiteer profit. Oranges vanished from the shops. Evacuee children streamed out of London and the big cities for the second time. Mrs Farthing joined the Women's Voluntary Service. Ned's regiment was sent to re-form near Catterick. Farthing joined the Home Guard. Nicholas and Emily rang up to say that their plumbing was all right now, would Rose like to come to lunch? Rose said, 'No, thank you.' Nicholas said, 'Too bad, we have both got jobs with the Ministry of Agriculture locally. Nice and safe. We can go on living at home and get a good allowance of petrol.' He sounded extremely chipper. By midsummer England faced the long hostile coastline of Europe and Rose would have felt, along with the rest of the population, rather exhilarated if only she could have heard from Mylo.

To stop her constant nagging anxiety she went to London for a few nights to help her mother and go out with Ned's regimental friends, Harold Rhys and Ian Johnson. They took her to dinner at the Czardas in Soho and to dance at the Café de Paris. They told her how brave Ned had been in the fighting, that he would surely get decorated (they were right; not so long afterwards he was awarded the Military Cross). Their vicarious pleasure in Ned's gallantry and courage mitigated the extreme boredom of their company. She felt like an adult listening to prattling children and gave them only half her attention while the unoccupied part of her mind mulled and digested the feelings she had for Ned since he confided his fear to her. She felt protective and was glad that he was brave. She tried to persuade herself that it would be sensible to forget Mylo and concentrate on her husband, that if she tried hard enough she would succeed.

Driving home through St James's Park, she passed banks of tulips lifting their heads to the moon and was reminded of walking hand in hand with Mylo the year before, of picnicking with him on a park bench, eating rolls, pâté and an apple between them, for they had not the money to go even into a pub, and her heart was wrenched back on course.

23

Rose paid the taxi and greeted the cats, lissom in adolescence. They twined in and out of her ankles, mewed, ran towards the kitchen, indicating that they were hungry, had not been fed. She followed. Two perfectly good cat dinners awaited their eating. They crouched down and ate, needing her company, needing an audience. And I need to be here, she thought, standing in the kitchen already grown familiar; it is after all easier to bear anxiety in my own environment. She admitted that Slepe was her home.

Farthing crossed the yard carrying a shotgun. He wore a Home Guard armband on the sleeve of his working jacket and his Sunday hat.

'Look a lot less foolish when you gets your uniform,' Mrs Farthing's voice from the cottage borne on the still air. Farthing shouted back, 'I shoot with the gun, love, not with uniform.' He sounded stalwart and jocular. Rose heard him mount his bicycle and clatter across the cobbled yard to the accompaniment of shrilly shrieked goodbyes from the little evacuees. She cupped her hands and shouted from the kitchen window, 'I'm back, Mrs Farthing.'

'Good. I fed the cats. Want anything?'

'Nothing, thanks, let you know when I do.'

'I'm going to have a big wash tomorrow. I won't be round for a day or two, if you can spare me.'

'I can spare you.' Enough to know the woman was there. From the back of the house she heard the Ministry of Information telephone pealing unanswered. The clerks kept office hours, they also kept to themselves, casting doubtful looks at Rose if they crossed her path, as though she had no right, did not belong. Ned had been irritated to find that they had fitted new locks on the communicating doors. He frowned when Rose said she neither minded nor cared. 'They should have asked permission,' he had grumbled. 'It's my house, dammit.'

What does it matter? thought Rose, amused by Ned's prickly attitude.

She found bread and cheese in the larder, ate standing in the kitchen, drank a glass of milk, poured a saucerful for the cats and went out to the garden.

A combination of dust in the atmosphere and evening mist coloured the moon like a blood orange. She stood on the steps leading to the walled garden and watched. In the distance she could hear the rattle and creak of harness, the rumble of wheels, the snort of carthorses as the Hadleys lifted the last load of hay by moonlight. Their lives were not much affected, thought Rose. They would not change as the Malones would be changed by their evacuees, and Ned and his friends by the Army. Even Farthing would change in the Home Guard, she thought, and smiled as she contemplated the self-importance already worn by Air Raid Wardens in the village. London was full of men joining the Fire Service or Ambulance, girls too. Uncle Archie and his Flora, to hear him talk, would run Scotland single-handed. Even her mother had said that the moment her flats were complete she would join the Red Cross. Rose wondered at all the activity, the stern enjoyment.

I want nothing to do with the killing, she thought, as she wandered under the lilacs, watched the cats crouch, freeze, leap after moths, miss. Yet I must do something; looking after Slepe and being wife to absent Ned is not enough to prevent me thinking. I must fight despair.

'The evacuation is over,' she said out loud. 'There will be no more news. It is over, over, over. I must do something to still my mind.' She walked through the door in the wall to the vegetable garden.

I will help Farthing here. Grow food. Perhaps the Hadleys will let me help on the farm? I will tire myself to sleep, prevent myself thinking, teach myself to forget. When she went up to bed the moon had lost its rosy look, resumed its gold. She drew back the curtains, undressed by its light, looked out at the cats still cavorting in the garden, got lonely into bed, supposed she would lie sleepless, slept.

Jerking awake she listened for a repetition of the sound. A pebble winged in through the open window to land with a skitter on the polished boards.

Springing to the window, she leaned out. Dark in the moonlight stood a man and a dog. The man, his face in shadow, stared up. The dog wagged, gently expectant.

'Rose?'

'Aah – Mylo,' she whispered. 'Mylo!'

'We will climb the magnolia,' he said. 'Come, Comrade, up you go.' He set the dog to climb, steadying her from below as he followed. The dog scrambled, scrabbled, the magnolia leaves clattered, man and dog came in over the sill in a rush. 'Are you glad?' Mylo held Rose in his arms.

'I had so nearly given you up.'

'You knew I would come.'

'I hoped, how I hoped – the telephone did not . . .'

'France is cut off for the duration.'

The dog flopped down on the floor with a sigh. Mylo, his arms around Rose, his face in her hair, swayed with fatigue. 'Get into bed,' she said, helping him off with his clothes. 'Are you hungry?'

'Later, later. Come close, take off that nightdress thing, let me feel you close.' She lay beside him, he put his arms around her, buried his face in her neck, fell suddenly asleep.

Overwhelmed by joy Rose gulped great draughts of air sweetened by new-mown hay, sweetened far better by Mylo's sweat. While Mylo slept exhausted and the birds in the garden tuned up for the dawn chorus Rose knew the intense happiness of relief. Curled up beside him she catnapped, waking to the delight of feeling him with her. She listened to his breathing, laid her hand on his heart, feeling its beat under her palm. On the floor the dog whimpered in its sleep, scratched on the boards with dreaming paws.

As the mistlethrush led the birds in noisy crescendo Mylo woke, turned, held her close, kissed her eyes, found her mouth, made love tenderly with fluent passion, lay back laughing.

'We managed it right this time.'

'Exquisite.'

What had she done, so wifely with Ned, so friendly with George? Not this, nothing like this.

'And again?'

'And again and again.'

Beside the bed the dog sneezed politely, craving attention.

'My poor Comrade. I brought her for you. I said if you must come with me, you will have to settle with Rose. She is probably hungry. We have travelled far.'

'I will take her down and feed her, let her out. Where does she come from?'

'France.'

'How?'

'She latched on to me. Followed my bicycle. I had a bicycle some of the way. She wouldn't go home. Has no home. She followed me from Conches to Perros-Guirec, leapt for the boat, fell in the water. I fished her out, she sneaked ashore with me at Brixham unnoticed and we came on here. Will you keep her?'

'Of course. I have been waiting for the right dog. I stocked up with tinned food. Ned would have liked me to have a labrador. What do you suppose she is? Or an alsatian.'

'A French mongrel.'

'I will feed her. What's her name?'

'I call her Comrade . . .'

Rose slid out of bed. 'Come, then . . .'

'Stand still a moment, let me see you properly.' Rose stood in the early light smiling.

'When you are old, you will look no different. Who is here? Are you alone in the house?'

'Yes. For the moment. The Farthings live in the cottage; he gardens, she helps when she feels like it; Ned's regiment is at Catterick.' She must mention Ned. He exists, she told herself without alarm.

'Got back from Dunkirk, did he?'

'Yes.'

'One wouldn't want one's worst enemy to be taken prisoner. I'm glad.'

Rose pulled on her nightdress and dressing gown. 'Must you?' Mylo protested.

'I will take them off when I come back.' (Mylo lay back.) 'Don't you change, either . . .'

'Hurry back.'

'I will. Come, Comrade.' Rose ran downstairs with the dog, let her out into the garden, watched her trot through the dew, crouch thoughtfully. I shall tell Ned she is a stray, that I found her lost. The dog scratched the grass, kicking little clods of earth behind her, came back to Rose full of cheer. In the kitchen she put the kettle to boil, opened a tin of dog food. While the dog ate, she laid a tray, made coffee, boiled eggs, made toast, found marmalade, butter and honey, carried the tray upstairs. The dog followed at her heels, ignored the cats staring balefully through the banisters.

Rose pushed open the door, carried in the tray. Mylo was asleep again. 'Come in, all of you,' she said. The dog lay down by the bed while the cats, every hair on end, their tails like bottle brushes, sprang for safety onto the windowsill, baring needle teeth, gaping with silent mews.

Mylo woke. 'Rose?'

She put the tray on the bed. 'I must keep you secret; I only brought one cup for us.'

'Take those things off.'

She dropped the dressing gown and nightdress to the floor, rejoined him in bed. They ate breakfast sitting close, sharing the cup. Then they made love again without haste, delighting in one another.

'You would think to see us now that we got it right the first time in that dismal little hotel.' He stroked her flank. 'I love you, love you, love you.'

'And I you.'

'You should see the expression of boredom on the faces of the girls I have regaled with my love for you. One yawned in my face.'

'Many girls?'

'You should not ask questions. How is Ned?' he countered.

'Ned is all right.'

'Isn't that *nice*.'

'Now then . . .'

'You are right, neither Ned nor other girls have anything to do with us.'

'No, nothing.' (Almost nothing, very little.)

'And do you speak of me?'

'Never. If I did, if I began, I should not be able to stop. I would go on and on and my love might dissipate in the process.'

'There is that risk.'

'Not really,' she said, 'how could it?'

'Ah, my love,' he murmured, kissing her, 'and yet in the nature of things it is better to keep me secret, nobody must know – my job.'

'What job?'

'To-ing and fro-ing.'

'What? Where? Not . . .'

'Yes. I shall be going back . . .'

'No!'

'I must. I shall come back often. Don't weep, Rose, don't weep. Nothing is easy.'

It was later she felt resentful.

24

Those precious days had set a standard difficult to adhere to, Rose thought, waking in the hotel bed, listening to the slap of water against the hotel jetty. The weather had been perfect; they had been so happy in their love, finding one another with passion, merriment, satisfaction. There had been no room for doubt or jealousy. They had resolutely shut out fear. The memory of those days in the midsummer of 1940 would endure strongly enough to bring the prick of tears, give courage in times of doubt or boredom, keep hope alive through disappointment, irritation, jealousy and anger. Do I dare hope, she asked herself; is hope a neglected habit which was strong in youth when I feared Mylo was gone from my life, had stopped loving me, loved someone else, was dead? There certainly had been times when hope guttered pretty low.

As a robin began to sing in a bush outside she looked across at the Bonnard hanging in view of the bed. 'I hoped you would keep it in sight,' Mylo had said that summer morning. 'You guessed that I sent it. You knew, of course?'

'Even though you wrote no word.'

'What is that garment she is wearing? A shift?' Propped on his elbow, he examined the picture.

'Camiknickers,' she said.

'Shift is a prettier word.'

'She has broken a shoulder strap.'

'Do you break yours?'

'I remember one snapping when you hugged me in the park. I thought if I protested it would spoil the moment . . .'

Mylo had laughed at that. 'Look at our Comrade,' he had said and they leaned together from the bed to stroke the dog's silky ears as she looked up at them, puffing out her lips with a whimper of devotion in the effort to express her affection, poor dumb animal.

I remember every moment.

'I feel like that about you. I am as inarticulate as the dog,' he had said.

'You are not doing badly,' she remembered saying with satisfaction. (Only temporary satisfaction, of course.)

We walked across the hayfields by the light of the moon. We lay on the grass in the walled garden under the lilac and syringa, we brought our meals out to the garden, we swam naked in the river. Why were we not interrupted or disturbed? I remember. Farthing was busy with his Home Guard; it was soon after that that he got his uniform; and Mrs Farthing had her big wash, an annual event of stupendous dimensions when curtains, covers, even rugs, were scrubbed clean; she probably made the little girls help her, so preventing them spying on us.

We lay in the bath and I told him about Nicholas and Emily; he said, 'Do not let them hurt you, keep them at arm's length; they will try to insinuate themselves into your life.'

'All very well,' she remembered saying; 'they have a gift of some sort.'

'A talent for finding your sensitive spot and prodding it?'

'Yes,' she had said. 'You put it exactly.'

'Then hide your sensitive spots.'

'I only have the one, you.'

'So?'

'So I hold my tongue, keep you secret. *I* shall not bore strange men telling them of you as you did those girls.'

'Now, now.'

'Who were they, anyway?'

'Does it matter? A girl in the Metro, another in a café, nothing to worry about – only girls.'

'But I do.'

'You must not be jealous; it would make more sense if I were jealous of Ned. I am, come to think of it.'

'How could you be?' she had said, amazed.

'How can I not be?'

'Oh, Mylo, stop. Ned – well, Ned thinks too much about

food; he is afraid of not having enough. He is really only interested in himself, not in me, except as a possession of some sort like the furniture, don't you see?'

'Nothing to fear, then?'

'Of course not.'

'But you have promised him . . .'

'He was afraid.'

'Hum.' Mylo was unsure.

'I cherish you, my secret.'

But was he so secret? She tried to remember. Had there not been a scene with her parents before she got engaged to Ned when she had suggested carelessly, to see what they would say, that she might marry Mylo? Was it imagination? Did she invent her mother's snobbish put-downs, her father's acid remarks? If it did not take place, it well might have, so the effect was the same. There might have been a scene even worse than she thought she remembered, blotted from her mind. Why else her mother's sneering remarks, 'people affecting workmen's clothes', 'people of mixed descent', derogatory remarks made by an envious insecure woman. Funny that they ceased when she read an article about Mylo in the newspaper lauding something he had done. But that was years later, just before she died. (I know where *her* ashes are, thought Rose, I tipped them into the Serpentine.)

So those few days, if not completely perfect, came pretty close, Rose remembered, stretching her legs in the hotel bed.

'Ow! God! Ow!' She is seized with cramp in her old age. Cries aloud and struggles out of bed to stop the muscles bunching in her calf, treads down to relax the agonised tendons. I never had cramp when we walked along the hedgerow hand in hand and Comrade startled partridges and their chicks from the long grass verges. She massages her legs to relieve the pain which, stopping as quickly as it came, leaves an echo in her mind. 'I suppose I am grown old,' she says out loud. Is joy still possible? There had been so many times when joy was in abeyance. And hope? What about hope?

*

Hope had been hard put to it when she had waked to find herself alone in her bed. The silence told her he was gone; only the dog Comrade leaping onto the bed to lick her face and grieve with her proved that he had been there at all.

25

Presumably, thought Rose lying in the hotel bed, the anguish of her cramped calf an echo, presumably it was during the late summer of 1940 that she plotted her future. Whatever she decided had been as deliberate as an act of taking out a life insurance policy. The surprise of finding Mylo there one minute, gone the next was something she was not prepared to endure.

She had once, as a child, bouncing as children do on her bed, bounced at an angle, hit her head against the nursery wall, concussed herself. Mylo vanishing left her equally stunned, she had not believed him capable of leaving without a word.

The first thing she had to do finding Mylo gone was to lie about the dog. She had found it, she told the Farthings, collarless, lost. It seemed quite an engaging dog, it did not chase cats.

'Got fleas?' enquired Mrs Farthing.

'Not so that you'd notice.'

She drove to the police station on her way to the shops, reported her trouvaille, arranged that if it were not claimed she would keep it. The lies tripped easily.

'That animal?' The sergeant looked dubious. 'I like a bit of class myself.'

'I like her.'

'It'll need a collar and a licence.'

'I'll see she gets both.' She drove back with Comrade on the back seat.

Ned, arriving on a week's leave, bringing Harold Rhys and Ian

Johnson, found Comrade installed. Quiet, house-trained, trotting at Rose's heels.

'What an appalling mongrel. What on earth can it be? You can't want a creature like that. I've never seen anything like it. Where did you find it?'

'She appeared. I found her in the garden, she attached herself.'

'You can't want to keep it?'

'I do.'

'I wanted to give you a decent dog. A labrador or an alsatian. That animal isn't anything.'

'A lot of things, I'd say,' said Ian Johnson. 'It looks like a scruffy sort of beagle mixed with terrier and a touch of spaniel.' Ian mocked Comrade.

'I wanted,' Ned exclaimed angrily, 'to . . .'

'I know you did.' Rose smiled at her husband, ignored Ian Johnson (not only boring, tactless also). She would keep Comrade's heroic retreat across France, her valiant leap from the quay to reach the boat (had Mylo intended leaving her?), her swim in the filthy dark water to be fished out by Mylo, her illegal entry at Brixham, to herself.

'If we were near the coast,' said Harold Rhys who, never famous for brains, yet had the knack of striking the nail on the head, 'I'd say it might be a French dog. There are dogs with a strain of hound in them all over France, supposed to be descendants of Wellington's foxhounds. I read a letter in *The Times* recently which said the French and Belgian refugee trawlers were bringing dogs and even cats across. Grandmothers too, apparently. It was calling attention to the dangers of rabies. One lot even brought a priest.'

'Rabid grandmothers, promiscuous priests,' mocked Ian Johnson.

'We are too far from the coast,' squashed Ned, staring at the dog. 'It does nothing for my home' (it was on the tip of his tongue to say ancestral), 'for Slepe,' he compromised. He had visualised, when Rose talked of having a dog, something elegant, pure bred, posing for the *Tatler*, Rose in tweeds, himself with gundog at feet.

'Oh, snobbish,' mocked Rose. Ned flushed. 'I was joking, only joking.' But he failed to keep the anger from his voice.

'Darling, of course. Come with me. I want to show you my war work. You won't mind, you two?' She led Ned away.

'Your what?'

'Work. I am helping Farthing on a regular basis in the garden and I'm working on the farm. The Hadleys say they can use me.'

'I don't think I . . .'

'It's so that I shall always be here when you come home, Ned.' She popped a plug into his objections.

'Oh,' said Ned, 'I see,' mulling the pros and cons. 'Oh, all right, if it's not too much for you, if that's what you want.' He wasn't sure he liked this but realised he could not stop her.

'If you don't approve I've been offered a job in the War Office.' This was a lie, but how was Ned to know?

'I don't want you in London, you are much better here, safer.'

'That's what I thought you'd say. And, Ned, when the war is over, we'll get you a labrador.'

Is she learning to manage me? Ned wondered as they walked through the vegetable garden. I must have a chat with Uncle Archie.

And, Rose thought, putting her arm through Ned's, as soon as I am sure Mylo is gone for good, I shall get myself pregnant. Mylo should have told her more, given her more hope, a child would be a sheet anchor through this dismal war, lessen her fear and insecurity.

It was years before Rose admitted she had opted as her father would have wished her to for safety, but at the time, since she was not completely ignorant, she also wondered resentfully where Mylo had learned to be such a good lover. She knew such things did not come naturally; had she not herself had to learn the mechanics with Ned? She discounted George, and bitterly resented Mylo's silent disappearance.

26

Far from subsiding, Rose's anger grew as weeks turned to months during the long summer of 1940. She resented Mylo's secretiveness, sneaking off without a word of farewell. He might have trusted her, she thought, as she hoed the vegetables, trundled her wheelbarrow, weeded the onion bed under Farthing's supervision. I would not have delayed him much, just enough for one last hug. Maybe he was hurrying away to other girls. The thought of other girls filled her with rage as she squatted among the onions, tearing up the weeds, filling her fingernails with grit. She gave small credence to his work, if it existed.

When Ned telephoned she babbled of her doings, giving him news of the farm, the garden, the village, making him laugh at the advice she received from Edith Malone. 'She wants to turn me into a lady of the manor; fortunately your uncle set no example. I can't see myself in the role. Some of her ideas are positively feudal.' She mocked Edith.

'Then keep a low profile,' said Ned, laughing, glad that Rose appeared happy, under the delusion that he would shape her to fit Slepe as he wished. And Rose enjoyed those conversations, looked forward to Ned's distant voice which distracted her from her hurt. But, at night, with her body lusting for her lover, she cursed Mylo, decided to forget him, sweep him clear. Then, leaning from her window at night, she breathed the scent of magnolia, remembered his climb, pushing the dog up ahead of him, heard the stiff leaves clatter and saw his gleeful, exhausted face.

(Why the hell had he not behaved like an ordinary person and rung the bell at the front door?)

When in late September Ned came on leave she surprised him with an affection which he took for love, with tenderness he mistook for lust, with friendship which was genuine. In her anger and grief for Mylo she saw nothing odd in turning to Ned for comfort. In later years she would consider that she might have exaggerated her search for consolation in the conceiving of a child. She did this on Ned's last night, simply ceasing to use the outfit provided by Doctor Helena Wright. She deluded herself that a child would erase Mylo from her mind. (Which goes to show, she would acknowledge in old age, what an idiot I was.)

Ned, driving down from Yorkshire in his large car so hungry for petrol, spent his leave hoisting it onto blocks, oiling and greasing it, disconnecting the battery, covering the whole with tarpaulin. From now on, he told Rose, he would use the railways and her car, should he come home on leave, economise on petrol. 'Shall you be all right with this little car?' he had asked. She guessed that he felt a twinge of guilt over its acquisition. (Nicholas and Emily could be seen speeding about the roads in their MG with petrol supplied by the Ministry of Agriculture.)

'I shall be perfectly all right with it,' Rose reassured him as she walked with him across the fields she had walked with Mylo, paused by the river where they had swum, watched Comrade flush partridges from the long grass as she had flushed them for Mylo. She held Ned's hand as they walked, daring herself to compare it with her lover's.

They sat, Ned's last evening, on the stone seat where on the morning of their honeymoon they had remembered diversely the winter tennis. Ned was to leave on the evening train. Across the fields John Hadley called his cows for the evening milking, 'Hoi, hoi, hoi,' his cry drowned suddenly by the roar of a plane.

'An enemy bomber?'

'No, a fighter. A Hurricane or a Spitfire. I cannot tell the difference.'

'The Farthings' evacuees can,' said Rose.

'Ah, children, children . . .' Ned looked across the garden where the first frost had yet to nip the dahlias. 'As soon as this is over I shall want children.'

'And not before?' Rose found her husband's selfishness amusing. 'I might want one before. Or never,' she teased, catching Ned's startled eye, 'or are you leaving me out of this caper?'

Ned flushed. 'You know I . . .'

'Should the war stop procreation?' Rose's voice was suddenly harsh, shouting at her husband.

'It's hardly the moment – with this battle going on – there's another plane, is it in trouble? – to my mind there is still danger of invasion . . .'

'Churchill is saying the battle is won . . .'

'So many pilots lost. I wish I had learned to fly.'

'I'm glad you didn't.'

'I am too old.'

'Are you too old to have a child?' Rose snapped.

'Don't let's squabble my last evening.'

'All right.' Partly she regretted her impulse of the previous night (perhaps nothing would happen). 'You will be on leave again soon.'

'I didn't want to spoil our time together so I did not tell you that I am on embarkation leave.' Ned stared at the dahlias, orange and red.

'*What?*'

'We are under orders for the Middle East.'

'Another one who does not trust me.'

'What?'

'Nothing, nothing. When do you go?'

'We don't know; it may not be for weeks, but tomorrow in London I must kit myself out with light uniform, visit my lawyer . . .'

'Lawyer, what for?'

'To check my will.'

'Oh, God, you could have trusted me not to spoil your leave,' she was bitter, 'you treat me like a child, a thing . . .'

'I am sorry . . .'

'I should bloody well hope so . . .' A future without Mylo and now Ned. 'I like you, Ned,' she said ruefully.

'And I love you.'

'I said like, not love.' Rose was sharp.

'I heard you. It's important to like the person you love. I both love and like you, dear.'

Rose breathed in, let speech out in a rush: 'I know it's silly, I

141

know I should have told you before, but I cannot bear being called dear, Ned, it makes me feel quite sick.'

Ned looked at Rose astonished; in a secret crevice of his mind there wriggled the suspicion that she did not love him. Rose went on, flushing as she spoke, 'Dear is what nurses call their patients, dear is what my parents called each other in hatred, dear to my ear is horrible. I'm sorry, Ned, but I simply can't stand being called *dear*.'

Across the garden the dahlias glowed orange and blood-red. 'I'd better get a move on,' said Ned, 'or I shall miss my train. I had not realised . . .'

Rose stood up, ashamed. (What a moment to choose.)

Ned went to fetch his luggage, his mind full of doubt. He had assumed that his feeling for Rose was reciprocated. Not usually given to introspection, he nevertheless thought as he drove Rose's car to the station that liking lasted longer than love, which to hear people like Uncle Archie talk was a flash-in-the-pan business. He was glad that Rose liked him, the thought amused him, and he laughed out loud. Rose forbore to ask, What's the joke? The train was puffing into the station; they had to run to catch it, Ned scrambling aboard with barely time to kiss goodbye.

When Rose went back to the car she had to adjust the driving seat which Ned had moved to suit himself. Manoeuvring it, Rose thought, Give him credit, if he had had time, not had to run for the train, he would have put the seat back without being asked, he was that kind of man; he would move car seats for her, but when it came to starting a family, he would only consider himself. Driving back to Slepe, Rose in her turn laughed, pleased to have stolen a march.

27

Restless in the hotel bed, listening to the chirrup of dawn birds, Rose was undecided whether to read her paperback until breakfast or opt for an early walk.

She thought, I miss the routine which formed life at Slepe. It had begun working with Farthing, digging, weeding, sowing, gathering. Increased with work on the farm, with its closeness to animals, the smell of cows at milking, the cluck of hens, grown with her gradual interest in the house, sharing Ned's pleasure in the pictures, furniture, porcelain, silver, and even rugs, as she evolved from ignorant girl into wife and mother. All the multiplicity of small jobs, recurring responsibilities, interests and irritations which added up to security and contentment snatched away by Ned's death.

But this is what I have looked forward to, she mocked herself, eventual freedom.

She got up, dressed in jeans and sweater, let herself out onto grass drenched with dew.

A brisk walk to 'stimulate the faggocites', her father's expression used in turn by herself, passed on to Christopher. What on earth are faggocites? She questioned the word as she set off along the creek. 'I hope,' she said to the hotel cat returning from its night foray, 'to walk off my gloom.' The cat dodged the hand she stretched to stroke it, proceeding indifferent on its way. 'So much for hope.'

As she walked she considered hope and what its loss let one in for.

Christopher, for instance?

Was Christopher the result of loss of hope? Probably. Blame him on Mylo? A plug against loss of spirit, fear, anger, jealousy, loneliness, or the result of a fondness for Ned and a maternal instinct stronger than herself?

Not that. She had never pretended to be excessively maternal, but how had Christopher, that lovely roly-poly baby, that delightful little boy, grown into the man chosen by Helen as husband. ('Let me take charge of that; I can see it upsets you. I will deal with it,' taking the urn with Ned's ashes which she had put momentarily next to the sandwiches on the dining-room table while she fumbled for a handkerchief to blow her nose. Interference or kindness? Don't think of Helen; she cannot help being like that; Christopher loves her; enjoy your walk.)

It had never been easy to unravel the skein of motive and emotion which resulted in the advent of Christopher.

Had it been something to do with the dog Comrade?

This is ridiculous, dogs are sympathetic to humans, not the other way about. And yet when she had realised that Comrade was in pup, must have been in pup when she followed Mylo across France, running by the bicycle, leaping to catch the departing boat when he might or might not have meant to abandon her. There had been fellow-feeling between herself and the dog when, Christopher little more than a pinhead in her womb, Comrade gave birth to puppies, one of which survived to sire the first of a long line of engaging mongrels which terminated abruptly when Christopher, squabbling with Helen, let them get squashed by a juggernaut on the main road.

First the dogs, then the urn.

Will this make Christopher feel guilty towards me, as I always felt towards my mother, my father?

'One hopes not,' Rose said out loud as she followed the path which led now through a wood.

There was the little matter of Mrs Freeling's ashes. (The official at the Crematorium had called them Mrs Freeling's ashes, not your mother's or your parent's ashes, handing her the parcel.) Ned would not have understood her feelings of guilt towards her parents. In his book, the dear uncomplex fellow, you loved your parents, even loved in-laws. Neither Ned nor Helen would have understood why she had tipped her mother's urn into the Serpentine, watching the ash drift down like a sash towards the water. It was done to placate Mrs Freeling's spirit, to keep her happy in death, separate from the husband she had outlived so cheerfully. Rose spared a breath to laugh as she puffed up the path as it turned uphill away from the water. It had done no harm to let Ned and Christopher bury the empty urn beside Mr Freeling. Not expecting her to lie, they had taken it that Mrs Freeling's wish had been not to have her urn opened. Christopher, taking the urn without much reverence, had said, 'Funny old Granny.'

She can't have been more than forty-five when I discovered just how funny she was, thought Rose. Forty-five and she had seemed so old!

She had discovered her mother's funniness when, on impulse the day after Ned's embarkation leave, she went up to London and took her mother out to lunch. It had certainly distracted her mind from harping on Mylo. Across the table she had seen a new Mrs Freeling. She no longer looked downtrodden, saintly, patient and forbearing, she looked lively; being widowed suited her.

As they ordered lunch, Rose observed her mother. She had had her hair properly cut; her hands were cared for; she wore new clothes. There was a rumour, she told Rose, that the government would ration clothes. 'I am stocking up,' she said. 'You should do the same.'

'I don't need much in the country, just lots of warm things. Slepe is pretty chilly.'

'I hope you won't let yourself get stuck in the country all your life as I did.'

'I thought . . .'

'You should get yourself something to do, like me. I have made a lot of new friends in the Red Cross. What are all your neighbours up to?'

'Mrs Malone has filled their house with evacuee children.'

'God help her, but perhaps she likes children? Have you noticed how delightful London is without them? I enjoy the quiet of the park without perambulators when I walk across it in the mornings.'

'What about air raids?'

'I have not much time for them, too busy by day and I sleep like a top at night. First time for years.'

'Really?'

'I get tired. There's the Red Cross, and I am still furnishing my flat. Did I tell you I have a lodger?'

'No?'

'A major who works in the War Office. He is mostly out, no bother, he pays his rent and keeps out of my way.'

'Oh.'

'You should come up oftener, I can put you up when I'm finally settled. There is plenty going on, concerts and now the theatres are open again, plays – you mustn't let your brain atrophy.'

'I hope not.'

'And I have taken up bridge, formed a regular four. My major plays when he's in, should one of us fail.'

'You seem to be having an interesting time.' Rose assessed this new parent who dressed smartly, went to concerts, played bridge.

'About time,' said Mrs Freeling with force, 'after all I endured with your father.' Rose had sat open-mouthed as there followed a diatribe against her defunct parent. His failure, his selfishness, his boringness; he was picked over bit by bit, no facet left unpecked. Once started her mother could not stop: she tabulated a lifetime of resentments. Her father's table manners, mean economies, treachery to friends, his assumption of gentlemanly Christianity, his sucking up to social superiors, his bitterly resented illness, the wasteful cost of the treatment for non-existent cancer, his snores, his impecuniosity.

'Mother . . .'

But Mrs Freeling had not finished, out came her horror of sex, her husband's insistence on his marital rights – brutal rapes.

'Mother, please . . .'

'And then,' Mrs Freeling made no effort to lower her voice, 'the unspeakable process of procreation!'

'I thought marriage, the Bible . . .'

'Written by *men*.' Mrs Freeling swept the Bible aside. 'Sensitive women like me should not be subjected to such – fortunately for you the process of childbirth is academic.'

'Is it?' Rose was astonished.

'Of course. A nice man like Ned would never . . .'

'Mother . . .'

Her mother's voice was clear; people at neighbouring tables munched with ears pricked. 'It's beyond my comprehension that women still put up with it,' said Mrs Freeling.

'The human race,' suggested Rose bravely.

'It's men who want it to go on. Sheer vanity. Give me one reason why it should.'

'I . . .'

'If it must,' said Mrs Freeling, 'the people who in earlier times had wet nurses should have gone the whole hog and let the husband couple with the wet nurse.'

Is she drunk? Rose looked surreptitiously round at masticating jaws.

'I trust you are not proposing to let yourself be hoodwinked by Ned into enduring the agony and humiliation of having a child? My dear Rose, the thing jumps about inside you, you have no control; your body is not your own, you cannot escape, it *heaves*!' Mrs Freeling's voice rose in disgusted recollection.

Crimson-faced, Rose muttered, 'Sorry, Mother, so sorry,' in apology for her foetal antics.

'Take my advice and make a stand.' The peroration was over. Mrs Freeling ate her pudding while her daughter wondered whether the exhilaration of widowhood had affected her brain. 'You must think I have changed.' Mrs Freeling put down her spoon, wiped her mouth with her napkin.

'A bit,' she had murmured cautiously.

'I have been bottled up all these years.'

'I wish I'd known.'

'What could you have done?' her mother asked sharply. 'You are just like him, you only think of yourself.'

'I could have . . .'

'You can do one thing for me. When I die, I do *not* want to be buried with him. Have me cremated and scatter me over water. I would like that. Can I count on you?'

'Of course.'

'Right. Is that the bill? Let's go Dutch.'

Mrs Freeling had never referred to the conversation. Rose sometimes wondered whether she had imagined it. The outburst had been cathartic; she remembered her mother's serene expression when they parted.

How grateful I am now, thought Rose, panting as she climbed the hill, that she refrained during my childhood and adolescence from alerting me to the horror of sex as she saw it and left me to make my discoveries with Mylo. (And of course Ned.) There had been an air raid, she remembered, as she left London and she had hastened to get back to Slepe where now, as she looked back over the years, she realised she had just spent a happy week with Ned.

28

Ned left his lawyer's chambers and set off on foot towards his tailor. There was an air raid alert; he had listened to the siren while discussing his will. His solicitor, already blasé, had said, 'You don't want to pop down to the shelter, I take it, it's the most fearful waste of one's time.'

'No, no thanks.' (He would charge me for time wasted in the shelter, knowing him, he's fly.)

'Good, then let's get on with it.'

'Right.'

'Your family trust makes it pretty plain sailing; it doesn't leave you much chance to settle old scores.' The solicitor had laughed.

As he walked Ned ruminated resentfully on the terms of the trust which had brought him Slepe. Thanks to the laws of primogeniture and entail he had inherited Slepe from a distant cousin, so far so good. But should he die without a son, Slepe would pass to another cousin. Perhaps, thought Ned as he strode along, he had been wrong in his approach to starting a family. Suppose one had a quiverful of girls, didn't manage a boy first shot? Rose had been angry, had not been easily mollified; he was not sure why she had been angry, but it made him feel guilty. When the war is over and she does produce my son, I will give her a jewel, he thought. Then he thought, turning into Bond Street, why wait, why not give her a present now? As he walked he glanced in at the jewellers' displays. If he bought her a jewel, she would at least have something to sell, should he get killed before she bore a son. He had practically no savings apart from monies tied up in Slepe. Rose had no money of her own. (The damn solicitor had tut-tutted about this at the time of his marriage.) All the jewels seemed tremendously expensive, but wouldn't their value increase? To buy or not to buy? Ned batted the idea back and forth. The principal snag in the family trust was that every penny, as well as the house, passed on his death to this imaginary son. Until this morning Ned had not taken much account of this clause. How would Rose manage? he had asked. 'The usual thing is that your son makes your widow an allowance.'

'But suppose they don't get on?'

The solicitor had said, 'They'd better,' his voice crisp and legal.

Poor little Rose, thought Ned tenderly, why don't I buy her a jewel now? Give her pleasure, something she can flog if I leave her a widow; she doesn't get on with her mother, not liking parents may be hereditary. Ned idled along, coming to a stop outside Cartier. (My God, I can't afford any of that! Our engagement ring was too pricey, one pays for the bloody name.) Ned walked on. Yet, he thought, I would like to give her something to remember me by. But suppose I did and she flogged it for no particular reason? Better to give her jewels when she's had my son, a reward, a thanksgiving. She hasn't done the job yet; it would be silly to give her jewellery now, especially if there were all those girls first and one had to keep at it.

And yet some sort of present? She likes pretty things, she has a good eye, she picked up that Bonnard she has hung in our bedroom, said she acquired it for love, to give it a good home. He had said, 'Like the dog?', joking, and she'd laughed. The dog was a pretty awful mongrel, but the Bonnard might easily turn into a canny investment. All the same I don't want to give her jewellery and have her flog it to buy pictures, you can come a cropper with pictures. The Bonnard might be just a lucky fluke.

He had arrived half-way up Bond Street and stared sightlessly at the window of the White House. 'God!' he focused, 'that's what the girl in her picture is wearing. Rose has no exciting underclothes, perhaps she bought that picture as a hint; my problem is solved.'

Ned went into the shop and chose six pairs of cream satin camiknickers, arranged to have them sent to Rose, writing, 'With all my love, Ned', on a card provided by the saleslady. He came out into the street relieved and generous. As he walked the All Clear sounded. He put thoughts of Rose aside and concentrated on his lightweight uniform. Should he go to Huntsman or Gieves? Just as he was in the habit of patronising two barbers, so it was with tailors, favouring now the one, now the other. His feet led him through Burlington Street to the corner of Savile Row and Vigo Street, and up the steps into Huntsman, the euphoria of his generosity making him decide on the more snob of the tailors.

Emily, sauntering down Savile Row, spied Ned emerging from the portals of his tailor, pausing to draw a satisfied breath, then running down the steps to the street with springing step.

'Ned, hi, Ned,' Emily shouted, breaking into a trot. 'Ned!'

Ned, recognising Emily, waved, waited for her to come up to him. 'Hullo, Em. What are you doing here? Long time no . . .'

'I was on my way to . . . what are you up to?'

'Having fittings for lightweight uniforms. Come and have lunch.' Ned surprised himself by his impulsive invitation. 'You are not doing anything, are you?'

'Just shopping,' said Emily. 'I'd love to. Thanks. Where shall we go?'

'Quaglino's? Why not?'

'Why not indeed.' Emily put her hand through Ned's arm, giving it a familiar squeeze.

They walked through the Burlington Arcade, crossed Piccadilly and descended into Jermyn Street.

At Quaglino's Ned was greeted with obsequious bows and scrapes. The maître d'hôtel enquired after Rose and watched

Emily from the corner of his eye while he handed Ned the menu. 'A drink while you wait?'

They sat in the hall for a pre-lunch drink.

'And how is Rose?' asked Emily.

'I have been buying her a present, six presents actually, she's in great form.'

'Oh, lucky Rose.' Emily smiled at Ned as she sipped her drink; Ned regarded her with quizzical eye. He wondered vaguely why there had been no time to get in touch during the past months.

'This is nice,' Emily sipped, 'isn't it?'

'Yes, indeed.' Ned stretched his legs, drew them back to let a couple in naval uniform pass, the girl in WRNS uniform looked a trim little piece. He swallowed his drink, ordered another. Emily refused, still busy with her first. He felt pleased with his morning, pleased with his uniform; part of the charm of joining the Territorials had been the uniform; he felt a better, a different man in uniform.

'Nice uniforms?' asked Emily.

'Mind reader. Yes, lightweight. I am posted overseas.'

'Oh, Ned, are we to lose you?'

'Not permanently, I am not gone yet.'

'What *will* Rose do?'

'She's working full-time in the garden growing food, and on the farm too; it's rum sort of war work but that's what she wants, it keeps her safe.'

'It will ruin her hands, but keep her out of mischief,' said Emily, spreading her fingers, inspecting her red nails, neat cuticles.

Ned laughed. What mischief could Rose get up to? 'Let's have lunch.'

They moved into the restaurant, sat on a banquette facing the room.

Emily scraped her nails on the white tablecloth, gritting her teeth at the thought of Rose's nails splitting and full of grit. 'What present did you buy her?'

'I bought her underclothes at a shop I found called the White House.'

'Underclothes!' Emily crowed with laughter, tossing back her head. 'Camiknickers, I bet.'

'Actually, yes,' said Ned stuffily. 'Come on, what are you going to eat?' He tapped the menu, bringing it to Emily's attention. Brought to order, Emily chose. 'And what are you and Nicholas up to these days; still the Ministry of Agriculture?'

'Yup. Still the Min of Ag. It suits me, lets me travel, as you know.' Emily slid a glance at Ned, who failed to respond. 'Tell me,' she said, 'about Dunkirk. I haven't seen you since. Everyone's saying how brave you were, got a medal, didn't you?'

'The M C.'

'Go on, tell me all about it, I really want to know. Rose told me about the gooseberries,' said Emily. This was not strictly true. Rose had told Edith Malone about the gooseberries in the tin hat; the tale travelled from mouth to ear by telephone, finally reaching Nicholas who had told his sister. (Imagine old Ned in danger, whatever next.) 'I should like to see you coolly reacting to danger,' said Emily, distracting Ned from thoughts of Rose. If anyone mentioned Dunkirk, he remembered standing in the queue in the sea, the hot sun on his head, the feeling that his legs were shrinking, the noise of the bombs. He had prayed to get back to Slepe and Rose, of course. 'I thought you never saw Rose,' he said.

'What makes you think that? I'm her neighbour, there's the telephone. Come on, Ned, tell me about being in danger, you are the only person I know who was at Dunkirk.'

'I'm in danger now,' said Ned, grinning.

'Ned, you are flirting.' Emily turned towards him, pressing her knee against his leg.

Ned put his hand on Emily's thigh, digging his nails in. 'Where are you staying?'

'Are you not going back to Slepe?'

'Up north on the night train.'

'I'm staying with a friend.'

'Is the friend out?'

'Away,' said Emily.

'Finish your lunch. I'll ask for the bill.'

'All right,' said Emily.

'I love Rose,' said Ned.

'Of course.'

'Bill, please,' said Ned to the waiter.

They sat in silence waiting for the bill; when it came Ned put notes on the bill and the waiter took it away to get change.

'I'll just telephone Euston and check my train,' said Ned.

'All right,' said Emily.

Ned went away to telephone.

The waiter brought the bill folded over Ned's change on a plate.

'He'll be back in a minute, just gone to telephone,' said Emily.

The waiter went away.

Since nobody was looking, Emily helped herself to some of Ned's change, putting it in her bag.

'Right,' said Ned, returning. 'We've got several hours before my train.' He pocketed the change without looking at it except to leave a tip commensurate with the splendour of his present to Rose.

Emily read this thoughts.

'I wonder whether she'll wear them gardening?'

Ned laughed, following her out of the restaurant, waving a taxi to stop. He handed Emily in. Emily told the driver the address. Ned sat with his arm around Emily. 'I wonder what it's like in Vienna these days,' he said.

'Why ever Vienna?'

'I was thinking of my Uncle Archie and his Viennese uncles.'

'Why?'

'They had quite a lot of fun, I gather.'

29

Emily found Rose breakfasting in her kitchen, Comrade at her feet.

'Hullo,' said Rose. The dog wagged her tail.

'I am on my way to your farm to get some Min of Ag forms filled in,' Emily said. 'My word, Rose, you do get up late. I had breakfast hours ago,' she said virtuously.

'I help with the milking and feed the pigs, then after breakfast I work in the garden. I'm up before six,' said Rose, matter of factly.

'I apologise.' Emily sat opposite Rose.

'Let's see the forms,' said Rose.

Emily put a protective hand on her briefcase. 'They are for John Hadley.'

'In Ned's absence I'm his landlord.' Rose held out her hand. 'Give.'

Reluctantly Emily brought a sheaf of forms out of her briefcase, put one back and handed the rest to Rose.

'Help yourself to coffee.' Rose perused the forms. 'Not too tiresome,' she said, 'they want us to grow more wheat. We shall have to plough another meadow, otherwise it's okay. Now show me the other.'

'What other?' Emily looked innocent.

'The form you put back, the one you didn't want me to see.'

'You won't like it.' Emily hesitated, then produced the form.

Rose read, eyebrows rising. 'No,' she said, angrily tearing up the form, 'certainly not.'

'You'll only get sent another,' said Emily with mock patience.

'Tell them it's not on,' said Rose. 'They can take me to court if they like. I am not having our rooks shot; they eat hardly any grain, they eat leather jackets and do a lot of good. You Min of Ag people are an ignorant lot. I love our rooks and so does Ned.' (Has he ever said so?)

'Tell that to my Ministry.' Emily was patient.

'I certainly will,' said Rose forcefully. 'Who is your boss?'

'Nicholas.'

Rose burst out laughing. 'Nicholas? Really?'

'Yes.' Emily was laughing too. 'Tell you what, we'll cook the books; nobody is going to check that you've complied with the order.'

'Cheat?'

'If you like. There's a war on, we're busy . . .'

'A war within a war. Have some toast and marmalade, more coffee?'

Emily refilled her cup. 'Actually you are not the only one to protest. The Malones nearly shot *me*. Then dear Mr Malone promised me two brace of pheasants a month throughout the season.' Emily drank her coffee, watching Rose over the rim of her cup.

'H-m ... and what bribe can I give you?' Rose eyed Emily with suspicion.

'Moral support,' said Emily gravely.

What's her game? Rose wondered. 'Me, give *you* moral support? Are you joking?'

Emily said, 'No jok.. I'm pregnant.'

Rose was silent, absorbing this news. Then she asked quietly, 'Getting married?'

'Out of the question.'

'Is he dead? Married already?'

'It's not a question of that . . .'

'Then what? Oh, Em, you're not . . .'

'I had an abortion once. Two years ago. There's a clinic in Munich. Nicholas came with me. We had a rather jolly time in the end. It cost the earth. We sold one of father's teapots; he's never missed it so don't breathe, but now with the war one can't get to Munich, can one?'

'Of course not.' Rose had an absurd vision of Emily and Nicholas infiltrating into Munich by parachute.

'I'm not in favour of back streets and knitting needles. I've tried gin and hot baths to no avail. You know us. Nicholas helped, he nearly boiled me alive, nothing!'

'There must be something, someone . . .'

'I've decided to have it.'

'Emily! How splendid!'

'I don't know what's so splendid about it.' The words were deprecating, but Emily looked pleased.

Rose had never received a confidence from Emily; she was tempted to confide in return, to expose herself, but long association with the Thornbys prevented her. She told herself that she was still not absolutely certain of her own pregnancy;

she might be six weeks late or something.

'I notice you don't ask who the father is,' said Emily demurely.

'It's not my business, is it?' said Rose.

The two girls thoughtfully drank their coffee. Comrade stretched out on the floor and yawned. She was heavy with pup.

'Do you feel sick?' asked Rose cautiously.

'Mornings,' said Emily. 'It's not too bad.'

'Does Nicholas know? Does he know you want to keep it, I mean?'

'Of course Nicholas knows. He thinks it's a great joke; he's already making plans for its future.'

'Oh.' Rose considered Emily. Emily with so many boy friends, Emily's visits to London, her popularity at parties. Then she thought of the brother and sister's closeness; was Nicholas perhaps pleased that Emily could not marry the baby's father, that she would not be leaving him? It was a lot to take in all at once. 'What shall you do?' she asked. 'Do you think Edith Malone would be helpful?'

'I told you. No abortion. If I turned to Mrs Malone, she'd think I was fathering the child on George or Richard.'

'Surely not, she's so kind.'

'It would be the first thing I'd think of in her shoes,' said Emily. 'No, no, we've decided to let people think and say what they please and have the baby. I shall ask my father for money. He can't refuse, he'd disapprove of abortion and he won't approve of the baby, but he isn't mean. Good Lord, bishops are supposed to be Christian.'

'I think you are most courageous, Nicholas too.' (Nicholas will love the drama.)

'Not really.' Emily stirred her coffee, then helped herself to more sugar. 'Sorry, I crave it, keep forgetting it's rationed.'

'Couldn't you say the father was a fighter pilot, shot down and killed?'

'Oh, Rose, how respectable you are,' Emily shouted angrily, 'the little soul of convention! I can't be bothered to lie. If it bothers you and people ask, just say you don't bloody know. I am not the first girl to get caught like this.'

'But . . .'

'I'm lucky,' Emily yelled, 'to be living with Nicholas in our own house. We've both got jobs, nobody's going to turn little Emily out into the snow. It will be a nine days' wonder. With the war going on, people have more interesting things to talk about. I wish now,' said Emily passionately, 'that I hadn't told you. You're so bloody pure, there's nothing disreputable about you, is there?'

On the floor Comrade whimpered in her sleep, flapped her tail against the flagstones.

'I'm glad you did tell me, didn't wait for me to wonder whether somebody was pumping you up with a bicycle pump.'

'Well, all right, let's shut up about it, shall we?'

'There's no need to be touchy; of course I'll shut up.'

'I'm *not* touchy,' shouted Emily, banging her cup on the table. 'Oh, curse it, I've cracked it, was it one of Ned's best?'

'No.' Rose fetched a fresh cup from the dresser, wiped the spillage, poured Emily fresh coffee and sat down to finish her breakfast.

For a while neither girl spoke, then Emily said in her usual tone of voice, 'When did Ned go?'

'He sailed from Liverpool nearly three weeks ago. It was cold and wet. At least he's gone to where the sun shines.' (It's funny how I miss him, that matter-of-fact voice.)

'I saw him in London, we met in the street, he gave me lunch,' said Emily.

'He told me, said you were most amusing, he's got a soft spot for you. Did he tell you,' asked Rose, 'that he'd gone bravely alone and bought me six pairs of camiknickers? From the White House, too, think of the cost!'

'Yes, he did. It made me laugh.'

'I would have thought him too shy and proper to do such a thing.'

'Much too shy, but he's brave, look what he did at Dunkirk; one would never have credited it. I made him talk. All that rearguard action before they got taken off must have been scary.'

'The war seems to bring out fresh facets in people; have you heard about my mother? She's settled herself in London, changed her appearance and become a bridge fiend. She's so changed, Emily, that she might turn out to be somebody who would help you.'

'I don't want help. I thought I'd made that clear,' snapped Emily.

'Yes. Well. Sorry.' Rose picked up her plate and cup and moved towards the sink.

'Ned told me when I met him in London that he loves you.' Emily reverted to Ned. Was the Ned she knew the same man who was Rose's husband, inheritor of all this? Emily looked around the large rather dark kitchen with its stone floor, draughts and inconvenient clutter. She felt no envy of Rose.

'I believe he does.' Rose rinsed her cup under the tap, not wishing to discuss Ned or dissect his love with Emily.

Emily watched Rose's back, the baggy corduroy trousers, the plain shirt under the thick sweater; when would she find occasion to wear the camiknickers? Not while milking, feeding pigs or gardening. 'Well,' she said, gathering up her briefcase, snapping it shut, regaining her poise, 'I must be on my way. Any chance,' she asked as they walked towards the red MG, 'of some extra butter now and again?'

Rose laughed. 'Blackmailer. Butter is rationed, pheasants are not. No chance.'

'Worth a try,' Emily said amiably. She kissed Rose's cheek and got into the car. 'The moral support will do.' She drove away.

Rose joined Farthing in the kitchen garden where he was trenching and manuring, preparing the ground for winter frosts. 'Shall I help?'

'You don't want to do this. It's too heavy. The cold frames need sorting out, you do that. They are full of weeds.'

'What's in them?'

'Parma violets and lilies of the valley. Come spring, you can post them up to Covent Garden or a posh shop like Constance Spry and make a packet.'

'What a lot you know.' Rose fetched a fork and trowel and began work, squatting by the frames. Does sly old Farthing guess that Emily is pregnant? Does he guess I am? He's heading me away from heavy jobs. Did it occur to Emily, or is she too absorbed in herself? Was Emily hinting, wondered Rose, her thoughts still on her friend, that Ned might be the father? Ignoble thought, she tried to push it aside but it turned this way and that in her mind. Emily would, but would Ned? Rose pulled up handfuls of chickweed, dug deep to extract a dandelion. Would Emily, if Ned? Would Ned, if Emily? Emily would, but would Ned? She pulled hard on the dandelion root which snapped, leaving a residue of root in the soil, buried deep to pop up later as persistent as Rose's suspicion of Emily. Would I mind? she asked herself. Mind much or mind a little? Not at all? The question does not arise, she scolded herself. Then she thought with surprise that Emily had looked vulnerable and then, even more surprised, she thought, I liked her this morning. I've never liked her before. 'What do you think of Emily Thornby?' she asked Farthing as he wheeled his barrow past her.

Farthing stopped, smiled: 'She's got spunk. They both have.'

'Ah.'

'Mind you, between ourselves, I wouldn't trust either of 'em round a razor blade.' Farthing gave his barrow a heave and moved on. Rose laughed, sitting back on her heels. 'Not a very flattering observation.'

'She'd be a bit of all right in a tight corner,' Farthing called over his shoulder, 'and her brother would too.'

'Their father is a trustworthy bishop, Farthing.'

'And who's he descended from? There's funny blood somewhere.'

'Are you suggesting pirates?' asked Rose, extracting a grub from among the weeds and throwing it in the direction of an attendant robin. 'Or gipsies?'

'I ain't suggesting nothing.' Farthing tipped the load of manure onto the ground by his trench.

Rose, remembering Emily's attack on herself, asked, 'Would you describe me as bloody conventional, Farthing?' rather cherishing Emily's description of herself.

'Wouldn't say bloody,' said Farthing, forking manure into the trench. 'The word conventional varies according to what you're doing in which social circle, I've heard.'

'What a philosopher you are,' said Rose. 'I think you and Mrs Farthing would be pretty splendid in a tight corner.'

'Might be at that,' Farthing agreed.

30

Mylo hoped to smell land. He stood, legs apart, balancing with the bounce of the ship. It was pitch dark and extremely cold. His fellow passenger, his charge, huddled below to keep warm; probably he slept.

Mylo strained his eyes across dark water, inimical waves leaping to mix their salt with rain sheeting from the west in a relentless torrent. The last words his fellow passenger had uttered before going below had been: '*Quel climat maudit.*' This in answer to the skipper's shouted information that they were two-thirds across the Channel, two-thirds towards their destination. Useless to point out that the weather had been equally foul in France.

Mylo fixed his eyes on a cloud, denser than the rest, trying to get his bearings. Afraid of showing his anxiety and fear, he refrained from joining the skipper in the wheelhouse. There had been an invitation, but Mylo judged it half-hearted. The skipper's job was to deliver them safe, not to entertain; if he was not happy on deck, he could go below. Staring into the mesmeric dark, ears buffeted by the wind, eyes watering from the cold, Mylo allowed himself to think tentatively of Rose as he had last seen her, curled in her bed, one hand pushed up under the pillow where his head had lately rested, the other flung wide across the bed. He had bent to kiss her, breathing the scent of her skin and hair; forcing himself to leave he had crept to the door, put out a hand to stop the dog, Comrade, from following, signalling her to 'stay', opened the door with stealth, gone swiftly downstairs and away.

For three months he had rationed his thoughts of Rose, lest day-dreaming he might drop his guard, speak a word of English, turn careless, risk capture, death, betrayal.

Had she been angry or sad? Had she understood? Could he or should he have warned her? Whichever way he left, it would have been painful; he had taken the mode least painful for himself. With his eyes fixed on the bank of cloud Mylo thought now of Rose, wished he could hear her voice, feel her body, taste the salt on her eyelids. In his heart he expected to find her exactly as he had left her. He would climb back into her bed; she would wake in his arms.

His mind jeered at the sentimental vision; months had passed since the parting.

'That's Start Point.' The voice startled him, banished Rose.

'I thought it was a bank of cloud.'

'We'll be in Dartmouth before daylight. Like some cocoa? Join us in the wheelhouse.' The voice was cheerful pitched against the wind, jolly even, gone the clipped accents used when he had taken them on board; it had been a nervous rendezvous. The tide had been too strong, tempers had frayed, almost there had been failure. Failure would have led to arrest, arrest to . . .

Mylo followed to the wheelhouse, accepted cocoa, answered smile with smile. 'Relax now, we'll be ashore in time for bacon and bangers. The crossing was a piece of cake.' The young officer was immensely relieved, tremendously pleased; so he, too, had been frightened. He hid it well, thought Mylo, drinking his cocoa. 'Your Frog's asleep; I looked in on him. Would he like some cocoa?'

'He's pretty tired, let him sleep.'

'They'll be meeting you, I take it?'

'Someone will be meeting us, yes.'

'Got a lot of nerve, you chaps.'

'I'm just a *commis voyageur*,' said Mylo, half offended by his own modesty, inwardly ridiculing it.

'What's that?'

'Commercial traveller,' both men laughed, 'and I am half Frog.'

'I say, sorry, I didn't mean . . .'

'We Frogs call you rosbifs.'

More laughter, the young officer laughing alone this time.

As the land reached out to block the wind, Mylo, back on deck, sniffed, hoping to catch the smell of home soil, a field under plough perhaps where seagulls swooped and foraged fresh-turned clods. Presently they anchored offshore; he woke his fellow traveller and they were taken off by a launch which whirled them away from the ship to land them at a jetty far up the harbour. They stumbled up slippery steps into the arms of waiting officialdom.

Mylo's companion showed no inclination to kneel and kiss British soil in the manner which years later would become de rigueur for His Holiness Pope John Paul. He gave a hoarse imprecation as his foot slipped on a scrap of seaweed which might have been construed as relief at reaching dry land if he had not before starting on the journey already made his dislike of things British clear, a dislike superseded only by his loathing of things German. They were led across a cobbled quay into a building which smelled of soap, damp uniforms and cups of tea, sifting through a cloud of cigarette smoke. Dazzled by the glare of unshaded lights, Mylo thought it would be at least forty-eight hours before he could attend properly to thoughts of Rose; his charge spoke no English, was still his responsibility.

They were offered tea by an attractive Wren. Mylo's charge accepted, sniffed in disbelief at the contents of his mug and put it aside.

Their escort disappeared through a side door while an Army officer wearing Intelligence Corps insignia came from an inner office carrying a sheaf of papers to shake Mylo by the hand and greet his charge.

'Does your friend understand English?'

'No.' Mylo followed the officer into an inner office.

'Bit short of interpreters at the moment, actually; our one and only is down with flu. No matter. We shall be sending you to London to be debriefed and when your passenger leaves Patriotic School he will be the Free French's responsibility. They insist on running their own intelligence.'

'Who will he be dealing with?' Mylo asked innocently.

'Chap who calls himself Passy, came over with de Gaulle. Haven't met him myself, of course. Do sit down, that pew's comfortable.'

'I have,' said Mylo. 'Extreme right wing.'

'Does that matter?'

Mylo shot a glance of wonder at the intelligence officer. Now I know I am in England, he thought, and burst out laughing.

'Joke? Did I make one? Cigarette?'

'No, no, it must be the relief at having got here.' Mylo leant back in his chair.

'Yes. I see. Dare say your job gets a bit hairy.' He picked up a telephone. 'Won't be a minute. I'll just rustle up your transport.' He spoke into the telephone, listened. 'Well, wake him up, Sergeant! Now, where were we? Your friend will be all right out there with Margaret, she's a bright girl.' He went back to the door which stood open. 'Keep an eye on our guest, Margaret, there's a good girl.' Then, raising his voice, 'You'll be all right with Margaret, Monsieur – er – Monsieur – er – forgive me, what's your name?'

'Picot,' said Mylo. 'Sit down,' he said to his charge, 'I won't be long; they are sending us to London by car.'

'*Tiens.*' Picot sat on a chair offered by the shapely Wren and looked about him. The intelligence officer closed the door. 'Not exactly forthcoming, your Frog friend.'

'Doesn't like the English.'

'Well, we don't like them, do we? Give me Jerry any day, he's not an hereditary enemy.'

'Well . . .'

'Yes, I know,' said the intelligence officer catching Mylo's eye. 'My name's Spalding, by the way. Not supposed to ask yours, am I? All this secrecy reminds me of my prep school days, games we used to play after lights out after reading too much John Buchan. Some of it makes a nonsense, though. I was dealing with a super secret chap last week, told to keep my trap shut by the powers that be. They didn't know we were cousins, did they, and been to the same school? Both of us did what we were told and kept mum, couldn't even make a date to meet for lunch on our next leave, wouldn't have done to make my brigadier look a fool. The Navy aren't half so stuffy. That's why I've wangled myself a Wren, by the way. Now then, mustn't run on; let's get the bumph work done, shall we?'

'Fine by me.' Mylo waited while Spalding shuffled through his sheaf of papers.

'Came to meet you carrying these, didn't I? I'm supposed to keep them locked up. Here we are, this is what we want. These are for you and I keep this and this. I'm supposed to ask you a lot of damn fool questions which you will be asked all over again in London, in triplicate I shouldn't wonder, and your friend Picot too, so I won't bother you now. Such a waste of time, God help the lot of us. Thank him, thank him, thank him, I'm due for a spot of leave. You two go up by car, but I go by train; it wouldn't be ethical to hitch a ride. Right? All done.' The intelligence officer smiled at Mylo across his desk and stood up.

'Thanks a lot.'

'I hear that Passy chap is a bastard, by the way,' said Spalding as he lit a cigarette.

'I've heard it too.'

'If your friend is a communist, tell him to keep it to himself.'

'- - - - -'

'The Passy chap, calls himself a colonel, isn't so much extreme right as blazing fascist, if you ask me, but please don't. I'm only here to do my modest job. You did say extreme right, didn't you?'

'Something like that.'

'Get the nuances right. Tip your friend.'

'I will.'

'There's a game within a game and it is not cricket. Am I being indiscreet?'

'Not at all. Of course not. What an idea.'

'Well, then. Right we are. Your car should be here by now.' Spalding shook Mylo's hand. 'I was never much good at hints.' They walked back to the outer office.

The shapely Wren was exercising her schoolgirl French. Picot was laughing as he corrected her accent. The Wren who was laughing too straightened her face and saluted Spalding. Picot got to his feet.

Mylo and Picot said goodbye and followed a military police-man who had materialised, to a military car.

'Wish we could give you a lift,' shouted Mylo, but the intelligence officer wasn't there any more. He got into the car with Picot, and they were driven off.

Picot watched the countryside of Devon, wet, brilliant green and ploughed, for half an hour, then turned to Mylo, 'Well?'

'You will, as I told you, be taken to Patriotic School and after that the French take you over. There's a snake called Passy.'

'Not a grass-snake?'

'No.'

'Thank you.'

'Eats communists for breakfast.'

'*C'est un flic, c'est tout.*' Picot much less glum than on arrival laughed. 'For an English girl that one was pretty. She moves soon to work in London; we are to lunch at a restaurant she likes, the Écu de France.'

'If you escape the Deuxième Bureau.'

'They do not bother me. And you, shall you be my escort next time? Shall we make a habit of this? Make rendezvous at your aunt in Paris and cross together to Dartmouth?'

'Possibly.' Mylo did not want to talk any more; he wanted to think about Spalding's fake asininity, he wanted to think of Rose. With an effort he dismissed both from his thoughts and concentrated on the report he must make on arrival in London. Try to make sense while protecting his back. My back is in France, he thought. All those friends and acquaintances continually at risk. How dare somebody as safe as Spalding be so frivolous? Shall I try telephoning Slepe from London? What happens if Ned answers, if Ned's on leave, what then? Well, here I am not concentrating on my report. I shall mention as few names as possible. Was Spalding planted there to look silly and drop a hint, when in London they play it straight? Not easy to switch quickly from the Gallic and Teutonic mind to the Anglo-Saxon.

'She says, that girl Margaret, that the food is not too terrible in London and that the rationing is fair.'

'Yes?'

'With us it is not so fair. I promised to bring my wife soap when I return; she has given me a list of things she wants.'

'I have two Camemberts I bought in Normandy as we journeyed.'

'There is no shortage there, the farmers do not suffer. Look at this country. Nothing is happening to your people, you do not suffer at all.' Picot waved his hand towards the pasture and plough they were passing.

'The towns have been bombed.'

'My friend, you have been listening to the German radio; your country is untouched; it is we who suffer, the workers.'

Let him wait till he sees London, thought Mylo; sometimes, listening to the Picots of this world, I think fuck the workers. Mylo pulled up his coat collar, leaned back and tried to sleep.

31

Mylo woke from an uncomfortable doze and recognising the contours of the hills realised that they were passing within a few miles of Slepe. He was furiously tempted to ask the driver to stop so that he could telephone, hear on the line Rose's hesitant, cautious, 'Hullo? Who is it?' When he said, 'Mylo,' her voice would swoop, bubbling up. But, he thought, looking at the driver's back, I shall do it later. The driver may have orders to report anything I do. I must wait until I am free, the job finished, then I can telephone or, better still, arrive quietly as I did before, find her asleep, let her wake in my arms and we shall be back where we left off.

It was getting dark when they reached the outskirts of London. The driver switched on dimmed lights and drove slowly. 'Raid's started, sir.' He sounded pleased.

'How d'you know?'

'Glow in the sky, sir. Very punctual, the Jerries come up the river same time every evening, can set your watch by 'em.'

'What does he say?' asked Picot.

'There is an air raid.'

'Can one see it? Is it dangerous?'

'No doubt we shall find out.'

Picot grunted, leaning forward in his seat to watch the glow in the east, the occasional flash, the lingering searchlights.

They were flagged down near Chiswick. 'Going far?' asked a policeman.

'Neighbourhood of Knightsbridge,' admitted the driver.

'There's a landmine in the Cromwell Road, an unexploded bomb in Queen's Gate, the Old Brompton Road's blocked. You will have to re-route via King's Road and Sloane Street.'

Mylo translated.

'*Tiens*,' said Picot, 'so it's true you do have trouble, what a mercy it is not Paris.'

'When you are free from your reception committee I will take you on a tour, show you the mess,' said Mylo.

'Good, we can invite the girl Margaret who has incidentally already offered and my little cousin Chantal who works with the French Navy. The girl Margaret knows her and I have messages for her from Maman.'

'Not written, I trust.'

'Of course they are written . . .'

'Idiot,' exclaimed Mylo. 'If we had been caught the letter would have led the Gestapo to the mother and then . . .' (I should have searched the bastard, what a fool I am.)

'But we were not caught.' Picot was amused.

'Your Colonel Passy will not be pleased to hear this.'

'Shall you tell him?' Picot was amused by this too.

'I don't expect to meet him, but in future no written messages. There is no need to take idiotic risks.' Mylo was angry.

'They did not search us at Dartmouth.'

'That will happen in London.'

'The Germans would search us before we left, half-way there, and on arrival,' said Picot, hating yet admiring the enemy.

'Why were you so careless? I cannot understand . . .'

'My cousin Chantal wrote to say the English are amateur.'

'Wrote? You got a letter?'

'We are not the only ones to cross the Channel, you must know that.'

'Is your cousin a Party member?'

'If she was, she would not have been so readily accepted by the Gaullistes. Her father was a naval officer, she has the *entrée*.'

It's useful that he has this cousinship to protect him, thought Mylo, he will need it; the Establishment's suspicion of communists is inbred, but so fortunately are family ties.

Separated on arrival from Picot, Mylo spent the following days being interviewed, questioned, re-questioned, de-briefed by the people who had sent him to France and by others he did not know. He felt resentful of these men who paced their offices or sat relaxed behind desks able to step out from Broadway, walk across St James's Park to lunch in their clubs, return to ask of their girl staff, 'Any messages, Diana, Susan, Jenny, Victoria?' (All the girls in all the offices bore the genetic stamp of colonels' or captains' (RN) daughters, safe fodder for Whitehall, the War Office and Broadway.) Not for these men and girls in bed at night the fear of the knock on the door. These are my people, yet must I protect my back, thought Mylo, they cannot know how it is for my friends in France; there are names and addresses they need not have.

'Now we come to your friend Picot,' said the man behind the desk. 'How would you rate him?'

'High.'

'Possibly, possibly. Party members are supposed to be more disciplined than your Free French enthusiast.'

'Certainly.' Mylo thought of Picot's cousin Chantal and her open letter borne by hand to Maman.

'He has, it seems, a cousin called Chantal in their Navy. Works for Soustelle. Did he mention her?'

So the bastard is at least well informed. 'Yes. Says he is looking forward to seeing her.'

'I dare say. Well, yes. We would like you, if you agree, to spend an evening with Picot and this cousin of his before we let the Free French have him. He also made friends with a Wren called, let me see, yes, Margaret, when you came ashore at Dartmouth.'

'A plant?'

'You could make a foursome. Show Picot London as it is, go out for a meal.'

'And?'

'Report to us, unofficially of course, whether Picot is working for others besides us and the French.'

'The Party?' Mylo put innocence in his tone.

'That's the sort of thing, yes.'

Mylo laughed. 'He told me his cousin is the daughter of an officer; she would be the same sort of girl as the girls you have here.'

'They are not as silly as your tone suggests.' There was a snip of huffiness.

'What exactly do you want to know?' (I hate this man, I hate his kind.)

'Anything that doesn't quite fit, you know the sort of thing.' (Non-committal, yet insistent.)

'Is this an order?'

'I should call it a request.' (Smiling now, bland.)

Mylo stood up. His questioner rose, too, walked with him to the door. 'Wasn't your father a communist at one time?'

Mylo grinned. 'My father thought all party politics ludicrous. He was not a joiner.'

'Wasn't there something he did in South Africa? I seem to have heard . . .' (The voice trailed.)

'He was asked to leave. He went to one or two Party meetings, he liked the songs.'

'Songs?' (Puzzled.)

'They were better than the Whites', the Black and Coloured songs.'

'Oh, dear. Here we get into colour.' (Pained.)

'Uncomfortable thing, colour.'

'Uncomforting too. Well! Have a good time, show him around. Let me know how you get on with the girls and so on.' (Hearty now.)

'I am not in the business of betrayal.'

'My dear fellow! What an idea.' He was pained.

'And expenses?' suggested Mylo.

'What? Oh, expenses. Oh, yes, well now. Victoria is the girl you need.' (Expenses are beneath me.) 'Victoria, sweetie?' They had reached an outer office. 'Yes, sir?' Victoria (a brigadier's daughter, perhaps) showed no pleasure at being addressed as sweetie.

'Fix Mr Cooper up with the proper forms and so on, he needs expenses.'

'Very good, sir,' snapped Victoria.

'Goodbye, Mr Cooper.'

'Goodbye,' said Mylo. They shook hands, watched by Victoria.

'This way,' said Victoria, 'follow me.' She led.

'Do you know whether the Hamman Baths are still open?' Mylo asked Victoria's back.

'People do come out of that office feeling they need cleansing,' said Victoria over her shoulder. 'Unfortunately the Turkish baths are closed, a stick of bombs fell across Jermyn Street a fortnight ago and demolished the baths and everybody in them.'

'Ah me!'

'It's all in the mind,' said Victoria cheerfully, 'nothing an ordinary bath can't cure. When I get that besmirched feeling, I buy myself a cake of expensive soap, that helps.'

Mylo laughed. 'I'll try that.'

'Used I not to see you at the Malones'?' asked Victoria. 'Aren't you a friend of George and Richard's?'

'It's a small world. I tutored George.'

Does she know Rose, too, Mylo wondered, has she heard her voice lately? He walked back to where he was staying, stopping on the way to buy sandalwood soap. On reaching his lodgings he telephoned Picot to invite him and his cousin Chantal to spend the evening, do some sightseeing first. He was not surprised to hear that the Wren, Margaret, had turned up in London and would join the party. What do the buggers take me for, he thought, as he lay in his bath before keeping the rendezvous. No amount of soaping washed away the feeling of grubbiness engendered by the smooth-talking man who had toyed with him in his office in the building in Broadway.

They met early, while it was still light, having planned to make a lightning tour of bombed London for Picot's benefit. Mylo hired a taxi (Victoria had been generous with her promises to reimburse). They drove through the city as office workers streamed away, anxious to get home before the air raids started. Picot leaned forward in his seat, staring at the faces of the crowd, trying to read their mood. 'They show so little; is it already a habit?' He chatted with his cousin, exchanging family news while Margaret sat silent on his other side. Why must we all spy on one another; it is unreal. Mylo longed for Rose, comparing her favourably with these self-assured girls.

As they drove round the docks Picot fell silent, stayed silent at the spectacle of the ruined Guildhall, smashed Wren churches, blocks of offices where firemen still hosed the smoking ruins of the previous night's raid, their faces grey with fatigue. Through the open window they smelled the stink of fire. Chantal, wrinkling her nose, asked for it to be shut. Mylo watched her sitting back in the taxi, looking unmistakably French in her perfectly cut uniform, her white shirt speckless against her young throat, her face so carefully made up.

Beside her Margaret in her uniform looked scrubbed and British. Mylo sitting on the jump seat wondered which of the girls would be best in bed and laughed inwardly at even asking himself the question. Bed was one thing, he told himself, but Margaret would make the most intelligent report on the evening. I wonder what soap Chantal uses, he mused, or is she spared any sense of guilt?

They dined presently at the Écu de France (spared by the stick of bombs which had demolished the Hamman Baths). The restaurant was Margaret's choice. Chantal sulked; she had wanted to go to the Café de Paris; it was safe, she said, it was underground, no need to fear in the raids which she confessed made her nervous. One could dance, she wanted to dance. 'It is the food I am after.' Margaret demolished the French girl's protest. When later that year there was a direct hit on the Café de Paris, the bomb falling through its glass roof and slaughtering many people, Mylo remembered Chantal on that first and only meeting.

As it was they dined pretty well. Margaret enjoyed her food.

Picot celebrated his reunion with his cousin and his first visit to England. Mylo drank steadily and too much to dull the impression of smashed London, to rid himself of the taste of betrayal and doublecross which he realised now to be endemic in the corridors of his masters. What the hell, he thought, as he grew bibulously cheerful, what the bloody hell. Coming out into the street he burst into song and seizing Chantal in his arms danced with her as he sang, 'Hitler has only got one ball/ Goering's are very very small/ Himmler's are somewhat simmler/ but Goebbels has no balls at all.' As they whirled along the pavement, Chantal pleading in French for a translation, an air-raid warden called to them good-humouredly and Margaret climbed into a taxi with Picot and drove away, shouting that it would be wise to take cover.

When a bomb fell within earshot Chantal took fright and begged to be taken home. In the taxi Mylo put his arm around her and kissed her; arriving at her flat she invited him in until the raid was over; she feared to be alone, her flatmate was away. Mylo followed her indoors. He had by this time reached the stage of intoxication when it was habitual for him to bore whoever he might be with with a description of Rose's charms and his love for her, and then since Chantal seemed an accommodating girl he would reward her for her charitable listening by making love to her; it would take her mind off the air raid.

When he woke, Chantal was already up and dressed in her uniform and offering restorative coffee. '*Vous etiez soûl mais gentil.*'

'Yes, thanks,' he took the cup. 'Nothing a ritual bath won't cure.' He sat up. 'Ow! My head! Ouch! Oh, Christ!'

'*Au revoir, je vous quitte.*' Chantal tripped away; he heard her heels click and fade on the pavement outside, looked at his watch, reached for the telephone, asked when a voice answered for Victoria.

'Tell your boss I did what he asked. There is nothing to report. The answer is nix.'

'Write in . . .'

'You joking? It was *unofficial.*'

'Margaret said you had a good time.'

'She reported in?'

'Two hours ago. Never mind, I'll tell him.'

'Can one still get American pick-me-ups at that chemist in Piccadilly?'

'Like that, is it?' A genial girl, Victoria.

'Don't tell me they've been bombed, too?'

'Heppells? No, they're still there. Did you sleep with the Free French Navy cousin?'

'What does *she* say?'

'She hasn't reported; we aren't on those terms with the French.'

In the unease of his hangover, Mylo was not sure whether Victoria was joking. Collecting his clothes, searching unsuccessfully for a razor (doesn't the girl even shave her legs?), he set off for his lodgings to soak in a hot bath, soap himself with sandalwood soap, forget about Chantal and Broadway, the trickiness of intelligence and dream of Rose, soon to be in his arms, back where they left off, a joyful reunion.

32

Standing in Heppells, watching the white-coated chemist mix the concoction known as an American pick-me-up, Mylo was filled with self-disgust. What had possessed him to try and sleep with Picot's cousin? She had yawned during his description of Rose, shown herself an unenthusiastic bedfellow, clearly only requiring his company to still her fears of the air raid.

Mylo took the nauseous brew handed to him in a tiny medicinal glass and gulped it down. As the liquid hit his stomach his system registered a revivifying shock which brought tears to his eyes; he remembered with humiliation that he had been too drunk to come, had fallen asleep, probably snored. He fumbled for money, paid the man behind the counter and stepped out into the street.

The sun shone as he walked along Piccadilly; he belched violently, startling a passer-by. The pick-me-up was working. His spirits began to rise, he was on leave, free to do whatever he liked, what he liked was Rose, but first to settle his mind as well as his stomach he went back to the office in Broadway to deal with his de-briefer of the previous days.

'I want to see your bastard of a boss.'

'He's busy. Will you wait?' said Victoria. 'His name is Major Pye, Peregrine Pye.'

'I know his name, find out if he'll see me, there's a dear.'

Victoria went away, came back. 'In about ten minutes,' she said non-committally.

'For a genetically trustworthy girl, you are rather nice.'

'A what girl?'

'Uncorruptible, bred full of patriotism, a colonel's daughter.'

'Brigadier, actually.'

'Genetically safe.'

'Oh.' Victoria latched on. 'I see.' She smiled. 'It does help with the Official Secrets Act. Did you go to Heppells?'

'Yes.'

'Feeling better?'

'Yes, thank you.'

'So glad.' Victoria picked up a folder, opened it and began to read.

'I got stinking drunk in the restaurant last night, then I sang and danced in the street.'

'Do you get drunk often?'

'It would be suicidal in my present occupation.'

'I imagine it would,' said Victoria.

'That's to say, I feel a bit foolish this morning.'

'Reaction to the strain in France? I'd say that's what it was – if I was asked.' Victoria had beautiful hazel eyes in an otherwise unremarkable face.

'What a sensible girl you are,' said Mylo. 'Do you ever get drunk? How do you know about pick-me-ups?'

'I have a brother and a fiancé in submarines. People have to let off steam.' Victoria stood up. 'Major Pye will see you now.'

'Hullo, Cooper. What's the trouble? What can I do for you this morning?' This morning Major Pye was genial. Mylo wondered why he had feared him during the previous days; he was ordinary, even nondescript in his blue pinstripe suit, gunner tie, horn-rimmed spectacles.

'Can it be quite clear that I do *not* spy on the people I bring across? That I am *not* interested in politics? That I am simply and plainly a guide?'

'My dear fellow . . .'

'Can it . . .?'

'Rather an odd request, but I suppose so, yes, can't see why not if you insist.'

'Thanks. That's all I wanted to know, just to have it clear.'

'Right, right. I'll circulate the news. You extract the people or persons, and have no interest after delivery. Can do. Happy now?'

'Thanks.'

'You are on leave now and will report in during the week?'

'Yes, I'll telephone.'

'Fine, fine. Goodbye.'

They shook hands. Mylo left Major Pye's office, went down in the lift and out into the sunshine.

Major Pye looked down into the street from his office window and watched Mylo cross the street and dodge into St James's Park Underground. 'I wish we had more like him,' he said to Victoria. 'Bit of an oddball.'

'Half French,' said Victoria. 'I've been reading his file. His mother was Jewish.'

'Both parents dead. Do we know where he spends his leave? Did he tell you? Did you ask?'

'No, sir.'

'You think it's not our business, do you? I wish you wouldn't call me sir, Victoria.'

'It distances me from the dirty tricks.'

'We can't all abjure politics like your friend.'

'Just an acquaintance, sir.'

'A good acquaintance?' pried Major Pye.

'You split hairs, sir.' (If Peregrine didn't pry so hard I would tell him Mylo Cooper tutored the Malone boys.)

'I thought I detected a soupçon of protectiveness.'

'I would imagine he's well able to mind his own back, Peregrine,' Victoria relented.

Jolting along in the Underground, Mylo gleefully counted the days of his leave, seven whole days with Rose, seven nights. Half a day wasted at Heppells and fixing Major Pye was no waste but a precautionary measure, and every minute now was bringing him closer to Rose. He would not, if he caught a train now, arrive to find her asleep as he had planned; no matter, arriving in daylight there would be the garden where they had strolled in scented twilight, the river, the woods, the fields; soon he would hear her voice, touch her, smell her, feel her.

At Paddington he jostled through the crowds to the ticket office, enquired the time of the trains, kicked his heels for an impatient hour before at last the crowded train pulled away from the platform and, gathering speed, carried him away from bombed London through undamaged suburbs into the Thames Valley. From the corridor he watched the ploughed fields, the copper and sulphur woods of autumn. The train stopped at every station, passengers crowded on and off, soldiers en route to Salisbury Plain, sailors to Plymouth, airmen to widely scattered airfields. Mylo watched, comparing them to the population of France with its expression of the watched and the watching; none of these Englishmen gave the impression of watching anything further than their noses, and why should they, Mylo thought in admiration, they had no need to. As the flat valley country changed to rolling chalk downland and again to brown plough and steeper hills Mylo's spirits soared. He arrived at his destination, left the train and boarded a country bus which carried him along familiar lanes to Rose's village; here, shouldering his pack, he set off to cover the last mile on foot.

As he walked he pictured Rose unaware of his imminent arrival, yet waiting for him. Comrade (until this moment he had forgotten Comrade) would recognise his step, bark with joy and alert Rose, who would hurl herself into his arms and then the hugs and kisses, cries of joy. Mylo walked faster, hurrying through the late autumn afternoon; it was clouding up, going to rain, he had left his mackintosh in London. Approaching the house from the back he felt uneasy, he was watched from a window by a woman with iron grey hair and suspicious eyes; he had forgotten the Ministry of Information. He waved a casual hand; the woman stood up to stare, a man came to stand beside her; Mylo could see their lips move. He waved again. They followed him with their eyes. Slightly disconcerted, wishing he had not taken a short cut but come the longer way up the drive, Mylo skirted the kitchen garden and arrived at the side door usually used by Rose. He opened the door, stepped into the stone-flagged passage, listened. Hearing voices in the kitchen he tiptoed forward, stopped in shadow to peer in unseen. There was a loud burst of feminine laughter.

With her back to him Rose sat at the kitchen table, at her feet Comrade in a basket suckling two puppies, across the table Emily Thornby laughing loudly at something Rose had just said, her head thrown back, eyes half closed, in her hand a cigarette. As she laughed she ejected little jets of smoke from her nose.

Rose was laughing, too. She did not see Mylo, spring into his arms with cries of joy, nor did Comrade like Argus recognise him with glad barks.

Since Emily was about the last person Mylo had hoped to see, he sidled quickly past the kitchen door across the hall to the library where he sat down on a sofa in a fury of disappointed rage.

It was forty minutes before a car drove up to the front door and Nicholas came running up the steps calling, 'Emily, I'm here, sorry I'm late. Rose, are you there? I've come to collect Em. Rose?'

'Here, we're in the kitchen; d'you want some tea?'

Mylo ground his teeth.

'No, no.' Mylo hated Nicholas's blithe voice. 'We must go. Come on, Emily, buck up.' Another ten minutes and a lot of laughter before Rose waved Nicholas and Emily goodbye and turning saw in the gloom of the hall a man. She sucked in her breath. 'Oh!'

'Rose?'

Rose stepped backwards. 'Who?'

'It's me, you idiot, Mylo.'

'How long have you been here?'

'Nearly an hour, I didn't think you'd like the Thornbys to see us together.'

'Mylo,' Rose whispered. 'Mylo.'

'You don't seem very pleased to see me,' said Mylo disagreeably. 'Perhaps you are not. Perhaps I'd better go. I seem to be labouring under a delusion.' His disappointment was whipping him into a childish rage. 'I thought, I . . . I thought we . . . What the bloody hell was all that laughter about?'

They were standing yards apart, both white-faced, now staring, shocked.

'We were laughing about the father of Emily's baby, a sort of guessing game, she's pregnant, she pretends not to know the father.'

' . . . '

'And so am I.'

'You? Pregnant? Who is the father?'

'Ned, of course.'

' . . . '

Rose drew herself up defensively, then whispered, 'Oh, darling.'

He did not hear her, just stood looking at her. She, growing aware of his fatigue, harsh disappointment, jealousy, anger, became afraid, dared not speak.

Comrade, disengaging herself from her puppies, came pattering into the hall to join Rose. She pricked her ears at the sight of Mylo's back, went up to him, sniffed his ankles, threw back her head with a warbling yowl, stood on hind legs to paw him, thrashed her tail, ululated with joy, making little upward ineffectual jumps.

Still Mylo stared at Rose. 'I wish it was mine, oh, God, I wish it was mine.' His voice bitter.

'I was so angry with you. So lost when you sneaked off without saying anything, so lonely, I thought . . .'

'And Comrade?' He stroked the dog's head.

'She must have been in pup when you brought her here.'

'So we don't know the father of the puppies, and Emily doesn't know the parent of her . . .'

'Nicholas says he knows, teases her.'

'Nicholas would.'

Rose put out a hand. 'Mylo, why are we standing here like strangers? Mylo, please.'

'Rose.'

They were laughing, crying, kissing, hugging while Comrade danced around them barking. 'I thought,' said Mylo between kisses, 'I thought I'd come in the night and begin where we left off, climb into your bed. Oh,' a kiss, 'my love,' a kiss, 'it would have been pretty funny if I'd climbed in with Ned.'

'He's in Egypt.'

'Then I can . . .'

'Of course! Come in, let's shut the door, it's icy. This is the coldest house . . .'

'I didn't want the Thornbys to see me.'

'I should hope not. You, we, are secret.'

'And the baby?' He held her away to look at her. 'Are you well? Shouldn't you be careful? Are you all right?'

'It's not an illness.'

'I wish it was mine. I wish . . .'

'I'll have yours next.' She was laughing, half serious. 'Come and get warm, your hands are freezing.'

'Darling, I was so excited at getting back, I got drunk last night, I . . .'

'Are you on leave?'

'Yes. A week.'

'A precious week.'

'I shall have to ring up, but yes, I have a week.'

'And then?'

'I shall go back.'

'To France?'

'Yes.'

'Oh, Christ. Must you?'

'There are people there I have to help. It's what I can do. It isn't killing people, it's not political.'

'Curse this bloody war,' Rose cried with passion.

179

'Oh, Rose, I do so want you.' He held her.

'Mylo, your tummy rumbled.'

'Sorry, I'm bloody hungry. I haven't eaten today, I had this hangover.'

'Come along, then. I'll get you a meal, then we'll go to bed.'

'Should you? Won't it hurt the little . . .?'

'No, it won't. A baby isn't measles, it's not dangerous, it's normal, lots of women do it.'

'Are you certain?'

'Yes, yes, yes. Come and eat.'

'Then I can pretend I arrived as I dreamed I would and we'll carry on where we left off?'

'Is that what you thought?'

'Yes, stupid of me. What was all that laughter I overheard in the kitchen? You and Emily . . .' (Suspicion creeping back.)

'Are you jealous?'

'I suppose so. Yes, I am. I felt so left out.'

'There is no need,' said Rose, leading him to the kitchen, making him sit down while she found him food. 'Neither of us should ever be jealous.'

There is no need to tell her about that bitch Chantal last night, she might not understand. I was, after all, drunk, thought Mylo. 'Of course, you are right. Oh darling, this looks delicious,' he said as Rose gave him a plate of food.

There is no need, thought Rose, watching him eat, to tell him what we were laughing at. If I told him we were laughing at my poor mother's horror of sex and particularly of pregnancy, her revulsion at the recollection of me in her womb heaving (Rose suppressed a giggle), it might put him off me in bed. 'Let's get to bed as quickly as we can,' she said.

33

They would remember four perfect days, four nights spent loving by the light of the fire. Falling asleep. Waking to make love again, then to lie close, each telling tirelessly, gently, of the immensity of love felt now, experienced now, to be cherished for ever.

Mylo would slip out of bed, put coal on the fire, balance another log on the coals, pat Comrade's head as she lay in her basket, puppies' noses pressed against her belly, stroke the cats purring in a ball on the hearthrug, return to hold Rose, lie listening to the breeze whispering round the house, to a restive cow lowing in the meadow, the shriek of a far-off train, the distant drone of a bomber. (The war stayed far away, did not impinge.) Time, though not standing still, passed with enchanted slowness. They loved, they slept, they woke to breakfast in the kitchen under Mrs Farthing's unsurprised eye.

'What have you told her?'

'She seems incurious so I say nothing, explanations can bog one down.' Indeed Farthing, Mrs Farthing, the evacuee waifs treated Mylo as a natural phenomenon, no odder than Ned's visiting friends or the Malone family when they came to care for Rose in her illness, treating him with reserve, a reserve more stringently applied to the Ministry of Information people, should they come round from their offices at the back of the house confessing that they had forgotten to order milk for their mid-morning cuppas, or, worse, had run out of sugar. (We will pay you back tomorrow when we get our ration). They were given sugar, made to feel they had stepped out of line, should have organised their sugar from their billets in the village.

On the fifth morning Mylo woke to hear rain smacking at the windows, rattling the leaves of the magnolia, wind whingeing and whining round the house, Comrade whimpering restless at the door asking to go out, and the knowledge that today he must telephone London.

Wrapped in a blanket, he went barefoot down to let the dog out, waited holding the door while she hurried out to squat, ears back, eyes slitted disgustedly at the rain, then finished, to scamper back into the dry, shake and patter fast up the stairs to her puppies. Creeping back into bed Mylo woke Rose.

'What is it? Your feet are cold. Where have you been? Why didn't you borrow Ned's dressing gown?'

'I don't want his fucking dressing gown. I have to telephone London, report in.'

'Oh, God! So soon. Oh, must you?'

'Yes. Yes, I must.'

'It's raining. Oh, Mylo, does this mean . . .?'

'No, no, three more days. Keep calm . . .'

'How can I possibly?'

'You must, my darling, we must.'

But the spell, if spell it was, was broken.

'If I drive you to wherever you have to go we can be together a little longer,' catching, snatching at time as it meanly accelerated. 'There's a hoard of petrol made by Ned for use in dire emergency. This is dire all right, of course it's dire. I can fill the tank, drive you to wherever, be with you a little longer.'

'It won't work. I am not allowed to tell anyone where I go.'

'Not even me?'

'Not even you.'

'Damn, damn, damn. Go and telephone, then,' she cried in fury.

Mylo telephoned, shutting the library door so that she could not overhear.

Returning, he said, 'We are all right until Saturday, three more days.'

'Two and a half.'

'I shall go up by train.'

'Can't I drive you to London?'

'No.'

'Why not?'

'Don't be silly, you know perfectly well that what I do, where I go, is secret. I have told you.'

'You haven't.'

'I am telling you now, then.'

'It's ridiculous.'

'It's the war. Come on,' he said, 'cheer up. Don't let's spoil our last days.'

'Could have been more happily put,' Rose said.

Mylo laughed, but the days were spoiled. Each tried to hide from the other that they counted time passing. Rose found herself comparing Mylo unfavourably with Ned. Ned had made no mystery about his doings, had been quite open about his posting to North Africa, why else would he need to stop in London en route for the north to buy lightweight uniforms? He wrote regularly, true, boringly, but he wrote. Mylo made it plain that there would be no communication once he was gone, no letter, no telephone, silence.

'How shall I bear it?' Rose wailed in petulant grief. Almost she enjoyed this grief, voiced it without let.

'You bore it before.' Here Mylo let the irritation up to now suppressed by the days of joy and love surface. Rose had changed since their last parting, grown assured. She was no longer the shy uncertain girl he had met at the winter tennis, she was mistress of Slepe, people responded to her, did what she asked, she took part in the farm, the gardens, village life. He had listened to her talk on the telephone, give orders disguised as suggestions, heard her gossip with Edith Malone, enquire after George and Richard, call Edith by her Christian name. He had seen her with the Farthings and the Hadleys; she had the strength and confidence given her by Slepe, she was happy in her environment, she had been happy without him.

When he arrived secretly to surprise her, she had been happy. She would laugh and be happy when he was gone. 'Don't spoil our three days,' he said harshly.

'I won't, I won't,' she cried passionately. 'How could I? They are ours, let's treasure them.'

But that night when they made love, she said, 'Don't do that, it hurts when you do that.'

He stopped kissing her breast, saying, 'What hurts? This?' and nibbled.

'It is because I am pregnant, my breasts are quite sore.'

He flung away from her, turning his back. And she not knowing what to say or do said, sniffing, 'I wish the baby was yours.'

'But it's not mine, it's bloody Ned's. Since you wouldn't leave Ned and come to me, you have his baby, not mine.'

'You've made it pretty clear I can't be with you. Don't be illogical,' she shouted in unhappy exasperation.

'I am not illogical, I am half French.'

'Besides,' Rose cried, desperate now, 'I promised Ned. I promised not to leave him. I can't break my promise, I'm funny that way.'

'You should have promised me, then there would not be this fuss.'

'You never asked me, you never asked for my promise.'

'There was no need. I assumed we loved each other. Ned only extracted your promise because he was unsure of you, he obviously felt he must pin you down.' Mylo was shouting now.

'Why are we quarrelling?' she remembered asking.

'Because we love each other.' Mylo pressed his face between her breasts, listening to her heart.

'We have got ourselves trapped, haven't we?' She held his head in her hands, kissing his dark hair. 'Perhaps we shall live to get out of the trap. I cannot wish Ned dead, though.'

'Ah, never.'

'Perhaps you will stop loving me, it's possible, people do fall out of love, wake to wonder what it was all about.'

'What about you?'

'I shall not change.' (But she has changed.)

'And nor shall I.'

'We are stuck, then,' she said with satisfaction.

'Yes,' he said. 'What about a little fuck?'

'What, now?' She pretended surprise. 'Oh, Mylo.'

Later she said, as the fire flared up and outlined his profile, 'When I am alone and miserably missing you, I watch your picture and remember your voice and the feel of you. I get terribly randy.'

'Thinking of me?'

'Of course, who else?'

'Ned. It would be reasonable for you to think of Ned.'

'He doesn't make me randy.'

'Some other lover you haven't told me about?'

'There is nobody but you.'

'. . . m-m-m.'

'Have you lain between other girls' thighs?'

'Silly girl.'

'Did I tell you about Ned's present just before he went overseas?'

'His sperm? Yes.'

'Not that.'

'What then?'

'He chose and had me sent six pairs of camiknickers from the White House.'

'What's the White House?'

'A grand shop in Bond Street.'

'So?'

'Mylo! Don't be dense. Camiknickers like the shift the girl wears in the picture. Do you think he noticed your picture is like me? Of course, I haven't worn them.'

'Why not?'

'Because the picture is you, yours.'

'Let me see those things.'

'Now?'

'Yes.'

Rose hopped out of bed, opened a drawer and brought the satin garments to Mylo in the bed. (Would he leap jealously out and cast them onto the fire? The smell would be awful.)

Mylo felt the silk, slid it through his fingers.

'Lovely. Put one on, let me see you in it.'

She stepped into the garment.

'Exactly like.' Mylo smiled at his love by the light of the fire. 'I didn't know your husband had brains,' he said.

'Of course he has brains.'

'And imagination.'

'I'm not so sure of that. Shall I wear them, then?'

'Yes, why not. Come into bed, keep it on. I want to compare the texture with the real thing.'

So, curiously, from his distance, Ned healed the rift between his wife and her lover, eased their last days, made the parting less agonising.

'How long will you be gone?'

'Don't ask, I don't know.'

'All right, I'll be good.'

'Take care of yourself and Ned's baby.'

I shall have yours next, she thought. 'If you send for me, I will come at once,' she said. 'You can promise me that much.'

'I shall come back,' he said with more confidence than he felt. 'I won't need to send for you.'

'Don't ever again creep away without telling me, that's all.'

'Don't nag.'

'I'm not . . .'

'Even if it spoils it for us, knowing the parting has to come?' he asked.

'Yes. This I can bear.'

'All right, all right, all right.' He rocked her in his arms. 'If I find a decent corkscrew in London, I will send it to you for Ned.'

'What a strange idea, has this some esoteric Freudian connotation?'

'It is just that he has no decent corkscrew. If I send him one, it will even out the camiknickers.'

'I love your jokes,' she said. She found the impending parting so painful she wished it was over so that she could apply herself to grieving, stop pretending to be cheerful.

34

When Mylo went away she had made herself busy, Rose remembered, as she stood on the hill letting her eye follow a flight of rooks as they wheeled and cawed down the valley. That was the trick, keep busy, keep occupied. Rose Peel working at the farm and garden, answering Ned's letters, caring for his friends on leave, learning to cook, clean, take an interest in the war, bear his child. That had become the norm. It used up time, energy and thought that might have been spent on Mylo, protected her from missing him physically, mentally, emotionally for long periods while she concentrated on her work, her child. It had not been possible, she thought, drawing her coat about her, turning away from the chill wind, to pine away. Just as well since the gaps between seeing him, being with him, were so varied, so long; and now she thought bleakly I have, in age, to think. It's hard to remember when I saw him last.

I used, she thought, letting her eye follow the distant birds, to believe we would always be in love, but now I don't know, I really don't.

Watching the rooks, blinking as the wind made her eyes water, she was reminded of her row with the Ministry of Agriculture, who had in spite of Emily's assurance arrived in a car armed with guns to shoot the Slepe rooks. She had hurried out, heavy with unborn Christopher, shouted at the men, ordered them away, made a considerable scene. Enjoyed it. Enjoyed embarrassing those men in a strident, authoritative voice, planting herself under the rookery, bulging with Christopher, born a fortnight later, ordering the men to 'get off my property', Ned's in fact, Christopher's now.

She had written in triumph to Ned, desk-bound by then in Cairo. He had replied, 'I can't see what the fuss is about; rooks do a lot of damage, you shouldn't interfere with the Min of Ag's work.' (She tore the letter up.) Nicholas and Emily had boasted around the neighbourhood of Rose's prowess. So unlike her mother, they said. 'Rose behaved like an old county warhorse, you'd never guess now she is mistress of Slepe that she is not true *hochgeboren*.' (Nicholas in the war liked to annoy by airing a meagre knowledge of German, reverting to the odd French expression on VE day.) 'Our Rose's vowels are perfect, unlike her Ma's which betray her lesser origins.' It was at this time, Emily being also pregnant, that the Thornbys cultivating Rose took to visiting her even without an ulterior motive. Emily's infant of unknown parenthood borrowed respectability from its mother's proximity to Rose, ponderously great with the child who would be heir to Slepe.

When Laura, a neat little baby, was born a week before Christopher it was natural that the mothers should be assumed to be friends as previously the same thing had been assumed of their mothers, although in actuality the only catty remarks ever uttered by Mrs Thornby when she was the rector's wife had been directed at Mrs Freeling; while Mrs Freeling, grown bold in widowhood, often lamented the tedium of hours passed in the company of Mrs Thornby. Lucky, thought Rose, watching the rooks disappear, that nothing came of Christopher and Laura's teenage scamper when they had thought for a day that they were in love and boasted of consummating their passion. Too soon the story had altered, their mood soured, Laura found Christopher boring, Christopher said Laura smelt!

Christopher takes after his father, thought Rose, yet he was such a darling little boy. She turned her back on the view and walked on. He had been a good and lovely baby; she had enjoyed his babyhood, enjoyed watching him grow into a delightful little boy. Had Ned been a charming infant, an adorable child? There had been no one to tell her, just a few photographs discovered by Aunt Flora at the back of a drawer when she was moving house, of Ned simpering beside his mother, of Ned looking sulky in baggy shorts aged about ten off to his prep school.

And Laura? Laura, looking exactly like Emily, had disappointed the curious who had laid bets, guessed at her paternity, run a sweepstake, naming all the men Emily was known to go about with, even including George Malone who at the time of her conception was in Moscow. Laura showed no likeness to anyone; her appearance gave no hint, nobody won the sweepstake. Christopher resembled Ned, there was no hint of Rose in his appearance; he had, as it were, rented her womb, taken nothing of his mother. I am quite prepared to accept that he is boring in bed, thought Rose dispassionately, as was Ned. If he slept with Laura so did Ned sleep with Emily, why he bothered to pretend he didn't defeats me. There are still people who think Laura may be Ned's child; somehow I have never thought so. Ned was quite fond of Nicholas. He was devoted to and proud of Christopher when he was small, maddened by him when he grew up.

Oh, the parental grumbles, thought Rose as she walked. She could hear in her mind Ned's voice droning and snapping down the years. 'Can't you teach your son to shut doors? He messes my newspaper before I have touched it.' (Ned, who never opened his *Times* until after lunch.) 'Can't you teach your son not to smoke? He stinks the house out with those filthy Gitanes.' (Like many who have kicked the habit, Ned was hard on smokers.) 'He's left an enormous turd in my lavatory, and now he wants to borrow my car.' What a fuss he had made when Christopher married Helen. 'Who *is* this girl, do we know?' What would he say if he knew she had taken charge of his ashes? Turned in the urn?

At times like that her promise to Ned sat like a lump of indigestible dough; she remembered Mylo crying, 'You can't bugger up our lives for a promise,' and regretted her insistence that she could, she must.

Yet Ned was a kind man. Kind to animals, kind to neighbours, considerate to his cars, he paid his bills, did not fall about drunk, made a success of his wartime career, loved an Opel motor car he acquired in occupied Germany (or was it the driver he loved?), was successful in the City when he returned from the war, was a consistently good landlord. He blamed me for his discontent, thought Rose; he needed choice, everything in pairs: two bankers, two tailors, two women (there was always a second woman, not necessarily Emily; several had appeared at the funeral with their husbands), two houses, two cars. He never said, but made it clear by hints, attitudes and chance remarks that life would have been 'all right' if he had had two children.

I had managed to forget Ned for several days, thought Rose, was quite successful handing responsibility to Christopher and Helen. I must not start thinking 'if only' and 'things would have been better or different'.

'All that crap!' she shouted out loud, startling a wheatear from

189

a gorse bush. Ned was not all that kind; he was on occasion accusatory and cruel. His permanent absence will not be so very different from his absence at the war, his frequent absences on business trips.

Just nicer.

35

The telephone woke Rose. 'Is that Mrs Cooper?' asked a distant voice.

'Who?' Her head came up from the pillow with a jerk.

'Rose Cooper? Am I speaking to Rose Cooper?' The voice was faint, furtive, impossible to tell how far away.

'I am Rose . . .' Only minutes ago she had given Christopher his last feed, she struggled awake from heavy sleep. 'What did you say, who?' Her heart was pounding.

'Your husband,' droned the voice, 'Mrs Cooper . . .'

'My *what*?' She was waking fast.

'. . . asked me to phone you. It strictly isn't . . .'

'Who – are – you?'

'Well, now, that's asking, let's say Truro General Hospital.' The man began to sound irritated, nervous. 'I'm not allowed, not supposed . . .'

'My husband?'

'Look. He asked me to ring you; brought in last night . . .' the line went dead, then the voice, reedy now, continued '. . . wounded.' It said, 'Nothing serious.'

'Wounded? Badly. *Not* serious?'

A high nervous laugh. 'You should have seen the others, they were dead.'

'Who are you?' shouted Rose, as if it mattered, but the line was dead now, blank. Half an hour later she got through to Truro General Hospital.

No, no information about new patients. Sorry. No, there was no doctor she could speak to, sorry, no matron, no sister, sorry. No, no, and again no. Quite polite but suspiciously guarded.

Why should they be guarded?

What were they hiding?

Mylo. Wounded. Mutilated. Dying?

'Only one way to find out,' said Rose to the sleeping baby. 'We must go,' she said to Comrade watching from her basket. 'I can take you,' she said to the dog, 'but not your puppies or the cats.'

She ran to the bathroom and bathed her face, she was trembling and drenched with sweat. Her hands shook as she dressed. 'Calm, calm, keep calm,' she muttered, pulling on her clothes. 'Must look respectable,' she exclaimed, tearing off the slacks she had put on, 'you never know who . . .' She took a coat and skirt from the cupboard, a shirt and jersey, combed her hair back, pulled on her last pair of silk stockings and best shoes, viewed herself looking respectable in the cheval glass. 'Right.' She had stubbed her toe pushing right foot into left shoe, the pain made her face look drawn.

She gathered the baby's things, stuffing spare nappies, clothes and shawls around him. Anchoring him in the deep basket, she carried him downstairs. 'Stay with him,' she said to the dog, 'stay.'

She ran round the house, her respectable heels clattering on the stone terrace. Reaching the Farthings' cottage she knocked, shook the door handle, shook some more, 'Oh, wake up, please . . .'

'Who is it?' Farthing, gruff.

'Me, it's me,' she shouted.

'Coming.'

Then Farthing was opening the door, as he buttoned his flies, the toes of his bare feet were widely separate, agile. 'What's up?'

'I have to go – now – at once to – to a – a friend, can you – hospital?'

'Want the car? Taking the baby?'

'Yes, yes, and Comrade – I . . .'

'Want it filled up, that it?' He had put a sweater on, inside out and back to front.

'Oh, yes, how did you . . .?'

'Half a mo, just get me shoes on . . .'

'But, do you know . . .?' Her voice was a suppressed scream.

'Where the petrol's hidden? Course I do.' Farthing laughed. 'Watched "the master" hide it, didn't we?' (Oh poor Ned, parenthesised master, mocked and such a kind man.)

'Want some help, love?' Mrs Farthing descending the stairs in an extraordinary sexy nightdress, pink feathered mules on her feet.

'It's the cats and the puppies and . . .'

'I'll mind them, don't worry.' Mrs Farthing pulled a sensible overcoat over the nightdress. 'Come in while Farthing . . .'

'No, I must . . .'

'Where shall I say you've gone?'

'Oh, Mrs Farthing . . .' Rose watched Farthing disappear around the house with a torch. If only he would run.

'Got to have something to tell people when they ring up, and the Hadleys.'

'Oh . . .' She found it hard to think. There was Mylo dying, what the hell did anything else matter? 'Oh, hurry . . .'

'I'll come and see you've got what's needed for the baby; Farthing won't be long.'

'I have everything. I must hurry, I . . .'

'I'll just check.' The woman was remorseless.

'Oh.' Rose clenched her fists.

'And if you are going far, you'd better take sandwiches and a thermos. You never . . .'

'Never?' Rose snatched at the word.

'. . . never know when you'll want a meal or something hot.' Mrs Farthing was walking Rose back to the house, her arm around her shoulders. 'He might like something hot.'

'He?'

'Don't be a muggins,' they had reached the kitchen, 'sit down while I get you a hot drink to set you on your way.'

'I don't want a . . .'

'Won't take a minute. Farthing hasn't got the tank filled yet.'

Mrs Farthing poured milk into a pan. 'Tea or coffee? I'll give you chocolate for the thermoses.'

'Anything.' Rose's teeth chattered.

'Listen to your teeth chattering. Got enough money?'

'I hope so.'

'Hope.' Mrs Farthing handed Rose a steaming mug. 'Drink that up, all of it.' She reached up to a jar above the stove, 'Now, here's fifty pounds, you won't need it all, but you never know.'

'I can't take your . . .' she was appalled, 'savings.'

'Yes, you can, Farthing and I will be happier if you will. Finished your drink? Good girl. Now take a few really deep breaths. That's right. Better now?' Rose nodded, she no longer felt clammy.

'Filled her up?' asked Mrs Farthing of her mate entering the kitchen.

'Petrol tank's full. I checked the oil, water and tyres, and put two jerry cans in the boot. You should be all right,' Farthing grinned at Rose, 'for a dire emergency.'

I wonder how much they listen to us, how much they guess. 'Thank you,' said Rose, 'oh, thank you.'

'We'll tell the Hadleys and anyone who asks that you were called away to help Mrs Malone with one of her friends, she couldn't manage on her own with all her evacuees, etcetera. That do?'

'Mrs Farthing! The brilliance of your mind.' Both Farthings smiled. They are my friends, she thought, they do not judge.

'Take care of yourself and the baby, now.'

Rose put her arms around the older woman and hugged her. 'Now, now,' said Mrs Farthing.

Farthing said, 'Shall I stow the baby in the car?'

While Farthing arranged the baby basket on the back seat, Mrs Farthing said, 'I don't really like being called Mrs Farthing by people I am fond of. My name's Edwina. It's not as if Farthing and I were married.' (Rose swallowed the second statement to digest later, feeling she would cry if she thanked Mrs Farthing for liking her.)

What extraordinary people, she thought, driving away. They seem to enjoy – she said she liked – they must approve of me, nobody's ever done that. She drove west along the roads of England passing the occasional Army truck and early farm cart.

When Christopher whimpered she stopped at the side of the road and fed him, changed his nappy and drank from the thermos. Fancy them not being married, she thought. I must remember to call her Edwina. What a privilege. She's even remembered Comrade's dinner. She put the dog's dinner on the grass and watched her eat while she held Christopher against her shoulder, waiting for him to burp.

She made no plan. She prayed that when she arrived at the hospital she would know what to do. She prayed that when she arrived she would not find Mylo dead. What had the man said, had she heard aright?

She reached Truro in the early afternoon, found the hospital, parked the car and stared at the lugubrious building.

Mrs Malone would know what to do, how to behave in these circumstances, not that she was the sort of woman to have a lover, but supposing it were George or Richard who was in there?

My mother wouldn't know, she never brought me up to deal with such a crisis. She was the cringing type, socially inferior, afraid of putting a foot wrong with authority; she's changed now, of course, but she never taught me the necessary oomph. What, thought Rose, would Mrs Malone do?

Walk straight in as though it belonged to her, right?

Leaving Comrade in the car, Rose checked the straightness of the seams of her stockings, squared her shoulders and marched in, carrying Christopher.

'I have come to see my husband,' she said to a man at the desk.

'What name?' He did not look up, she could see no face, only a smooth, bald, pink skull.

'Cooper.'

'Cooper. Cooper.' He ran a slow finger down a list. 'He'd be in ward seven by now unless he was one of the RAF with the flu, oh, they are in seven. You try ward seven.'

She climbed stairs, walked corridors, passed wards full of women, another full of children. Wards one, two, three and on to six, where was seven? She did not want to ask the nurses squeaking along on their rubber-soled shoes, starched cotton aprons, clacking voices carrying clear enough to echo in the long institutional corridor. Ah, ward seven.

She stared through a glass panelled door into a long ward full of active young men in pyjamas and dressing gowns. Laughing, talking, wandering about, hugely restless, none of them looked ill or wounded. The noise was worse than the parrot house at the zoo. About to turn away, nerve herself to ask, she spied a still lump in a bed in the far corner. She pushed open the door and walked in.

As she walked between the double row of beds, the volume of noise decreased, the tempo of conversation changed. There were one or two whistles, quick exchanges between the men as they totted her up, following her with their eyes. She felt the blood rise traitorously to her neck and face. She held the baby as a shield, stiffened her back. She was afraid of the men who turned and stared, some of them stepping forward like curious cattle in a field. None of them looked ill or wounded.

Just as she felt her nerve might crack and her impersonation of Edith Malone desert her, she recognised Mylo.

Reaching the bed, she stood staring down at him.

'Sister's off duty.' One of the men had followed her; he was bolder than the others, smoking a cigarette. He stared openly at her breasts, large with milk, straining at her blouse.

'Thanks,' said Rose. 'Are you allowed to smoke in here?' she asked coldly in the spirit of Mrs Malone. 'Fetch me a chair.'

A chair was brought; she sat. The walking wounded retreated to resume a slightly muted brouhaha at the far end of the ward.

It was eight months since she had seen Mylo. They must have been rough months. He lay on his back, deep green smudges under his eyes, his cheeks thin, the colour of cheese. She could trace the curve of his jaw under the stubble of his beard, see the presage of lines running from nose to mouth. His brows were knit in pain, he had a large bruise on his temple, his lips moved as he muttered something. Rose bent close to listen.

'I will shoot the . . .' He was reaching a hand up under his pillow, gripping a hidden object.

'Mylo,' said Rose very quietly, 'it's me.'

Mylo's eyes opened with a snap. 'Rose?'

'Yes.'

'So you got here?'

'Yes.'

'I was just going to shoot them, the . . .'

'Why?'

'The noise, the fucking noise. I have a revolver.'

'I'll ask them to be quiet.'

'They don't know what quiet means. They are all quite well, they only had flu. Young RAF servicemen bursting with health and high spirits.' Mylo's voice was venomous. 'How long have you been here?' Why was he not washed and in pyjamas like the others? Had he persuaded authority that he had a revolver? This was no time for games and the spirit of Edith Malone. 'We were brought ashore the night before last, got our lines crossed with another party. The other fellows were killed in the cross fire. Get me out of here, darling.' He shut his eyes.

'How badly wounded are you?'

'Nothing much. Leg wound and concussion, it's the bloody noise I can't bear . . .'

Somebody whooped at the far end of the ward, a chair was knocked over. 'Pack it in,' said a voice which might have been male or female. There was a succession of, 'Sorry, sister, sorry, sister, sorry . . .'

'What's going on here? These are not visiting hours. Who are you?'

The sister was short, brisk, intimidating, busty and strong. She wore a watch pinned to her chest like a medal, she glowered at Rose, took Mylo's wrist to feel his pulse. Mylo snatched his wrist free and reached again under the pillow for what appeared to be a revolver.

It was a revolver.

If Rose had had difficulty in recognising Mylo, he was frankly incredulous of the woman who now appeared. Gone was the shy girl he had met at the winter tennis, reduced to tears by the Thornbys' teasing, ill at ease in company, afraid of the Malones' guests, scared of her parents' disapproval, immature, a prey to indecision, constantly in need of his protection. This new Rose drew herself up and spoke to the sister in a clipped authoritative voice. She asked, nay demanded, that Mylo's bed should be moved into a side-ward. (Do you want your other patients shot?) She walked beside the bed in which he lay holding the revolver. Two nervous nurses pushed and pulled. Away from the noisy ward she bent close to Mylo and in a low voice asked, 'What's your boss's name? Quick.'

'Pye, Major Pye, but don't . . .'

'Right. Shan't be long. Don't speak to anyone, hang on to the revolver.' She went away. As she went she handed the baby to a nurse. 'Hold this, please,' and 'Take me to Matron,' she said to the Sister.

Mylo was left alone in the side-ward. He felt bemused and very weak. From the ward he had left he heard renewed shouts and baying laughter. Poor devils, he thought, they feel perfectly well, they have only had a touch of flu, they have not encountered fear.

Then there came the clack of heels, the crackle of Matron's starch, the pinched nose of Sister holding her breath in disapproval. The amused yet grave expression of a white-haired doctor who inspected the dressing on his leg, courageously felt the pulse in the wrist of the hand which held the revolver (chauvinistic bravura in front of the nurses, he looks at least sixty-nine). The doctor nodded and smiled, turned to speak to Rose standing there remote and dignified.

Then two orderlies were easing him into a dressing gown (their breath hissed as he changed the hand that held the revolver, watching it with swivelling eyes) transferring him from the bed to a wheelchair, propelling him down the corridor to the lift, down, out through the hall, out of the hospital, to help him into the front seat of Rose's car, wrapping a blanket around his legs.

While this was going on he was aware of Rose beside him. She had at some stage regained the baby, which she put into a basket on the back seat beside Comrade who was furiously wagging her tail and moaning in pleasurable recognition.

'Don't faint yet,' Rose murmured, leaning into the car. 'Are you comfortable, darling? Where's the revolver?'

'Here.'

'Better give it to me now.' She took it from him. 'Goodbye,' she said to Sister (Matron had not come out with them), 'and thank you so much. What?' She leaned towards Sister, who was explaining something in a low voice. 'No, of course you couldn't, no, I understand perfectly,' and 'Goodbye.' She shook the old doctor's hand. 'Thank you for all your care and help.' She got in beside Mylo and started the engine. She put the revolver into the glove compartment and drove. As she drove she let out a crow of laughter. 'That poor Sister said they hadn't dared wash you because of the revolver.' Mylo did not answer. 'You can faint now,' said Rose after half a mile. Mylo closed his eyes. After two more miles, Rose said, 'I think they thought it was loaded.'

'It is.'

'Good God.' Rose pulled into the side of the road. 'You might have killed somebody.'

'I meant to shoot those yahoos. I would have if you hadn't arrived, they were driving me crazy.'

'Unload it at once.' Rose reached into the glove compartment and fished out the revolver. 'You must be out of your mind.'

Meekly Mylo unloaded the revolver. Rose threw the bullets into the ditch. 'Really, Mylo,' she was trembling, 'I thought you were averse to killing people.' She was near tears.

Mylo was interested to see that her hands shook. This was the Rose he knew. 'I'd rather like to kiss you,' he said. Then he said, 'How the hell did you find me?'

'I got your message; a man rang up.'

'So I didn't dream it.'

'No.'

'Whose baby is that?'

'Mine.'

Mylo felt confused; he had forgotten that she had been pregnant. 'The man said he wouldn't telephone you unless I paid him. I had no money.'

'He must have thought better of it.'

In his basket on the back seat Christopher began to scream.

'Sorry,' said Rose, 'he's hungry. I must feed him, won't be

long.' She moved the car closer to the side of the road and got out. 'You'd better have a run,' she said to Comrade.

Mylo watched the dog sniffing about in the grass, then Rose was sitting beside him with the child, undoing her blouse and thrusting her nipple into its violent mouth, silencing the screams. Her breast was swollen, marbled with veins. 'Will they recover?'

'What?'

'Your breasts, will they . . .?'

'Back to normal. When I wean him.'

'So that's how it works.'

'Yes.'

'Ah.' So peaceful. Only what, two days ago? The violence in the dark on the rough sea, the pain, fear, seasickness . . . and now. 'This is all rather unreal.'

'I don't think you should talk. That doctor said you should be kept quiet at home, and rest.'

'Is that so?' (Soon I shall be able to laugh. Home.)

'Yes.' She moved the baby from left breast to right.

Mylo watched the child's gums bite on her tender nipple. 'You said it hurt when I . . .'

'One gets used to it. You mustn't talk. I'll give you a hot drink in a minute. Mrs Farthing lumbered me with supplies. She asked me to call her Edwina and, guess what, she and Farthing are not married, isn't that a turn-up for the book?'

'Nor, alas, are we.'

Rose did not answer. He watched her burp the baby, change it and settle it back in the basket, then as they sat drinking hot chocolate he said, 'Excuse me asking, but where did the extraordinary bossy act you put on with the nurses and doctor come from? You ordered those dragons about and twisted the old doctor around your little finger.'

'It's not an act. It's me. If sufficiently frightened or enraged, it comes naturally. I found I could do it when the Min of Ag sent people to shoot our rooks.'

Mylo noted the our.

'And what did you tell them that allowed them to release me into your charge?'

'I said you were top secret, working hush-hush for General

Pye (I promoted him), and that since you were fit to move, it was better all round for you to be at home with me. Your revolver had rather unnerved them, they are not really a military hospital.'

'Did they think you were my wife?'

'Of course.'

'You are not far wrong.'

'How so?'

'The intelligence bit. I shall have to contact the bastard, let him know I'm not dead.'

'Let him go on thinking it for a bit,' said Rose. 'I'm in no hurry to lose you again.'

'The war.'

'Let the war wait.'

Rose screwed the top back on the thermos. 'Now shut up and let me get you home before Christopher starts screaming again. He's terrible when he puts his mind to it, he's been good so far.'

Some time later, waking from an uneasy sleep, Mylo asked, 'Did we eat the Camembert?'

'What Camembert?'

'The Camembert I brought you last summer when I brought Picot over ...' She did not ask who Picot might be, but she remembered the cheese. Delicious, a little squashed on its travels, over-ripe. They had eaten it in bed, washed down with a bottle of Ned's claret, what a peculiar thing to remember now. 'Yes,' she said, 'I remember. I remember it well. Try to sleep, darling, it won't be long now, we are nearly home.'

Home, thought Mylo wryly. What home, whose home?

36

Time was, thought Rose, pausing out of breath to sit on a granite boulder, when I would have reached the top of this hill without effort. But then, she thought as she stretched her legs, I would hardly have noticed the view.

Noticing the view comes with age, she thought, looking down the valley where mist still laced around the tops of the trees she had walked under, drifted across the waters of the creek, reluctant to give way to the sun which now warmed her back. It was going to be a perfect autumn day, blue and gold, no breeze to ruffle the water, pewter flat and deep, or loosen the leaves of oak and beech on the turn from dark green to rust to gold. Unaware of the view, one missed a lot in the hunger of youth, one wasn't prepared, one was taken by surprise, she thought, casting her thoughts back to the day when in weather of sleepy beauty she had arrived back with Mylo from the hospital in Cornwall to cherish and heal him in privacy and love.

What possessed me, what gave me the nerve to kidnap him from the hospital, over-ride the objections of the staff? What did I think I was doing? It is difficult at sixty-seven to recall the emotions of twenty. I wish I still had the nerve, the mix of bloody-mindedness and innocence. Have I quite lost it, she wondered? Am I blunted, am I too aware?

She had not that day been aware of anything other than Mylo's need. It was vital that he should have peace and quiet, to protect him. If his nerves were shaken by whatever embroilment had resulted in his wound, she would heal them. They would be together, her passion would revive him. Had he not in distress sent for her? Beyond this she had no plan.

It was a shock and surprise to be met on arrival by Edwina Farthing wearing an air of warning, drooping the corners of her mouth, raising her eyebrows, whispering, 'Watch out,' as she leaned into the car.

'What's up?' asked Rose, startled, pulling on the handbrake, switching off the engine.

'Mr Loftus and Mrs Malone,' hissed Edwina. 'I have made up the gentleman's bed in the yellow room,' she said loudly, 'and the other gentlemen, the young chap from Down Under, the pilot, is quite happy in the blue room. Mr Loftus and Mrs Malone think that will do very well. That's what you ordered, isn't it?'

Blue room? Yellow room? What was the woman up to putting on this air of servility? Rose was amazed to see Edwina semaphore with her eyebrows, hiss breath in through her teeth. She had not previously particularly noticed Edwina's teeth. Large and slightly crossed, they brought to some errant corner of her mind a likeness to the evacuee waifs when they would not admit an urgent need to leave the room and go to the lavatory in case they missed something of interest. Edwina's act of an old retainer was putting a message across: she was under strain.

But then Archibald Loftus had come hurrying from the house: 'Rose, my dear! Good girl! Great minds think alike.' He had kissed her as she got out of the car. 'When Edith told me – when I suggested – when we found you had thought of the same scheme and gone to fetch – it *is* young Cooper, isn't it? That's what Edith said. I wasn't quite sure myself. We'd better get you into the house, my dear fellow, let Mrs Farthing give me a hand with you, you look just about done in, they should have kept you a while longer, shortage of beds, I dare say. Ah, here is Edith – now give me your arm – oh, I see, you can manage with a stick, jolly good.' (Had Mylo winked as he caught her eye?)

As Edith Malone embraced Rose she watched Mylo hop and hobble into the house between Uncle Archie and Edwina. He did not look back as he adapted himself to the unexpected. (This is how he survives doing whatever it is he does in enemy France.) Rose let Edith press her to her breast. 'I *thought* I had sent you all the particulars of the scheme, you must have answered but in my usual stupidly vague way' (Edith vague? Come on!) 'I mislaid your letter. I was so enraged with Emily and Nicholas I tore their letter up. I must have destroyed yours with it.' (Oops, clever one.) 'They really are too selfish for words; they have at the very least two spare rooms in that house of theirs; people with far less convenient houses have joined the scheme and are putting themselves out, and look at you, living alone and willing. Nobody will persuade me that one small baby and part-time work – she's only part-time now at the Ministry of Agriculture, I took the trouble to find out before asking her – take up all her time. Why, look at you with Christopher, you took him with you to fetch – oh, by the way, my dear, *don't* take me amiss, but it was a *little* over-zealous to fetch him yourself. Where, by the way, did you get the petrol? Another time, leave it to the ambulance people, it is their job, you know, all the forms and so on. Never mind, you'll know another time . . .'

Tactfully, a quality he lost as he grew up, Christopher had begun to scream. Comrade, anxious to be of use, licked the baby's face, switching Edith Malone onto another tack. 'Do you think it's a good idea to let the dog lick him? I know there is a school of thought which says it doesn't matter, but when you think where dogs put their noses and the things they pick up and eat – please don't think I am interfering . . .'

'Oh, no, of course not, not at all. I think he is hungry.' Rose had picked Christopher out of his basket, grateful that he saved her the necessity of answering Edith's flow (she is gabbling to hide her embarrassment, to save me from mine. Why should I be embarrassed?) 'Gosh, he's soaking, rather overdone his jobs too, needs changing, would you like to hold him a minute?' She had offered Edith the bundled, stinking baby.

'No, thanks, my dear. I am no good with babies.' Edith backed away. 'I had Nanny for George and Richard; I like children when they are older.'

'House-trained?'

'That's it. I think you girls who look after your own babies without help are wonderful.'

'Emily?'

'Most extraordinary, that brother Nicholas helps her, baths the baby, I hear . . .'

'They are keen on baths.' Rose shouted above Christopher's yells; he was working himself up into high gear. 'How are the evacuees?' she bellowed. 'Hush, hush, won't be a minute.' She held hungry, smelly Christopher as a shield between herself and Edith.

'Marvellous, my dear. Tremendous fun. They all go to the village school, bright as buttons, they don't get on with the village children who simply loathe them, but all ten are pretty well behaved, bless them, that's why I haven't a chink of room for the chaps on leave. I started you off with an Australian, by the way, he's a nice young man, broke his leg learning to fly.

Such a shame, though it's probably saved his life, they say far too many bombers are getting lost. I'll just go and see he is settled now you are back, then I must fly, Archie has our only spare bed. He was coming back by bus after talking to you, but perhaps you could run him back, you seem pretty flush with petrol?'

'I . . .'

Edith Malone hurried ahead into the house, mistress of the situation.

Rose took the baby to her room, changed him and sat down to nurse him. Mylo had been taken from her, she was afraid to protest.

Alone with the child, she found herself trembling with a mixture of anger and fatigue. She tried to compose herself while Christopher sucked and nuzzled at her breast, fat tears wet on his cheeks. He looked old and pathetic; he snatched and grabbed at her nipple, strenuous with hunger and anxiety, reminding Rose of Ned when he feared the war and its unknown consequences. 'Hush,' she said, 'there, quiet baby, quiet. Don't be in such a hurry, you'll get wind. Take it easy. Take it slow.' When Edwina put her head round the door, she said, 'Come in, tell me what the hell's going on. Is this a plot?'

'Got it in one.' Edwina came in and shut the door.

'Sit down and tell.'

Edwina sat. 'Your fellow's all right. He got straight into bed without a word. Wants sleep, I'd say, and quiet.'

'Thanks. And?'

'People are more observant than you give credit,' said Edwina.

'What if they are?' snapped Rose.

'Someone, some busybody in the village maybe, sees you and him together the last time or the time before, it doesn't matter who. They talk. Talk spreads, see? The master's Uncle Archibald . . .'

'I wish you wouldn't call him that . . .'

'Just our joke, Farthing's and mine. Well, his Uncle Archie gets a sniff, smells a rat. When he called by chance, he said it was by chance, and found you gone. You follow me?'

'Oh, yes.'

'He didn't say anything, nor will he, but he acts, takes advantage of this scheme of Mrs Malone's for officers and men from all over on leave with nowhere to go and, what ho, bingo, it's done. He pops an Australian into the house, and you've got yourself a chaperon.'

'Damn him, curse his guts,' said Rose.

'He's protecting your name from gossip. Instead of playing with fire and singeing your reputation, thanks to him and Mrs Malone you are doing important war work.' Edwina cackled with laughter, 'Can't say it's not funny.'

'Most droll. Bloody hell, how could . . .?'

'You are so wrapped up in yourself, you never think anybody notices what you are doing, do you? You are too young, they think, to be on your own with him overseas. They watch . . .'

'Curse them.'

'They commune.'

'They what?' Rose laughed now and the child at her breast eased perceptibly.

'They commune,' Edwina repeated, enjoying the word, 'that means nothing gets said, but a lot gets thought and with those sort of crafties, they act. Sort of sly.' Rose could see that Edwina admired Archie and Edith.

'Does Mr Malone play any part in this?'

'No, no. Driven out of the house by the evacuee children's noise, he spends a lot of time in London these days, says he'd rather have the air raids.'

'What a lot you know,' said Rose sarcastically.

'Well, Farthing and I are over the initial stage, you might say. We can see beyond our noses. Hear too, stopped being blind.'

Rose giggled, she held the baby up to pat and stroke his back. 'Come on, my pretty, don't go to sleep. Burp for mother.' Christopher obliged so violently a mouthful of curdled milk trickled out. Rose wiped his mouth and put him to her other breast. 'So we have an Australian lodger. What's his name?'

'Jack Bowen. He's harmless enough. I think, on the whole, those two did right.'

'Traitor. Tell me one reason,' said Rose in fury.

'You don't want to burn your boats so far from land, that's one.'

'I believe you and Farthing want me to be respectable, to conform to . . .'

'There's such a thing as compromise, too.'

'Ugh.'

'He's not exactly offering you security, is he, your young fellow? You have the baby to consider.'

'I do . . .'

'The house. The farm. The place . . .'

'You and Farthing?'

'I didn't say so.' Edwina flushed.

'Oh, Edwina, I'm sorry.'

'It's got to be said; he comes and goes, you never know where you are with him; let's face it, one of these days he might not come back. You don't even know where he goes, do you?'

'I do,' said Rose bravely.

'Somebody had to say it, love.'

When Edwina left her, Rose sat on with the child dozing on her knee. She had felt trapped, she remembered in age, sitting in the sun near the top of the hill looking at the view. She had viewed the trap she was in with sorrow and, she admitted now but not then, with resignation. Even if Uncle Archibald and Edith Malone had not interfered to frustrate her by the tacit use of their social act, she would have been self-snared by her promise to Ned. We had enough obstacles without them butting in, she thought. I hope I am wise enough not to interfere between Christopher and Helen.

She remembered that she had put Christopher down to sleep, washed her face, brushed her hair, and gone down carrying the dirty nappies in a pail. Archibald Loftus had been hovering in the hall. 'Hullo, everything all right?' he had asked, rather bluff.

'Yes, thank you. I'll just get rid of this lot, then I'll drive you home,' she had said.

'Oh, yes, ah well, thank you.'

One supposes she had thought unkindly that he wants to have his say too, otherwise he could perfectly well have gone home with Edith; I shall not ask him to stay for tea.

He had settled himself beside her in the car; Comrade had leaned from the back seat to sniff and breathe on his neck. He had winced and Rose had not restrained the dog, taking petty pleasure in his annoyance. 'You're a cat lover, aren't you?' she had said pertly.

'Would you stop in the village, I want to buy a *Picture Post* for you to take back for your visitors.'

'That's kind of you. They must not be allowed to get bored,' she had said crisply.

'Don't be like that.' He had shown a tinge of weakness and for a mile or two she thought he might withhold whatever he had that he wanted to say, but in the end he had circumnavigated his indecision: 'I am not saying you are unwise, I am saying that you looked as though you might be, which amounts to the same thing.'

'Yes, Uncle Archibald.'

'Your friend Emily appears to have been a great deal more indiscreet than you (a touch of bad luck there, one assumes). Edith, an old old friend you know, Edith knows and I know you have done nothing reprehensible. Of course not, of course not! But it looked wrong.'

I wouldn't call it reprehensible, Rose had thought, you silly old man; if you think I am an innocent ninny, think away. 'Is that all, Uncle Archie?' she had asked sweetly.

Uncle Archie had shot her a look which had she been older and more experienced she would have interpreted as an invitation to something very reprehensible indeed, but being only twenty at the time all she said was, 'We can buy a *Picture Post* at the newsagent,' and Archibald Loftus thanked her. Now at sixty-seven Rose chuckled in recollection. Uncle Archie was such a devious old man, he could not imagine her other than straight. He was funny that way. Or, she thought, frowning at the view, looking back along the years, was he even craftier than I thought? Did he guess I was tempted by security?

37

Mylo woke sweating. The weight of the bedclothes oppressed his wounded leg. He was handicapped. Visions of police, Gestapo, suspicions of unreliable friends raced through his mind, then, fully awake, he remembered where he was. He lay back, perspiration cooling on his chest as the heart which had thundered in terror slowed its pace.

He looked at his watch. He had slept seven hours since Edwina Farthing undressed him, manoeuvred legs and arms into pyjamas and rolled him into bed. He lay listening to the silent house, then cautiously got out of bed, limped to the window. A full moon lit the garden; across the fields an owl hooted. Under this moon he had held Rose after the winter tennis, kissed her as they listened to the vixen screech.

Pricked by desire, he hobbled into the passage, listened again. A board creaked as the house cooled; from a neighbouring room the Australian snored; he remembered his arrival with Rose, her expression, mixed astonishment and irritation, as Mrs Farthing imparted her news, her eyes wild as Archibald Loftus helped him into the house, the old man's grip firm, compelling, her expression changing to hopeless resignation as command of the situation was whipped from her. He had guessed that she was outmanoeuvred, was best left alone, but now – he made his way along the passage, opened Rose's door and walked in.

She lay as he had left her that first time, her hair tousled, one arm flung across the side of the bed he had just left.

From her basket Comrade thumped her tail as she had when, departing, he had told her to 'stay'. On the rug the twin cats curled entwined, emerald eyes watchful. It was the same, everything was all right, nothing was changed.

In his cot Christopher sighed, whimpering in his sleep.

Ah. That . . .

Mylo hesitated as the events of the last few days surged back. The fear, the chase, the pain, the grotesquely noisy hospital, the rescue by Rose.

'Darling.' She was awake. 'Get in.' She held out her arms. 'Careful with your leg. Can you manage?'

'I can manage.' He struggled out of the pyjamas.

'You manage pretty well,' she said contentedly when they had made love. 'Very well, I'd say. Shall we do it again?' She kissed his throat, feeling his pulse under her tongue, while he breathed the scent of her hair. 'Oh, my love, I have missed you so.'

'If I were blind, I would know you by smell.'

'If I were blind, I would know you by feel.'

'Your voice.'

'Your dear voice.'

Christopher waking, wet nappies cooling around his parts, raised an aggrieved yowl.

'*His* voice! I have to feed him.' She sat up.

'At this hour?'

'Yes.'

'Tyrannical.' He watched her get out of bed, snatch a wrapper around her shoulders, pick up the child, change it, bring it back to bed, sit propped by pillows, put it to her breast. Watching, Mylo felt a surge of jealousy, a murderous rage against Ned who thus in the guise of Christopher imposed himself, wedging him apart from Rose. 'What does your husband think of his heir?'

'He hasn't met him yet.'

'But he knew you were pregnant?'

'Oh, yes. I wrote. Yes, I wrote and told him.'

'Wasn't he delighted?'

'He had gone overseas when I wrote, so . . .'

'So he was delighted?' (Why do I insist?)

'Not exactly,' she answered carefully. 'Pleased. Yes, I suppose he was pleased.'

'You suppose?' Mylo was puzzled. 'He knew it was his.'

'Of course. He would not have supposed otherwise.'

'He trusts you.' Mylo lay on his back, put his hands behind his head.

'Of course.'

'So he must have been enchanted, proud, delighted.' (My wound is throbbing in time to the baby sucking.)

Rose glanced at Mylo over Christopher's head, his dark eyes looking at the ceiling glinted in the moonlight. I can hardly tell him having a baby was my idea, my decision, not Ned's, that Ned played no part, well, very little, was not consulted.

'I wrote and told him,' she repeated.

'And what did the happy father say?' Mylo hoped the jealousy did not sound in his voice, knew his choice of words was unfortunate, too late to retract them. 'He must have been thrilled to bits,' he amended.

'He said, Let's pray it's not a girl.' Rose kept her voice neutral.

'Primogeniture?' Shocked and appalled, Mylo sensed her pain.

'Yes,' she said, 'exactly.'

'So, when he was born, what did he say then?'

'Thank God it's a boy. I trust it's strong and doesn't squint or anything.'

'Anything?'

'Some distant Peel was born with a harelip,' she said.

'He telegraphed this?'

'He didn't telegraph. He wrote.'

'Bastard.'

'He can't help it,' she defended absent Ned, 'he's a man of property, he's a kind man.'

'So you say.'

'So they say.'

'Look, he's had enough, he's falling asleep. Put him back in his cot, come back to me.' (One should not dislike an innocent infant.) Propped on his elbow, Mylo watched Rose settle the child in his Moses basket, stoop to kiss the top of its head.

'He can't help his nature,' she said.

Did she mean the child or its father? There was something in the tone of her voice which filled him with elation. 'I believe,' he said laughing, 'that you are a survivor.'

'I hope you are too,' she said.

Rose back in his arms, he stroked her hair, pushing his fingers up her scalp, cupping her ears in his palms, bending to kiss her mouth. She heard the roar of the sea as one does when holding a conch to one's ear and shivered close up to him, reminded of the Channel which so recently separated them.

'When I am about my business in France,' he said, 'on the rare occasions I allow myself to think of you, I see us as those two in the Bonnard.' He raised himself to peer at the lithograph.

'We have already grown older than those two,' she murmured.

'Not in our hearts, never that.'

'Of course not,' she agreed robustly.

'She has no husband to come between them,' he said enviously.

'He has no job to take him away from her,' whispered Rose. 'Away, to get shot in the leg.'

'All her attention is for him. She has no house to look after, no farm, no garden, no handsome Australian visitor to care for.'

'Is he handsome?'

'Stunning. I caught a glimpse as I was frog-marched to bed. She has no interfering in-laws and friends, no baby. If she had a baby it would be her lover's.'

'Oh,' Rose turned away, 'don't. That *hurts*.'

'My darling, I wouldn't hurt you for the world. I only beef because I am so lucky to be here at all, I love you.'

'And I love you, but I don't suppose,' she too looked at the lovers in the picture, 'that they spent all their lives he naked, she in camiknickers.'

Perhaps what held me most strongly to Rose, Mylo would think in later life, was the laughter we shared. It was a stronger tie than promises of eternal love, more lasting than jealousy, more binding than lust.

38

Rose was angry with Ned's Uncle Archibald and Edith Malone. She had not felt the interference of relations and friends so strongly since she had been manoeuvred into marriage. Now all her resentment came flooding back. Later she would learn to frustrate her elders' benign force, recognise and mock their divine right to know what was best for her. She would learn much from the Thornbys who, thick-skinned and selfish, yet managed to appear compliant and agreeable should it suit them, while doing the opposite of what was suggested.

The imposition of an Australian visitor, which infuriated Rose at the time since it deprived her of her privacy with Mylo, was to lead via Edith's scheme to other visitors, French, Dutch, Polish, Canadian, Belgian, American. For the rest of the war Slepe was seldom free of guests; Mylo faded from people's minds, was lost in the crowd. If it was hinted that she might be having an affair with one of her visitors Rose would laugh, guessing that the suggestion came from Nicholas, put about as a smokescreen for his sister, for Emily soon latched on to the hospitality scheme, offered their spare rooms and was not above poaching the more attractive and sensual of Rose and other hostesses' visitors, leaving the more boring and boorish for hostesses less spry than herself, so that by the end of the war it was general knowledge that Emily received more CARE parcels, was better stocked with cigarettes and nylons than anyone in the county, and that, in this the period of dried egg, spam and whale steak, she learned to cook from her polyglot guests (and other less tangible arts).

But all this was to come later. Coming in from her morning's shopping, aglow with the beneficence of the night's love-making, her mind busy with plots to get Mylo to herself during the day as well as at night, Rose was furious to find Emily, Nicholas and baby Laura making free with her tea ration in the kitchen, talking and laughing with the Australian pilot who dandled Laura on his knee while Nicholas drew a naked lady on his plaster cast. ('This is my sister Emily at her best.')

Rose was even more furious to find that without telling her Mylo had telephoned London and informed Major Pye of his whereabouts and was even now closeted in the library with Victoria. When Mylo introduced them she shook hands; meeting Victoria's remarkable eyes in her plain bun face, she felt a premonition of doom.

'Victoria is from my outfit, come to do a spot of de-briefing,' said Mylo.

'It's very good of you to have Mr Cooper to stay, you rescued him for us before we could get around to it.' Victoria's smile was friendly, showed more than passable teeth. (Who does she think she is? Who are 'us' and 'we'? He's mine.) Victoria re-seated herself beside Mylo and looked up at Rose. (She expects me to leave them together. I am *de trop*.)

'I have to brief Victoria with the results of my trip,' said Mylo. He did not want her to stay, did not call her darling, was distant.

'Then I'll leave you to get on with it,' said Rose, then forced herself to say, 'I hope you can stay to lunch?'

'I should love to, but I must get back to the office and I mustn't impose on your rations.' Victoria's manners were as perfect as her eyes.

'But you must stay, I insist,' said Rose. 'We have a broken-legged pilot who needs cheering up and we have masses to eat since we have a farm. Please stay.' Perhaps, she thought wildly, this girl will succumb to the charms of the beautiful Australian.

In the event Victoria stayed and was amused by Nicholas and Emily who entertained the lunch party, telling them that their father, the bishop, refused to baptise Laura, making a good story of their parents doubting the validity of baptism when the child was of father unknown. 'Isn't it barbaric? Isn't it a typical churchman's attitude? He's a bishop and yet so unchristian.'

'He's a nice old man and I bet he hasn't refused to baptise Laura. You've invented the story to be snobbish and show off'

(What am I saying? I'm behaving like a child back in the nursery.) 'that your father is a bishop.'

'No, no, we haven't invented. He makes all sorts of excuses. Emily doesn't know who the father is, either. What would you do Down Under? You wouldn't be beastly to a little Pom bastard, would you?' Nicholas drew Rose's guest into his net, enjoying signs of embarrassment. 'Come on, Rose, you must help us.'

Rose backed away from what she suspected was a Thornby trap. 'I never knew your father all that well,' she excused herself.

'Then can you lend us a gallon or two of petrol?' Nicholas revealed the real reason for their visit.

'No,' said Rose, 'certainly not.'

'Oh, come on, Rose, I'm sure you can spare some. Our friendly blackmarketeer has dried up.'

'What about your Min of Ag?'

'They are being a little difficult.'

'It's still no.'

'What must you think of us blackmarketeers with illegitimate babies?' Nicholas turned to Victoria.

'It happens,' said Victoria calmly, then, 'I must go, I'm afraid.' She turned to Rose. 'Many thanks for lunch.' Mylo limped with her to her car while Rose followed. 'Goodbye,' said Victoria, shaking Rose's hand, and, 'I'll have you fetched tomorrow,' she said to Mylo as she got into her car. 'Can you be ready by ten?'

'Yes, of course.' Mylo watched the car go down the drive. 'Nice girl that,' he said, 'very capable.'

Rose felt a fierce pang of envy. 'You can't go tomorrow, your leg isn't fit enough.'

'I'll get it checked in London.'

'You can't leave me, I've only just got you back!'

'I must go . . .'

'Why?'

'You know why.' He was not going to argue or explain his job, was forbidden to anyway. That night they had a row.

It began, as rows do, over a matter on which normally they would have agreed, Edith Malone. Rose, smarting at being jumped into hostessing a number of strangers for an indefinite period, complained when Mylo joined her in bed of Edith Malone and Archibald Loftus' interference. There would be a constant interruption of precious privacy, a crowd of visitors with unknown needs. The imposition was outrageous.

During the day she had fuelled her annoyance, letting her mind run over the occasions, real or imaginary, that her life had been impinged on by her elders. Forgetting that, had it not been for her mother's persistence, she would never have met Mylo at the winter tennis, she dwelt on the meeting with Ned. If it had not been for her mother and Mrs Malone she would never have met, never have been cajoled into marriage with Ned, would not now be trapped, lassoed into this hospitable role. She would like to be at peace, to be alone with Mylo, her love, her darling, to copulate. (This word, sometimes used with effect by Nicholas and recently added to her vocabulary, she tried now on Mylo who appeared unmoved by it.) Hurrying on, she said she would be bored and bothered by the uninvited guests, foresaw much irritation from Nicholas and Emily. 'Look how they barged in on us today,' she grumbled. 'It is all Edith's fault, our day ruined.' She dared not voice her real fears, Mylo's imminent departure. Where to? How long for? Would he be killed next time? Might she never see him again?

And Victoria.

Since the morning she had been devoured by a jealousy so intense it upset her milk, which in turn upset Christopher who now whinged with stomach ache, drew up his legs, clenched infant fists, and either could not or would not sleep as was his usually angelic mode. If Mylo was on these terms (she could not, of course, define *what* terms) with Victoria, who might there be in France to draw him back like a magnet? One girl in particular? Many girls? All that talk of boring French girls with expressions of his love for her, Rose, was obviously all my eye. So her thoughts and fears raged as for the umpteenth time she soothed Christopher, hopefully spooned gripe water into his mouth.

'Edith Malone is an old busybody. Since Mother went to live in London, she has appointed herself watchdog over my morals. I wish to God she would mind her own business instead of poking her nose into mine and dragging Ned's uncle along. Why can't they leave us alone? How on earth did she guess about you and me, we've been so utterly secret?'

'I don't think she has the remotest idea about you and me,' said Mylo equably. (If only Rose would get that baby to be quiet, we could cuddle up in bed and listen to the night.)

'What do you mean by that?' snapped Rose.

'Mrs Malone is a snob, it would not occur to her that you would sleep with her son's tutor.'

'What nonsense. She's not a snob,' (Of course he's right, she *is*) 'that's nonsense,' Rose repeated.

'It is not. She's kind. You have told me how kind she has been to you, how she looked after you when you were ill, sent George – by the way, what about George?' A whisp of doubt slid across Mylo's mind, but he went on treading the track of Edith's kindness. 'She was kind to me when I worked for them, she even bought me clothes when she couldn't stand my French workmen's blues. I never told you that, did I? She is being kind to all these homesick servicemen you are going to entertain – don't go over the top with them, will you? – she just happened along with old Loftus in tow because he is staying with them. He possibly smelled a rat, she didn't.'

'Don't be silly.'

'I am not. As far as your glossy reputation is concerned, it's safe with Edith Malone, and Loftus won't gossip; it wouldn't be in his nephew's interests.'

'How wouldn't she? Why?' Rose, tired and already irritable, resented Mylo's tone. She laid Christopher back in his cot.

'As I said, I'm her son's tutor, a servant, not someone a person like you would sleep with.'

'How can you talk such rubbish! How can you be so ridiculous?' Rose's raised voice roused Christopher, who had been on the point of sleep. He rallied his strength, filled his lungs, whined, changed gear, screamed.

Sitting on the side of Rose's bed Mylo clenched his fists in exasperation. He didn't blame the baby, he told himself, he blamed Ned. During the lonely months in France when he dreamed of Rose, gentle, pliant, gloriously roused to passion, he forgot Ned's existence, but now – he eyed the screaming infant with distaste. He had wanted to make love to Rose as he had the night before, he had come to her room full of erotic anticipation, he felt choked with jealousy and frustration. 'If that were my child, I'd drown it,' he said.

Rose grew quite pale.

'What I meant,' said Mylo, 'was that I wish I could drown your husband Ned.'

'No, you didn't. You want to murder my innocent baby.' She had to shout to make herself heard above Christopher's screams. 'And, if you must know, I love my husband,' Rose yelled. (What devil possessed her to voice this patently obvious lie which Mylo, gorged with jealousy, chose to believe?)

There followed charges, counter-charges, tears, remorse, apologies, forgiveness, explanations and, since Christopher tired before they did and hiccoughed himself to sleep, fucking.

Next morning Rose shivered as she watched Mylo being driven away. What happened to us? she asked herself. We must never let such a thing happen again. She felt quite sick and ill as she stood on the steps and waved to Mylo; then the car turned the corner and was out of sight.

39

During the following weeks Rose suffered. The words and tones of the row reverberated and echoed through her mind. They had been too shattered by their own violence to have a satisfactory love-making. Mylo, hampered by his wounded leg, climaxed too soon. Rose was too tense to have an orgasm. They lay wakeful for the rest of the night, too distraught to sleep, clinging together in silence.

When he left her bed in the morning Mylo looked sourly at the Bonnard and the ideal it represented.

Watching him drive away in the car sent to fetch him Rose felt an astonishing spasm of relief.

During the next week she attended assiduously to her Australian guest, telephoned the person in charge of the hospitality scheme to arrange for a succession of visitors, re-arranged the house to make room for them. By filling her life to the brim she thought she could endure Mylo's absence. She worked harder than ever in the garden, increased the hours spent on the farm. Attended by her dogs, she carted Christopher about with her so that for ever after he would wonder why in times of stress he would smell the scent of cow-byres and think of his mother.

When Mylo telephoned she felt their separation fiercely. Listening to his voice, she craved his physical presence. When their short conversations ended she was more lonely than before. The conversations were of necessity brief, most of the three minutes allowed by wartime restriction, in retrospect, wasted. When next he telephoned she knew by his voice that he was leaving the country.

'You are going away again?'

'Yes, darling, tonight.'

'Your leg, how is your leg?'

'Quite healed. However long I am gone, don't forget me.'

'As if I could. I love you.'

'And I love you. Keep watch over the girl in the camiknickers for me.'

'I will. I will.'

What else did they say? Take care of yourself . . . come back soon . . . come back safe . . . don't forget, oh, don't forget . . . I could never love anyone else . . . Words, just words. Did he hear the catch in her voice? She thought she heard a hint of uncertainty in his. Did she doubt him? How was she to know that he was to be dropped by parachute into France that night and the prospect turned his bowels to water?

'When will you be back?'

'I don't know. I can't tell you. Don't worry.'

What a bloody stupid thing to say: don't worry.

She put the receiver back and went to the kitchen. Edwina was making tea for the postman. The Australian visitor was peeling apples to make apple rings for apple pie in the coming winter. 'Hullo,' he said. 'Come and join us. Mrs F doesn't believe in idle hands.'

'Good morning,' said the postman.

'Cup of tea?' suggested Edwina. 'Here's your post. Three letters from his highness.'

The Australian looked up. The postman snubbed a grin.

'Don't call him that.' Rose took the letters. 'His highness is worse than "the master".'

Edwina raised her eyebrows. The postman put down his empty cup, muttered goodbye and left.

Rose slit the airmail letters open with a knife. 'I have written,' said Ned, 'to put my son's name down for my old school. It is important to get his name on the list for a good house. I have written to Uncle Archibald to find out the best housemaster for when my son is fourteen, if he is bright, thirteen. I have also provisionally put his name down for my old prep school.'

Rose picked up the rest of the letters and left the kitchen. In the library she sat on the sofa and re-read the letter. Her eyes had not deceived her. Ned wrote, 'my' not 'our' son, not Christopher, nor even 'our baby'. He wrote 'my son' twice. Comrade, sensing that there was something wrong, leaned against Rose's leg. Her pup, still juvenile, lay on his back, exposed his stomach and wagged a beguiling tail.

In the next letter Ned gave news of his health (excellent), that of various friends (passable), hinted of imminent promotion to Major (excellent also, since he was not a professional soldier) and 'now for the good news, it is highly probable that I shall be back with you ere long'.

Rose wondered whether her heart, already ebbing, could sink any lower. She opened the third letter. 'Dear Rose,' he wrote, 'my bank manager is worried . . . you seem unaware . . . before spending so freely you should . . . while I am away fighting for my country . . . (Fighting? At a desk?) . . . not earning as much as in peacetime . . . now I have a child to . . . Is it necessary to cash such large . . . try to be economical as . . . is it, for instance, necessary to buy so many books? Hatchards account is . . . try please to imagine what it is like for me out here to . . .'

She was grateful for Christopher's cries. Time for his mid-morning guzzle.

'I don't seem to satisfy him,' she said presently to Edwina. 'He's fearfully collywobbly and he has not been fretful before.'

'Being worried dries your milk. How about a supplementary feed?'

'A bottle?'

'Yes. Shall I mix him one?'

'If you think it will help.'

The older woman went away. Rose brought up Christopher's wind. Squinting with indigestion, the baby looked remarkably like his father. 'He's putting your name down for Eton. His son! Poor little sod.' Christopher belched. 'That's better. Ah! Here's Edwina with an itsy bitsy bottle, try it.' Rose put the teat into Christopher's mouth. 'My God! He loves it! I've been starving him. Look, he's uncrossing his eyes.'

'Loves it . . .'

'In that case I shall wean him, and the Major can complain of a remarkably heavy bill from Cow and Gate.'

'The Major complaining of extravagance?' Edwina, latching on, let her eyes swivel towards Ned's letters. 'Been promoted, has he?'

'About to be.'

'Send on the bills from his tailor, then. He told me to keep them back when he went overseas; re-address them, shall I? They are in the kitchen dresser drawer.'

'Edwina!' Rose was lost in admiration. 'Yes. Please do.'

'All right. Leave the baby with me for a bit. The children can push him round the garden. You take the dogs for a walk, you'll feel better when you've been on your own for a bit.'

'Shall I? Do you really think so?'

'Give it a try.' Edwina swooped on the baby. 'Come with old Edwina then, we'll push your pram to the post and shovel Dada's billsy-willsies into the postbox.' Christopher chuckled as she carried him off.

Rose pulled on rubber boots and a jacket, whistled up the dogs. Walking up the river, watching the trees shed golden leaves into the water, she tried to imagine Ned in Egypt. His letters brought no mid-Eastern vision, he might as well be writing from his London club, she thought resentfully, and anyway what I want to see is France, Mylo in France. Will he be wearing his workmen's blues, melting into the French crowd? Will he be singing as he sings in his bath: *Par les routes de France/ de France et de Navarre/ Je fais ma révérence/Je m'en vais au hazard*. Will he sing? Watching the leaves fall, running to catch one and missing it, she heard Mylo's voice in imagination and cried out in the empty meadow, startling the rooks feasting on acorns in an oak tree. 'I am lonely, lonely, lonely.' But she was not to be lonely long. Five weeks later she realised she was pregnant.

40

Having believed the old wives' tale that it is not possible to conceive while breast-feeding Rose could not at first believe her predicament. She left Christopher with Edwina Farthing, travelled to London for the day and had a pregnancy test in a hospital, giving an assumed name and telling glib lies. A week later she received an intimation through the post that the test was positive.

Mylo was gone, there was no means of communicating with him. He had volunteered no address; she had been too proud to ask whether messages could be transmitted via Victoria. She had no means of knowing when he would be back or, coldly she faced up to it, whether he ever would come back. She must manage alone.

Who could she ask for help?

If she asked for help it meant she thought to get rid of the child.

No need for help if she had it. Ned would be home soon. She could, with a lot of luck, present him with a little brother or sister for Christopher (born prematurely). He would speak of 'my' daughter, 'my' younger son. This scenario was ridiculously and improbably silly.

She could not bring herself to involve childless Edwina. The permutations of help which could be offered were endless.

Emily? Would Emily be the right person to ask? Had she not recently presented the neighbourhood with Laura and had not 'the talk' already died away? Emily had Nicholas's backing. People feared Nicholas, kept on the right side of him. Rose too feared Nicholas, shrank from putting herself in his power. Neither he nor Emily had rumbled Mylo, nor must they.

Should she confide in Edith Malone? No, said her inner voice, she is too close a neighbour. She would be too kind, too bossy, she would gobble me up, baby and all.

When last year she had told him she was pregnant Mylo had cried, I wish it were mine; in her mind's ear she could hear his voice. She daydreamed that she had not married Ned, that Mylo had not vanished into France, that she had money of her own. Sleepless at night, her thoughts plagued her; however busy she was by day the fears, the arguments for and against pursued her.

Her milk dried up and Christopher prospered on Cow and Gate baby powder, growing chubby and contented.

It is cowardly and ridiculous to be afraid of 'talk', Rose argued in robust mood. What have I to lose?

Everything, said the voice of sense. Husband, home, child, work, good name (whatever that means), security. Oh, ah, security! 'Fuck my good name, fuck security,' she said out loud.

At the sound of her voice the dogs looked up, wagging their tails. 'I might even lose my dogs,' she thought.

On impulse, in desperation, she telephoned Flora Loftus, the most improbable person she could think of.

After enquiring after Flora's and Uncle Archibald's health, she said, 'I need your advice. We only have three minutes. Our landgirl is in trouble. So tiresome – yes, that kind of trouble. What?'

Flora Loftus' voice fluted from Argyll, clear, confident, cheerful. 'Funny thing,' plump laughter, 'Archie's landgirl had the same thing; it's all the fresh air, these town girls are not used to it. I'll send you the address on a postcard. She'll need eighty pounds in cash, that's the price apparently, take it or leave it. Archie grumbled but, as I told him, a good landgirl's price is above rubies. You telephone the man for an appointment and the service is immediate, I gather. How is your darling baby? I long to see him. What a bore the war is, everything so difficult and – oh, dear, are we about to be cut off, these telephone operators could teach Hitler a thing or two, they enjoy their power, I'll post the address . . .'

'Oh, thank you . . . so sorry to bother you . . . with Ned away I'm supposed to be responsible . . . you are always so kind.'

'Not at all, my dear. Not to worry, Archie will catch the evening post for me, he's just off to his Home Guard. What fun the old boys are having! Did I tell you the man is in London? Archie grumbled about the fare down there. It'll be less expensive for you, of course, than for us . . .' This time they were cut off.

Three days later in the train to London Rose looked out at the passing landscape and thought bitterly, 'Put your trust in the Establishment, for sheer hypocrisy they are peerless, unbeatable.' Then she thought, 'I can't beat them, I am joining them.'

She counted the telegraph poles as the train thundered past, one, two, thirteen, eighteen, twenty, forty . . . one hundred, one hundred and one. A man opposite her who had been reading *The Times* watched her lips move, thought her eyes sad: 'I watch the fences, this lot are well cut and laid, and think myself onto a good hunter and jump them effortlessly behind the hounds who are in full cry, the fox only a field away.'

'I don't hunt. I'm afraid of horses.'

'Ah,' he said, 'surely not.' A pretty girl like you, he wanted to say, should never need to be afraid, but being English he merely said, 'Ah,' again and picked up his newspaper defensively.

'I am afraid. Full stop,' said Rose distantly. 'Here we are in the suburbs. Your ride must end. My telegraph poles go on and on.'

'Ah, yes,' he said, 'I see.'

'You don't see *anything*. Do you see, for instance, that I am about to drown in Establishment soup?' Rose hissed.

The stranger was glad when the train drew into Paddington; it was folly to speak to strange girls, one should have remembered.

The man in the white overall put the money in a drawer, washed his hands at the basin.

'If you will take your knickers off,' said his assistant, 'and lie back on the chaise.' (Why did she call it a chaise?) 'Have you brought some STs? You will need some STs.'

'Yes.'

'Open your legs wide,' said the assistant, 'while I swab you with antiseptic. You like the smell, yes?' She too wore a white overall. It all seemed very clean and efficient. The surgical instruments cooking in that tray thing. He was pulling on what looked like new rubber gloves. Full marks for cleanliness.

'There will be just a little prick of local anaesthetic, it won't hurt, takes a minute or two to work. Take a taxi home and go to bed for at least twenty-four hours; if you have pain or excessive bleeding, take these pills. Two, every four hours. Now, just a prick.' It stung.

'I tie your legs apart like this so you keep quite still,' said the assistant.

She had yelled, 'No, no, no.' Sprung off the chaise, grabbed shoes and stockings, pushed the assistant aside, rushed to the door, opened it, torn down the passage, put shoes and stockings on in the lift as it went down, run clattering out into the street.

It was dark, she couldn't see a taxi, she walked fast over the bridge into Chelsea, into the King's Road. She struggled onto a bus. She was numb, her vagina was numb, there was no feeling there, none at all, local anaesthetic he had said. I wish he had pricked my mind.

'Oh, the bloody buggers,' said a woman beside her. 'Here we go again, another fucking raid.'

'Knightsbridge. Everybody off,' shouted the bus conductor. 'Into the Underground with you.' He sounded glad.

She was swept along with the crowd down steps onto the moving staircase. Warm air blew up her legs from far below. (I left my knickers in that place.) She let the crowd sweep her with it onto a train. She stood, held upright by the press of people, struggled free at Piccadilly. 'I'm feeling funny,' she thought. 'If I could get some air, if I could sit down somewhere – all these people.' She walked slowly, picking her way. The crowd frightened her. People were getting settled for the night, wrapped in blankets, cramped several together on mattresses, reading books by torchlight, drinking out of thermoses, playing cards, singing, snoring. A drunken man whooped. The tube trains chuntered into the station – 'Mind your backs, mind the doors' – and out again. She craved air. Half-way along the platform the wrenching pain began. She was outraged, cried out. (How *can* it? I didn't *let* him, he didn't *do* it. I *saved* it. I haven't *had* an abortion.) She doubled up, bending over. (Oh, God, this is awful, what a place to – Oh, my knickers, I'm not – oh pain, the pain.) She felt blood oozing out of numb vagina, pouring, streaking down her legs. (I left my STs in that place, oh, Jesus Christ.)

'Look, Nance! That girl – I call that disgusting,' said a voice. 'I mean. Look here. In the tube with people trying to sleep, taking shelter like decent . . .' And other voices said other things. Her legs were not helpful, not managing the one foot in front of the other job, quite simple really.

'Needs help,' another voice, a young sailor. Then she was being wrapped in a blanket and was this a stretcher? Try everything once – and an ambulance, bright light, voices, 'Don't try to stand, just lie quietly, we'll soon . . .' and rumble, rumble on rubber wheels, very fast along a corridor. 'The raid's over, jolly good.' And an icy swab on her arm, an injection and away roaring in her head, woom–womb–woom–womb. Those bills, what was he worrying about in his letter? The lovely smell of new books, oh, Hatchards, obviously Nicholas and Emily had been up to their usual tricks charging books to Ned's account, rather comical, quite a joke. What or who else had they charged to his account? one wondered. She was talking out loud now. 'I wonder what he'll say, whether he'll notice that last cheque cashed for eighty pounds. Did you put it on a horse?' she gasped.

'She's coming round now. It's all right, dear, all over, you're okay now. Try a sip of water, bad luck, getting caught in a raid like that, poor dear. You've been nicely tidied up.' Tidied up, is that what they call the baby who escaped life into the Underground, running down my legs in a slodge of blood? Tidied? That was my baby, his name was Tidy, funny name for a boy, well, perhaps it was a girl, it didn't wait for me to see. (I was nearly born in the Piccadilly tube station.)

There was a grey-haired doctor in a white coat standing by the bed; he looked very tired (well, everybody does these days, it's the war).

'I am afraid you lost it, Mrs Peel.' They knew her name, must have looked in her bag. 'We did what we could, I'm very sorry.'

'So am I.' (Oh, so am I.)

'We'll keep you here for a few days just to be on the safe side.'

'Thank you.'

'Like us to get in touch with your husband? If you tell Sister, she . . .'

'He's in Egypt.'

'Your mother?'

'I haven't got a mother.' (How pat it came, but, no, enough's enough, I could not bear to have her come to see me.) 'I should love just to be quiet, please.'

The doctor smiled: 'Being quiet in a London casualty hospital is a contradiction in terms,' (what a lovely man) 'but we'll do our best.'

They let her go home after a few days.

Edwina Farthing folded her in her long bony arms and gave comfort, comfort, comfort.

Up in Scotland Flora Loftus said one night to Archibald, her husband, 'I wonder, should I have asked the landgirl's name?'

'No, no, leave well alone,' he answered.

A year later on her annual shopping foray, which even the war could not stop, meeting Edith Malone for lunch at the Cordon Bleu in Sloane Street, Flora asked, 'How is Ned and Rose's landgirl?'

'They've never had a landgirl,' said Edith. 'It's Rose who works on the farm.'

Flora Loftus stood corrected, held her peace.

41

When Picot came to write his memoirs and attempted to explain his conversion from the anti-British feelings of a normal Frenchman to the Anglophile warmth of his latter years, he found himself describing an incident which took place in Occupied France in the middle of the war, en route to London. It had to do with the English taste for milk puddings, he wrote, a taste discovered for him by his guide Mylo Cooper, a brave man.

There had been the rendezvous in a small town where Mylo masqueraded as a plumber, occupying himself over a period of weeks with small jobs such as changing washers, checking cisterns, advising on drains. The local plumber had disappeared into the Resistance; Mylo had access to the man's tools, thanks to a friendship with the plumber's sister, a waitress in a café at the corner of the Place.

The morning after their rendezvous Picot sat with Mylo outside the café watching the *va-et-vient* of police and soldiery at an hotel along the square used by the Gestapo as their headquarters.

Picot was extremely nervous – he did not write this in his memoirs, taking it for granted that his readers would know that anyone engaged in the Resistance would inevitably be tense, to say the least – but on discovering that Mylo proposed to go on sitting around in the café flirting with the waitress instead of proceeding on their journey as they had on previous occasions, his nervousness turned to rage. He had never particularly liked Mylo; now he detested him.

'You are risking both our lives,' he said. 'We sit here and if we sit much longer someone will remark and inform on us.' (In his memoirs Picot had earlier explained that his guide whose job it was to get him safely to England had in mind to help a woman at present in the hands of the Gestapo.)

Mylo answered, 'It's possible.' Sipped his acorn coffee and exchanged looks with the waitress lolling against the bar counter.

'You know they have her? You have yourself checked?' Picot queried. He had asked this before. Mylo nodded, shifted the bag of tools at his feet to let a customer pass, winked at the waitress who tossed her head.

'How you dare be so foolhardy when so many of us are at risk when she talks,' said Picot.

'She won't talk.' Mylo rubbed the scar on his leg through the heavy cotton of his trousers.

Picot laughed. 'Everybody talks. If not sooner, then later. We should be on our way.' Then, since Mylo said nothing, 'Is she so special?'

'She is my aunt,' Mylo murmured. (She had been so gentle and kind to Rose that morning, made jokes, jollied her up.)

Picot lit his miserable wartime cigarette. 'Now you tell me.' He sighed.

'Jewish. My mother's sister.'

'They all go to the camps,' muttered Picot.

'Not this one,' said Mylo.

'So where does she go?'

'With us. England.'

'Jesu. Holy Mother. Optimist.' In his fear and nervous state Picot would remember later that he was tempted to leap up, shout out loud to the people in the café, for all those passing in the street, 'This man is English. This man risks my life, arrest this man.' Sometimes he dreamed that he had done this, woke screaming, upset his mistress (his wife never woke, she slept like a rock). He debated whether to include this temptation in his memoirs, did not, regretted it later, liking to be thought human.

'If you are so impatient,' Mylo had teased, 'go on on your own.'

'You have the contacts. All in that mad head of yours,' said Picot.

'Two, at most three more days,' said Mylo.

'Then what?'

'They,' Mylo nodded imperceptibly towards the hotel, 'move out.'

'They move *out*? You *crazy*?' Picot, ever suspicious of his masters, wondered whether they had deliberately entrusted him to a lunatic. It was whispered in London that Colonel P. was not above arranging the disappearance of communist party members. He put this in his memoirs in another context, a later chapter.

'Then she – er – um – joins us and we go on our way,' said Mylo, grinning.

'And what is this way? We have missed the boat thanks to your auntie, there is no other boat for a month, the tides . . .'

'Bugger the tides. We walk,' said Mylo.

'Over the Pyrenees, I suppose.'

'Right.'

'And are taken prisoner by Franco's lot on the other side?'

'It's probable.'

'*Merde.*'

'Better than being handled by our friends in there.' Mylo picked his teeth with a match.

'Handled . . .?'

'I am partial to euphemisms.'

Picot sighed. 'All right. Explain the situation with your aunt. How did she get herself arrested?'

'Who knows? A tip-off? She's in there is all that matters.' Mylo's eyes were half closed. He scraped the match along his jaw, he had not shaved for a week. 'She's my mother's sister. She has a perfectly good house in Bayswater.' He sighed, remembering how Aunt Louise had given them a splendid breakfast (he could smell the coffee). She had lent Rose the train fare home, comforted her after her own aunt's coarse accusations. 'She's daft,' he said with affection. 'Reminds me of Mother.'

'Bayswater? London?' Picot let smoke trickle from his open mouth. 'And she came back here?' He couldn't believe the idiocy.

'Volunteered. We are a heroic family.' Mylo pretended to look modestly down his nose.

'There are heroes in mine, but we are not also fools,' said Picot, sneering.

'*Mademoiselle, deux cafés, s'il vous plaît.*' Mylo caught the waitress' eye.

Watching the girl move away, swinging her hips, Picot said gloomily, 'One wonders what it does to one's guts, this coffee.'

'What I did to monsieur the proprietor's drains.'

'Which was?' Picot watched the Germans down the street, alert, bored, alien.

'Scoured them out,' said Mylo, 'but our friends in the hotel had a faulty ballcock; the noise of the cistern kept the gentlemen awake when they wished to nap between bouts of interrogation.'

'They believe you to be a plumber?'

'They do.' Mylo bent to pat his bag of tools.

'How many more days?' Picot was resigned.

'We should notice some unease tomorrow. Two days later, exodus.'

'What makes you so sure?' asked Picot.

'I put sago down all the lavatories, sinks and washbasins. The guard who watched me thought it was soda.'

'And?'

'Sago swells,' said Mylo.

Telling the story Picot would say, 'Of course, I recommended him to the General for the Croix de Guerre,' and roar with laughter. In his book he wrote that he had been instrumental in getting a gallant friend decorated for acts of supreme courage and sacrifice, which was re-writing history but more dignified than the truth.

42

As time went along without news of Mylo, unbearable pain dulled to an ache. It became reasonable to be grateful that fate had robbed Rose of Mylo's child (it had probably disposed of

Mylo as well). Her hope ebbed low. The child, she told herself, would have grown up cleverer and more attractive than Christopher, her loyalties would have divided. She told herself harshly that she should thank God for small mercies; she had been spared an embarrassment she was well without.

She surprised herself and used an unexpected fund of common sense, taking pleasure in the predictable and mundane, admitting to a taste for the security and convention she had hitherto despised as evidence of her unloved parental background. With a mix of grief and relief she put her true nature into reverse. She was still too young to know that it is possible to operate on several planes at once.

During the months between the miscarriage and Ned's return she consolidated her defences, teaching herself to manipulate life at Slepe to her own ends, the work among the vegetables and on the farm. The role of mother, host and housewife which up to now had been mere camouflage became, she persuaded herself, her true persona.

When she looked at the Bonnard she saw a picture she liked; it no longer spelled the image of Mylo putting his arms around her preparatory to some delicious act of erotica. In some lights, such as when she was dressing on chill winter mornings, the couple's lack of sensible clothes made her chilly body shiver as she pulled on woolly vest and longjohns. If she looked closely at the girl she could perhaps be disagreeing with the boy, drawing away from him. But more often she dressed in such haste she did not notice the picture at all. Her days were crammed with Christopher's needs. The constant stream of foreign visitors. Instead of country solitude, mooning about dreaming of love, she made friends with the people who worked in the Ministry office in the back wing: at meals she absorbed homesick accounts of life back home in Australia, Poland, the USA, Holland, and even France without necessarily making any connection with Mylo. How was she to know he was really there, or even alive?

When her visitors flirted with her, she encouraged them, boosting their egos and her own, stopping short of going to bed with them, for was she not faithful wife to absent husband? She even stopped discouraging Emily and Nicholas who came to

Slepe often, bringing infant Laura, making blatant use of the facilities of Slepe when they wished to economise on their own (they had not had the forethought to stock up for the war like Ned; they had mocked him at the time). Should her visitors' randiness become unbearable Emily could, indeed would, oblige.

Rose was at that time so busy growing a scab over her wound she felt no sense of disloyalty. If there was an occasional mad longing for Mylo, she scotched it.

When Ned did arrive home (wearing Major's tabs now and a red band around his hat), he was delighted to find that the wife whose capability he had previously questioned had a firm grip on his estate. He was miffed as well as amused to discover that even after his return Hadley continued to consult Rose about milk yields and pig production, that she was hand in glove with Farthing. He did not say so. (Perhaps it was then he decided that when the war was over he would switch to sheep and cereals about which Hadley knew nothing and get rid of Rose's precious pigs and dewy-eyed jerseys.) Meanwhile he praised her care of Christopher, laughed at her losing battle with the draughts, promised central heating when the war was over, and applauded her talent for manipulating the guests into helping with the washing-up, tinkering with the innards of the bishop's car and refilling the log baskets.

It was Rose who brought up the subject of money. 'You hurt my feelings when you wrote accusing me of extravagance,' she said. 'As you see for yourself, I have not done too badly.'

'I did not accuse. When I wrote I was warning you to be careful, thinking of the future . . .' Ned said touchily.

'I have been careful. Since you complained, I no longer pay the wages in cash; the change hasn't pleased people, who distrust cheques.'

'Why not?'

'Never heard of fiddling income tax?' Rose laughed. 'It's such a joy to people like the Hadleys. The shopkeepers, too.'

'I can't approve. I don't see anything funny.'

'No. Well. I stopped your accounts with Hatchards, Penhaligons and Trumpers.'

'Good God.'

'I thought you would prefer to deal with your tailors yourself – why do you have two?'

'Aren't you being rather . . .?'

'Bossy?' Rose met his eye. 'Interfering?'

'Yes.' He had not expected her to turn out bossy.

'It was you who complained. I acted as I thought best.' (Is she teasing me? Ned wondered.) 'Perhaps you had better tackle Emily and Nicholas yourself.'

'What have they got to do with it? What do you mean?' Ned bristled, this was no child wife.

'Wake up, Ned. Nicholas uses your accounts; he's a great reader, and look how nicely cut his hair is. He's a dodger, you must have known.'

'If it's true, I'll put a stop to it,' cried Ned, angry now.

'And Emily?' asked Rose mildly.

'What about Emily?' Ned took a step backward.

'Oh, well . . . you know . . . I wouldn't blame . . . I wouldn't put it past . . . I . . .' Rose let her gaze sweep out across the dark fields. She would be gentle with Ned, as he would not perhaps have been with her if he had asked what a cheque cashed for eighty pounds had been used for and she stupid enough to tell him. Ned did not ask what Rose was insinuating; he had already studied infant Laura's physiognomy with trepidation; he watched Rose with respect, undecided on what line to take, then she said, 'I should just take it a bit easy if I were you,' on a closing note.

'Rose, I . . .'

'It doesn't matter all that much, does it?'

'If you are thinking what I think you are thinking . . .' Ned began.

'I think nothing,' and I care less, she thought; if I was in love with Ned it would be different. 'It's late,' she said. 'Let's go to bed.' Mylo did not intrude in Ned's embrace. Rose congratulated herself. I shall yet become like Edith Malone, she thought, or Ned's Aunt Flora. I have regained my balance, I should be happy.

But standing near the top of the hill in old age, looking out at the view, she remembered that she had nearly lost that balance when a much-censored letter arrived from Spain. What was left of the message read: 'Stuck here playing bridge stop je n'oublierai jamais les lilas et les roses stop.' Never having heard of Aragon, she had not recognised the quotation. She passed the letter to Ned, who was watching her curiously. He turned it this way and that, and guessed, 'One of your guests, d'you think? Shot down and brought out along the escape route? Have you had many Free French to stay?'

'Lots.'

'The address on the back is Miranda, that's a prison camp; I've heard of it, chap in my club told me. They get caught coming over the Pyrenees, put in jug, then the military attaché in Madrid sets about extracting them via Gibraltar. Did any of your visitors play bridge?'

She said, 'There were several who were keen on cards.'

'That would be it, then. Chap must be bored, so he writes to you.' Then, 'You didn't have an . . .'

'Don't be silly, Ned, I don't have affairs with the visitors. Try not to be idiotic.' She had spoken quite harshly to hide the lurch her heart had made, to still its hammering, crush hope, stifle her feeling of guilt and disloyalty to Mylo, who was, she supposed, dead, must be.

How wobbly and wavery her faith had been, Rose thought in old age. Oh, the swings and roundabouts of hope.

It had been about that time, she remembered, that Ned, catching her on a low, weeping at the loss of one of Comrade's puppies, shot by a neighbour's gamekeeper hunting his pheasants, had shown his nicest side. He had telephoned the neighbour in furious rage (he could not bear to see Rose cry), threatened never to invite him to a Slepe shoot, told the crusty squire to bloody fuck off, banged down the receiver. Emily, imposing herself for an unrationed meal, had shrieked with laughter, been rounded on, told to remove herself and her bastard brat from Ned's house, to cease darkening his doors.

Ned's rages were rare and always left him afraid he had gone too far, made himself vulnerable to reprisal. He had been afraid on that occasion that Emily would repay in spiteful measure.

The neighbour, from whom he would later buy a labrador pup, would understand his outburst, condone his spleen. Not so Emily. It was fear of Emily, Rose remembered, which made Ned insist she renew her promise never to leave him and she, sorry for him, aware of Emily's hold, knowing that while keeping up his relationship with Emily he must have her to act as buffer, had promised yet again not to leave him, and she had not left him. It had been quite amusing over the years to thwart Emily and now it was Ned, dead and cremated, who had done the leaving.

43

From where he sat in the Palm Court Mylo had a good view of people coming into the Ritz from Piccadilly. Each person paused to adjust from the blackout in the street to the bright lights inside the hotel. It was raining outside; people shook their umbrellas as they came in, hesitated, then dodged according to sex through the doors of the cloakrooms. Mylo watched Peregrine Pye, who had just left them, go into the men's lavatory and come out wearing a bowler hat and carrying an umbrella. As he headed out towards the street he passed Archibald Loftus coming in with his wife Flora. 'I know that old buffer,' Mylo said.

'Does recognising a person make you feel you are really back,' asked Victoria, sitting beside him, 'at last?'

'Yes, it does.' What an understanding girl; he must get to know her better over dinner. It would have been easier tête-à-tête, but Picot was firmly of the party. They were celebrating their safe, though belated, return from France and Spain, had that day finished their de-briefing with Pye and his cohorts; there had been no fuss over Aunt Louise. On the contrary Mylo had been congratulated. Mylo smiled at Victoria. 'Have another drink?' he suggested. 'Picot?'

'No thanks,' said Victoria.

'Un whisky,' said Picot. 'I hear, by the way, that the Royal Automobile Club have a store of Pernod. The barman did not know what it was, all the Gaullistes try to get themselves invited there, some idiot spread the news. The indiscretion of my compatriots is appalling. The Pernod won't last two days.'

'All the more reason to hurry up and end the war,' said Victoria, laughing.

'Where shall we have dinner?' asked Picot. Mylo did not answer; he was watching Ned, who had come in by the Arlington Street entrance, greet Archibald and Flora. They stood blocking the hallway, heads nodding in confabulation.

'Let us start. Flora and I have our train to catch; we've managed to get sleepers, don't want to miss it.' Archibald's voice carried into the Palm Court.

'All right,' said Ned. 'I'll leave a message with the page.'

Mylo watched Ned walk towards the restaurant with the Loftuses.

'I can show you quite a passable place in Frith Street run by some Free Greeks,' said Victoria. 'They have a pâté which resembles liver and sometimes they have venison rumoured to come from Windsor Great Park.'

'Sounds fine,' said Mylo. '*Ça te convient?*'

'*Oui,*' said Picot, 'any food is marvellous after prison. Apparently we are persona grata with your boss, Victoria? I had never cared for him until today but now he acts as though he had absolved me of a mortal sin, makes himself agreeable, or at least tries.'

'Probably playing a new game with the Free French,' said Mylo, laughing. 'Playing Party members against Colonel Passy's bureau.'

Victoria giggled.

'They are talking of a man called Mitterand who has been over to see the General; he left last week from Dartmouth, my cousin Chantal tells me,' said Picot, drinking his whisky.

'Oh,' said Victoria, 'you are not letting the grass grow.' She turned towards Mylo. 'Are you catching up on gossip, too?'

But Mylo's eyes were on Rose, who blinked as she came in from Piccadilly. She had no umbrella, her hair sparkled with rain; she had grown it longer to a pageboy cut, its ashblonde was silvery and smooth, her eyes looked dark in the strange light, darker and larger than he remembered. She bent her head, accepting the message left by Ned. She did not go into the cloak-room but walked straight on and turned right along the hall to the restaurant.

'Shall we make a move?' suggested Victoria. 'I don't like get-ting to bed too late these days. The air raids taught me to treasure sleep, and I must get to the office early.'

'But there is no raid,' said Picot.

'One never knows when they will start again.'

'Let's go, then.' Picot stood up. 'Ready, Mylo?'

'There is a person I have to contact.'

Victoria stood up. 'See you later, then.' She walked away with Picot.

As they climbed into a taxi which had just deposited its fare at the Piccadilly entrance, Picot said, 'You did not tell him the name of the restaurant. Shall I run back?'

'No,' said Victoria, 'it isn't necessary.'

No conversational spark lit the table where the two couples sat. Talk had been desultory, continually returning to the subject of food and the dreariness of wartime menus, Archibald's recollec-tions of gastronomic delights between the wars falling flat as a dover sole. When he embarked on a description of a dinner at Sachers in pre-war Vienna with an aged uncle, Flora Loftus said, 'Oh, Archie, do shut up,' and Ned looked down his nose, wondering when these famous old gentlemen's sexual powers had waned or whether they had been carried intact into their graves. 'I hope to be cremated when it's my turn,' he said.

'Put it in your will, dear boy.'

'Rose will remember.'

The party fell silent while they finished their uninspired pudding.

'Well.' Archie looked at his watch. 'It's later than I thought, we must rush to catch our train. Come along, Flora, get all your things. I shall be buried to the sound of the pipes on the hillside, that's in my will, one shouldn't leave these things to chance.

Flora might boggle at the expense. Come on, Flora, hurry up.'

'Don't fuss.' Aunt Flora none the less snatched up her gloves and bag, pushing her chair back with her ample behind. 'There's plenty of time,' she said. 'Well, dears, it's been lovely to see you.' She reached up to kiss Ned, kissed Rose also. 'Pity it had to be for such a sad occasion. I wish Archie wouldn't hurry me so, he's afraid of not finding a taxi, he thinks just because he can't see them in the blackout that they aren't there.'

'I'll see you get one,' said Ned.

'It's raining buckets,' said Archie. 'One would have preferred the funeral to be in the country.' He had said this at dinner but was not afraid of repetition. 'But Edith said – one wonders sometimes what's got into her . . .'

'Henry lived in London latterly. He couldn't stand the house full of noisy children,' said Rose. This had not been said before. 'So Edith arranged the funeral in London, she thought the funeral at home would disturb the kids.'

Flora pursed her mouth. 'Did she actually say so?' Her eyebrows rose in shock.

'Yes,' said Rose. 'They have become her principal interest. She likes them better than she did George and Richard when they were little. With Henry out of the way she can concentrate on them entirely.' This had not come out at dinner either.

'You should not say things like that, even if you think them,' said Ned repressively.

'Even if they're true?' asked Rose pertly.

'Let's get you a taxi,' said Ned to his aunt and uncle. 'I have to get back to my office, there's a bit of a flap on. Look, Rose, if I give you the money, will you pay the bill?' He fumbled for his wallet.

'Of course.'

'See you later, then, don't wait up.' He took money from his wallet and gave it to Rose. 'I may catch the night train home,' she said, taking the money. 'I'll remember to give you the change,' she said. 'Goodbye.' She resumed her seat and watched Ned, Archie and Flora dwindle down the hall until they went through the revolving doors into Arlington Street.

The waiter, hovering with the bill, laid it now in front of Rose.

She glanced at it perfunctorily, put money on it and sat back waiting for the man to bring change.

How sordid the table, greasy knives and forks, wine-stained glasses, crumbs, bits of food dropped off forks waved in conversation, crumpled napkins, coffee half drunk. She sipped water from her glass. They had buried Henry Malone in an immense cemetery on the outskirts of London; neither George, who was in Moscow, nor Richard, somewhere in the Indian Ocean, could be there. The rain had persisted throughout the afternoon in a race to fill the grave before the coffin was lowered into it. She had taken Edith, impatient to get back to the evacuees, to Paddington before joining Ned and the Loftuses for dinner.

The waiter brought the change. The restaurant was filling up, it was time she left, others would want the table. She calculated the tip. 'There's a note for you, Miss.' Nobody had called her Miss for ages; she picked up the note: 'Waiting for you in the Palm Court,' it said.

The blood rushed up into her face, retreated, leaving her very pale. She felt sick, ridiculously weak. Under the starched white tablecloth her knees shook. She stood up. The waiter pulled back her chair, she ran. Mylo held her hands crushed in his: 'You are doing your hair in a new way.'

'I thought you were dead.'

'What is Ned doing here? I thought he was in Cairo. I've been watching you while you had dinner.'

'He was. He's in the War Office now, plotting the Second Front.'

'You've grown thinner, more beautiful.'

'You are thin, too, and, oh, a white hair.'

'I've been in prison. I wrote – did you get . . .?'

'I couldn't believe it was you, it was so censored, something about lilacs, I dared not . . .'

'Are you living with him?'

'He's in London during the week; we have a flat; he's home at weekends.'

'Home?'

'Well, it is home.'

'And your baby?'

'Fat and well, he's waddling about now.'

'That's good.'

'Mylo, there's . . .'

'So if I joined you and Comrade in the middle of the night, climbed up the magnolia and in at your window, I might find Ned in bed with us?'

'Sometimes.'

'Not always?'

'During the week he's in London.'

'With his mistress?'

'Or me . . .'

'That girl Emily?'

'Well . . .'

'Does she blackmail him?'

'Why should she? How did you guess?'

'Her child might be his.'

'So it might, but I do not think so. Mylo, there's . . .'

'I love you so.'

'And I love you. Mylo . . .'

'Yes?'

'We buried Henry Malone today, that's why we were all here.'

'A nice old boy. I'm sorry. How is your mother?'

'So happy! She lives in London, loves every minute of life, has a stodgy lodger, they swim in the emergency water tank in her street when it's hot. And your aunt?'

'We brought her back from France.'

'My God! Was she there, how terrible!'

'She was working in the Resistance. She's all right now, staying with friends. Somebody dropped a bomb on her house in Bayswater.'

'Mylo?'

'Yes, darling.'

'Is this really you? Go on holding my hands like that, tightly, tighter.'

'I want to undress you.'

'Here? Among all these people?'

'I could and would make love. Even on top of a bus.'

'So could I, oh, so could I . . .'

'Does your promise to Ned still stand?'

'Yes. It does.' Rose stared into Mylo's black eyes; he was so thin, there were lines now, a sharp line between his eyes. One tear swilled out of her left eye, ran down to her chin: 'Oh, darling, I am so happy.'

'The first time I met you I asked you to marry me. Within minutes.' He touched the tear.

'You said we'd have to wait.'

'So you married boring old Ned and are stuck with him and protect him and mother him and defend him from blackmail.'

'Oh.' How it hurt to hear this. 'Oh.'

'If it's not Ned's, whose is it?'

'Does it matter?'

'No.'

'Secretly Ned worries but she's the spit of Emily and Nicholas. The bishop eventually baptised her; she's called Laura.'

'I'm not interested. Where shall we go and fuck?'

'I was going home on the night train . . .'

'Shall I come?'

'Of course.'

'What about Ned?'

'Working.'

'Why are we wasting time, then, in chitchat?'

'There is so much I want to tell you . . .'

'Can't it wait?'

'I suppose it can . . .'

'Let's be on our way, then.' He pulled her to her feet. 'I can't really concentrate properly with people around staring.'

'Comrade will be so glad to see you.'

'Then I shall start believing I am really back.'

44

The wind was cold at the top of the hill. She looked out across strange country. There is something daunting in a view seen for the first time, its concealments manifold, a challenge that mocks. She turned away, retraced her steps. As she walked she retraced her life.

Why had she not told Mylo, during those days and nights they spent together, about her miscarriage? It should have been easy, but for four days, while their love bubbled and boiled, frothed and spilled over, distilled into an essence of happiness, she could not risk spoiling it.

When Mylo left, she retreated into the familiar minutiae of everyday life at Slepe, drowning herself in domestic detail, relying on it for consolation until he would reappear.

He told her hardly anything of his part in the war; she accepted that he to-ed and fro-ed to France, that other lives would be risked if she talked. Ned, too, made a mystery of his work; secrecy was normal at that time. With the bulk of the population, she relied for news on a diet of newspapers and radio, remained in virtual ignorance. When, after the war, she read its history, she was amazed at what had been going on, that dull men like Ian Johnson, Ned and Harold Rhys had performed feats of courage while she and thousands like her stayed at home complaining of draughts and minor deprivations.

She had told Mylo about the miscarriage when she saw him next. He had telephoned, suggesting blithely that she drive him into Cornwall 'for a job', that they picnic on the way, possibly spend the night together, that they use some of the petrol set aside for emergency. (The days when the Germans were expected to invade were long gone; the boot was now on the other foot.) Ned was in London. Rose leapt at the chance. She filled the car with petrol, packed an overnight bag, met Mylo off the train and drove off.

Comrade stood on the back seat, her head thrust through an open window, ears flapped back by the wind, a long and perfect day stretched ahead.

They drove across Devon, left Exeter behind, took the high road over Dartmoor. They were happy; there was no need to talk; sometimes they sang, pleased at the sound of their own voices. They stopped at a moorland pub for a drink, ate their sandwiches in the car near a high tor, watched Comrade chase a rabbit.

'Where are you going in Cornwall?'

'Newlyn. We could spend the night in Penzance. I may find I have to go on to the Scillies.'

'Why?' she had asked stupidly. 'Whatever for?'

'To catch my boat.'

'A boat? You didn't tell me you were off again – you said a job. A boat?'

''Fraid so.'

Taken by surprise she had heard herself whine, 'I don't want you to go.'

'Don't be silly, darling. It's my job.'

'Must you? I shall never get used to this constant wrenching apart.'

'I must.'

'Can't somebody else go?'

He had said harshly, 'Shut up, don't spoil our day. If I'd thought you would be difficult, make a scene, I wouldn't have suggested this outing. I thought it would be wonderful to be with you. I was supposed to go down by train anyway, not joyride with a girl.'

'If you want to go by train, I can drop you at the station at Plymouth,' she had said acidly, 'and go home.'

They had glared at each other, fearing and hating each other and what they did. She remembered screwing the top of the thermos on so hard she had difficulty in getting it off later. Mylo had walked away from her. When she looked after him he was urinating in the bracken. She packed the picnic basket, called

243

Comrade sharply, sat waiting for him in the car with the collar of her coat turned up. When he rejoined her she slammed the car into gear and drove on. Neither of them spoke for some miles.

When the road forked and turned south to Plymouth, she asked neutrally, 'Plymouth, then?'

Mylo said, 'Not unless you want it that way.'

'I don't.' She drove on west through Tavistock. After some more miles they both spoke at once, saying, 'I'm sorry.' Laughter eased their gloom slightly.

Going over Bodmin Moor, Mylo said, 'I'm sorry I was so short. I was told some lousy news yesterday.'

'What?'

'Victoria. You know, the girl in Pye's office?'

'What about her?' She remembered Victoria's disturbing eyes all too well.

'She got news that both her fiancé and her brother have been killed.'

'On the same day?'

'The news was on the same day. They were both in submarines. No great future in them.'

'Oh, poor girl . . .'

'It casts a cloud. She's such a splendid girl.'

A splendid girl, a splendid girl, a splendid . . .

'Is there anything one can do?' she said.

'You could ask her down for the weekend or something, if your house isn't too full.'

'I'll ask her to dinner next time I'm in London.' (I could not bear those eyes at Slepe.)

'She'd probably like that,' he said.

'Is she fond of that French friend of yours?'

'Picot?'

'Yes.'

'She's not keen on him. I believe he made a pass and got rebuffed . . .'

How ungenerous I am, she had thought. 'What a horrible war this is,' she had exclaimed.

'But today is not horrible, is it? We haven't spoiled it insuperably, have we?'

244

'No, no.'

But it was spoiled. Victoria's sorrow intruded on their day and as she drove over the rise and could see Mount's Bay she matched Victoria's grief with her own, told Mylo about her miscarriage.

What a time to choose; Mylo had gone quite green.

That night they lay in an hotel bed clutching each other, unable to sleep, unable to comfort, unable to make love. In the morning she had driven him to Newlyn. 'Wait a moment,' he had said. He had gone through the gate onto the quay, returned carrying a box of live lobsters and crawfish. 'Take these home with you. They are off a Belgian boat.' He put the box on the back seat with Comrade who sniffed, recoiled, jumped into the front of the car in alarm. 'Go now, darling, don't look back.' He had taken her face between his hands and kissed her fast – eyes, nose, forehead, mouth. 'Go, go, go.'

Walking back down the hill by the way she had come Rose remembered those kisses, his hands salty from the box of lobsters, his mouth salt from her tears. She had driven as far as Truro before noticing where she was; for the rest of the drive she tormented herself with visions of Mylo crossing to France on a trawler or a submarine or a motor-torpedo boat; getting drowned, shot, disappearing for ever.

Ned had been at Slepe when she got back. 'Where the hell have you been?' he had shouted. 'Where have you put my corkscrew? I can't find it. I've a bottle of decent wine and I can't find . . .'

'It's there, under your nose,' she had said and it had been there under his nose, giving her a shot of one-upmanship (what silly things one remembers) and 'Lobsters for dinner,' she had said. Ned, seeing the lobsters and hearing where she had been and how much petrol she had used, had said admiringly, 'You must be out of your tiny mind.'

After the invasion of Normandy a year later, she lay in Mylo's arms in a small flat he had been lent in Chelsea. A new and sinister noise disturbed their copulation. They stood on the balcony and watched the first V1 rocket doodling its noisy way across London to explode in Harrow.

That summer of 1944 he brought her Aragon's poems from Paris, told of the explosion of talent from people bottled up under the Germans, talked to her of Sartre and Anouilh. Growing restless in the country she came often to London, drawn by the fear and excitement of the bombing, the feeling that the end of the war was in sight, the need to walk recklessly on the broken glass in the gutters. Then Mylo was off again, to Northern Italy she was to learn later, where he spent the winter with the Partisans and she, with no news of him, grew melancholy, pacing in the park with Comrade where German prisoners of war swept the dead leaves of the plane trees in a grey drizzle, in their grey uniforms, with long grey sweeps of their reluctant brooms, watched by indifferent guards while the wet heavy air pressed the smoke of aromatic bonfires down to nose level.

She went back to Slepe for the coldest winter of the war yet, where she was for once without visitors, they naturally preferring warmer London. Ned, who was by this time in France, complained of the cold, wrote frequently asking for comforts from Fortnums, cigars and coffee. He gloried in his staff job, his authority and the power he dared not use as he was unable to sort collaborator from Resistance fighter when working with the French. He could not speak the language. He was happily moved to Paris to liaise with the Americans, among whom he made contacts useful to him later in peacetime business.

At Slepe the pipes froze. Rose fetched drinking and cooking water from a well; Christopher caught measles, Farthing slipped on ice and broke his leg, Edwina fell ill with shingles, and Emily, sensing that she might be asked to come and help, dumped Laura at Slepe ('It would be a good thing if she could get measles, save an awful lot of trouble later.') and moved to London to live with an American colonel who had a centrally heated flat off Grosvenor Square. Nicholas sulked, closed the Rectory and moved into a pub close to the Min of Ag.

Struggling with the children, the farm, the shortages and the cold, Rose should have had little energy to pine for Mylo, yet still she watched for the postman, ran whenever the telephone rang, dreamed of a time when worries would evaporate and they would be together.

It was during that horrible winter, Rose remembered as she retraced her steps downhill, that Ned, coming home on leave, extracted yet another renewal of her promise. Finding *Horizon* and the *New Statesman* in the house he accused her of having a 'Pinko lover'. She would not, he reasoned, have discovered such reading matter for herself, thus insulting her intelligence. 'It will be that bugger J P Sartre next or the cad Kafka . . .' He had raised his voice (he had not in fact said the cad Kafka, Rose added it later to make a better story), made a scene in front of Christopher and Laura. There had been other indications of infidelity listed but Rose forgot them. She remembered, though, doing something she had never thought to do: she hit Ned, made his nose bleed. Poor Ned. She realised later that he was shaken by Emily's deviation from her norm of availability and infected by a malaise rife among his associates who, returning from the war, found their marriage ties loosened, in some cases bust. While applying ice to his nose she had apologised; by hitting him she was diminished, weakened, more closely tied to him and he, putting his arms around her, had said, 'Of course you have no lover. How could I suggest such a thing? You are not that sort of girl. You promised never to leave me; to suggest you sleep around is idiotic. A girl like you would not dream of it.'

Instead of being uplifted by Ned's estimate she had been irritated. What did he know of her dreams? Did he take her for gormless, dreamless? (In this mood of irritation, having run out of clothes coupons, she helped herself to his dinner jacket suit and had it cut down by her own tailor into a coat and skirt which she wore with white hat and blouse at George Malone's wedding and later at Richard's.) That she was too meek to be suspect rankled, put ideas into her head which had not been there before, ideas which she was later to put into effect.

Remembering that period, Rose chuckled as she walked downhill. The wind was freshening, stirring the treetops, making her eyes water. In tandem with her irritation she had developed a fondness for Ned and he for his part stopped his nervous requests that she renew the promise. She reviewed life as it might be without him and shied away.

About that time Emily parted with her American colonel,

returned to live with Nicholas. Thinking about it in old age, Rose wondered whether her decision to grow up, shut up and stick to Ned was arrived at partly to thwart Emily taking over her husband and home (the idea was there in Emily's mind; one could not be certain whether, given the chance, she would have acted upon it) or had she been daunted, just as minutes ago she had turned away from the unknown, retraced her steps to the known path she had climbed that morning rather than explore new country?

Dogs in the manger are presumably lying comfortably.

45

Leaving the open ground Rose re-entered the wood, treading now on beech mast which split crisply under her shoes. Often in woods similar to this she had stood with Ned whistling, then listening for the sound of Comrade hunting with her pup, for the betraying yelp which would signal their whereabouts, their ineffectual effort to capture rabbit, fox or badger. Ned, his patience matched by his admirable labrador's, would stand beside her. 'They will find their way home,' he would say. 'They always do.'

'They may get trapped or shot,' she would answer. Never once did Ned say, 'Serve them right, if they do,' although he must have felt it. She remembered his tolerance; her dogs were always naughty, his well behaved.

It was easier to remember the Ned of the early days of marriage than of later years. Her memory of him in youth was much clearer than that of the middle past when time concertinaed into old age until finally death reduced him to ash, releasing her from her promise.

She could see him on those occasions when at last she found her dogs. He would grin, take off his glasses, polish them with his handkerchief, ask, 'Satisfied now?' and they would walk home to an enjoyable tea by the fire with Christopher. But if Laura had come to spend the day, to be fetched by Emily at dinnertime, Ned would watch Laura uneasily, hasten when Emily arrived to offer her a drink, help himself to whisky to keep her company, chatter, laugh a particular laugh, glance towards Rose for reassurance. It was years before Ned was convinced she would not allow him to be gobbled up by Emily.

For her part Emily was content with the role of part-time mistress, that was what she enjoyed. If she extracted the occasional hand-out towards Laura's upkeep, Ned could afford it. Rose knew about it, nobody suffered. When the time came for Cheltenham Ladies' College fees and Ned moaned, he received no sympathy. Rose never fully believed Laura to be Ned's child. At first Ned fostered the myth himself, partly from guilty panic, partly from a liking to be thought a bit of a dog. But, Oh my, thought Rose as she threaded her way through the trees, that promise still meant something in 1948.

Half-way through dinner with Harold Rhys and his new wife and her mother who was visiting for the weekend, Edwina Farthing put her head round the door and said, 'The pup's back,' but there was no sign of Comrade. Two days later the water bailiff found Comrade where she had become entangled in brambles at the river's edge, been trapped and, when the water rose in flood, drowned. Fond of Rose, the bailiff brought Comrade's body himself, stood awkwardly watching her white face while Ned thanked him for his trouble, offered him a drink. When the telephone rang Rose picked up the receiver, said, 'Hullo?'

Mylo asked from long distance, 'Does that bloody promise you made to Ned still hold?' And she, watching Ned standing a yard away, said, 'Yes, it bloody does.'

'That's it, then.' Mylo rang off abruptly and she, she remembered as she walked, had broken into terrible weeping. Ned had been kind. He had not offered to buy her a pedigree dog, he had continued to put up with the puppy, and later the puppy's puppy. If he thought her grief exaggerated, he did not say so. He presently took her on trips to Bath and Edinburgh (the exchange control precluding travel abroad), to theatres in London. He stopped quibbling about the expense and installed central heating. He sold his London flat which Rose had always rather looked on as Emily's preserve, and together they chose a cheerful little house in South Kensington which was to be their London base, a London home for Christopher as he grew up. For more than a year he hardly saw Emily. And I, thought Rose looking back, was grateful; I put away thoughts of Mylo; it was as though with Comrade's drowning love for Mylo waned. When a year later she heard by chance from Richard Malone that Mylo had married Victoria, she too said, 'That's that, then.'

What a lot Emily contributed to the keeping of that promise, thought Rose, treading carefully now down the steep hill; it was a triumph that to this day she was unaware of her hold. But she was not alone; Mrs Freeling also fuelled Ned's discomfort, kept Rose determined to defend him.

While Christopher was an infant and for as long as he looked in any way baby-like, Mrs Freeling eyed her grandchild with distaste. Any baby reminded her of the horrors of procreation and child-bearing she was persuaded she had suffered. But when Christopher grew into what she termed a human being she enjoyed her status of grandparent and looked on Ned with a kindly eye. 'Christopher is exactly like his father,' she would say. 'One can see he takes after you, Ned, he has your eyes, your nose. I can see nothing of Rose in him,' and Ned would preen. By contrast when Laura was at Slepe, which she constantly was, playing or fighting with Christopher, Mrs Freeling would stare at the child, draw her son-in-law's attention to her: 'Look at little Laura, one would hardly credit that child had a father. She's exactly like her mother, has no resemblance to anyone but Emily, Nicholas of course, but he is Emily's twin. It's odd, don't you think, Ned? Children take after their fathers; Christopher looks like you; Rose looks like her father.'

'That's your theory,' Rose would say.

'It's a fact.' Mrs Freeling clung to her opinion. 'I'd say that child might not have had a father. What do you think, Ned?'

(Did she or did she not do this on purpose? Surely she was not clever enough to invent such a tease?) And Ned would flush, say, 'Ah, well – I don't know,' try and change the subject, while

Rose, aware of his distress, suggested an immaculate conception or on one occasion, 'Perhaps Emily siphoned up someone's spunk in the bath,' disgusting her mother, earning a scandalised but grateful glance from Ned. ('You went too far there, dear.' He was never cured of the word 'dear'.) And Laura, who liked being discussed, would stand close to Ned staring up at him with her mother's bright and wicked eyes. Then Ned, his guilt fuelled by his mother-in-law, would soon be reminding Rose of her promise, if not outright, by hints. Small wonder, thought Rose, descending the hill, that there were no false pretences when Mother died. But let me be honest now, thought Rose grimly, while to thwart Emily was fun, a good motive in its way, that wasn't what kept me with Ned all those years. His insecurity was matched by my need for security.

46

At the Festival of Britain in 1951, early for a rendezvous with Ned and Christopher up for the day from his prep school, Rose watched the crowds enjoying the gaiety, the atmosphere of optimism. Coming up behind her Mylo said, 'Why did you hang up on me three years ago?'

Rose span round: 'It was you who hung up. *Why* did you marry Victoria?'

'Because we hung up, perhaps . . .'

'Ned was beside me. I had just heard Comrade was dead, she was drowned, her body . . .'

'Our little friend! So that was it!'

'You need not have rushed off and married Victoria . . .'

'There was no exact rush. You were stuck with Ned, and your child, living in that house. You love that house, I know you do. Getting used to it all. It seemed the thing to do. You didn't expect me to hang around indefinitely.' (She had.)

She searched his face: 'You have several new lines, more grey hairs.'

'I see birds' feet ... Your eyes ...'

'Oh, Mylo.'

'I love you.'

'I am meeting Ned and Christopher for lunch.'

'How are they?' He grinned at her.

'Very well. Ned and Christopher have been to the dentist, we are meeting here.'

'I love you, darling.' He did not bother to lower his voice.

'Have you any children?' She fended him off.

'Victoria has a daughter.'

'A daughter. How lovely for you.' She stiffened.

'She's not mine ...'

'Oh.'

'She's Picot's.'

'But she didn't *like* Picot.'

'*You* didn't like Ned.'

'What a stickler you are for truth.'

'No need to be bitter.'

'Is that why you married Victoria?'

Mylo said, 'Cut the lunch. Come and spend the afternoon with me. Please.'

'If I did ...'

'I haven't changed and nor have you. I want to hold you ... come on, just a little fuck for old time's sake.'

Weakening, Rose giggled. 'What about Victoria?'

'What about Ned?'

'It wouldn't help. It would only make things worse.' She fumbled for her resolve.

'Are things bad, then?'

'No, no, of course not. I've got everything I ...'

'Except me.'

'Except you.'

'We used to think having each other would be enough for eternity ...'

'There they are, I can see Ned and Christopher.'

'Nice-looking boy.'

'Victoria has lovely eyes.'

'Yes.'

'Mylo . . .'

'Yes?'

'Don't touch me.'

'All right, I won't.'

'Thank you.' She felt desolate.

'Perhaps you would explode if I touched you.'

'Yes, I would.'

'Good. Some day I will telephone and you will come.'

'Here they are . . .'

'Who was that you were talking to, Ma?' asked Christopher.

'Um . . . he's called . . . I think he's called, er . . .'

'I've booked a table.' Ned pecked her cheek, took her arm. 'All the restaurants are terribly crowded, we don't want to lose it, come on.' (If Mylo had touched me, I would have gone with him.)

'Yes, yes, I'm coming. How sensible to book a table.' They started walking. Mylo was nowhere to be seen.

'What does that man do, Ma? Where does he live?'

'I don't know, darling. What part of the Exhibition do you want to see?'

'I'd really rather go to the Fun Fair. Who was he, Ma?'

'Who was who?'

'That man . . .'

'I don't know.'

'How funny, it looked as though you knew him well.'

'Well, I don't.' (I don't know where he lives or what he does, only that he's with Victoria. Those eyes!) 'He was only asking me something I don't know the answer to.'

'This is such an easy place to get lost,' said Ned. 'This way, I think, ah, here we are, here's the restaurant. I hope they've kept our table. In spite of the signposts.'

'Like life, any number of signposts, yet one still gets lost,' she had said lightly. Ned had laughed, called her a philosopher. 'You didn't know your mother was a philosopher, did you?' He was so proud of Christopher in those days; his fury came later during Christopher's adolescence and later still during the era of long hair and screwball jeans.

She had sat at the table, picked up the menu, while Christopher switched his curiosity to the food. He lost his precocious inquisitiveness as he grew up, growing into the incurious man he was today. If he'd kept it, thought Rose, he might not have married Helen.

She came out of the wood, stepping onto the footpath along the creek. She remembered with a pang how fast her heart had beat as she looked at Mylo that day, how she had felt sick with desire.

I feel sick with desire now just thinking of him. At my age! I've had no breakfast, perhaps I am confusing my hungers. She stood staring at the still water and across the water to the trees on the far side.

47

A few years later, travelling up Knightsbridge on a bus, she had looked down on Mylo walking with Victoria. As she craned her neck to get a better view of him he burst out laughing at something Victoria said and took her arm. The pain she felt was out of all proportion.

In an effort to blot him from her mind she experimented with lovers. If other men could give her enjoyable orgasms, she argued, it would cauterise her pain. Long ago Mylo had suggested that whereas the act of sex with him would be sublime, with Ned or others it would be quite otherwise. She decided she would prove his arrogance wrong.

She had been circumspect, mindful of Ned, not wishing to hurt his feelings, discreet and secret, wary of Emily and Nicholas. She experimented over a period of several years with different types of men. She tried quite hard.

Standing on the path looking across the still water of the creek she remembered ruefully that all that she had learned from these experimental efforts was that the act of sex so joyous with Mylo (tolerable with Ned) became something rather messy, the postures ridiculous if not obscene, at best laughable. 'These calculated adventures must cease,' she remembered thinking; she could not even recapture the frivolous charm of the tonic brush with George Malone. 'I am sorry,' she had said to her current experiment, 'but there it is.'

'But you slept with me last Wednesday,' he had complained. He had been angry when she said, 'Not this Wednesday, it's early closing.' Not finding her feeble joke amusing he cut her for ever after at parties or in the street.

Hurrying along in the rain one day, head down, she bumped into a man walking the other way. 'Sorry,' she apologised.

'I am not.' The man put his arms around her. She recognised Mylo. 'Where are you going in such a rush?' He held on to her.

'I was leaving a lover.' (This was not the case.)

If she had hoped for a rise, she did not get it.

'Come along in here.' Mylo kept hold of her, led her into the lobby of an hotel, made her sit on a sofa. 'I saw you belting along the street, waited for you, you walked into me as if I wasn't there.'

'You are *not* there,' she had said angrily, '*ever*.'

'I am at the moment, darling.'

'What?' (I can't bear this, she had thought, I can't.)

'I *am* here, Rose, *now*. What's the matter?'

'I told you. I have just left a lover. I'm late.'

He had laughed. 'So now we have lovers.'

'Yes,' she snapped.

'Is it enjoyable?' Amused and teasing, he made her turn to look at him.

'It's terribly boring,' she had burst out and Mylo said, 'I am glad to hear it.' As he examined her face, 'You are looking very beautiful,' he said. 'I like it when your face is wet from the rain.'

'Actually I was hurrying because I came out without an umbrella,' she admitted.

'You hadn't just left a lover?'

'No.'

'Thought not.' He held her hands. 'You don't lie very well.'

'I did have lovers . . .'

'Why?' His voice had been harsh. 'Why?'

'Victoria.' She whispered the name defensively, then repeated it louder, 'Victoria.'

'And what about Ned?'

'Ned doesn't know I . . .'

'You know what I mean, Rose, don't prevaricate, what do you imagine I feel about Ned?'

'It's not the same for men.'

'A stupid remark not worthy of your intelligence.'

'You are hurting my hands.' But she had not drawn them away.

'You know I married Victoria because of her child.'

'You never said so,' she had said huffily.

'You did not give me much opportunity.'

'I saw you with her from the top of a bus. You were laughing,' she accused.

'Laughing's not a sin.'

'And you love her.'

'Who said so? Yes, I love her in a way.'

'There you are, then.' The pain of meeting him made her sulky.

'And Ned?'

'We are friends.' Did she at that time admit to herself the love of security?

Mylo murmured, 'M-m-m-m friendship, yes.'

They had sat there on the sofa in the hotel lobby turning towards each other, her hands in his, searching each other's face, oblivious of people coming and going, bringing a whiff of petrol-fumed rain from the street, muffling into their scented furs as they ventured out. Standing now on the muddy path by the water's edge Rose could remember the smell of the leather sofa. Mylo had asked very gently, 'What else?'

She had whispered, leaning towards him, 'I cannot bear to think of your cock inside Victoria.' And he, still holding her hands, had leaned forward and kissed her mouth. 'That won't get us anywhere.' She had tried to draw away but he held on to her hands.

After a while he had said, 'Listen, darling. It would be better for both of us if we could meet sometimes. We need not make love if it ... well ... no, wait, let me speak ... we can be more normal ...'

'What's normal, for Christ's sake?' she had exclaimed in anguish.

'Lovers can be friends, my darling. I am not here often. I live in France. If we met occasionally it might stop us tearing each other apart like this ...'

'*I'm* not torn!'

'Rose, stop it, listen to me. We could lunch together sometimes, go for a walk, visit a gallery, how about it?'

'I don't know.' She had been afraid then, tempted.

'Lovers should be friends, too. You know that as well as I do. We have mutual interests. We could discuss books, films, plays. What do you say? Give it a try? Pretend we are civilised?'

'I ...' Still she feared the unbearable.

'You could tell me about your child, your garden, your cows.'

'I have no cows. Ned switched to sheep ...'

'Those lovely cows ...'

'Well, it's his farm' – she defended Ned – 'not mine.'

'Yes, of course, but why should we not talk about it? Your dogs, for instance?'

'I have Comrade's descendants.'

'There you are, a safe subject for discussion, there must be others. Give it a try?'

'You are wheedling me.'

'I am.'

'Won't it hurt?'

'Not as much as never seeing, never knowing ...'

'So you mind, too?'

'Idiot, you bloody idiot,' he yelled at her.

'Darling!' How her spirits had soared.

'Can't get you out of my system. Don't want to, don't even try.' (People had stared, looked away.)

'I have tried,' she admitted.

'Wasted effort, wasn't it? Waste of lovers. I could machine gun the lot.' This rang true.

257

'There were not enough for a machine gun . . .'

'So . . .'

'We should see a bit of sense at our age.' She had given in, reaching for the freaky lifebelt of good sense.

'Not always to be trusted, too much sense got you into your fool promise to Ned.'

'And your marriage to Victoria.'

'Enough.' He pulled her to her feet and holding her close kissed her. 'Eyes, nose, mouth,' he muttered as if renewing acquaintance. 'I mind very much that Ned . . .'

'What?'

'What you said about Victoria applies also to Ned.'

'Ned mostly goes up Emily Thornby.'

'Such coarse words to pass these lips.' He kissed her again. 'And what about those lovers?' he asked jealously.

'Over. My heart wasn't in it,' she said smugly.

'So if I telephone . . .'

'Yes, yes, yes.'

'We shall have each to treat the other with care . . .'

'That goes without saying.'

'It won't be often, alas . . .'

'It will have to do . . .'

'Resigned?'

'I shall never be resigned.'

'Nor I.'

As they walked out into the rain she said, excusing her pusillanimity, 'I feel I must protect Ned, and there is Christopher.'

'And I,' said Mylo opening his umbrella, 'have to protect Victoria and Alice.'

'That's that, then.'

'Yes.' They stood on the pavement unwilling to part. 'So we won't ever turn into one of those awful old couples who hate each other like my Pa and Ma?'

'I dare say we won't.'

'So it's looking on the bright side, is it?'

'Yes.'

48

So they met at intervals over the years. Of a generation used to the concept of rationing (food, clothes, petrol), they spaced their joy. In the nature of things each meeting held potential disaster, it being dangerously easy for either of them to feel jealous or possessive, resentful even. They walked a knife-edge, teetering as they nursed a passion, which could so easily have died as an adolescent obsession, into a love conjoint with friendship.

With trepidation they learned to speak of Ned without resentment, of Victoria without fear. Discussing Christopher and his friends or Alice and hers brought the alternative partner into the conversation at a neutral level. But chiefly they discussed books, plays, films. While Rose felt passionately about politics, expressing fury and despair at the lies, hypocrisies and evasions of governments, Mylo distanced himself as his father had and made Rose laugh at her own righteousness. If she had been on holiday with Ned to France, Greece or Italy, she did not tell Mylo how she had longed to be with him instead of Ned, and Mylo took care not to say, 'Oh, but you should have seen . . .' or 'When I went there with Victoria . . .'. She told him about Christopher as he grew up into a mirror image of Ned, to be finally yanked from her orbit into yuppydom by Helen. She talked about her garden, her dogs and cats, her neighbours. And Mylo talked of his work, a freelance like his father, of his interest in abstruse European writers, teasing her into reading Julien Benda, Teilhard de Chardin and Michael Polanyi so that she could keep up with what he was talking about.

When her mother died he comforted her for not having loved her, understood the little problem of the ashes. When Edith Malone died they regretted her passing, reminisced about the winter tennis. When in 1956 during the Suez Crisis petrol was rationed once again and Ned, remembering his wartime hoard, found all the jerrycans empty, they shared nostalgic recollection of their wartime drives. Mylo, asking where all the petrol had gone, for they could not have used up all those gallons, was amused when she confessed to using them over a period when Ned was being parsimonious with housekeeping money, buying instead of petrol plants for her garden. She did not tell him of the scene Ned had made or the wounding things he had said, nor that he had gone off to Paris for an extravagant fortnight with Emily. In her efforts to be fair to Ned, Rose made herself feel quite sick, but she would persist as long as Mylo stayed loyal to Victoria.

Those meetings over the years, two at most a year, often less, were always hard to contrive. Twice she was ill and could not meet him; once she was away with Ned, staying with his relations in Scotland, when Mylo telephoned and they did not see each other for eighteen months. For some reason they never discussed, they never wrote letters, fearing, perhaps rightly, the easy betrayal of the written word.

Always when Mylo telephoned, Rose nearly choked with joy, having superstitiously feared that their previous meeting was the last. While they battled for continuity there was never any certainty, she never felt secure. So when one day in 1960 sitting at a corner table in a restaurant Mylo put his hand over hers and said, 'Rose,' she was instantly alert.

'What is it?'

'There is a plan – a job in the States.'

'And Victoria wants to go?'

'No, she doesn't particularly.'

'You want to go?'

'In a way.'

'Don't let me stop you.'

'Rose . . .'

'You want to go. What's the job?'

'Lecturing, teaching, an interesting university, it's . . .'

'Go on, go. Why on earth not? What's to stop you?' She had controlled her voice while her stomach churned in alarm. 'Have a great time, make a lot of money . . .'

'Don't be like that.'

She withdrew her hand: 'They haven't worked, these civilised meetings, have they?'

'I can't do with half a cake . . .'

'It was your suggestion.'

'A bloody stupid one.'

'All this popping in and out of my life like a jack-in-the-box doesn't amuse you, then.' The finality refused to sink in.

'You never look for *me*.'

'No, I don't. Why should I? I've got my life, quite a busy one as it happens. I have Ned, it's my choice, I abide by it. You have Victoria; about time she was considered, isn't it? Time we grew up.'

Mylo had riposted, she had struck again.

My word, thought Rose, standing on the bank by the creek watching the breeze riffle the water, how we hurt each other that day, how we let rip, how well each knew how to wound the other. It was suicide. They had parted leaving the wounds raw. They had not even said goodbye. Split.

It had been a fight to come to terms with her loss. She had become quite ill, grown thin and snappy. When Ned, worried, took her to a specialist he said it was not the menopause, although she was of that age, suggested a psychiatrist. Refusing a shrink, Rose set herself tasks which she called fresh interests. She made a new lily border in the garden, planted more magnolias, took on voluntary work in the neighbourhood, tried hard to like her daughter-in-law, behaved, as Nicholas remarked, like a widow. 'Anything wrong, Rose dear? You are behaving like a widow.'

'I am easing myself into a role I may never have to play,' she had replied, 'so that, should the need arise, I can enjoy it.' Then she found that she was enjoying her role, was being nicer than she had ever been to Ned, that people came from far and wide to admire the garden. The only failure was her lack of enthusiasm for Helen. Helen's fault, thought Rose, watching a pair of swans cruising up towards her. She should have suppressed her longing for dead men's shoes; one did not have to be a mind reader to know what Helen intended doing to Slepe once she got her hands on it. Well, thought Rose, she's got it now but if she had not annoyed me so I would not have looked after Ned so well, she would have got it years sooner and I, unbraced by my dislike of her, might have moped into a decline, not considered myself cured of Mylo.

So what had she felt when, picking up the telephone nine years later, Mylo's voice said, 'I have tickets for Venice tomorrow, pack your bag.' She had felt she had come alive again.

'Are you still grumpy?' he had asked.

'I . . .'

'To be honest with you, all those civilised meetings drove me mad, darling. I was like a randy dog.'

'And now?'

'Randier than ever.'

'What time's our flight?'

49

The subtle smell of warm drains. St Mark's Square at two in the morning, empty by the light of the moon. Wandering along the narrow alleys. Quizzing the peeling stucco. Leaning over bridges to read each the other's face reflected in the murky water. Mylo's hair grey now, beginning to recede, his face thin and lined. Hers, eyes deep-socketed in reflection, pale (she had had no sun that summer), hair dusty wheat-coloured.

They had leaned towards the water, their reflections joggled into one by passing barges carrying vegetables to the markets. They had sat speaking sparsely, eating prosciutto with figs, large plates of pasta, drinking cold wine at tables by the canals, light dappling their faces. Wandered on to drink bitter espressos near the Accademia. They had swum lazily from the Lido in water soupy with sand and Lord knows what else; they had lain nights rediscovering each other's bodies in a state of happiness neither dared remark on so perfect was it, so tender, such fun.

They were too wise to say, 'If we never have anything else ever again, we shall have had this.' When strolling along a small canal they heard through the shutters of a room high above the water Paul McCartney sing, 'Will you still love me/ Will you still need me/ When I'm sixty-four?' Too wise to catch each other's eye. Too wise when they parted to make arrangements to meet again.

We got it right that time, Rose said out loud to the swans paddling past, their wings cupped over their backs. Stooping she picked a pebble from the path, threw it, broke her single reflection.

50

Then they exchanged the occasional cautious letter. Just to keep in touch, he said, writing to congratulate her on Christopher's marriage, an event he had learned from a casual meeting with George Malone in New York. 'I hope she is a nice girl, that she will make him happy. I remember him in his Moses basket on the back seat of your car with Comrade. You stopped the car to suckle him. Alice, Victoria's daughter, has two children. I don't much care for babies,' he wrote.

'Would you have cared for ours?' she wrote on a postcard which she tore up on the way to the post. (Many of the letters she wrote him got torn before posting.) She wrote instead a scrawled sheet enclosed in an envelope, 'She is not a nice girl, but she will make Christopher happy.' It seemed of paramount importance to be honest, not to pretend to him as she did with the rest of the world that she liked Helen.

Over the years Alice, Victoria's child by Picot, aged twenty-five at the time of the Venetian meeting, played the part of invisible go-between. 'How is Alice?' Rose would enquire and news came back that Alice and her family were spending the summer at Cape Cod or, the year that Picot, rich, growing elderly, retired now from his post in Monsieur Pompidou's government, had finally acknowledged parenthood and settled a lump sum on Alice, they, this included Mylo and Victoria, spent part of the summer in the Ardèche. (Not a great success. Picot needed help with his memoirs which Mylo had not been willing to give.) Rose tried to imagine Alice, searched between the lines of information about Alice and her family for Mylo hiding like a sea anemone in the weeds of his stepdaughter's mundane life. Alice was helpful when Victoria was away (where?) and Mylo had jaundice./ Alice had done some useful research for him. What research?/ She kept her mother company while he was in Peru. What was he doing in Peru?/ She was helpful when they moved house. Where to? Where from?

Rose sent her sparse letters c/o Mylo's publishers, distancing herself deliberately. So, sparingly they wrote but did not meet; several times she suspected that he had spent time in England, not made contact. The years flew on or dragged by, according to mood and state of health. When she thought of it, reminded perhaps by a tone of voice in a crowd, a whiff of drains, Rose congratulated herself that their love had ended on such a high, not dwindled as most loves do into habit. 'Shall we go to Venice this year? You've never been to Venice,' Ned once asked.

'I don't think I could bear the smell. Why don't you get Emily and Nicholas to go with you?' Would Ned admit that he had already been twice with Emily alone?

'I find Nicholas rather trying in large doses. One used to get Emily to oneself – not any more,' he answered grumpily. He knew that she knew all about Emily.

'Yes. She cleaves to Nicholas more than ever. Poor you.'

Ned said, 'What? Can't hear you. Wish you'd speak up, not mumble.'

Virtuously Rose held back the words often shouted these days by Harold Rhys and Ian Johnson's wives, 'You're getting deaf.' *Unberufen*, as Nicholas would have said during the 1939–45 war, that she should grow like those boring old women.

'About time we invited what's-his-name, oh, Arthur and

Milly, to dinner,' said Ned, dredging round for substitute company.

'All right, if that's what you'd like. I'll ring them up.' I must not allow myself to be beastly to Ned.

The note on the hall table in the cleaning lady's script (the Farthings were long since retired, living in a granny flat in the erstwhile evacuees' house) said, 'A Mr Cooper will be waiting for you on platform one, Paddington Station, mid-day – 12 o'clock – tomorrow.'

When the train pulled in he was sitting on a luggage trolley waiting for her. 'I need to talk to you.' He put both arms around her, kissed her mouth. 'That's better.'

'What has happened to you?' He looked terrible.

'Perhaps we could walk in the Park, or is it too cold for you?'

'No, no.' She walked beside him to the taxi queue. He looked gaunt, she thought. He has lost weight, his hair more white than grey now.

'Lovely cockatoos!' His face lit up as they passed a group of punks with rainbow hair and painted faces. 'In Molière's day it was the women who did that, they were known as *Les Précieuses Ridicules*. Her 's a taxi, jump in.'

In the taxi he sat looking straight ahead, he held her hand. 'Thank you for coming,' he said.

They walked under bare February trees in the east wind. 'Shall we sit for a while?' They sat on a bench and looked across the grass to the wintry Serpentine. A group of children bounced along the Row on plump ponies.

'Loosen that curb rein, Samantha, don't tug his mouth,' shouted the riding instructor.

'How is Ned?' asked Mylo.

'Well. Getting a bit worn. He's over seventy, gone a bit deaf, trouble with his teeth. That sort of thing, otherwise . . .'

'Victoria died,' said Mylo quietly.

'Died?' Those lovely eyes.

'It took a very long time.' His cheeks were deeply furrowed, what she could see of the stubble mostly white.

'Oh, dear God. Cancer?'

'Yes.'

'What can I say?'

'Nothing. Shall we walk for a bit? You mustn't get cold.'

'When was it?'

'Nearly a year ago. It's terribly unfair. She never hurt anybody. It took such a bloody long time. She was in such pain. I kept wishing I had the nerve to kill her. She asked me to kill her, she asked me to ask the doctors – I even got the drugs, bought them from a junkie. Alice, her daughter, was being marvellous – you know how they are? Kept on at the doctors to try this, try that . . . It's grotesque what the marvels of modern science come up with to prolong suffering, keep 'em alive. Who enjoys that life? Certainly not Victoria.'

'No, no, no, she had such wonderful eyes.'

'Yes, weren't they? Wonderful eyes in a plain face. Used to remind me of Comrade.'

'So that's why . . .'

'I married her? It may have played a part. You are cold.' He took her hands and rubbed them between his. 'Haven't you got any gloves?'

'I was in a hurry.'

'The shameful thing was that all those months . . . I am so glad to see you, darling . . . the terrible thing was that all the time Victoria was dying I kept thanking God it wasn't you.'

Rose stared at him.

'One can't control those obscene and shabby thoughts. Then, too, I had the drugs. I had the drugs without the nerve to administer them. I should have made the opportunity but there was this – it was not you dying, you see, so I lacked the urgency, the whatever it takes, I just couldn't – anyway, I didn't.'

'No.'

'Are you glad she's dead, darling?' (Gently.)

'No, oh, no.'

'Nor am I, except that her pain is over.' He stopped his stride, bent to kiss her. 'Are these tears?'

'The wind. The east wind.'

'M-m-m. Shall we walk on? We don't need to catch pneumonia. D'you know my Aunt Louise caught pneumonia

266

almost immediately I got her back to England and died? Really, sometimes one wonders – I had to tell you about Victoria, needed to.'

'Thank you.'

'Then there's Ned. What will you think when he dies? Probably you won't know what to think. There's so little emotion left after a prolonged ... do forgive me boring on like this ... then there's your promise never to leave him. What could have been more idiotic? Do you truly believe you stayed with him because of that? Of course you don't. I don't. I think you did promise. I've always accepted that, and it's been useful.'

'You think I chose cake?'

'Does it matter now?'

'What are you going to do?'

'Oh, I've been commissioned to write a book about Thailand. I fly off tomorrow.'

'It will be nice and warm there,' she said sadly.

Mylo did not answer. They were walking now with their backs to the wind.

'Oh, hell!' Rose exclaimed. 'We have people coming to dinner and I'd clean forgotten.'

'I'll take you back to Paddington, there's a train at two forty-five.' He swung her round towards the Bayswater Road.

'What will you ...?'

'I have to meet my agent. It's all right, darling.'

'Mylo ...' The wind whipped at her.

'One thing.' He still held her arm. 'If it had been *you* dying, I would not have hesitated, I would not have let them stop me, I would have killed *you*,' he took her face in his hands and kissed her, 'however difficult. Here's a taxi, pop in.'

Sitting in the train she reproached herself bitterly. She had said so little, not known where to start with the torrent of pent-up words. As the train put on speed, the voice on the intercom informed her that the bar was open now. The buffet could provide tea, coffee, toasted sandwiches and soft drinks. People stood up and began to push past her, swaying with the movement of the train. Watching them go by she mourned the cold comfort she had given Mylo. I failed him, I failed him, I failed

267

him, her thoughts chugged in time with the train. Contrapuntally she started to fuss about Ned's friends Arthur and Milly coming to dine. Once before she had forgotten people were coming, another pair of Ned's friends, she had made no provision. At the last moment they had taken the surprised guests to a restaurant. Ned had been so cross, made a scene, nursed a grudge, gone on about her incompetence for weeks. I don't think I can bear that again, she thought, not after seeing Mylo today. Then, remembering that the day was Wednesday, early closing for her local shops, she let out a wail. The couple sitting opposite looked at her askance. 'Just a twinge.' She smiled falsely like a dog about to bite, got up, made her way to the buffet car to buy an expensive paper cup of tinged water, changed her mind when she saw it and had a double brandy.

Arrived, she retrieved her car from the station car park, drove into the town. Surely some shop somewhere would be open? How stupid can you get, she thought, walking up the empty street, all the shops shut on Wednesdays. I am only putting off the evil moment of telling Ned I have no dinner for his friends and him asking whether I have lost my marbles *en permanence*.

As she walked, pulling her shopping trolley behind her, empty and likely to remain so, a Land-rover passed, pulling a trailer. Catching a salty sniff, she peered into the trailer and beheld boxes of crabs. The Land-rover hesitated at the turning into the High Street to let a couple of lorries go by. During this pause Rose reached into the trailer and helped herself.

As the driver of the Land-rover changed gear and accelerated Rose walked sedately back to her car, her only worry now whether to crush garlic into the mayonnaise she would make and turn it into aïoli, or have it plain.

Presently, the guests departed; duty done, she would gain her bed, shared now with Comrade's great-great-grandchildren (Ned had years ago moved into a separate bedroom) and if she felt like it, weep for Mylo.

And did I weep? Rose questioned, standing by the water's edge. Most unlikely. Our parallel lines had grown past weeping and the theft of the crabs had a curative effect, quite a boost.

It takes a happening like Christopher and Helen squabbling

two days after Ned's funeral, their decision to take my dogs with them when they decided to walk off their spleen, allowing them to get crushed by a juggernaut as they argued, probably about me, instead of keeping an eye on my dogs, my company, my last links however tenuous with Mylo to make me cry.

'I shall catch my death standing here,' Rose said out loud.

She stamped her feet on the path to warm them, squared her shoulders.

51

Rose was aware that her feet were cold. A fog rolled up the creek, invisible hands pulled a wispy duvet along the water. She watched its advance billowing along quite fast, distorting the few sounds left by winter, twigs dropping in the wood behind her, the cry of a coot across the water. Far above, a plane flew leaving an unravelling vapour trail. Did it come from Thailand?

Fool, I am sixty-seven, not seventeen.

Looking down she found herself shoulder deep in vapour. Her body was chilled, she wanted to pee, she shivered. Irrationally she feared that if she stepped out of sight into the wood she would twist her ankle crossing the ditch, slip and fall. Her walk had been so peopled by thoughts, she had not noticed how alone she was.

She unzipped her trousers, squatted on the path, disappearing below the fog. Standing up she heard a man's voice calling: 'Mrs Peel? Mrs Peel?' The sound was muffled but coming closer. 'Mrs Peel?' She could see his head and shoulders reared above the fog. 'Mrs Peel?' It was the owner of the hotel.

'Here I am,' she said, stepping towards him. 'What is it?' She did not want him to scent her urine on the path.

'We thought you might have got lost. These fogs roll up from the sea so quickly it is easy to become disorientated.' He was irritated, anxious, obviously he didn't want to lose a foolish guest. Any mischance would damage the reputation of the hotel; he blamed her for his anxiety.

'As you see I am not lost, though I may well be disorientated, but thank you.'

'You have had no breakfast. My wife was worried.' Still he blamed her. The head and shoulders visible above the fog attracted pearly drops from the deafening atmosphere.

'How kind, I am ravenous.' And so she was, now she thought of it, walking beside the hotelier. 'Do you like being a hotelier?' she asked, hoping to raise their chat to a more frivolous plane. She had to talk; it was not possible to walk in silence, which would have been preferable but ill mannered.

'It has its moments. Would you like the full breakfast or coffee and croissants? My wife . . . We close at the end of the week for a winter break.'

'That will be an important moment. Just the coffee and croissants, please. Sounds delicious.' She hurried beside him in the fog (I could perfectly well have found my way back by myself). 'Ah, here is your cat come to meet us. We met last night and again this morning.' She stooped to caress the animal as it did its best to trip her by winding melodiously round her ankles. 'She's talkative, too.'

'Do you have cats?' Her host's voice was affectionate towards the cat. He had not forgiven her for causing unease.

'Not now. Nor do I have dogs. Nor garden – no ties at all, come to think of it. Nothing to restrain me. It's really rather scary, takes getting used to, being loose.'

'Oh,' he said, looking at her sidelong. 'Um.'

'M-m-m . . .'

'I will see about your breakfast; we call it *petit déjeuner*,' he rallied.

'Of course you do.' (She must not laugh.)

'Would you like it in your room?' he asked.

'Yes, please. And thank you for coming to look for me.' (Had an unwary guest once fallen drunk into the creek?) 'I must pack my bag. And might I use your telephone? There is a call, maybe several calls, I have to make . . .'

'I will have it plugged into your room.'

'And have my bill ready.'

'Certainly.'

Certainly the bill. One paid the bill, the tally, the reckoning. One settled one's account at the end. 'I shall swallow my pride with the croissants.' She smiled at the man.

'Er?'

'I may not be able, now that I am free, to pay what I owe.' They had reached the hotel now and the fog was lifting. She watched the cat run ahead, pat the door with an arrogant paw, raise its whiskered snout to yowl: 'I observe that there's a perfectly good cat flap,' she said.

'She's too bloody proud to use it, she won't stoop. We take all the main credit cards, naturally, if ...' He stressed the last sentence.

'Aha!' said Rose laughing. 'Credit! Of course.'

The manager wondered what there was that was so funny. 'Even Eurocheques,' he said.

Avec le petit déjeuner, thought Rose. 'Don't forget to charge me for my phone calls,' she said.

52

The church had been packed. The young couple, popular single, would be popular as a pair. One or both of them had an inordinate number of relations. Although they had arrived early Nicholas, Emily and Laura had been relegated to a pew a long way back.

'That usher can't have known who we are,' said Emily as they regained their car.

'Of course he did. That was Richard Malone's youngest. He knows us all right,' snapped Nicholas.

'I thought he was still at school,' said Emily.

'Time passes, Mama. He left university years ago; he works in the City.' Laura spoke from the back seat.

'I thought the bride almost indecently virginal,' said Nicholas. 'Are those cars ever going to get a move on? I need a drink.' The Thornby car was stationary in a line waiting to get free of the village. A number of people had parked inconveniently, causing a jam on the route to the reception.

'It's the mode to be virginal,' said Laura.

'Barbara Cartland?' questioned Emily.

'AIDS,' said Laura.

'In spite of being stuck at the back I quite enjoyed the spectacle,' said Nicholas and tooted his horn. 'Don't know many of the people here, though.'

'No use hooting, Nicholas, consume your soul in patience like everyone else,' said Emily.

'You misquote, Mama; it's "possess ye your souls . . ."'

'Don't be such a know-all, Laura, *my* soul is consumed.'

Laura raised her eyebrows.

'There was a fine turnout of elderlies,' said Nicholas. 'The finest collection of lines, wrinkles, scraggy necks, crêpey skin, bags, bald heads, dowagers' humps, arthritic limbs, shuffling, hobbling, rheumy-eyed old crones and cronies I've seen in years. A wedding is better than a funeral for a geriatric turnout.'

'Your generation,' said Laura caustically.

'We do not suffer from cachexia,' snapped her mother.

'And there are others besides us,' Nicholas allowed, 'there's poor Rose. There were several in the church carrying their years with decorum, not to say panache.'

'Move on, Nicholas, can't you see the queue's moving? Rose was not there.'

'Of course I can. Shut up.' Nicholas clunked into gear. 'I didn't say she was there; my point was that she has worn remarkably well, as well if not better than us.'

'Look out, Nicholas, you'll hit that car . . .'

'God! Emily. Must you? Actually the old boy who gave the bride away was pretty trim.'

'I thought him quite a dish,' said Laura. 'That shock of white hair with black eyebrows and eyes is stunning. Marvellous figure, too.'

'Who was he?' asked Emily. 'They should write these things on the hymn sheet. I couldn't display my ignorance to the people near us, they were all strangers.'

'No idea,' said Nicholas. 'I always think, reverting to Rose, that the reason she looks as she does is that she hasn't suffered the extremes of joy, grief, or anxiety the rest of us have been through. A few worries over Christopher, nothing desperate, and Ned. Well, let's face it, Ned wasn't of the stuff to make any woman's face sag, was he?'

'Wasn't she the lucky one?' said Laura on the back seat, finding Nicholas's obsessive interest in Rose Peel entertaining.

'When Rose eventually shows her age she will look like a fossilised rose in a dead flower arrangement,' said Emily, ignoring Laura. 'Faded, yet crisp. Go on, Nicholas, they are moving again.'

'I can see they are. Would you like me to stop the car, change places and let you drive?' asked Nicholas nastily.

'Now, now, you two, don't squabble,' said Laura.

'We are nearly there,' said Emily, sensing that she had goaded her brother too far. 'I too need a drink, we all do. All those uplifting hymns and watching that beautiful pair has made me quite thirsty. That girl, the bride, has extraordinary eyes.'

'They run in the family,' said Laura.

'I like the looks of the groom; he's improved no end since I last saw him. If I'd been twenty years younger I would have been tempted to . . .'

'More like forty,' said Laura on the back seat, 'or fifty.'

'What did you say?' asked Emily sharply. Laura did not reply.

'All those promises,' said Emily after a pause, 'are pretty ridiculous. Who on earth can be expected to cleave – correct me if I'm wrong, Laura – cleave indefinitely? It's unreasonable.'

'Cleave will do. Is that the reason neither you nor Nicholas ever ventured into Holy Matrimony?' Laura asked a question which had rattled around her mind for a lifetime. Neither Nicholas nor Emily answered.

'Here we are. At last! Now we can get at the booze,' said

Nicholas. 'There's nothing to prevent you embracing that mode of life, though I would think you've left it a trifle late now you've almost reached your half century.'

It was now Laura's turn not to answer.

'Fancy having a marquee in winter. I hope we shan't catch our deaths,' said Emily. 'I personally shall go into the house. Come on, buck up, Nicholas, what are you staring at?'

'I thought I saw Rose Peel's car up there in the yard.'

'Don't be silly, she's miles away in some luxury hotel; her car's a mass-produced job, it might be anybody's. Let's find the buffet. I say, there's that old man who – I agree with you, Laura, let's find out who he is.'

'She won't be able to afford luxury hotels for long,' said Nicholas, parking the car. 'I only heard this morning what a mingy annuity Ned left her.'

'Everything's entailed on Christopher, everybody knows that.' Emily stretched her leg out of the car. 'Give me a hand, Laura. Thanks.'

'Presumably Ned imagined Christopher and Helen would supplement it,' said Laura. 'Aren't you going to lock the car, Nicholas?'

'Nag, nag, nag,' said Nicholas, turning back to lock the car. 'Can you see Rose accepting a penny from Christopher? She *loathes* Helen.'

'And we all thought she'd be left rich! Well, well, beggars can't be choosers,' said Emily. 'She has her old age pension, hasn't she?'

'I can't see Rose begging,' said Laura.

'Well, I can't help her, can I?' said Nicholas. 'You could have,' he rounded on Emily. 'You must have known what Ned planned, Ned was in your pocket, you could have pointed out to him the decent thing to do. He may have been stupid but he wasn't all that mean, look what he did for Laura.'

'Was Ned my father?' asked Laura, walking between Nicholas and Emily.

'Good Lord, no!' Nicholas burst out laughing.

'What a suggestion,' said Emily primly.

'I thought not,' said Laura. 'I did ask Rose once and she said she thought not.'

Watching the Thornbys go into the reception, Rose ducked out of sight. She had not foreseen when, by a series of astute telephone calls, she had discovered where Mylo would be at lunchtime, that there would be a large marquee, a hoard of wedding guests. When she had come upon the house by a back lane she had hoped to catch Mylo coming away from a quiet lunch with friends and possibly speak to him. This half-baked plan flew out of the window when, leaving her car in the stable yard, she had rounded a corner, seen the marquee and been almost instantly swamped by a rush of cars bearing bride and groom, parents, guests and various press and onlookers, and, worst of all, Emily, Nicholas and Laura back from the church.

Crouching down behind the wheel, hiding her face until she judged the Thornbys out of sight, she decided that what she had hoped for was not feasible, she must drive away, escape from this potentially embarrassing situation.

Then she thought with a gasp of relief that she had come to the wrong house, had been misdirected, natural enough in the circumstances of the wedding. She had been stupid, she would return to the village and ask again.

She sat up.

While she had ducked out of sight several cars had parked blocking her way out of the yard; she was, to all intents and purposes, trapped. Cursing her luck, she thought all she need do was wait until the owners of the cars came to remove them. But then, she thought, it will take hours and hours and meanwhile Mylo will finish his lunch at the other house and go. Damn Emily and Nicholas and all these people, she thought. Then she thought, What do I care about Emily and Nicholas? I care nothing, nothing at all, all the ways they can hurt me have been incinerated with Ned. All I need do, she told herself, is to go calmly in to this strange house, interrupt the wedding feast, explain my plight, my silly mistake and ask for whoever owns these cars blocking my escape to come and move them. Easily done. Very easily done. She sat in the car telling herself how easy it would be. So she sat.

She sat in her car telling herself how easy it was to walk in alone to a stranger's wedding party in a rather grand house, wearing her comfortable old jeans and sweater and muddy shoes, barge into a room where everyone was dressed in their high-heeled best and important jewellery, the men in grey morning suits drinking champagne and making yuppy speeches. But never mind that, it would be perfectly simple to find the bride's mother or father or the best man or an usher and explain – I got here by mistake, I am really looking for another house where someone called Mylo Cooper is having lunch. You see I *have* to find Mylo Cooper. With her hands over her face she rehearsed this speech, nearly crying with rage and frustration as she muttered out loud . . .

'Who are you talking to?'

'I was rehearsing a speech.'

'So I heard. Did I hear right? You have to find Mylo Cooper?'

'Yes.'

'And then what?'

'Perhaps,' she said stiffly – her whole face felt stiff – 'you could help me find the owners of these cars which are blocking me in and then I can get out. I was rehearsing the speech I have to make to someone responsible, the bride's mother or father or the best man or an usher to ask the owners of . . .'

'I heard that bit.'

'Oh.'

'Would the bride's step-grandfather do? I gave her away in the church just now.'

'Ah.'

'I just stepped outside to get a breath of air.'

'You are looking wonderfully well, Mylo Cooper.'

'You are as lovely as ever, Rose Peel. How did you find me?'

'I telephoned your publisher who put me on to your agent, who told me the hotel you are staying in, and they told me you had a lunch date here.'

'Very clever. I saw in *The Times* that Ned is dead.'

'Yes.'

'It would be untrue to say I am not delighted.'

'Ah.'

'I intended coming straight on from here to Slepe to gather you up and Comrade's descendants and take you away.'

276

'They are dead too, they were run over.'

'I mind about that very much.'

'You would not have found me there.'

'You would have been looking for me?'

'I can't deny it.'

'I am terribly pleased.'

'Well . . .'

'I won't say I love you as much as I did at the winter tennis party — isn't it extraordinary that Victoria's grand-daughter should be marrying one of George Malone's grandsons? One of the things I love about you is that you don't answer, "It's a small world," that sort of bilge — but I will say that I love you differently and more so, much more so.'

'Oh. Does she have Victoria's wonderful eyes?'

'Yes, she does.'

'I am glad.' (His voice had not changed, a little deeper perhaps.)

'I can't think what I am doing standing here while you sit in there in the warm. I am too old to hang about growing stiff, risking hypothermia. Open the door, darling, and let me in. I want to hug you.'

She opened the car door, moved over to make room for him beside her. 'I have our picture in my overnight bag, I did not bring anything else.'

'Quite right. What else would we need? I say, isn't this nice, I love kissing you.'

'Not forgotten how?'

'If you must know, I'm as hungry as I ever was. I just space the meals out a bit.'

'Do that again,' she said. 'I very nearly did not come to look for you.'

'Pride, I suppose. Thank the Lord you swallowed it. I would never have forgiven you if you had not.'

'I might have choked.'

'In such a good cause.'

'Do you have to go back in there?' she asked presently, listening to the distant hubbub of the party. 'Nicholas and Emily are in there.'

'So I saw. Pickled in time. Never mind them. I have to say my goodbyes. Then we are off.'

Watching Nicholas and Emily circulating among the crowd, Laura reflected soberly that it would be she who would be driving the car home. Nicholas's hand reached repeatedly towards the trays of drinks, Emily's followed suit. They ignored the temptings of vol-au-vents stuffed with shrimps, caviare on strips of toast, and other succulent eats offered by perambulatory waiters. Their tour ended, they rejoined Laura by the buffet. 'Having fun?' asked Emily.

'Bored,' said Laura, 'there's nobody I want to talk to.'

'And very few we want to talk to either, but it's not a bad party as parties go.' Emily's voice had risen several decibels above her norm. She's tippled into drunkenness, blast her, thought Laura. 'Why did none of us marry?' Emily asked the world at large. '*We* would have had the most marvellous parties, the best champagne, not this stuff. *You* could have married, Laura. You could have married Christopher Peel. Why did you not marry Christopher, Laura?'

'I was under the impression he was my brother,' said Laura tightly.

'Oooh? Then, when it was too late, you checked with Rose?' Emily's once brilliant eyes focused on her daughter's, still brilliant. 'You could have had Slepe, couldn't you? Think on that.'

She's not quite as drunk as I thought. 'Stupid old bitch,' said Laura with wintry intensity.

'Poor Rose Peel. *I* should have married poor Rose,' exclaimed Nicholas, ignoring his females.

'Would she have married you?' asked Laura tightly.

'We should have brought her with us today,' cried Nicholas, 'jollied her up. We used to be so kind to her when we were all young.'

'Would she have wanted to come?' asked Laura.

'We teased her, admittedly,' said Emily, reminiscence overriding Laura's tone, 'but we were very kind. We took her to the party where she first met Ned.'

'If I had married her I would have sophisticated her, made much more of her than Ned did.'

'Jolly nice for Rose,' said Laura, 'that would have been.'

'Poor Rose. Nothing ever happened to her. I hate to think of her holed up in some hotel alone and palely masturbating when she could have married me – if I'd asked her of course ... Where's all the drink gone?' Nicholas looked around but no waiter passed.

'You are disgusting drunk and pretty disgusting sober,' said Laura.

'Don't speak to Nicholas like that,' Emily shouted shrilly.

Laura smiled, mouthed, 'Don't speak to your father like that,' watched Emily look blankly around in pretence to the people near her, that it was not she who had shouted, but somebody else. 'Why did you never marry, Mother?' she asked.

'I could have married, perhaps I should have married,' Emily answered portentously, 'but there was such a wide choice, one ...'

'You could have married absolutely anybody,' said Nicholas, switching to a fond gargling note. 'Even a man like that dishy old example of humanity who gave the bride away. Have we discovered who he is? Does anybody we know know?' Nicholas fumbled for his glasses to scour the room better. 'We really should find out.'

'You'd better look sharp then,' said Laura. 'He's just leaving. Look, he's over there with Rose. *She* seems to know him.'

The Camomile Lawn
Mary Wesley

'A very good book indeed . . . has the texture and smell of real life,
rich in detail, careful and subtle in observation, mature in
judgement'
SUSAN HILL

'It is hard to overpraise Mary Wesley's novel . . . exceptional
grace and understanding . . . so tingly and spry with life that put
a mirror to the book and I'll almost swear it will mist over with
the breath of the five young cousins'
THE TIMES

Behind the large house, the fragrant camomile lawn stretches
down to the Cornish cliffs. Here, in the dizzying heat of August
1939, five cousins have gathered at their aunt's house for their
annual ritual of a holiday. For most of them, it is the last summer
of their youth, with the heady exhilarations and freedoms of lost
innocence, as well as the fears of the coming war around the
corner.

The Camomile Lawn moves from Cornwall to London and back
again, over the years, telling the stories of the cousins, their
family and their friends, united by shared losses and lovers, by
family ties and the absurd conditions imposed by war as their
paths cross and recross over the years. Mary Wesley presents an
extraordinarily vivid and lively picture of wartime London: the
rationing, imaginatively circumvented; the fallen houses; the
parties, the new-found comforts of sex, the desperate humour of
survival – all of it evoked with warmth, clarity and stunning wit.
And through it all, the cousins and their friends try to hold on to
the part of themselves that laughed and played dangerous games
on that camomile lawn.

'Extraordinarily accomplished and fast-moving . . . plotted with
great deftness and intelligence'
MARTIN SEYMOUR-SMITH, FINANCIAL TIMES

'Nothing old-fashioned or even ladylike about it. With the verve
and jollity of youth . . . a book as scatty and chatty as a gossip
column'
MAIL ON SUNDAY

'Delightful . . . wholly believable and exact. I like the mixture of
warmth and wit . . . More, please'
DAILY TELEGRAPH

0 552 99126 0

BLACK SWAN

Harnessing Peacocks
Mary Wesley

'Delightful, intelligent entertainment'
THOMAS HINDE, SUNDAY TELEGRAPH

Hebe listens in the darkness of the hall to a family
conference. The stern hypocrisy of her grandfather is
winning the day. He has summoned her three horsey
sisters' successful husbands and they are discussing
Hebe's unexpected pregnancy. The decision, unanimous,
is that it be terminated. Hebe, dissenting, flees into the
night.

Twelve summers later she is living happily alone with her
son in a seaside town in Cornwall. He is receiving an
expensive education. Hebe has organised her life oddly
but well. She has two chief talents in life – cooking and
making love – and these she has exercised with dignity, in
privacy and for profit.

It is when the separate strands of the web of Hebe's life
become entangled that the even tenor of her days is
threatened, and her life is changed.

HARNESSING PEACOCKS, Mary Wesley's third novel,
is suffused with freshness, warmth and wit. The author's
delightful literary skills are here fully engaged in a story
of independence, honesty and sensual charm.

'Mary Wesley goes from strength to strength . . . She has
a great zest for life . . . The book is tremendously lively,
very funny, touching, spirited'
SUSAN HILL, GOOD HOUSEKEEPING

0 552 99210 0

BLACK SWAN

A SELECTED LIST OF OTHER BLACK SWAN TITLES

The prices shown below were correct at the time of going to press. However Transworld Publishers reserve the right to show new retail prices on covers which may differ from those previously advertised in the text or elsewhere.

BLACK SWAN